Praise for *A Traitor in Whitehall*

An Amazon Editors' Pick for Bes'
Aunt Agatha's—One of the Best I
Bookreporter—One of the F

"A very good historical novel . . . I
that this is the first novel in a series!"
—*The Wall Street Journal*

"If you like to mix history with your mystery, then this propulsive novel set in World War II London should be on your TBR list."
—*Oprah Daily*

"In Winston Churchill's London underground bunker, Kelly spins an Agatha Christie–esque mystery featuring—who else?—one of Mr. Churchill's whip-smart secretaries, of course! A thoroughly delightful and well-researched novel of London during the Blitz."
—Susan Elia MacNeal

"Evelyne Redfern is exactly the kind of intrepid, plucky heroine I love to root for, and the details of Churchill's cabinet war rooms were spot-on and fascinating. *A Traitor in Whitehall* will keep you guessing as to who the killer might be as the pages fly by."
—Madeline Martin

"*Call the Midwife* meets *Mr. Churchill's Secretary* in this riveting and atmospheric mystery set in wartime London. . . . Sharp, charming, and fast-paced, *A Traitor in Whitehall* marks a stellar debut for a winning and original heroine."
—Mariah Fredericks

"A cast of opinionated side characters and a wealth of fascinating historical details add to the fun in this engaging, atmospheric series kickoff."
—*BookPage*

"This was a blast of a read. . . . Pacing, suspense, and a wonderful mystery make this book a real standout in a crowded field of WWII books."
—*Aunt Agatha's*

ALSO BY JULIA KELLY

The Lost English Girl
The Last Dance of the Debutante
The Last Garden in England
The Whispers of War
The Light Over London

A TRAITOR IN WHITEHALL

An Evelyne Redfern Mystery

Julia Kelly

MINOTAUR BOOKS
NEW YORK

Published in the United States by Minotaur Books, an imprint of St. Martin's Publishing Group

www.minotaurbooks.com

Designed by Gabriel Guma

The Library of Congress has cataloged the hardcover edition as follows:

Names: Kelly, Julia, 1986– author.
Title: A traitor in Whitehall / Julia Kelly.
Description: First edition. | New York : Minotaur Books, 2023. |
    Series: The Parisian Orphan
Identifiers: LCCN 2023025182 | ISBN 9781250865489 (hardcover) |
    ISBN 9781250327345 (Canadian) | ISBN 9781250865502 (ebook)
Subjects: LCGFT: Detective and mystery fiction. | Novels.
Classification: LCC PS3611.E449245 T73 2023 | DDC 813/.6—
    dc23/eng/20230526
LC record available at https://lccn.loc.gov/2023025182

ISBN 978-1-250-86549-6 (trade paperback)

Our books may be purchased in bulk for promotional, educational, or business use. Please contact your local bookseller or the Macmillan Corporate and Premium Sales Department at 800-221-7945, extension 5442, or by email at MacmillanSpecialMarkets@macmillan.com.

First Minotaur Books Trade Paperback Edition: 2024

10 9 8 7 6 5 4 3 2 1

For Arthur, my partner in crime

A Traitor
in Whitehall

PROLOGUE

September 7, 1940

M iss Redfern!" snapped Miss Wilkes, causing me to jerk up and
my pencil to skitter across the page of my notebook.

"Yes, Miss Wilkes," I said, slowly reaching for an old dispatch to pull over my shorthand practice in hopes that she wouldn't
notice.

I needn't have bothered. My supervisor looked distractedly at a
clipboard she held in her ringless hands. "You're due for your first
sunlamp treatment."

"Sunlamp treatment," I repeated.

"All of us are required to go. It helps keep us healthy, what with the
amount of time we're underground," Miss Wilkes explained. "I'm certain that one of the other girls must have mentioned this while training
you."

I fought the urge to protest that, in the few days I'd been employed
in the typing pool at Prime Minister Churchill's secret underground
bunker, there had been so much information to take in that I hardly
knew which way was up any longer. The cabinet war rooms had security protocols, shift patterns, air raid and ground invasion warnings.
Working there was like being dropped into a foreign land without a
dictionary.

"I apologize, Miss Wilkes. I became caught up in my work, and it
slipped my mind," I fibbed.

Miss Wilkes shot me a look that seemed to say, *A likely story.* "Go now while there is a lull before the evening shift change. And remember to secure your notes."

I hurried to tidy my desk. My notes and the old dispatch went into the locked container with a slit at the top that would be taken to the incinerators later so that all potentially sensitive materials could be burned. I had no handbag with me—there really is no need for one when your bed and your desk are separated only by a veritable rabbits' warren of tunnels. Instead, I flung my pistachio green cardigan over my cream-colored blouse with the rounded collar, slung my brown leather gas mask case over my shoulder, touched my hair to make sure the dark brown curls were in place—you never knew whom you would meet in those corridors—and set off with purposeful steps.

Around the corner from the typing pool, however, I hesitated. I'd been warned that taking a sunlamp treatment would require stripping down to my unmentionables and then standing in front of the blasting ultraviolet light with my eyes firmly shut. During busy times, this could mean waiting in queues that stretched down the corridor, and I was not going to stand around without a book. I changed course and headed to the Dock.

I knew the risk I was taking with this extra trip to the barracks, where all of us more junior staff who made up the nerve center of Britain's most secretive, sensitive wartime hub slept during our three-day shifts. I didn't know how things were on the men's side—it was made explicitly clear to me that I would never see that part of our barracks—but descending into the women's Dock meant I was just as likely to find myself alone as I was to be caught up in an assessment of the attractiveness of a newly sewn siren suit, a heated debate of our military strategy in Europe, or a detailed discussion of why some half-wit boyfriend had just left a crying typist or switchboard operator who was clearly the best thing that had ever happened to him.

Really, going to the Dock with a deadline on one's hands was a fool's errand. However, I was fifty pages from the end of *Busman's Honeymoon* by the incomparable Dorothy L. Sayers, and I needed to see if I was right in my suspicions about who had killed Mr. Noakes.

I was in luck. As I descended the stairs, I found myself nearly alone except for four girls I recognized from the typing pool's night shift playing a rubber of bridge. I nodded a polite but quick hello and scurried over to the bunk that I'd claimed that morning when I'd come underground for my shift.

When I'd taken this job, I'd retained my room with my best friend, Moira, which meant that most of my clothes were still crammed into the wardrobe at our digs on Bina Gardens. I did make sure to take my knitting and bundle up five mystery novels with a leather belt like a schoolgirl to keep me occupied through the sometimes-long nights. I could go without many things during a time of war, but I could not abide the thought of being without books.

With *Busman's Honeymoon* in my hand, I retreated from the Dock, happy as always to leave the damp, slightly moldy air and the lingering funk of the chemical toilets behind. I'd been told that I would become accustomed to the stench over time, but I very much doubted that.

The corridors were unusually quiet that afternoon, although I passed a pair of clerks ladened with folders and a stone-faced Royal Marine stationed at the base of one of the staircases who barely batted an eye despite my choice of a particularly bold shade of lipstick that day.

After making two right turns, I finally found the room where the sunlamps were temporarily set up. I was understandably grateful when I found no queue waiting for me. I'm not, as a rule, a woman who is embarrassed by her own nakedness—I spent too many years at boarding school for that. However, I didn't relish being starkers around my colleagues even if they were firmly behind a locked door. If I hurried, I hoped I could finish the whole process before anyone came along.

I banged on the door of the temporary treatment room to make sure I was alone and then hauled it open. The room had been cut into two with a set of screens, to create makeshift changing and treatment areas. Since this was my first go-round with the sunlamp, I skipped past the dressing room to investigate the device. Better that than standing shivering and nearly naked, trying to make the bloody thing work.

I rounded the screen to the treatment area and stopped short. A woman in a crimson and white cardigan sat on a metal folding chair in front of the card table holding the sunlamp. Her head was pillowed on her arm, asleep.

"Hello there!" I called. I knew enough about the cabinet war rooms to know that sneaking a quick kip on the job would not be tolerated.

The woman didn't respond. With a sigh, I edged closer.

"I hate to be a terrible bore, but I can't imagine you want to be caught—"

A drop of red liquid dripped off the desk and onto the floor in a pool at the girl's feet.

"Oh my God!" I cried, dropping my book as I rushed to her. I grabbed her arm, and her jumper gave under my grip like a wet sponge. Her head lolled forward, revealing a short, slim-handled knife protruding out of the side of her neck.

All at once, everything went black, and the room's metal door crashed behind me. I whipped around in the dark, the sound of something scraping against metal chilling me to my core. Someone had shut the door and thrown the large metal bolt on the corridor side.

Nausea rising, I tried to think past my rising panic. Logic told me that the light switch must be near the door on the other end of the dark, unfamiliar room, but there was a much closer light at hand.

Trying my best to avoid where I thought the body was, I felt along the partition screening off the treatment area until my fingers hit the table. There must be a switch somewhere . . .

The full blast of the UV lamp stamped a black void ringed with brilliant yellow across my field of vision. I stumbled to the door, catching my foot on the partition and sending it tipping drunkenly in my wake. Still, I didn't stop until I reached the door handle.

I yanked at it.

Nothing.

Again.

It didn't even budge.

I slid down to the ground, the cold metal of the door raking up my cardigan and shirt. Someone had locked me in with a dead body, and I had no way out.

ONE

August 27, 1940
ELEVEN DAYS EARLIER

If I had to look at one more tray of anti-tank shells, I was going to scream. A full-throated, head-thrown-back, ear-piercing bloody scream.

Now, I'll admit that this threat was more metaphorical than literal; however, I am my mother's daughter and *Maman* was predisposed to the occasional display of dramatics.

Gripping the workbench in front of me with both hands, I took one or two of the deep meditative breaths my dearest friend, Moira, swore by and reviewed the facts at hand.

One: I was nearly done with my shift at the royal ordnance factory.

Two: Mrs. Jenkins expected me to pay my usual rent at the end of the week.

Three: There was a war on.

Taking all of these factors into consideration, I had to admit that it would be neither prudent nor patriotic to find myself sacked. We were all supposed to be doing our bit in the war against Nazi Germany. I just wished my bit wasn't quite so mind-numbingly dull.

The trouble, I reasoned as the huge factory clock mounted to the far wall ticked slowly closer to the end of my shift, was that almost anyone could fill racks of half-empty shells with powder to the same precise measurements every time, ensuring that the shell detonated as expected and blew up its target. I'd mastered that challenge in my first half day on the job six months ago, and even Sheryl four down the row from me was coping while nursing a head sore from a night's drinking at the pub around the corner from the factory.

Somehow I managed to last forty-one more minutes without running amok on the factory floor, and when the shift change bell rang I pushed away from my table, nearly elbowing my fellow lady workers out of the way in our daily sprint to the changing rooms.

Munitions is a messy, dangerous line of work, so we all wore stiff boiler suits, tight turbans, and steel-toed shoes, and we were checked every time we came onto the factory floor. One errant hairpin could cause a spark and blow the entire place to kingdom come. The changing rooms at a royal ordnance factory, therefore, are a magical place of transformation where women morphed from canvas-covered caterpillars into cotton, linen, and even silk-clad butterflies.

Even though it was only Tuesday, my colleagues were already making plans for the weekend while they dressed. I'd tagged along to a couple of dances when I'd started back in February, but I'd quickly lost my taste for nights out where the ratio of men to women would be woefully skewed by conscription. It wasn't any fun dancing a foxtrot with another girl when we both kept forgetting who was meant to lead and who to follow.

At my locker, I gave a few polite nods and demurred when several women next to me asked where I was off to in such a hurry. *Maman* had taught me at an early age that, whether they be male or female, it was best to cultivate an air of mystery by leaving a curious audience wondering.

The reality was that my plans for that evening were no more ambitious than to curl up with the brand-new copy of *Death at the Bar* by Ngaio Marsh I had picked up on my way into work from the news agent around the corner from the factory. You see, I simply *adore* detective fiction. Each new story contains within it the tantalizing possibility of a puzzle so fiendishly twisted that the solution may elude me until the final pages.

I began reading detective fiction at sixteen. Finally allowed into the village my school was nestled in, I'd taken the meager allowance Aunt Amelia bestowed on me out of pity and purchased a subscription to the local lending library. It was really just two bookcases angled toward each other in the corner of the shop that served as post office, news agent, and sweets counter, but to me it represented a world of literary possibility. At first, I tried a little bit of Dickens, some Wolfe, and even a romantic novel or two. They were all well and good, but it was a beaten-up copy of *The Mystery of the Blue Train* by Agatha Christie that I could not put down. I read it so quickly I was left with days to wait until I could return to the village and change it for another. I checked the publication dates of the few Christie copies on the shelves and was delighted to return to the beginning of Monsieur Poirot's stories with *The Mysterious Affair at Styles*.

Now, at twenty-two and with years of reading under my belt, it was rare that an author could stump me—the great exception being Christie, who had shocked me with the dastardly twist at the end of *Murder on the Orient Express*—but I relished the hunt for a fictional killer, nonetheless.

At my locker, I finished pulling on my wide-legged tan trousers and cream shirt. On went *Maman*'s gold watch and her pearl earrings. Unwrapping the cotton turban that kept my hair out of my face while I worked, I shook out my dark brown curls and settled my tan beret at an angle on the crown of my head. Even on my best day, I would never draw attention away from Moira when we stood side by side, but I had a certain flair that could attract the occasional appreciative nod from a passing soldier. Not that I was particularly interested.

I waved goodbye to my fellow munitions ladies, sending Sheryl and her sore head a sympathetic nod, and let myself out of the factory door. This, I decided, was a lucky day because the bus was on the corner and the driver—a fellow woman doing her part to "free up a man for the force"—waited while I sprinted up on my short brown heels. I gave my money to the ticket collector and settled into a seat in the back corner, where I knew I wouldn't be disturbed.

I was twenty pages into my book when the driver called out my stop. I pulled the cord and clambered up and out onto the pavement down the road from my digs.

I lived in a tall redbrick building that would be unremarkable to any passerby unless they were to glimpse inside. Then, they would be assaulted by a wall of giggles and the occasional shriek, as well as the constant, comforting scent of laundry. Mrs. Jenkins, who lived on the ground floor and reigned over the sitting room, kitchen, and dining room, had split up the other three floors into rooms to let sometime after the last war. Installed into these six rooms were twelve young women, including myself.

When I'd moved in, Mrs. Jenkins had told me that she only let rooms to respectable ladies. However, I'd soon learned that respectability was not the only requirement for living in digs with Mrs. Jenkins. A woman needed the ability to merrily bump along while crammed into a rickety, madcap building. Being able to sleep through all manner of snores, shouts, and other noises also helped.

Moira and I had a room two flights of stairs up, across from Cynthia, a secretary working a mysterious job in Whitehall she rarely spoke about, and Jocelyn, a model-turned-journalist whom Moira had met on a photo shoot and recruited for the house just before this beastly war kicked off. Moira had promised Cynthia and me that Jocelyn would be a vast improvement on Cynthia's previous roommate, Sally, a postal worker who spent nearly an hour in the bath each morning if you didn't pound on the door and demand your fair share of the hot water. So far, Moira had been proven right. Jocelyn worked such long hours on Fleet Street that we hardly saw her.

That evening, I climbed the stairs with my book in front of my face, pausing only to sweep up a set of stockings hanging from the banister in front of my room. I twisted the doorknob, pushed inside, and found Moira on the edge of her bed, leaning out the window with a cigarette in her hand.

"I wish you wouldn't do that, darling," I said as she hastily hid her cigarette around the edge of the blackout curtains, only to bring it out again when she realized it was just me.

She pulled a face. "I can't very well run down to the road every time I want a smoke."

"You're going to land both of us in trouble," I said, letting my gas mask holder slide off my shoulder and drop in a heap on a chair along with my brown leather handbag. They nearly knocked a stack of paperbacks to the floor, but I managed to catch the pile with my foot and right it just in time.

"I'll swear to Mrs. Jenkins that you never smoke," said Moira.

"And the stockings?" I tossed them at her. "She thinks it lowers the tone of the place when you leave them out to dry."

"I only do that because it's so bloody damp in this room that nothing dries. Even in August," said Moira, plucking the stockings out of the air before they could drift down to the carpet.

I flopped on the bed, my book on my chest, but didn't open it. "How was your day?"

Moira sighed. "Ghastly. It was another one of those awful dumb doll parts again."

Moira had been toiling in bit parts for the Ministry of Information's propaganda films in hopes that they might prove a stepping stone to her first role in a proper film, but it didn't mean that she necessarily liked the jobs thrown her way.

"What was it this time?" I asked.

"Oh, I had to pretend to gossip to my husband in a club of some sort. Except that instead of going to an actual private club, which would have been very lovely I'm sure, we were on a set at a poky studio in Ealing," she said. "You?"

I shrugged. "More shells."

"Ghastly," she said again, and I couldn't help but agree with her.

"Shall we go out tonight?" Moira asked, immediately brightening.

"I'm planning to spend an evening with Roderick Alleyn," I announced, holding up my book.

"Evie, if that is a fictional detective, I'm going to scream."

"Scream away, darling," I said, cracking the book's spine.

Moira snubbed out her cigarette and stood, planting her hands on either side of her slender hips. "No. We are going out. I have an invitation from Robert to go to the Ritz."

I grimaced. Robert was nice enough, but he spent all of his time gazing adoringly at my friend, rendering me wholly unnecessary in any conversation. "Take Jocelyn."

"She's working," said Moira.

I sighed. "She's always working. I'll go next time."

"No, you'll go tonight."

I put my book down with a huff. "I've had a very long day, Moira."

"You've had a very boring day, and now you're feeling sorry for yourself."

"I have a new book. How could I possibly feel sorry for myself?" I asked.

"You're becoming positively agoraphobic. I won't have it." She marched over to the wooden wardrobe we shared and wrenched open the door, which gave a shriek of protest.

"Careful! There's not much wood left to rescrew the hinges into," I said.

"Right. Do you want the rose satin bias-cut with the cowl or the black and gold net?" Moira asked, pulling my two evening dresses out for inspection.

"I'm not going," I said, opening my book again.

Over the top of the page, I spied Moira glancing between the two dresses before giving the rose satin a nod. "This one."

She dropped the dress—hanger and all—on my legs and then marched to our shared chest of drawers that was spilling over with clothes. Over her shoulder she winged a girdle, bra, and knickers.

I gave a yelp as I batted away the girdle just before it smacked me in the face. "What are you doing?"

"Helping you dress. If you're nice to me, I'll put your hair up too. I know how much you hate pinning it," she said.

"Moira . . ."

My best friend in the world spun around on her bare feet and gave me the sort of very stern look I imagined made men quake in their boots. "Evelyne Redfern, what would your mother say?"

Never let life's moments pass you by, ma chérie.

I gave a sigh, found a place for my book among the stack of detective novels already littering my small bedside table, and hauled myself upright, grabbing at the dress to keep it from slithering to the floor. "Will there be champagne?"

Moira grinned and tossed her platinum blond hair over her shoulder. "It's the Ritz, darling. If there's champagne to be had in London, that's where it will be flowing."

TWO

I had to admit, Moira had outdone herself.

One of the perks of living with an actress and sometime model was that she was an expert at hair and makeup. And because Moira was a generous soul who tolerated my literary clutter, she had done as promised and sat me firmly down to tug, poke, and prod me into the most appealing version of myself. Now, among the unimpeachable glamour the Ritz managed to exude even in wartime, I was glad for her ministrations.

When we arrived, the place was abuzz as King Zog I and Queen Geraldine of Albania glided through the lobby accompanied by various bodyguards on the way up to the floor of the hotel that had been set aside for them. As we were seated for dinner, I thought I caught a glimpse of the famous hostess Lady Cunard as well.

Most of our fellow guests, however, were normal people like us who had the good fortune to be with someone who had too much money and too little sense to think twice about the exorbitant price of dining at the famous hotel. I will admit, I loved it there. Even though rationing and shortages had curtailed the menu slightly, the dining room still exuded luxury with its mirrored wall reflecting the soft lights of the chandeliers that hung over us. Men too old to serve in the war made up most of the room's male population, although the dashing dress uniform of a soldier, sailor, or pilot occasionally punctuated the space. However, it was the women who provided the real color with our gowns.

The women of Britain had escaped the much-feared prospect of a clothing ration so far; however, neither Moira nor I would have been able to afford a wardrobe more varied than we currently had on our wages. This necessitated sharing. Neither of us minded much, although sometimes, when we'd drunk enough wine to be philosophical, Moira would point out that if only she could have countenanced being a debutante and nothing but, her circumstances might have been different. You see, Moira's well-intentioned mother had taken her to the cinema at the impressionable age of eleven, and she'd fallen hopelessly in love with the silver screen. Her father, however, didn't understand the passions of his young daughter. When she'd refused to make her debut and informed him she intended to become an actress instead, he'd cut her off without a shilling, assuming that would be enough to scare her back under his roof. He clearly understood very little about his daughter because she hadn't returned to the family home in Mayfair since.

The circumstances surrounding my own fall from wealth and familial grace were in some ways far less dramatic, but that never stopped Moira from treating me like a fellow woman scorned by parental displeasure.

"How do you know Moira?"

I jerked a little, pulled out of my thoughts by the man seated next to me. He was Robert's friend, Charles something or another. Moira might have done my hair and eyes that evening, but she certainly hadn't warned me that Robert had arranged a date for me.

Meddling woman.

I set down my champagne coupe and fixed a smile on my face before turning to Charles. "We met at boarding school."

"Is that right? Which school?" he asked.

"Ethelbrook School for Girls. I was sent there at thirteen after growing up in Paris. I was new and alone, and Moira was the first girl who was kind to me," I said.

"Paris? You don't have an accent at all," he said.

"*Mais bien sur je n'ai pas d'accent. Je suis anglaise aussi,*" I rattled off.

He threw his head back and laughed in such a way that I could hardly tell whether he understood me or not. I might have my moments of wit, but I'm not *that* funny.

"My mother was French. I spent most of the year with her, but when I was a child I would stay with my father's sister during the summers," I explained. I think Aunt Amelia believed that these visits tucked away in Hampshire would somehow keep me from becoming *too* French, as though that were an ailment that needed preventing.

"Until you went to school presumably," Charles said.

I nodded. "My father thought it would be for the best. He wanted me to have an English education."

That might have been the one thing my father hadn't lied to the judge or the papers about. The man was mad for an English education, and I suspect that, had I been a boy, I would have been carted off to Eton at the first moment possible.

"Whereabouts is your family from?" he asked.

"Buckinghamshire originally," I said.

I saw the moment that everything clicked into place for Charles. "You're not Sir Reginald Redfern's daughter, are you?"

I managed to stifle my cringe and gave a clipped nod of acknowledgment instead.

"I remember reading about you in the papers. 'The Parisian Orphan,' they used to call you. What an extraordinary thing," he said with a laugh.

"Yes, it was extraordinary to be written about in all of the papers from the age of ten until thirteen," I muttered, glancing at Moira. I knew she would come to my rescue—we'd done this dance often enough over the years—but Robert was currently playing with the gold bracelet her mother had given her and whispering sweet nothings in her ear.

"That was quite the custody battle. The knight and the French—"

Courtesan. Party girl. Prostitute. Whore. Although Charles had stopped himself before he said something truly indiscreet, I'd heard it all before.

Maman hadn't cared what people called her, instead telling me with a shrug, "I live all of life, *ma chérie*. Some people do not like that. They would rather I was small."

Now, left with only the memory of her, I also tried not to care too much.

"I'm sorry about your mother's death. That must have been terribly difficult for you," Charles had the good manners to say.

"Thank you," I said quietly, because it had been.

I had found *Maman* in bed in the hotel suite we called home. The doctors blamed her death on an overdose of laudanum. The police had concurred—the empty bottle had been found on her bedside table after all. The investigation had been clean, neat, and over in a matter of days—just as my father, who had swooped in clad in false grief, had wanted it. It had also, conveniently, ended the three-year custody battle my parents had been locked in. No matter how you looked at it, my father had won.

In a matter of weeks, he'd flown off to resume his gallivanting ways, and Aunt Amelia was tasked with collecting me in Paris and running me around the shops of London to prepare me for boarding school in the English countryside. I remember all too well standing at my dormitory window at Ethelbrook, miserable as I watched Aunt Amelia's chauffeured car drive her away. Alone and armed with nothing more than a pair of suitcases full of new clothing I didn't want and a crushing case of grief, joy only began to creep back into my world when, a week into the school term, Moira plunked herself down on the edge of my dormitory bed and announced that we should be friends.

"Your father was right, though," said Charles, bringing me back to the table at the Ritz. "At least you received an English education."

Right.

I inhaled sharply, threw back my champagne in one great gulp, and rose, snatching up my gold beaded evening bag as I went. This abrupt movement was enough to break the spell between Moira and Robert.

"Is everything all right?" Moira asked, shooting a look between Charles and me.

"Perfectly. I'm simply tired," I said. "I'm going home."

"I am sorry if I offended you, Miss Redfern," said Charles at the same time Moira said, "But the blackout," and Robert protested, "But I booked us a table next to the dance floor at Café de Paris."

I shook my head to silence all of them. There were two types of people in this world: those who thought my father was right to do what he'd done, and those who didn't.

I knew whom I wanted to spend my time with.

"I'll take the bus," I said.

"The bus?" asked Robert as though he'd never heard of anything so shocking in his life. "At this time of night?"

"I'll come with you," said Moira.

I shook my head emphatically. "You stay with Robert. Go dancing. I'll be fine. Good night."

Before anyone could say anything further on the matter, I turned on my heel and made my way out of the dining room.

I stopped in the lobby of the Ritz. The doorman gestured as though to ask whether I would be leaving. I gave him a small shake of my head. I wanted to go, but with the blackout plunging all of London into a strange darkness, I needed to count out my bus fare before I left the light of the hotel.

I had just unclasped the top of my evening bag when a light touch on my elbow startled me. I whipped around, fully expecting to find that Moira had chased after me, but instead a short, neat man with a white mustache and a pair of rimless spectacles stood before me in an inky black dinner jacket.

"Miss Redfern?" he asked.

I squinted a little. There was something familiar about him.

He touched his chest with short, square fingers. "Lionel Fletcher. You won't remember me. I was a friend of your parents when they lived in Paris."

But I did remember him. He had been at one of the last dinners that *Maman* and my father had hosted together. Even as a nine-year-old child I'd known that things were falling apart, but for that night, when I'd been taken around to meet the guests during cocktails, my parents had seemed happy. I recalled that Mr. Fletcher had rather dramatically produced a pound note and folded it for me into the shape of a little paper bear. My father had clucked that it was too much to give a little girl, but *Maman* had simply kissed Mr. Fletcher on the cheek and stooped to tell me that I must thank the kind gentleman.

"Of course, Mr. Fletcher." I held out my hand to shake. "How do you do?"

"Very well for having seen you, Miss Redfern. I was just saying to my wife last week that I must look you up," he said, nodding to a small, sturdy woman in black sequins and silk who hovered by a column a few feet off.

"What a coincidence that we should both be at the Ritz tonight," I said.

He gave me a little smile and raised his eyebrows, and I had the strange sense that this was not a man who believed in coincidences.

"What are you doing these days, Miss Redfern?" he asked.

"I work in a royal ordnance factory," I said.

"Munitions? Very worthy war work." He paused. "But perhaps not as diverting for a young lady of your intelligence as it could be."

I shifted on my heels. "I'm very happy to do my bit."

Mr. Fletcher reached into his jacket pocket and pulled out a slim gold card case. He flicked it open with the edge of his trimmed nail and pulled out a buff card. Handing it to me, he said, "If you fancy a change, come to this address at half past nine tomorrow morning."

I stared at the card for a moment. Something about the way he said it, with a casualness that felt affected, made me pause. But I couldn't just leave the poor man standing in the lobby of the Ritz, holding a card out, could I?

"I'm due at work at eight," I said.

He waved a hand. "I'll see to it that your foreman understands."

How intriguing. Who was this man who seemed so assured that he could wave away a little annoyance like my regular shift?

"Are you offering me a job?" I asked, finally taking the card.

"I'm simply proposing a conversation," said Mr. Fletcher, a twinkle in his eye. "Now, I must return to Gertrude. Finding a taxi these days is its own unique challenge."

I watched Mr. and Mrs. Fletcher make their way to the door, his hand lighting on the small of his wife's back. Then I looked down at the card:

54 Gosfield Street, No. 4
Fitzrovia

Questions formed on my lips, but when I looked up again, the Fletchers were gone.

THREE

The following morning, I arrived at Gosfield Street two minutes before Mr. Fletcher's appointed time. It was a discreet, quiet road very near the looming presence of the BBC's Broadcasting House, and there was hardly a soul around as I carefully checked the lines of my slim black skirt, white collared shirt, and neat plum jacket I'd pinched from Moira's side of the wardrobe while she was still sleeping off the effects of Robert's generous attitude toward champagne. Over my freshly combed hair, I wore a black beret that showed off *Maman*'s pearl earrings nicely, and I'd painted the bow of my lips bloodred for confidence. I felt as ready as I could without knowing exactly what this "conversation" Mr. Fletcher had invited me for would entail.

At precisely half past nine, I rang the polished metal bell for number 4. There was a long pause before the freshly lacquered black wood door creaked open, and a tall, willowy older woman in a gray belted knit suit peered out at me over the top of the spectacles she wore on a thin chain.

"Can I help you?" she asked.

"I have an appointment with Mr. Fletcher."

I produced the card he had handed me the night before. The woman stared at it with a furrowed brow as though disbelieving that Mr. Fletcher would ever deign to give it to me. I pulled my shoulders back. If I'd survived the constant scrutiny of the teachers at Ethelbrook

School for Girls who had been aware of my "past," I could stand up to one suspicious secretary.

Finally, the woman tucked Mr. Fletcher's card into the square pocket of her jacket. "Follow me, Miss Redfern."

For a fraction of a second, I hesitated, knowing full well that I hadn't provided my name. Then I shook off the unsettled feeling. It was completely logical that Mr. Fletcher would have told his secretary who I was when informing her that he had a morning appointment.

Up the carpeted stairs we went until the woman stopped on the second floor and pulled out a large ring of keys. She unlocked the door and let us both through into the entryway of an office.

The office reception was done up in wood paneling with tasteful oils of country vistas hanging on the walls and a Persian rug reaching from the door to an empty cherrywood desk.

The woman led me past the desk without glancing in its direction, disabusing me of the notion that she might be Mr. Fletcher's secretary, and through a hidden door in the paneling to a room dressed only with a small wooden table, a pair of chairs, and a lamp with a green glass shade. On the table sat a closed file and a pen.

"Sit, please," said the woman, gesturing to the chair that faced away from the door.

I did, trying my best not to notice that she had the incredible ability to make "please" sound less than polite.

The woman also sat down, adjusted her spectacles, and opened the file. She read in silence for a minute, her long, tapered fingers slowly turning the pages. She wore her nails free of polish and buffed to a shine, the only flaw a depression around the fourth finger of her left hand.

"Miss Redfern, I am Miss White," the woman finally said, folding her hands on the table in front of her. "Mr. Fletcher is indisposed and has asked me to speak with you to assess whether you are suitable for some work that he has need of."

"Is this a job interview?" I asked, just as I had the night before.

Miss White glanced down at the file and touched a line of what I could see was neat typing with the tip of her pen cap. "I see that you currently work on the line for a royal ordnance factory."

There was a pause, which I assumed was my cue to speak.

"That is correct," I said.

She nodded once and made a note. "And what is it that you manufacture there?"

"Whatever is useful for the war effort," I said with a smile.

Miss White glanced up at me. "Can you be more specific?"

I certainly could. I'd been haunted by anti-tank shells from the first day I arrived in Woolwich and entered the Royal Artillery. However, if there was one thing that had been drilled into us women on the line from the moment we'd begun filling shells, it was that we could not speak in detail about what it was that we did within the factory's walls.

"Loose lips sink ships" and all that.

"Oh, I don't really know," I said, playing a little dumb. "It's all Greek to me."

"But you must know what it is that you do every day. Your work record is exemplary."

I gave a little laugh even as the hairs of the back of my neck stood straight up. How detailed was that file?

"That is good to know, isn't it?" I asked, with more good humor than I felt.

"Why is that?" asked Miss White.

"Everyone wants someone to notice when they're doing a good job."

"Certainly." Miss White gave me a thin smile. "How is it that you travel to work?"

"Like any else, I suppose. On the bus."

"Which one?"

"Whichever will put me closest," I said.

"You must have a regular bus," said Miss White.

I kept my smile firmly in place. "Nothing really is regular about things these days, is it? One of the women in digs with me had three route changes in as many days because there had been so many smashups due to the blackout. No one can see a thing at night."

"This would be"—another glance down at my file—"Mrs. Jenkins's establishment on Bina Gardens?"

I fought to keep concern out of my expression. This woman I had never met before knew where I lived. She knew where I worked. I didn't like to think what else might be in that infernal little file.

"Miss Redfern," Miss White prompted.

"I'd like to speak to Mr. Fletcher," I said.

"Mr. Fletcher isn't here," Miss White said.

I started to rise from my seat. "Perhaps I can come back another time."

"Please, Miss Redfern. Sit down," said Miss White, gesturing again to the chair I'd just occupied.

Despite my better judgement, I sank down into my seat. I didn't trust this woman—not one bit—but I needed to know what it was that Mr. Fletcher wanted with me after all of these years.

"I assure you, I am only asking questions that Mr. Fletcher himself would want answered," said Miss White with a real smile this time that transformed her face from pinched to warm. "Perhaps you could tell me about Mrs. Jenkins's establishment."

I mirrored her folded hands and fixed her with a look. "What would you like to know?"

"How did you come to live there?"

"I needed a place to live," I began. Miss White nodded encouragement, so I added, "My friend from school and I went in together because she also wanted to live in London."

"What is your friend's name?"

I tilted my head a little, studying her. Finally, deciding that there was no harm in sharing a detail that could easily be known by anyone, I said, "Moira Mangan."

Miss White noted something down in my file. "And you met at Ethelbrook School for Girls, you said?"

"Yes," I said, very aware that I hadn't mentioned Ethelbrook at all.

"When did your parents send you to school?" she asked.

"My father sent me when I was thirteen."

"Why?"

That question made me curious. Among my father's class—too upper crust to be satisfied with a local school but not wealthy enough to be able to justify including a governess on the household staff—it wasn't so unusual to send girls away for their education. From her clipped accent to the quiet nature of her clothing, Miss White seemed like the sort of woman who shouldn't require explanation of this.

"My mother died, and my father didn't know what to do with me," I said.

Normally when I said things like this, most people stumbled over themselves trying to walk the fine line between curiosity and awk-wardness. Miss White, however, was proving to be very unlike most people.

"Your mother died in France, is that right? A tragic accident?" she asked.

"You know so much about me, you must know that."

She looked up. "I beg your pardon?"

"I don't mean to be rude, Miss White, but I was under the impression that I had come here for a conversation, not an interrogation to confirm things that are already written down in that file. Perhaps you could ask me the questions you really want to know the answers to."

The right corner of Miss White's mouth twitched, and I couldn't help feeling like the mouse who thinks it can outwit the cat.

The woman closed the file and capped her pen. "All right, Miss Redfern. How much do you remember of your life with your mother?"

"Not enough. As I said, I was thirteen when she died."

"That must have been difficult for you," she said, not an ounce of sympathy in her voice.

"It was," I said, not seeing the point in trying to hide the truth. Losing *Maman* had been the worst day of my life.

"I can't imagine that things were exactly easy before her death either," said Miss White.

I forced my hands to stay folded on the table, unmoving, even though I wanted very much to hug myself. "I'm not entirely sure what you're referring to."

"Your parents' divorce was a very public *affair*." The way she said the last word told me she'd read—and likely believed—all of the headlines about their very public separation. *Maman*'s allegations that my father liked to do immoral things with every willing woman he came cross in Paris and elsewhere. My father's slanderous claims that, after their separation, *Maman* had taken up with gentlemen for more than just the pleasure of their company.

"And then you were right in the middle of it," said Miss White.

"Yes. The papers called me 'The Parisian Orphan,'" I said with a wry smile, wanting to claim the wretched nickname before she did. "I know I wasn't an orphan, having two living parents and all, but I can hardly blame the papers. 'The Parisian Orphan . . .' It has a certain ring to it, doesn't it?"

"You lived with your mother throughout the divorce proceedings?" Miss White asked.

"Yes," I said.

"And you were called to give evidence in court?" Miss White asked.

I couldn't help squeezing my eyes closed. I hadn't wanted to—I'd begged *Maman* not to make me—but she'd held my face in her hands and said, "Please. For me, *ma chérie*. So that you may stay with me."

"I was," I told Miss White.

"Your father's attorneys asked you about your mother's social activities," she said.

There was another pause, but unlike the beginning of our interrogation, I didn't move to fill it.

"They asked you if she entertained many different gentlemen," said Miss White. "And you said yes."

I nodded my head a fraction. It had been my mother's downfall, her underestimating the ruthlessness of my father's attorneys. They'd sought to take her apart piece by piece until they shamed an unshamable woman and separated us forever. It was only her death that stopped them.

"They also asked if you had ever seen any of those men give her gifts. Jewelry, furs, that sort of thing."

I dug my nails into the palms of my hands. "My mother was a beautiful woman. People always gave her things, even if she didn't ask for them."

Miss White raised a brow. "Money?"

I lifted my chin, knowing how I had answered as a child. Knowing that, even though *Maman* was gone, I would not answer the same way again and stain her memory any further.

"Miss White, I believe that my time here is done. Please tell Mr. Fletcher that I would be happy to come back another day."

"If you will just sit down—"

"I don't think I will, actually," I said.

"This is all a matter of public record," said Miss White.

"And I am choosing not to speak about it," I said. "Just as I imagine you choose not to speak about your own marriage."

Miss White looked stunned. "My marriage?"

I pointed to her left hand. "You wore a wedding ring long enough that you have a permanent imprint on your finger despite calling yourself 'Miss' rather than 'Mrs.' Now, you either took it off for this interrogation or you yourself are divorced."

Miss White swallowed once, but then her cool mask slid back in place. "How very perceptive of you, Miss Redfern."

"Thank you," I said, feeling a little more in control.

Miss White picked the edge of the file up again and looked inside. "Perhaps we can speak more about your father."

"That will be a rather short conversation. I haven't seen him in years," I said.

"Nevertheless—"

"It's all right," came a tinny voice. "I've heard enough."

I looked around, casting about for the speaker. "Is that Mr. Fletcher?"

"Don't bother looking. You won't find it," said Miss White.

The door opened, and Mr. Fletcher strode in. He was much the same as I'd seen him the day before, except that he'd traded his dinner jacket for a gray wool suit and navy silk bow tie.

"I apologize, Miss Redfern, for the line of questioning, but these things are sometimes necessary," said Mr. Fletcher.

"Necessary for what, exactly?" I asked.

Mr. Fletcher looked to Miss White. "If you please, ask Miss Summers to bring tea into my office."

Miss White dipped her head. "Yes, sir."

The older woman scooped up my file and her pen but then hesitated and looked back at me.

"You did very well," she said. Then she left.

"I did very well at what?" I asked, looking to Mr. Fletcher.

"Why don't we go to my office? It's more comfortable there, and we can have a cup of tea while we discuss why I asked you here today."

FOUR

I was brimming with questions—and more than a little ire—as Mr. Fletcher led me out of the small room, past the empty secretary's desk, and through the oiled wood door. His office was small but comfortable, with a set of brown leather armchairs facing a sofa, a wide, well-made desk, and bookcases lining one wall. It being August, the coal fire wasn't lit, but the room exuded a sort of cozy warmth nonetheless.

Mr. Fletcher gestured for me to sit as a petite woman in a pale blue suit I presumed to be Miss Summers came in with a tea tray. There was even a little plate of shortbread biscuits set to one side. The sight of them, full of butter, sugar, and flour, made my mouth water in a way it never would have before rationing had come into place.

"I don't suppose you mind me playing mother, do you?" asked Mr. Fletcher with a smile as he leaned to take up the teapot.

"Not at all," I said, keeping my voice polite and unobjectionable—even if what I really wanted to do was to toss his tea tray onto the ground and demand to know what he was playing at.

He glanced at me as he poured. "I suppose you are angry with me. Milk?"

"Yes, please," I said, accepting the cup and taking a sip before adding, "I suppose that you were trying to make me angry."

"Not angry necessarily. Mrs. White was trying to elicit an emotional reaction with her line of questioning."

A Traitor in Whitehall   25

"She managed that very well. I reacted," I said.

"In a very controlled manner. You did not lose your temper."

I cocked my head to the side. "What if I had burst into tears at the mention of my dead mother or my absent father?"

"Then I would have given you tea and sent you on your way," said Mr. Fletcher.

"That isn't what you're doing right now?" I asked.

"No."

I studied him. "Why?"

"You were right. I do have a job for you, but first I wanted to know what sort of metal you're made of," he said.

"Why not simply ask?"

"In my experience, people are rarely good judges of their own character. It takes a moment of stress to bring out their true nature. Biscuit?" he asked, holding out the plate.

I accepted a piece of shortbread because if I had been made to re-hash old wounds, I was bloody well going to enjoy my tea along the way.

Mr. Fletcher took a biscuit for himself and leaned back in his seat, the leather creaking as it settled around him.

"Before I tell you about the job, Miss Redfern, I must ask you to sign something," he said.

He set his biscuit down on the edge of his saucer and stood to retrieve a piece of paper from his desk drawer.

"This document is a statement saying that you understand that the information I am about to give you is covered by the Official Secrets Act," he said as he handed it to me. "This conversation, this job, anything related to what we discuss, is not to be shared with anyone. Not Miss Mangan or any of the other women in your rooms. Not your father."

"I can't see that my father will be a problem," I said as I took the statement. "As I said earlier, I haven't seen him in years."

"No?" he asked.

I looked up from the document. His tone was casual, but it was underpinned with something approaching curiosity.

"No," I said firmly. "I've laid eyes on him precisely twice since I was sent off to board."

Once had been an awkward lunch at a coaching inn near school the term after I'd arrived. We'd sat across the table from one another in near silence, neither of us knowing what to say to one another, until mercifully the bill came to release us from our familial obligations.

The last time had been a similarly awkward affair four years later, just before I was about to leave school for good. My father had roared up the front drive in a smart SS Jaguar 100, hopped out, and swanned into the headmistress's study as though a visit from him wasn't something extraordinary. I didn't know any of this until the secretary, Miss Clarkson, came to fetch me from my somewhat redundant French lessons and related it all in breathless tones as we hurried to the headmistress's office. A few minutes after I'd been discussing *Le chanson de Roland*, I'd found myself standing in front of the man, hale and handsome—just like his newspaper photographs.

"You look well," he barked. "You take after my side, I think."

"Thank you, sir," I said, even though I knew that my dark hair and pale complexion were far more *Maman*'s traits than his.

"Right. I'm taking Miss Redfern to lunch," he announced.

The headmistress stammered something or another, clearly smitten. It was mortifying, of course, but I could hardly blame the woman. Sir Reginald Redfern was a famous adventurer, knight of the realm, playboy, and general man about town, and the headmistress was only doing what so many women before her had done.

As I'd climbed into my father's car, I'd thought he'd take me for a reprise of our meal at the coaching inn, but instead he'd pointed the Jag toward the road to London and roared off in a cloud of spitting gravel and dust.

We were destined for his club.

"They let women in these days," my father announced as we passed the reception desk. "Not as members, of course, but to dine. Dashed row it caused among the members when it happened."

As we climbed the clubhouse stairs and crossed the dining room, I felt distinctively conspicuous in my schoolgirl's uniform, my skinny limbs sticking out every which way from under my navy wool skirt and blouse. However, the men of his club hardly looked up from their newspapers as we settled in a quiet corner.

Once the waiter had taken our orders, my father fixed me with a look and asked, "What do you intend to do after school?"

I raised my brow. Once *Maman* had died, rendering their custody battle null and void, my father had never shown the littlest bit of interest in me. End-of-term holidays were spent with Aunt Amelia, who I'd always assumed took me in more out of obligation than love.

"I thought to go to university," I said.

"Can't give you an allowance for that," he said with a shake of his head.

"I never dreamed of asking for one," I replied. Aunt Amelia was always going on about how her dashing brother wrote frightfully successful books about adventure and derring-do, but couldn't manage his own affairs if he tried.

Three years later, when I left Edinburgh with a first, I wrote to Aunt Amelia to tell her about my degree—my own sense of obligation, I suppose, since she had surprised me with a small allowance that was enough to keep me in digs and decent food if I minded my shillings. However, it was Moira who'd been my true rock, collecting me from at the train station in London and moving me into the rooms she'd found us at Mrs. Jenkins's that very same day.

I didn't send my father my address or my news, and as far as I knew he hadn't asked his sister for either.

"Will you sign, Miss Redfern?" Mr. Fletcher prompted, pulling me back to reality.

I took the pen he produced from his jacket pocket, uncapped it, and scribbled my signature with a flourish, and then set the document aside to dry.

When I returned the pen, he smiled sadly. "I used to be a Montblanc man, but with the war on I've had to switch pens. German company and all that."

"Mr. Fletcher, will you tell me what this is all about now?" I asked.

He cleared his throat. "Right. There is need of an intelligent girl working in the prime minister's offices. I thought you would be well suited to the role."

"You want me to work for Mr. Churchill?" I asked, a little taken aback.

"In the typing pool. There may be some light secretarial duties too. It's 'all hands on deck' down there, and they need young women who are willing to muck in where needed."

Immediately, I was torn. On one hand, working for Churchill—even indirectly—would be far more exciting than my days on the line at the Royal Artillery. However, I could see a problem with Mr. Fletcher's plan.

"Mr. Fletcher, I haven't worked as a secretary before," I said.

He frowned. "You took secretarial courses, didn't you?"

"Yes," I said carefully. "I did when I first arrived in London. However, I never did work as a secretary or a typist. I wrote copy at an advertising firm. It's a very different skill set."

"And yet you managed to make a go of it, didn't you?" asked Mr. Fletcher.

I shifted in my seat. "Yes, but—"

"Miss Redfern, there are a number of girls already working in the civil service who could take on this job. However, it needs to be the *right* girl."

"Why is that?" I asked.

"Because this isn't just a job in the typing pool. You must also keep your eyes and ears open at all times. I want you to take note of anything that might be untoward or out of place. I need someone observant in the role, and I think that is you to a T," he said.

"You want me to spy on the people I'll be working with?" I asked.

He shook his head. "Not spy. Monitor. This war, more than any other, is about information. Even the smallest detail could be vital to turning the tide in our favor.

"You will be working on shift, spending three days on and two days off. When you are on, you will live in the women's dormitory."

"Live there?" I asked. "In 10 Downing Street?"

"Not quite. You will be employed in the cabinet war rooms."

"I've never heard of the cabinet war rooms," I said.

"That is intentional. The PM was concerned about security and safety in case of an air raid. He's moved the vital operations of the war underground into a secret bunker built under Whitehall. Miss Summers will give you all of the details of where you should present yourself. I suggest packing a small case ahead of your first shift.

"Your first day of work will be next Monday. Use your first three-day shift to settle in. I will expect to see you at this office in two Tuesdays, after your second shift. After that, you can arrange with Miss Summers to make your weekly report."

My brow quirked. "I start next Monday? Then it has all been arranged?"

"I had a high degree of confidence that you would stand up to Mrs. White's questioning," said Mr. Fletcher. "I would suggest that you use your now free days brushing up on your shorthand and typing. Miss Summers will lend you a typewriter. She will also equip you with the pass you will need to make it through the building's security checks and any other details you need to know."

"All right." I rose, sliding my handbag over my left wrist. "I will be sure to do my best."

"Good, Miss Redfern," he said, sticking his hand out for me to shake. "I'm counting on it."

I turned for the door but then stopped. "Mr. Fletcher, you called Miss White 'Mrs.' several times."

"I did," he said.

"Is she not divorced?" I asked.

"Widowed. Her husband died four years ago in a boating accident. I believe you'll find that she uses 'Miss' during interrogations to maintain a degree of distance. It is sometimes easier to intimidate a subject if they cannot establish a connection with or empathy for their interrogator."

My stomach fell. "I should apologize."

Mr. Fletcher shot me a bemused look. "I suspect that, if you do, Eleanor will lose all respect for you. She enjoys a good interrogation with a worthy adversary. Go home, Miss Redfern, and prepare for your assignment. I will see you again in two weeks' time."

FIVE

―――――――

Monday morning, I stood in front of the New Public Offices on Horse Guards Road, clutching one of the two cases I'd moved to London with in my left hand and a piece of paper with the address of my new job in my right. It was ten to nine, and all around me, people were going about their normal days. However, this was not a normal day for me.

I hadn't been nervous about my new job until I'd woken up to wash and dress that morning. There had simply been too much to do to prepare. The previous week, I'd hurried home from Mr. Fletcher's office with the heavy typewriter Miss Summers had presented me with awkwardly clutched under my arm. When Moira returned from some shoot or another that evening, she found me surrounded by scraps of paper.

"You're home early," she said, dropping her hat on the edge of her unmade bed.

"New job," I said, typing up the bit of shorthand I had taken while listening to the wireless downstairs.

"You're not at the factory any longer?" asked Moira.

My fingers froze on the keys. I had signed the Official Secrets Act. I wasn't allowed to tell Moira—my best friend in the world—what it was I would be doing at work every day.

"That's right. I'm going to be working as a secretary in one of the Whitehall offices. I'm sure it will be dull, but at least I won't have to hear the ups and downs of Sheryl's love life any longer."

"That should suit you, I would think," said Moira, turning to peel off the rest of her things.

"The shifts are long, so they want us to bunk there while we're working. Three days on, two days off," I said.

Out of the corner of my eye, I saw Moira's face fall. "Are you moving out, Evie?"

I swung my legs out from under the little card table I'd perched the typewriter on and gave her a big hug. "Not a chance. I'll be back here for my days off, so don't even think about asking Jocelyn to move across the hall to take my place. And no taking over the entire chest of drawers."

Moira's shoulders relaxed. "I can't make any promises. Tell me, what do we need to do to make sure you're ready for your first day?"

Now, staring up at the entrance to my new job, I wished I could have Moira there with me.

"Pull yourself together, Evelyne," I muttered to myself. I unsnapped the handbag that hung against my case, deposited the paper inside, and fished out my security pass.

As soon as the Royal Marine standing guard just inside looked at my pass, a prim, birdlike woman called out my name. She might have been forty, so fresh was her skin, or sixty, so dowdy was her hair. She wore a pair of wire-rimmed spectacles, and two silver pins connected by a chain at the throat of her cardigan.

"I am Miss Wilkes," she said when I came to a stop in front of her.

"How do you do?" I asked.

Her eyes raked over me, and then she gave a nod. "Do you have your pass?"

I held up the orange piece of card I'd just presented at the door. On the front was written:

C.W.R.
On presentation of this Pass the holder
EVELYNE REDFERN
is authorized to enter the C.W.R. on official duty.

"Good," said Miss Wilkes. "You will need that pass every time you enter or exit the building. You must also carry it—and your gas mask—on your person whenever you are working.

"It is very important that you are on time for your shifts. Not early, not late," she continued as we began to climb a flight of stairs. We stopped at a door on a landing, presented our passes, and then found ourselves at another staircase.

"This is Staircase 15," said Miss Wilkes as we passed by a sober Royal Marine stationed at a large set of doors. "Take note of where you are at all times. The building can be confusing at first, and it is important that you do not wander off anywhere you are not meant to be."

"What is behind that door?" I asked, glancing over my shoulder.

"Nothing of your concern," snapped Miss Wilkes. But then she glanced from side to side and lowered her voice. "That is the entrance to the No. 10 Annex flat."

"Does Mr. Churchill live there?" I asked, more than a little impressed.

"Not presently, but I've been told that there is talk of it being readied for him, should he need it."

Miss Wilkes led me down a staircase made of concrete. I imagined that this was a little like what descending into the hull of a ship felt like. Everything was fluorescent light and ugly pale yellow tile with lino flooring. At the bottom of the stairs, we showed our passes again and were allowed out into a long corridor studded with red-painted steel beams overhead that made it impossible to forget the weight of the ground pressing down on us.

The corridor was a hive of activity. Men in every uniform of the armed services strode forth with purpose, while besuited civil servants of every variety sped up and down with file folders in hand. A harried-looking woman in a tweed skirt, brandishing a notepad and pencil, followed a mustachioed man, quickly scribbling down dictation as they went.

"Is it always this busy in the cabinet war rooms?" I asked.

"You may find that calling it the CWR will save you time. This is a normal day," said Miss Wilkes, with a satisfied smile—the first I'd seen since meeting her. "If there's a flap on, it can feel as though all of London is down here with us."

As though to punctuate the controlled chaos, we managed only a few more feet before a bespectacled man with a receding hairline ran up to us, waving a set of papers.

"Miss Wilkes, this cannot go on!" he cried.

"Mr. Faylen, what is the matter?" asked Miss Wilkes with what sounded to me like a weary sigh.

He thrust the papers forward, making them crinkle. "The duplicates that I requested. They haven't been done."

"Mr. Faylen, I know that you are not suggesting that my ladies are not diligent in their work," said Miss Wilkes. He opened his mouth—I suspect to say that very thing—but she put up a hand. "Yesterday you rushed into the typing pool three times, insisting that we stop what we were doing and work on a different set of duplicates for you. *Three times.* We did what we could, but my ladies are not machines."

"But, Miss Wilkes, these are important," he protested.

"Everything that we do in this office is important, Mr. Faylen. The reason that your duplicates have not been typed yet is because something came in directly from the PM," said Miss Wilkes.

Mr. Faylen seemed to deflate at the mention of Churchill, and when he tried to muster a, "But these are vital," his heart hardly seemed to be in it.

Miss Wilkes stuck out her hand. "Let me see."

The man handed over the documents. I watched Miss Wilkes's eyes flick over them and then narrow.

"Mr. Faylen, I'm sure you must be mistaken. Cathy duplicated this memo two days ago," said Miss Wilkes.

Mr. Faylen's ears turned beetroot red. "That can't be. I'm certain I—"

"I assigned the work. I was there when you collected the pages," said Miss Wilkes, handing them back to Mr. Faylen. "I'm sure if you search your desk, you'll find them."

After shooting Miss Wilkes a stern glare, Mr. Faylen marched away without another word.

"Who was that?" I asked, watching him go.

"Harold Faylen. He is an assistant secretary to the Minister of War. He doesn't seem to be adjusting to his time in the CWR. Apparently, before the war, he was neat as a pin, calm and composed. Now he has a nasty habit of losing things and storming about when he can't find them," said Miss Wilkes, tugging at the hem of her jacket. "As though that is anything to do with my department."

I glanced back at Mr. Faylen's retreating figure, and was just about to turn away when another man caught my eye. He was dressed in a brown suit with a Fair Isle vest that would have seemed out of place in August save the constant roar of what I assumed were enormous air conditioning units that kept the air moving underground. He wore his light brown hair combed in a deep side part. In his hands, he carried an open file; however, he seemed far more intent on studying the interaction between Mr. Faylen and Miss Wilkes than he was in the contents of his folder.

Then, almost as though he felt me watching him, he glanced my way. Our eyes met. His lips quirked as he snapped the file shut and retreated in the opposite direction.

"Who was that?" I asked in a low tone.

Miss Wilkes glanced at the man's retreating back and frowned. "Miss Redfern, it is strictly forbidden for typists or switchboard operators to fraternize with any men, civilian or military, in the CWR."

"I would never dream of it, Miss Wilkes," I said, putting on my most innocent expression.

I'm not entirely sure she bought it because she huffed, but then she went on: "That is David Poole. He is relatively new—he's been just two months with us. He assists the minister of information, Mr. Duff Cooper."

"I see," I said.

"Come along," ordered Miss Wilkes.

I fell into step with her again, stopping only when we arrived at a door marked 60 on the top of its frame. On the door itself hung a sign that read "Typing Pool."

Miss Wilkes opened the door. I could hear the occasional giggle as two women with their backs toward us leaned close to gossip, their fingers still flying over the keys. The room smelled of freshly struck ink and five different perfumes. Yet something was wrong. After a moment, I realized what it was: the lack of noise. I could see six typewriters—five occupied—yet none of them made the incredible clatter I expected.

"They're noiseless," explained Miss Wilkes. "Mr. Churchill had them imported especially from America. He can't abide unnecessary sounds."

"I see," I said.

"Ladies," called Miss Wilkes as she clapped. Almost immediately, the typing stopped. "I would like you to meet Miss Redfern. She will be taking Gloria's place."

There was a a chorus of mostly cheery hellos.

"Miss Travers, will you please take Miss Redfern to the Dock to store her things? Then you may show her how we do things here," said Miss Wilkes.

A glamorous woman, who had raven's wing black hair and wore a claret-colored suit that managed to be both modest and stylish, popped up from her typewriter.

"Gladly, Miss Wilkes." Miss Travers turned to me and grinned. "Follow me."

The moment we were out of the typing pool door and into the corridor, Miss Travers spun around on her high heel to face me.

"I'm Irene. What's your name?" she asked.

"Evelyne."

"Good. We only call each other Miss Travers and Miss Redfern when Miss Wilkes is around. She's frightfully old-fashioned, don't you think?" asked Irene.

"Perhaps a little," I said carefully, not wanting anything to make its way back to Miss Wilkes but not disagreeing with Irene at all. Miss Wilkes had the air of the Victorian about her.

Irene leaned in. "Did she already warn you about not seeing any of the men down here?"

I laughed. "She might have mentioned it."

Irene rolled her eyes. "She is always going on about that, but that isn't as though it stops anyone. Why should we when there are hardly any decent men left around in London these days? Bloody war."

"Bloody war," I murmured in agreement.

Irene gave me a cheerful smile. "Come on, I'll show you where we all sleep when we're on shift. It's called the Dock, and I hope it won't scare you off too much."

SIX

I followed Irene through the corridor to another metal door—the place was filled with them and they all looked the same—and another staircase. This one descended to a level below our underground offices. A wall of stench hit me immediately, and I scrunched up my nose.

"It's the chemical toilets," said Irene. "I'd tell you that you become used to the smell over time, but that would be a lie.

"This is the women's dormitory. The men sleep separately from us—of course—and that really is a hard and fast rule. If you're caught on the men's side for any reason, you'll be out of the job faster than you can try to apologize."

Irene led me down a row of wooden bunk beds before stopping in front of one of them. "This is where I try to bunk when I'm on shift. It's the farthest away from the entrance, so you have fewer people knocking into you when you're trying to sleep. If you can become used to the air conditioning and the other noises, it's really not so bad sleeping here. Just try to keep as far away from Cathy as you can. She snores. Joanna on nights does too."

I suspected that if I had survived years of sleeping in a dormitory with a dozen other girls at school, I would be just fine sleeping in the Dock.

"Which one should I choose?" I asked.

"Any one but that one," said Irene, pointing to the top bunk two down from hers. "That's Jean's."

"Who is Jean?" I asked.

She pulled a face. "Oh, you'll have the joy of meeting her soon enough. She's in the typing pool as well."

"You don't get along?" I asked.

She gave a short laugh. "No, we don't."

I wanted to know why, but I didn't want to push my luck with Irene too early. Instead, I settled for asking, "Why does she have her own bunk if they're meant to be unassigned?"

Irene rolled her eyes. "She isn't supposed to, but she makes everyone's life miserable if she doesn't get it. It even stays open when she's not on shift. Here." She took my suitcase from me and hauled it up onto the unclaimed bunk to the left of hers.

"Don't mind the rats, by the way. They're practically harmless," she said.

I jerked back. "The rats?"

She shrugged. "You'll become used to it. We are living underground, after all."

I supposed that was true, but simply because it was logical didn't mean I had to like it.

"Did you bring a dressing gown?" Irene asked.

"I did." Living at Mrs. Jenkins's, I was used to traversing the corridors blurry eyed in the mornings on my way to wash my face and brush my teeth in the loo the next floor down.

"Good. You never know who you'll see in the corridors," said Irene.

She watched as I popped open my suitcase and stored a few personal items and my handbag in the cubby next to my bunk.

"Never leave anything personal out, and make sure you take everything with you at the end of your shift. Some people have light fingers," said Irene.

"There have been thefts?" I asked, locking my things away.

"Not thefts so much as girls claiming that things have moved around when they've been on shift. Hairbrushes being in the wrong spot, hairpins falling out of their tins, things like that. Not that anyone would be able to make it out of the CWR with anything they stole. The Royal Marines will check your bags each time you leave, and sometimes a supervisor like Miss Wilkes will go through your pockets, so be sure that you aren't carrying any documents or paper out with you. Even a scrap of notepaper can be a fireable offense," Irene said.

"Really?" I asked.

She nodded. "It's one of the security measures they put into place in June. I was in a meeting taking shorthand and one of the deputies started talking about it. Apparently they're worried about leaks."

My ears perked up. This could be something Mr. Fletcher might want to know about.

"In the typing pool, we have locked boxes at each of our desks where we deposit all of our notes, mistakes, typewriter ribbons, anything that might have any sensitive information on it," she continued. "At the end of each shift, Jean is in charge of taking it all to the incinerator. And, of course, we're not meant to talk about what it is that we're working on—even down here, although it does happen from time to time. Just don't let Miss Wilkes or Caroline catch you."

"Who is Caroline?" I asked.

She sniffed. "She steps in when Miss Wilkes is pulled away. She's just a typist like the rest of us, but she follows the rules so closely that Miss Wilkes deputizes her sometimes. She's a tattletale so I would stay on her good side if I were you."

"That's good to know. Thank you," I said.

I thought Irene might tell me that it was time to return to the typing pool, but instead she crossed her arms and looked me up and down. "You know, usually the new girl ends up working nights with a floating desk. You ended up with a day shift and a permanent desk. You must know Churchill himself."

I laughed. "I promise you, the prime minister and I are in no way acquainted."

However, I sent up a silent little thank-you to Mr. Fletcher for whatever arrangements he'd made that meant that I was on a humane schedule.

"Who is the girl I'm replacing?" I asked.

Irene waved her hand. "Oh, Gloria. She didn't stay long. She was engaged when she joined us, and when her fiancé came back on leave from the Royal Navy they got married. There are no married ladies in the typing pool, so she had to go. It was a shame really. We don't seem to be able to keep anyone in Desk 1."

"Why is that?" I asked.

She shrugged. "I don't really know. First it was Charlotte, then Gloria. Now there's you.

"Let's see, what else do you need to know?" Irene continued before

I could ask more about Charlotte or Gloria. "Never agree to switch a shift with Anne. She works nights, and she's desperate to be on days. Caroline, Patricia, and Edith are all working today, and Rachel and Cathy are our swings, so they'll be coming in next. Swings hop around to whatever desk is free at any given moment. Most of the girls really are sweethearts, and if you ask nicely Edith will give you a spiffing haircut."

Irene fluffed her hair and preened, so I made admiring noises.

"Betty will take over on your desk most nights. You'll be briefing each other when you go on and off shifts. The rest of the girls on nights are nice enough, but we don't see them much."

I did a quick mental calculation of all of the names that Irene had rattled off and then frowned. "And I gather the sixth woman is Jean?"

Irene looked at me sharply. "You're a quick one, aren't you?"

"I try to pay attention," I said.

"Miss Wilkes will like that. Just remember, Jean is like Jekyll and Hyde. Sometimes she'll be sweet as can be, but if she thinks you've crossed her, she'll lash out faster than an adder. She's also always sniffing through other people's dirty laundry. And don't pretend you don't have any. Everyone does, it's simply a question of how well you've hidden it."

Oh, I had dirty laundry. It wouldn't take long before one of my fellow typists recognized my name—or my father's. Long after his very public divorce trial from *Maman*, Sir Reginald had gone on making headlines. Motorcycle racing through the Alps. Trekking across the Namibian desert. Sailing single-handed through the Indonesian archipelago. The odd party here and there in Kenya or New York, Shanghai or London, each time with a different glamorous woman on his arm. The newspaper reports were the only way I kept up with him—not that I devoted too much attention to his pursuits.

Others might see the glamour in my adventurer father. I saw him for what he was—a selfish man who cared little for anything but hedonism in all forms.

I knew that I would have to choose my moment—preferably when a number of my colleagues were around—to address my family name in the most matter-of-fact way.

"Thank you for the advice," I said to Irene.

"You're welcome." The edges of her mouth tipped up. "Now let's hope you can keep up."

═══════════

I was only three hours into my first shift with the typing pool, and I was already exhausted. It was a hive of activity, the dull thump of six noiseless Remington keys the odd score to the wartime drama playing out around me.

It was incredible how rapidly paper flew in and out of the room, with everyone from clerks to ministers' secretaries hauling open the metal door to demand things of us. Miss Wilkes was quick to intercept them, listen to what was required, and then rattle off instructions to whichever typist was next in the queue for work. Sometimes the requester disappeared into the corridor again, but other times they stood against a little gap of free wall in the small room, arms crossed and feet tapping until the work was done.

I was infinitely grateful for Mr. Fletcher's foresight in lending me a typewriter to practice on. I was nowhere near as fast as the other women, but at least when I handed over my typed documents for Miss Wilkes to check, she'd only had two corrections on my work for the day so far.

Irene had told me that when the night shift girls relieved us in the evening, we would be released to go to the canteen or—if there was no flap on—the Lyons Corner House on Coventry Street for a bite of supper. With rationing in place, I didn't expect that the meal would be much, but I was already dreaming of the relative calm that would accompany it.

The typing pool's metal door handle clanged and Edith rushed in, breathless. "Miss Wilkes! Mr. Dean would like to see you."

"See me?" Miss Wilkes asked.

Edith clutched her pad and nodded, sending her short blond curls bouncing. "He says it's urgent."

Miss Wilkes rose stiffly, brushed down the front of her skirt, and announced, "Caroline, you are in charge of assignments."

Caroline, whom I'd found to be a little serious for my taste when I met her after Irene's tour of the Dock, nodded and resumed her typing.

As soon as the door shut behind Miss Wilkes, the thud of type-writer keys resumed. Edith slid into the desk next to mine, glancing over at Caroline.

"The PM was in that meeting I've just come from," Edith whispered in her little girl voice. "He was in a rage. Apparently part of a memo marked 'Secret' made its way onto a German propaganda broadcast."

"What?" I asked. If that really was true, it sounded as though the CWR had very good reason to be concerned about leaks.

"You've heard of Lord Haw-Haw?" asked Edith, eyes wide.

Who hadn't? Lord Haw-Haw was the pseudonym of the presenter of the English-language propaganda show that the Germans broadcast out to Britain. He sounded like your garden-variety British aristocrat, but the things he said could be downright nasty. I will admit, I listened because sometimes Lord Haw-Haw had more information about what was happening in Europe than the papers and the BBC, although what he broadcast was always favorable for the Germans. However, Mrs. Jenkins disapproved of the broadcasts, so all of us had to wait until she was otherwise disposed to turn on the wireless and wait for Lord Haw-Haw's signature opening "Germany calling, Germany calling" to come crackling over the airwaves.

"How did he even learn the information?" I asked.

"No one knows. There are probably spies all about," whispered Edith, casting her gaze about as though an enemy agent might pop up from behind someone's desk. "Can you imagine? It's like something out of a book."

Behind us Caroline cleared her throat. Both Edith and I snapped to attention, our fingers instinctively flying to our keyboards.

However, only a few moments later, another voice cut through the noise.

"Evelyne."

I twisted in my seat and found Jean Plinkton standing just a few feet from me, a smirk etched on her face. She was objectively stunning, with enviable hair that was a sun-kissed strawberry blond. She wore a thin-knit, baby pink jumper and a light gray skirt topped with sky-high heels, exuding an effortless glamour that made the rest of us typists look somehow flat in comparison. Despite Irene's warning, I'd sensed nothing sinister in the way Jean had smiled sweetly during Miss Wilkes's introduction, saying, "How do you do?" as pleasant as could be. Now, however, without Miss Wilkes's supervision, her tone sounded syrupy as a flytrap.

I could feel every other woman's eyes on me, waiting to see what would happen between us.

"Yes?" I asked.

"You must tell us *everything* about yourself. We're all so curious. Did you work for a minister before this?" Jean asked.

"No, I was on the line in a royal ordnance factory," I said.

"We really should be working, Jean," Caroline tried to cut in.

"What about before the war?" Jean asked, ignoring Caroline.

"I was a copywriter in an advertising agency."

"But that means you're not a typist or a secretary?" she asked, aghast.

"I trained as a secretary after I left university, but I found the copy-writing job shortly after I finished that course. It suited me, so I took it," I said.

"Then what is it you're doing here? Surely you should be in the Ministry of Information, shouldn't you?"

I lifted one shoulder a fraction. "I am happy to be placed wherever I am needed."

"Oh dear, but we don't need a copywriter," said Jean with a trilling laugh, glancing around at the other women for support. "You see, all of the other ladies here are well trained and experienced. In fact, many of us have skills that go far beyond typing. I, for one, am frequently called upon to take shorthand for meetings."

"Leave her alone, Jean," said Irene.

Jean's beautiful features darkened. "I'm simply asking questions."

"Is that right? Because it sounds rather like you're staking out your territory," Irene grumbled.

Jean pouted. "I want to know a little more about our newest typist. That's all."

"That's not what it sounds like," said Patricia, tugging the edges of her cardigan close around her.

"I swear I never thought I'd live to see the day I'd actually hear you speak again, Patricia!" Jean exclaimed.

"Jean, stop," said Irene as Patricia shrank back into her chair.

"Excuse me, but Patricia and I are having a conversation. Aren't you hoping to learn more about Miss Redfern, Patricia? Maybe you'll get along just as well as you and Charlotte did. Although maybe this time when Evelyne leaves you won't cry quite so much."

From where I sat, I could see Patricia's cheeks flame tomato red.

I had had enough of this sort of childish competition in boarding school to last me a lifetime, so I fixed Jean with a stare. "If you wish to speak to me, you may speak to me. There is no need to involve anyone else."

Jean gave me a thin smile. "We're a typing pool. We're meant to work together, although I can understand that you wouldn't know that given you haven't done this job before."

To my side, I heard Irene snort in disgust.

"I can assure you that I will work hard and do my share," I said. "Now, is there anything else you wished to know about me?"

"Really, there's no need to be defensive," said Jean.

"I'm not being defensive. I'm simply clearing the air. I understand I'm new and that you're all curious about me. You'll find that I'm actually rather used to people asking me all manner of questions."

"Evelyne, you really don't need to—"

I cut Irene off by holding my hand up, my gaze never leaving Jean's. "At some point, I have no doubt, someone will learn that my father is Sir Reginald Redfern, the adventurer. Many years ago, my mother initiated a divorce from my father while I was living with her in Paris. It caused rather a lot of bother and some of the newspapers wrote about it," I said, brazening my way through the slightly taken aback stares.

"Well," said Jean, "that's very forward of you to tell us that."

"I've always found it best to lead with these things in case someone decides to blow them out of proportion," I said. "Now, you know everything there is to know. If you will allow me to return to my work . . ."

"Yes, that's what we should all be doing," Caroline interjected.

Jean gave that light little laugh again. "I was only trying to learn more about our newest colleague."

"Learn more about her when you're not on shift," said Caroline.

Jean held her hands up and turned back around, but I didn't miss the almost thoughtful glance she sent me over her shoulder as she settled into her desk.

SEVEN

fter my initial encounter with Jean, the rest of my first three days in the CWR were relatively uneventful. Out of necessity, I became faster at typing, and I snuck moments to practice my shorthand on the steno pad I kept next to my typewriter while Miss Wilkes checked my work. Every time I left my desk, I locked my notes up, and at the end of the day I dutifully slipped my documents into the bins Jean carted off to the incinerator.

Both in and out of the typing pool, I steered clear of Jean. It wasn't particularly difficult as she seemed to take every moment she could to be away from her desk, jumping up whenever someone telephoned to request assistance with dictation or meeting notes. And apparently the typing pool wasn't the only place Jean was keen to leave.

On Tuesday evening, long after our shift had ended and we were all meant to be in our bunks, I awoke to see Jean slipping out of bed. She carefully slid her feet into a pair of slippers. I thought I saw the flash of her light gray wool skirt under her quilted dressing gown, but I couldn't be sure in the dimmed lights.

I considered asking Irene about it, but my fellow typists hardly had a good word to say about Jean, with Irene the harshest in her criticism. However, I found none of their animosity aimed at me. Indeed, the other ladies seemed content to adopt me as one of their own, inviting me to join in when they took meals. In the Dock at night, I played gin for matchsticks with Irene and a bright-eyed woman named Rachel, and listened to Edith perform her best impressions of the prime minister's distinctive voice, blond curls trembling as she shook her pretend jowls.

However, when on Wednesday evening I stumbled out into the dimming light of the gently falling late summer night, I was grateful for my two days off to rest my whirring brain. I practically sleepwalked to the bus that took me home to Bina Gardens. Fortunately Moira was in and the moment I put my case down she shoved me toward the bath to wash off the residual memory of the Dock before setting me up in bed with a bowl of soup and one of Margery Allingham's Albert Campion novels.

A girl never had a better friend.

My time away from the CWR did wonders for reviving me, and by the time I showed my pass to the Royal Marine at the top of the stairs and descended into the CWR's underground tunnels on Saturday morning, I was ready and looking forward to my second shift at work.

"Miss Plinkton," said Miss Wilkes from across the typing pool about an hour after I'd settled in at my desk. All of us turned our heads to watch while we continued to type. "Do you find yourself missing the bunks of the Dock when you are not at work?"

Jean frowned, her lips pushing out into a pretty little pout. "I beg your pardon, Miss Wilkes?"

"I suggest that you make better use of your time away from this office so that you do not continuously yawn at your desk."

A titter rose up through the typing pool as Jean's gaze hardened. "Yes, Miss Wilkes."

"Ladies," Miss Wilkes said, casting a stern gaze about the room, "if you do not have enough to do, I'm certain that Mr. Faylen would be happy to send you more work."

All of us snapped to attention.

There was a flurry of activity when a Mr. Conley, tall and impressive in a navy suit, strode in with an armful of file folders stuffed with enough work to keep us occupied until lunch.

A few hours later, in the canteen, I sat with Irene, Caroline, and Edith, wiggling my fingers to try to alleviate some of the soreness that had built up in them that morning. As soon as Miss Wilkes released us for lunch, Jean had headed straight for the staircase to go aboveground.

Meanwhile Patricia, who had walked in with us, set herself up in a corner with a book firmly held in front of her face as a barrier.

"Doesn't she want to join us?" I quietly asked the others, even if I was a little jealous that Patricia got to read while I had to chat.

Irene leaned in. "Patricia never sits with anyone."

"That's not true. She used to sit with Charlotte," said Edith. "They were thick as thieves."

"Charlotte is one of the women who used to work here?" I asked, recalling Irene's mention of her.

"She quit," said Caroline, lifting her nose as though the very idea of quitting the CWR was distasteful.

"But why?" I asked.

"No one knows," said Caroline.

"Surely Patricia would if they were such close friends," I said.

Edith shook her head emphatically. "Patricia was devastated when she found out. At first, I thought it was because she'd typed a memo about a lost ship with a brother or a boyfriend on it, but it was just because of Charlotte. We tried to tell her she would be able to see her friend outside of work, but she wouldn't be consoled."

"I always wondered if they had a row," said Edith, taking a bite of her thin cheese and cress sandwich.

"We really shouldn't be speaking about this," said Caroline, eyes darting to Patricia. "Whatever happened was a private matter."

"Oh, don't pretend that you aren't just as curious as I am," Irene said.

Caroline straightened her shoulders primly. "What my colleagues do outside of work and the choices they make isn't my affair."

Irene raised a brow. "You mean to tell me that you never wonder where Jean goes every lunch?"

"She truly never eats with us," Edith told me.

"No," said Caroline.

"Or how about how she can afford to eat out lunch and dinner every time she's in the CWR," said Irene with a raised brow.

"We don't know anything about her. She could be living at home and saving money," said Caroline.

"But that's just it. We don't know *anything* about her other than she passed the same security checks that we did," said Irene.

"And that she types seventy-five words a minute. Oh, and she's all of the men's favorite substitute to take meeting notes when their own secretaries are occupied," said Edith before taking another bite.

Irene made a dismissive sound.

"Maybe she goes for a bit of fresh air and then comes back. There's always a spare room somewhere," said Caroline. "Just look at the sunlamp treatments."

"Have you gone for your first sunlamp treatment yet?" Irene asked me.

I shook my head.

"Enjoy that little delight," she said with a snort.

"What do you mean?" I asked.

"Working here, we spend far too much time underground without any sun, so we're required to have ultraviolet light treatments," explained Caroline.

"They find a spare room and you are assigned a time to go, strip down to your unmentionables, and stand in front of one of the treatment lamps," said Edith.

"There's no dignity in it," said Irene.

"It's meant to help us with all sorts of diseases," said Caroline.

"Like what?" Irene challenged.

Caroline rose to her feet and gave a firm nod. "We do it because we're told to do it. Now, I am going back to work."

"We have five minutes," said Irene, glancing down at a rather lovely slim gold watch stacked next to a gold bracelet that just peeked out of her cardigan's sleeve.

"I like to be early," said Caroline.

Irene, Edith, and I watched her go.

"I'm so glad you're working with us, Evelyne," Edith said with a bright smile. "It's nice to have someone fun around here. Now, I think I'll just run to the Dock and fix my lipstick. I never can make it stay through a meal."

As soon as Edith left, Irene shot me a smile. "And then there were two."

I tipped my cup of tea slightly in a salute.

Irene shifted to lean forward and close the space between us. "Evelyne, I wonder, would you be an absolute doll and do me the biggest favor?"

"A favor?" I asked.

"It's nothing really." However, Irene still lowered her voice, a sparkle in her dark eyes. "If someone asks whether you saw me in the Dock this evening during our overnight, all you need to do is say yes."

That certainly didn't sound like nothing. It sounded as though she wanted me to lie for her.

"Where will you be instead?" I asked.

Irene gave a shy smile, a wave of her black hair falling across her eye as she dipped her head. The gesture struck me as so contrary to the bold, confident character I'd come to know. "There's a man."

"A man?" When she hesitated, I hastened to add, "Your romantic life really isn't any concern of mine. I'm only worried that you might be caught."

"Oh, don't worry about that," she said.

"But surely the guards—"

She waved a hand, dismissing my concerns. "Oh, you leave that to me."

With her confidence back, she sounded more like one of the girls I went to school with rather than a woman working in the nerve center of Churchill's war effort. Yet I couldn't blame her. Everyone felt the urge for some normalcy these days—a break from this wretched war.

I knew I'd had it easier than some. I didn't have a brother or cousin in uniform to worry about like many women. There was no boyfriend, fiancé, or husband off fighting when he should have been home with me. I didn't know where my father was or if the army, which he had fought in in the last war, would even want him back at his age.

Still, I dreamed of little things from my pre-war life. A meal bought without thinking about how many ration coupons it would cost me. A night out planned without having to decide whether or not to carry my gas mask along with my evening clutch. Silk stockings that weren't hoarded like gold dust.

What I wouldn't have given for a cup of tea filled with real milk!

All every sane person in this country wanted was for the fighting to stop and life to go back to the way it had once been.

"If anyone asks where you are, I'll tell them that the smell in the Dock gave you a headache and you went to splash some water on your face," I said.

"Oh, Evelyne, you really are a doll," Irene practically purred.

"Don't give it another thought," I said. "Although I really don't see how you'll be able to get around the Royal Marines on guard. Won't they report that you passed them by on your way out if anyone asks?"

Irene grinned. "I think you'll find that some of them are willing to look the other way from time to time. Especially if you flirt with them a little."

"Which guards are those?" I asked.

Irene waved a finger at me. "That, I'm afraid, is information that you'll have to find out on your own, but if I were a wise woman, I would keep an eye out for a particularly good-looking one."

I returned Irene's grin even as I filed that little tidbit of information away for later.

EIGHT

That afternoon, there was a rare lull in assignments. Patricia and Jean were on deliveries, a request had come in via telephone asking for Irene's assistance with a memo, and Caroline had practically snatched the last assignment out of Miss Wilkes's hands. Edith was busy cleaning her typewriter, while I practiced my shorthand and let my mind wander.

I couldn't shake the feeling that Irene's plan to slip away that evening was unnecessarily reckless and would likely one day cost her her job. I suppose, now that I think about it, I was exposing myself to risk as well by agreeing to fib for her. Perhaps it was my own propensity for skirting the rules at school coming back to me. I remembered how Moira and I used to egg each other on to climb out the window of our dormitory bathroom and make our way out into the wood on the edge of the school simply to toe the line of what was allowed.

It also struck me that Irene asked me, a woman she'd only just met, rather than one of the other typists. When I'd entered the CWR, I'd expected a workplace of harmony—everyone laboring diligently under the nose of the prime minister for the sake of the war—but what I'd found was fractious. Some girls, like Edith, seemed perfectly content to accept the goings-on of the typing pool, but I could feel that something was off from Jean's aloofness to the abrupt disappearance of Charlotte. Even Irene seemed to be acting a part, shifting from bold career girl to shy ingenue in a matter of moments to secure what she wanted from me.

Would Mr. Fletcher really care about any of that? He had given me very little direction about what I was supposed to be looking out for, saying only, *Even the smallest detail could be vital to turning the tide in our favor.*

Well, if there were any useful details to be found, I was determined to be the woman who unearthed them.

"Miss Redfern!"

My head snapped up as Miss Wilkes approached my desk, clipboard and pencil in hand.

"Yes, Miss Wilkes," I said, pulling an old dispatch over my steno pad where I'd been practicing my shorthand.

"You're due for your first sunlamp treatment," said Miss Wilkes.

"Sunlamp treatment," I repeated.

"All of us are required to go. It helps keep us healthy, what with the amount of time we're underground. I'm certain that one of the other girls must have mentioned this while training you."

"I apologize, Miss Wilkes. I became caught up in my work, and it slipped my mind," I fibbed.

"Go now while there is a lull before the evening shift change," Miss Wilkes ordered. "And remember to secure your notes."

I locked away my notes and notepad before hurrying out of the room. If I didn't dally, I could stop at the Dock to pick up my book, and then—

Well, you know all of this bit and how it was that I found myself, on my fourth day of work in the CWR, locked in a spare room with a dead body.

Back plastered against the door, I stared in shock at the body at the end of the room. That was all I could think of it as: "the body." But I knew exactly who had bled out on the floor of the room.

Jean.

We were never destined to be friends, but there was no part of me that had wanted to see her harmed. Now she lay there lifeless on the desk.

The last time I had seen a corpse . . .

My wits came back to me in a rush. I needed to find help. I needed out of that room. I pushed off the ground and began to scream.

"Help! Help! Let me out! Help!"

I banged on the door and tugged on the handle. Nothing. These doors were designed with strength in mind, and a woman just a shade over five foot seven was not going to batter one down anytime soon.

"Help!" I went on screaming, hoping that the doors of the CWR weren't also soundproof.

I almost collapsed with relief when I heard the scrape of metal against metal and suddenly the softer light of the corridor mixed with the sunlamp device I'd turned on. I pushed past my savior and staggered out, gasping for breath.

"What the devil is going on?"

I looked up through the dark curtain of my fringe and saw that it was that man who had stared at me in the corridor on my first day. David Poole. I managed to pull his name from somewhere in the recesses of my brain, even while the panic and adrenaline of finding Jean's body coursed through me.

"She's dead," I said, raising a shaky hand to point back to the room.

He stared at me. "Dead? What do you mean dead?"

The doubt in his voice snapped me out of my shock.

"Someone's killed her." She was dead. What more did he need to know?

Mr. Poole pushed by me, and stopped as soon as he passed the partition now wobbling dangerously on its side.

"Bloody Hell," I heard him mutter. In a flash, he was at Jean's side, lifting her wrist to check her pulse. He dropped her hand and gave a shake of his head. "She's dead."

"That's what I just told you! Did you think I would miss the knife sticking out of her throat?" I cried, my voice rising. I'm not a hysterical woman by nature, but I do think that stumbling across a dead body is justification for dramatics.

"How did you find her?"

"I had come in to do my sunlamp treatment. I thought I was alone until I walked farther into the room. Then I saw her."

"She's one of the typing pool girls," he said, reaching up to switch off the ultraviolet light I'd turned on in my panic.

I nodded. "Jean Plinkton. Right after I realized what I'd found, the lights went out. The door banged shut behind me. When I tried it, I realized someone had locked it from the outside."

"You think someone was here with you and they locked you in?" he asked.

I shivered and hugged my arms across my chest. "I certainly didn't lock myself in."

He stared at me for a moment longer before brushing by me to make for the door. Over his shoulder he threw a, "Stay here."

"Oh no," I said, casting a look back at the body. "I'm not going to risk being locked in again. The killer could be waiting nearby for another opportunity to strike."

Mr. Poole leveled a look at me. "I find that very unlikely. If he wanted to do that, he would have killed you already."

"Oh, thank you very much for planting that pleasant thought in my mind. I'm sure I'll sleep very well tonight. Where are you going?"

He hesitated, and I could see a flash of uncertainty there. He didn't know what to do any more than I did. But just as fast, it was gone.

"Stay here, and guard the body. Don't let anyone in. I'll have someone call the Corps of Military Police. I'm sure the investigators will have questions for you. You might want to make sure you have your story straight," he said as he opened the door again.

My story straight? I'd told him exactly what had happened with no embellishments, and yet it sounded as though he didn't trust me.

Mr. Poole left, kindly leaving the door ajar this time. However, as soon as he was out of sight, I slipped off my shoe and stuck it into the gap between the doorframe and the door. If someone was going to shut me in again, they would have to figure out a way to clamp down on a heeled Oxford or kick it out of the way, which would at least alert me to their presence.

I turned back to Jean, wringing my hands. It felt wrong leaving her there, blood pooled underneath her. I edged closer, steeling myself to try to look past the knife sticking out of the side of her neck.

After I'd disturbed her, she hadn't quite settled back where she'd lain when I found her. Now, her right shoulder and arm leaned on the table, her head resting against them at an unnatural angle. Her legs, I saw now, were akimbo, as though she'd tried to push up and then fallen back into her seat when she'd been murdered.

I frowned. Jean was seated in front of a sunlamp light, but she hadn't undressed. Had she not had the chance to begin the mandated ritual, or had she never intended to?

I thought back to the last time I'd seen her. It had been that afternoon. She'd been in the typing pool, volunteering when Miss Wilkes began to speak about a delivery that needed handling. As always, Jean had jumped at the opportunity to leave her typewriter. Had I seen her again?

No. I was certain of that. I closed my eyes and tried to recall the room as it had been when I left for the Dock. Irene had just gone out to take shorthand, and Patricia had been on a delivery to an assistant secretary of the Joint Planning Committee. Caroline had been hard at work on memos for the Home Forces, and Edith had been idling at her typewriter. Jean wasn't there, I was certain of it.

I opened my eyes again. The blood on the floor and on Jean's jumper was still bright red. I was no coroner, but I reasoned that meant that it hadn't had time to oxidize yet. It was likely that Jean had been killed very recently, but was it before or after she'd made her delivery?

There was a bang somewhere down the corridor, and I heard distant footsteps. Soon the military police would arrive. I had no doubt that the fact that a murder had happened in Mr. Churchill's supposedly secure and very secret cabinet war rooms would motivate them to solve this case quickly. They would poke around and ask their questions. They might even find the killer in the process.

However, these investigators didn't know what I knew. Something was rotten enough in the CWR that Mr. Fletcher had wanted an inside observer. He must have known that something was going to happen. I just wondered whether he could have guessed it would be this deadly.

I stared at Jean's body, my mind whirring. If Jean had made her delivery, someone likely would have seen her and could narrow down the time of death. If her documents were still with her, she could have been killed anytime between being called out to make the delivery and when I found her. It would also prompt the question of why Jean had come here before carrying out her task.

I stooped to look under the table, but saw nothing. I pushed back my revulsion and peered around to see if a file folder or envelope had been trapped under her body.

Nothing.

The footsteps were louder now. I was just about to turn around when a flash of white writing paper under the spill of Jean's strawberry blond hair caught my eye.

I carefully brushed her waves away. The edge of the paper was already stained with the pool of blood creeping ever closer. It was just a long, thin scrap, but on it someone had written "Grove House SW" lightly in red pencil. I peered a little closer, trying to make out the rest of the postal code.

"Step away, Miss!" a man shouted behind me.

I dropped the lock of Jean's hair, doing my best to angle my body to block the view from the door. I edged back and then turned, painting what I hoped was a contrite look on my face as I greeted two men in uniform.

"I'd hoped that maybe there might be a chance she would still be alive," I said. I knew that it couldn't possibly be true, but it sounded like something a pair of men would want to hear from a woman stuck in a room with a body.

The older of the two men marched ahead, stopping next to me. He peered down at Jean's body, shaking his head. "I'm sorry, Miss. It's not a fit sight for a lady."

His counterpart looked over his colleague's shoulder but didn't say a word. Instead, he pulled out a notebook and pencil from inside his uniform jacket and began to write.

Out of the corner of my eye, I saw a flash of gray suiting in the doorway. Mr. Poole lingered just outside the threshold. Our eyes met. I almost raised a hand to hail him, but he twisted away and vanished around the door.

"Miss," said the older man.

"Miss Redfern," I said. "Who are you? I was told only to let in investigators from the Corps of Military Police."

"That would be us. I'm Sergeant Maxwell. This is Corporal Plaice," said the man with a nod to his notebook-wielding compatriot.

Corporal Plaice, who had the misfortune of resembling his fishy namesake, gave me a little nod before going back to his notes.

"If you will step aside, we will begin our investigation," said Sergeant Maxwell.

"Don't you want to know who she is and the circumstances in which I found her?" I asked, remembering all too well the questions the Parisian detectives had for me when I'd found *Maman*'s body.

"We will interview you in good time," said Sergeant Maxwell, placing his hand on my elbow and steering me toward the door. "In the meantime, a Royal Marine will escort you to the canteen, where you can have a nice cup of tea for the shock."

I bristled at the implication that I was not handling the shock of finding a body well, but before I could say anything, Sergeant Maxwell added, "I must insist that you do not speak to anyone until we have the opportunity to question you."

I generally hate being managed, and I could spot a man trying to do it from a dozen paces. However, I had questions of my own and they would only likely be answered after Sergeant Maxwell and Corporal Plaice had the opportunity to examine the crime scene themselves.

"Fine," I said as we reached the door, me half hopping next to the sergeant as I was only wearing one shoe.

"Very good. This is Lieutenant MacIntyre. He will take you to the canteen," said Sergeant Maxwell, gesturing to a Royal Marine hovering in the corridor just outside.

"I'm very capable of finding the canteen on my own." It was one of the few places in the CWR I could reliably find that early in my tenure.

"Nevertheless," said Sergeant Maxwell, nodding to Lieutenant MacIntyre.

"Come along, Miss," said the Royal Marine.

"Perhaps you would be so kind as to return my shoe to me," I said. "Unless you've decided that is evidence."

Sergeant Maxwell looked as though he was seriously considering keeping my shoe back, but finally he nodded and I scooped it up off the floor to slip it on.

"We will speak soon, Miss Redfern," said Sergeant Maxwell.

I gave him my most dignified nod, and then turned toward the canteen. To his credit, Lieutenant MacIntyre waited until we were around a corner before saying, "I hope you don't mind me asking, Miss, but who was it?"

"You don't know?" I asked.

He gave me a sheepish smile. "I know that someone died, but my orders were just to accompany the investigators."

"Jean Plinkton from the typing pool," I said.

The young, rather handsome man sucked in a breath, his eyes gone wide. "Jean?"

"Did you know her?" I asked, curiosity piquing.

He cleared his throat. "I know all of the girls. My word. I never would have thought anyone would—" He cut himself short as we reached the canteen door. "I should leave you here, Miss. My duties. I should be getting back."

I watched him walk away, wondering how long it would take for word to spread around the CWR that Jean was dead.

NINE

My second cup of tea in the staff canteen had long cooled in my hands before Sergeant Maxwell called me in for questioning. When he finally reemerged at half past four, he took me to a small, nondescript office that had been requisitioned for use as an interrogation room.

I wanted to know why Jean had been in the sunlamp room. Had she intended to meet someone there or had the killer surprised her? And what about Grove House? Where was it and was it significant to her death? If not, why did she have a note with the name and part of a postal code written on it?

Even more than any of those questions, I wanted to know how the women of the typing pool would react to the news of Jean's death. I didn't want to suspect any of my new colleagues, but knowing that Jean wasn't widely liked meant they couldn't be discounted as suspects.

"Miss Redfern," said Sergeant Maxwell, settling into the metal chair across from me. "Thank you for your patience as we secured the crime scene. These things are necessary when there has been a death."

"You mean a murder," I corrected.

The two men exchanged a glance.

"There's no need to sugarcoat things on my account, gentlemen. I was the one who discovered the body, and when you see a knife sticking out of someone's throat, there can be little doubt that there was foul play involved," I said.

Sergeant Maxwell cleared his throat. "As you say, Miss Redfern. Can you please tell us what happened?"

"This afternoon around a quarter to three, Miss Wilkes, who manages the typing pool, sent me for a sunlamp treatment," I said.

"Is there a particular rota for sunlamp treatments?" asked Sergeant Maxwell.

"I can't be certain. I'm the newest typist here. This only my fourth day on the job."

Corporal Plaice glanced up from his notebook, and Sergeant Maxwell said, "That's a bad streak of luck."

I nodded in acknowledgment just as the sound of an air raid siren pierced the air around us. The two investigators looked nervously at the steel beams in the ceiling.

"Don't worry," I said, a bit of bravado making me feel a little more sure-footed after my horrible discovery that afternoon. "We're underground with a roof of steel and concrete over our heads. We're safe as houses down here."

I'd heard the reassurances several times, and I crossed my fingers under the table, hoping they were true. As a typist, I was supposed to simply type the information that I received without any need for remark. However, I knew from the documents I'd processed in my first days on the job that the Ministry of Information was forcing the newspapers to underreport the number of dog fights between the RAF and Luftwaffe planes that had happened all over Southern England since August. It was probably only a matter of time before London felt the effects, but so far, the greatest danger to our safety was blacked-out buses and cars driving down dark roads at night.

"You were saying that Miss Wilkes sent you off for sunlamp treatment?" Sergeant Maxwell prompted.

"That's right."

"Was Miss Plinkton in the typing pool with you at the time?" he asked.

"No."

"When was the last time you saw her?" he asked.

"Jean had been sent off to make a delivery. I believe it was to Mr. Conley," I said.

"Who is that?" he asked. When I didn't answer immediately, he added, "Given the sensitive nature of this case, you can speak freely about the movements of people in this office. It will not be considered a violation of the Official Secrets Act."

I knew that even acknowledging that I'd signed the Official Secrets Act could land me in a great deal of trouble, and the truth of the matter was that I hadn't yet decided whether or not to trust these men. I'm the sort of person who is inclined to believe actions far more than words, and so far, neither of them had shown themselves to be a competent detective. I hoped that they would prove me wrong, but until that day came, I decided I would reserve my judgment and give them only the most necessary information for their case.

"Mr. Conley is a clerk in the Ministry of Information," I said.

"In your short time working in the typing pool, have you seen him often?" Sergeant Maxwell asked.

"He has come in at least once a day to drop off documents that need to be duplicated or typed up. Memos, orders, things of that nature," I said.

"Did anything about his behavior strike you as unusual?" Sergeant Maxwell asked.

"No. So far it seems that requests come in waves. Sometimes there will be a high volume from a number of different departments. Other times it will be quieter," I said.

"Is it unusual for yourself or one of the other girls in the typing pool to hand-deliver documents once they are completed?" asked Corporal Plaice.

I glanced his way, surprised to find he had a voice.

"I'm given to understand that so much work is processed by the typing pool that Miss Wilkes prefers the documents to leave as soon as they are done. If we waited for clerks and secretaries to pick up every memo, directive, or set of meeting notes, the paper would pile up, so if anyone doesn't have an active assignment, they are often asked to make a delivery. Other times, departments will request a delivery," I explained.

"I see," said Sergeant Maxwell. "Do you remember the time that Miss Plinkton left for her delivery?"

"Approximately two o'clock."

"You say that Miss Plinkton left at two o'clock. Earlier you said that you left your station at approximately a quarter to three. You seem very sure about these timings, Miss Redfern," commented Corporal

Plaice, still scribbling away in his little notebook. I was tempted to snatch the thing away and find out what exactly he was writing in there.

"I have a habit of looking at my watch," I said, pushing back my cream blouse's cuff and holding up my wrist to show them. "I did so just before you fetched me, Sergeant Maxwell, wondering how long I had been made to sit and wait."

Sergeant Maxwell ignored my jab, instead giving a low whistle. "That's an elegant watch, Miss Redfern. Is it gold?"

I pushed my cuff down again. "I wouldn't know. It was a gift from my mother."

The two men exchanged looks again, and I knew what they were thinking. *Posh girl.* They weren't wrong, but that certainly wasn't the entire story.

"What did you do when you left the typing pool?" asked Sergeant Maxwell.

"I stopped for a moment by the Dock, where we bunk when we are on shift, to fetch a book. I had been warned that sometimes there is a queue to use the sunlamp machines, and I didn't want to be caught out without something to read."

"Which book was that?" Sergeant Maxwell asked.

"*Busman's Honeymoon* by Dorothy L. Sayers." I waited for a flash of recognition for the title, but there was none.

"Is it any good?" Sergeant Maxwell asked.

"It's different than her older ones. Her characters have more occupying their time these days," I said.

This earned me an uninterested grunt.

"What happened when you found the body?" asked Sergeant Maxwell.

"I walked into the room. I understand that the ultraviolet light devices can be moved about so someone constructs temporary walls for a dressing room to give us some privacy when we use the machines," I said.

"Why is that?" asked Sergeant Maxwell.

I leveled a look at him. "Because in order to receive treatment, we need to undress."

Red shot colored both men's cheeks, and Corporal Plaice made a very concerted effort to keep his eyes on his notebook.

"What happened after you entered the room?" asked Sergeant Maxwell.

"There was no queue. However, I thought it best to check I was alone before changing. I walked around the partition leading to the treatment area and I saw that someone was seated in a chair. I thought she might be asleep and was worried that if someone caught her she would be punished, so I went to see if she was all right. That was when I realized there was blood all over her jumper and the floor," I said.

"Was the sunlamp device on or off?" he asked.

"Off."

"What did you do then? This is very important, Miss Redfern. You must tell us exactly what happened," said Sergeant Maxwell.

"I cried out—'Oh my God,' I think it was—and dropped my book. Then I rushed to the body. I grabbed her arm and I saw the knife sticking out of her neck."

"Go on," said Sergeant Maxwell.

"The lights went out, the door slammed behind me, I heard someone lock the door from the outside."

Sergeant Maxwell looked up sharply and Corporal Plaice lifted his watery eyes from his notebook to ask, "You're certain that someone locked the door?"

I leaned forward. "I'm positive. The metal bar ground against the door's latch."

Corporal Plaice took a note as Sergeant Maxwell asked, "What did you do then?"

"It was pitch black, but I managed to find the switch on the sunlamp machine and turned it on. Then I ran back to the door and tried to open it. It was locked, as I feared," I said.

"Why didn't you turn the regular lights on immediately?" he asked. "Surely it was a simple straight line back to the door."

"I was rather more preoccupied with the fact that I'd been locked in an underground room with a freshly killed corpse than I was with the overhead lights," I replied sourly.

Sergeant Maxwell put his hands up as though accepting this point.

"After I tried the door, I began screaming and banging on it. I hoped that someone would come along and let me out," I said.

"How *did* you free yourself?" he asked.

"I didn't. An assistant secretary heard my shouting. He unlocked the door and turned on the light," I said.

"This would be David Poole, the man who alerted the Royal Marines to contact the military police?" asked Corporal Plaice, flipping back through his notes.

"Yes," I said, wondering if they had already spoken to Mr. Poole.

"Were you acquainted with the man before this?" Sergeant Maxwell asked.

"No, we've never spoken before," I said.

"How do you know his name?" he asked.

"My supervisor pointed Mr. Poole out to me on my first day in the CWR," I said.

"What did Mr. Poole do when you told him that there was a body in the room?" asked Sergeant Maxwell.

"He went to check her pulse. Then he said, 'She's dead.'"

"Even though you'd already told him that she was dead?" asked Sergeant Maxwell.

"Yes."

"What then?" he asked.

"He told me to guard the body," I said.

"*You* were to guard the body?" he asked with a laugh of disbelief. "Why?"

My eyes narrowed. "I suspect that it is because Mr. Poole isn't the sort of man who believes that women will dissolve into hysterical messes just because they've been confronted with something grizzly."

"If Mr. Poole left you to guard the body, where did he go?" asked Sergeant Maxwell.

"He told me that he was going to alert you," I said.

"When we arrived, you were standing over the body. Why?" he asked.

"I was looking at her," I said.

"In my experience, most women shy away from death," he said.

"I can only speak for myself, not the other women you've met, Sergeant."

Although the mechanics of Jean's death—from the knife protruding from her neck to the soft give of her sodden jumper—appalled me, there was something intriguing about the entire thing. I will admit that I was curious—morbidly so—and having adjusted to the reality of there being a dead body in my presence, I had been drawn to investigate.

"You shouldn't have done that," Sergeant Maxwell said.

"Whyever not?" I challenged.

"There can be important pieces of evidence that can be disturbed by any interaction with the body. These can hinder us in solving a crime swiftly," said Sergeant Maxwell. "Fortunately, nothing of significance was found on the body."

The hairs on the back of my neck stood up. "Nothing?"

"There was—what was it, Corporal?" asked Sergeant Maxwell, indicating to his partner.

Corporal Plaice flicked the pages back. "In Miss Plinkton's pockets there was an orange security pass and two hairpins. On the desk, we found a torn piece of paper soaked in blood. Nothing else."

That had to be the scrap I'd seen "Grove House SW" written on. By the time that these two had arrived, the blood must have rendered the faint pencil marks unreadable.

I was about to mention what I'd seen on that scrap of paper, but then Sergeant Maxwell asked, "Miss Redfern, if you already knew that Miss Plinkton was dead, why did you approach her again?"

"I was wondering whether she still had her files with her," I answered honestly. When they both stared at me, I added, "To see whether she had finished her delivery before she was killed. It would be helpful in establishing a time of death, wouldn't it?"

"It might be," said Sergeant Maxwell slowly. "It also could be that the killer took the files."

"Do you think that she was killed for the information she had on her?" I asked.

"I don't wish to speculate," he said.

I tilted my head in concession and tried another question that had been nagging at me since I'd sat down in the canteen to wait. "It is interesting that Jean was killed in such a violent way, isn't it?"

"What do you mean?" asked Sergeant Maxwell.

"Well, she was stabbed—and in the throat no less. It's such an act of aggression and requires a great deal of strength to do it, but it's also an intimate act," I said.

"Intimate?" asked Corporal Plaice.

"You can't stand across a room, at a distance, as you would with a gun. Stabbing her means that whoever killed her must have been close enough to touch her. They either physically dominated her, or they were an intimate she trusted very deeply to allow them so close. I imagine that, if the coroner finds that she has no defensive wounds, you might explore that theory," I suggested.

A sly smirk spread over Sergeant Maxwell's features. "I understand now."

"I beg your pardon?" I asked.

"The book that you mentioned, Miss Redfern. What was it?" he asked.

"*Busman's Honeymoon*," I said.

"If I'm not mistaken, that's one of those detective novels that offer cheap thrills to girls like you."

"Girls like me?" I asked, an arctic chill entering my voice.

"We see it all the time in our profession," said Sergeant Maxwell, sliding a look at Corporal Plaice, who gave a brief nod. "Girls who don't have anything better to do than to sit around and read that sort of rubbish. They think murder is a thrill, a game even. I can assure you that this case is not a passing amusement. All we want from you are straight answers. No theories about what the killer might have been feeling."

The man might as well have reached out and slapped my wrist before giving me a pat on the head like I was a precocious child. He actually thought that since I was a woman who read detective novels, I was going to be the sort to make things up. That my observations weren't valid.

My stomach sank as I realized it was Paris and the investigation into my mother's death all over again.

"If there is nothing else, I think we are done here," said Sergeant Maxwell.

"You're done questioning me?"

"You may go back to work. If we have any further questions, we will send for you," he said.

I rose. I knew that I should tell them about the pencil scratching of "Grove House SW" that they'd missed, but I doubted they would pay me any heed. They had as much as they wanted from me: an account of what happened and a timeline of the events. I had served my purpose and now was only a hysterical woman speculating wildly.

"Will you be speaking to the rest of the women in the typing pool?" I asked through gritted teeth.

"You can be reassured that we will be questioning everyone who may have a connection to this case." Sergeant Maxwell rose. "Now, if you don't mind . . ."

But whatever he wanted from me, he didn't have a chance to ask because in that moment all Hell broke loose.

TEN

The ring of the CWR's warning system pierced the interrogation room, making all three of us jump. The bell rang again. Then again.

Sergeant Maxwell grabbed my arm. "What does that mean?"

"Intermittent bells mean imminent danger overhead," I said, looking around me automatically for my gas mask.

"What?"

"It's the CWR signaling system," I explained distractedly. Drat. I must have left the gas mask in either the sunlamp room or the canteen. I couldn't hear any rattling handbells—the signal for a gas attack—but if the Nazis managed to gas me, I was going to be bloody annoyed.

"What do we do?" asked Corporal Plaice as Sergeant Maxwell demanded, "Where do we shelter?"

"Stay where you are," I said, striding toward the door. "Remember, you're safe as houses down here."

I rushed out the door without another word, entering the frenetic but surprisingly orderly stream of people in the corridor. Everyone at the CWR had a place—I was told this in no uncertain terms on my first day. In the case of an air raid or a ground attack, it was vital that we all knew what we were meant to do. Those of us who were on duty were to go to our posts. Those who were not were to remain in their accommodation.

As I was still technically on my shift, I headed for the typing pool.

I was working against the flow of most traffic in the corridor. Taking advantage of the extra height my shoes afforded me, I angled my shoulder down and did my best to push my way through the crowd, saying "beg your pardon" as though it were a crowded train platform. It was ridiculous, but when I had been working at the factory it had been drilled into us that to panic among volatile chemicals could mean disaster for an entire shift. It was best to remain polite and calm.

"Excuse me," I said, doing my best to push past a smartly dressed man in RAF blues who had boxed me in as I approached an alcove. If I was pushed aside, I risked becoming stuck until the crush of people passed, and I was not going to give Miss Wilkes a reason to scold me during my first air raid with the CWR.

"Excuse me," I said again, pushing a little harder against the man's back. However, rather than making the forward progress I'd expected, I found myself tipping to my left, pulled by an anonymous hand.

I gave a yelp and fought to stay upright even as another hand clamped around my waist.

"I've got you. You're all right. I've got you," a man said.

"Let me go!" I insisted, pushing forward out of his arms.

The man immediately released me, and I spun around to find myself staring into the calm, collected expression of Mr. Poole.

"Why did you do that?" I demanded.

"I need to talk to you," he said in a voice just loud enough for me to hear above the din around us.

"I have to go to my station," I said.

He put an arm out to block me. "This is more important than that."

I crossed my arms over my chest.

"What happened after I left you?" he asked.

"Nothing really. The investigators arrived. I was escorted to the canteen and set up with a cup of tea. After longer than I would have liked, I was questioned," I said.

"Who were the investigators?" he asked.

"Sergeant Maxwell and Corporal Plaice," I said.

"Never heard of them," he muttered.

"Had many run-ins with the Corps of Military Police?" I asked sweetly.

He looked up sharply. "What?"

"Why should you know who they are?" I asked, removing the sarcasm from my question.

"Did you see or speak to anyone else?" he asked, ignoring my question.

"No. Wait, yes, I did. A Royal Marine escorted me to the canteen."

"Who?" he asked.

I wracked my brain before coming up with the answer. "A Lieutenant MacIntyre."

"How did he react when you told him what had happened?" he asked.

I raised a brow. "Why do you want to know?"

"Miss Redfern . . ."

"Tell me why you want to know, and I'll tell you what he said."

He looked up at the concrete ceiling as though gathering strength. "Miss Plinkton could have been murdered by someone in the CWR, but the minister is particularly concerned that there may have been a breach of security—unlikely as that might be. He is eager that all avenues are explored."

I knew he was lying. It was unlikely that the minister of information was any more worried about the security of the CWR than the other cabinet ministers, and Mr. Poole's unwillingness to admit the real reasoning behind this curiosity was setting off alarms just as loud as the one ringing above us. Still, I decided that it might be a good idea to keep Mr. Poole in my good graces because I had questions of my own.

"He seemed surprised," I said. "He indicated that he knew all of the women in the typing pool. He also said something like, 'I never would have dreamed anyone would,' but then he cut himself off."

"What do you think he was going to say?" he asked.

I lifted my shoulders. "It could have been all manner of things."

"But what do *you* think he was going to say?" Mr. Poole pushed.

I studied him, weighing the urgency behind his words. "I think he was going to say that he couldn't believe anyone dared to do it."

"Why would he say that?" he asked.

"Jean wasn't well liked. At least not by the women of the typing pool."

"Enough that she was murdered for it?" Mr. Poole asked in disbelief. "Women as a rule don't murder their colleagues simply because they aren't temperamentally suited."

"No, we do not."

"What did the investigators want to know?" Mr. Poole asked as the alarm continued to blare above us.

"They asked me about my movements, about what happened when I found the body. They asked about you."

His eyes narrowed. "Me?"

"They wanted to know if I knew who you were," I said.

"What did you tell them?"

I shrugged. "The truth. You'd been pointed out to me, but nothing else. The first time I met you, you were springing me from a locked room."

This seemed to satisfy him enough because he pressed on, asking, "What else?"

"They were particularly concerned about when I remembered certain things happening." I shrugged. "Other than that, they weren't interested in what I had to say."

He screwed up his brow. "Why is that?"

"I think that Maxwell and Plaice are laboring under the misapprehension that women are either unobservant or useless. Both of which, of course, are untrue."

"Idiots," Mr. Poole muttered under his breath.

"Do you think—"

The low, unmistakable rumble of a far-off bomb exploding shook up from the floor, through my feet, and straight into my soul.

My throat went dry. "They're actually doing it."

"They're bombing London," he agreed, expression grim. "You should go before someone misses you."

"What about you?" I asked.

"What about me?" he asked.

"Aren't you meant to be somewhere right now?" I asked.

He seemed almost amused at the suggestion as the ground vibrated again, more forceful this time. I stumbled, catching myself against the wall.

"I'll be all right," he said. Then he stepped out into the crowded corridor and slipped away.

———

The intermittent bells hadn't stopped as I rounded the corner of the typing pool's corridor. Ahead of me, two telephonists I recognized but hadn't yet met hurried into the switchboard room, tails of their nearly identical navy suit jackets flapping behind them as they went.

"Evelyne!"

I glanced over my shoulder to see Patricia hurrying up, her normally perfect hair falling out of its clips and the edge of her jumper pulled out of her belted skirt. She clutched a stack of files in her arms, and I could see her fear-widened eyes behind her glasses.

"Are you all right?" I asked.

"Where have you been all afternoon?" she asked, ignoring my question.

"I was detained," I said, marveling at the fact that that six-word question was the longest sentence she'd ever spoken to me.

"Never mind. Miss Wilkes will be furious if we aren't in before the bell stops," she said.

Since Patricia's arms were full, I pushed open the typing pool door to let us both in. Miss Wilkes stood in the center of the room while Edith and Caroline sat at their desks. Behind them stood Betty, Joy, Jill, Claire, and Anne from the night shift. My eyes flicked up to the clock on the wall. They must have been about to do the regular handover from day to night shift when the alarm sounded. Irene, I noticed, was nowhere to be seen.

"Miss Redfern," said Miss Wilkes, her voice almost soft. "Please close the door behind you."

I saw now how Betty clung to Jill, and Claire had tears forming in her eyes. Miss Wilkes's knuckles were white from clutching the back of her chair, and Edith looked as though she was about to faint.

"This is most unfortunate timing," said Miss Wilkes, sending me another glance. "Something terrible has happened this afternoon. I'm afraid there's been a horrible accident."

"An accident?" I muttered in disbelief even as gasps sounded all around. It wasn't possible for anyone who had seen what I had seen to believe that what happened to Jean was an accident.

"Oh, I can't stand it any longer!" cried Betty. "What's happened?"

Miss Wilkes sucked in a breath and then said, "Miss Plinkton is dead."

There was a distinctive pause as everyone seemed to look to one another for cues about how to react.

"What happened?" Edith asked first.

"Was it the bombs?" asked Caroline.

Miss Wilkes glanced at me, this time her expression concerned. "I don't know yet. There are two inspectors here from the military police. These gentlemen may wish to ask all of you some questions."

I would hardly have called Maxwell and Plaice gentlemen, but that was only my opinion.

"She was murdered, wasn't she?" asked Betty, fear creeping into her voice.

"Miss Lewison, please. Control yourself," Miss Wilkes admonished. "When the investigators speak to you, you must answer truthfully and precisely. This is not a time for wild speculation. I trust that all of you will behave in the manner I have come to expect from my typists."

Miss Wilkes straightened the hem of her jacket. "I know that it might feel heartless to some of you, but this tragedy cannot prevent us from doing our very important work." The bell overhead stopped as though punctuating her point. "And neither can an air raid. Those of you on the day shift will brief those on the night shift. Remember, gas masks must be kept to hand, and those not working will be confined to the Dock."

"Miss Wilkes," said Edith meekly, "my shift is meant to be over tonight. I'm supposed to go home."

"Don't be ridiculous, Miss Tierney. You cannot go out in an air raid," said Miss Wilkes. "Use one of the spare beds in the Dock."

"What if there aren't any?" Edith asked, but I hardly paid attention because I noticed the typing pool door edge open. Irene inched inside, caught my eye, and gave me a cheeky wink even as the floor reverberated with another bomb fallen somewhere on London.

Cries rang out, and a couple of the girls clung to desks even though the room hadn't shaken much.

Miss Wilkes drew in a steadying breath. "We are safe underground, ladies."

There were a few murmurs all around. I felt the warmth of someone edging close to me. Irene had drawn near.

"What did I miss?" Irene asked in a low whisper.

"Jean was found dead," I said.

I heard her quick intake of breath before she managed a shaky, "What?"

Across the room, Anne stuck her hand up as though she was in school. "Miss Wilkes, what will happen to Jean's shift?"

"I imagine we'll need to find a replacement for her. In the meantime, I will assess the rota and see where we have weaknesses in Miss Plinkton's . . . absence. I will make my decision in the following days as to who will take her shift."

Miss Wilkes was matter-of-fact and blunt, and I strangely found that comforting. If the stern, straightforward woman had fallen apart in the middle of the typing pool, I don't know what I would have done.

"Now, you will all do your handoff as you normally would. Remember, ladies, we are at war," said Miss Wilkes.

I hurried over to Betty, who took my desk for the night shift. It felt strange reaching back into the recesses of my brain to think about what I had been doing before I'd found Jean's body, but I did my best.

"We're waiting on corrections for two memos from the Ministry of Labour. And Mr. Swearting came by again looking for the duplicate of the RAF communication earlier," I said.

"What do you think happened to Jean?" Betty asked quietly.

Given the elevated volume of chatter around me, I suspected that there was very little handover and a lot of speculation afoot. I had no doubt that the moment they learned I had found the body I would be soundly questioned. I suspected that the women of the typing pool would do a far more thorough job than Maxwell and Plaice.

"Miss Redfern," Miss Wilkes called out, saving me from having to answer Betty's question.

"Yes, Miss Wilkes?" I asked.

She gestured toward the door. "A moment of your time, please."

Outside in the corridor, the scene was quieter, people having taken to their stations during the air raid.

"They're bombing East London," said Miss Wilkes, as though reading my thoughts. "I just received word before I spoke to the girls. This is what we've been preparing for since the start of the war."

Then she took a deep breath. "Miss Redfern, what happened to Miss Plinkton?"

"You mean they haven't told you?" I asked.

She crossed her arms and looked up at the ceiling. "They said that Miss Plinkton died, and that I should call all the ladies together to tell them as much. They also said that you found her body. Nothing more."

"I did find her in the sunlamp room. Someone had stabbed her in the throat. Jean was murdered."

I searched her face for a reaction to make sure she understood what I was saying. Something flashed across her face, even though she stood remarkably still, only her lips moving to whisper, "I feared as much."

"Why do you say that?" I asked.

The older woman's soft brown eyes snapped open. "I know that I cannot ask you to keep what you saw from the other ladies for very long, but no doubt you will already have noticed that we have some excitable personalities in the typing pool. I would not want them to find fear where there is none."

"A woman was murdered, Miss Wilkes. I imagine it would be a very sensible thing for her colleagues to be frightened," I said.

Miss Wilkes straightened her shoulders. "Miss Redfern, we may not be in uniform, but we are helping to win the war. I will give you a moment to think on that, and then I will expect you back at your desk to brief Betty."

She pulled open the typing pool door, leaving me alone. It might have been her intention to leave me to ponder my responsibilities in the CWR, but two thoughts kept turning over in my mind:

When I'd told Miss Wilkes that Jean had been murdered, she hadn't been at all surprised. And if I didn't know any better, I'd say that the look I'd seen cross her face had been relief.

ELEVEN

That night of Jean's murder and the first of what the world would later come to call the Blitz was one of the longest of my life. I'm certain that no one in the Dock slept. It would have been hard enough knowing that outside, London was being bombed and all of us were worried about our loved ones, but on top of that, one of our own had been violently killed. The ladies were strangely subdued and tense at the same time, with no one even suggesting a game of cards. Instead, we all climbed into bed and pulled the covers over our heads like children trying to will away a bad dream.

Around two o'clock in the morning, I heard Edith crying softly while the usually buttoned-up Caroline, who slept in the bunk underneath her, softened enough to try to whisper comfort to her.

About an hour later, Irene reached over and gently tugged on my blanket.

"Are you awake?" she asked.

I pushed up onto my elbows. "Yes. I can't sleep."

I couldn't stop wondering who would have wanted to kill Jean and why. But even if those questions hadn't kept running through my mind into the late hours of the night, the memory of finding Jean would have. I could still smell the faintly metallic, organic tang of her blood, and I didn't think I would ever forget the feeling of her sodden jumper under my fingers.

"Who do you think did it?" Irene asked.

"I don't know," I said honestly.

Irene looked down for a moment, and when she raised her eyes again there was real fear there.

"It couldn't have been one of us in the typing pool, surely," she said.

"I suppose everyone in the CWR is a suspect."

Irene jerked back a little. "But you don't really think—"

"It's a closed environment. There are checks at every door leading down from the street. We all have passes that need to be presented. There are Royal Marines stationed at all of the staircases leading aboveground."

Irene lowered her voice to barely a whisper above the roar of the air conditioners. "Even if one or two of them is willing to look the other way every once in a while?"

Logically, she was right, but the chances of someone from the outside infiltrating the CWR without detection and then slipping out again were incredibly slim. No, I was certain that Jean not only knew her killer but that she likely worked with them as well.

"You didn't sneak out tonight," I said, pointedly. "Won't your fellow be disappointed?"

"No man is worth being blown to kingdom come for," Irene snorted, but I saw the moment's doubt in her eyes.

"You'll see him again," I said.

Irene let her head fall back onto her pillow. "You're right. I will."

I settled back too, thinking that was the end of the conversation, but after a moment Irene asked, "Do you think those inspectors will want to speak to all of us in the typing pool?"

"I suspect they will."

From the other bunk I heard a long, shuddering breath in the dark.

———————

The next morning, everyone on the day shift looked worse for wear, and there were more than a few grumbles as we queued for the showers.

Cathy and Rachel, who had only just come in for the start of their three days in the CWR, were bursting to speak when we all gathered for our shift handover in the typing pool.

"It's horrible," Cathy said. "There's smoke pouring out of the East End. The whole sky glowed orange all through the night. No one knows yet how many people were hurt or how many buildings were damaged."

"We spent the entire night in the Anderson shelter Dad dug out in the back garden. It was horrid. It was moldy because it floods during the rain, and my sister kept screaming because she thought bugs were crawling on her," said Rachel.

"The buses this morning were a nightmare too," said Cathy. "So many roads are closed."

"The whole area around Charing Cross is a mess," Rachel agreed. "Fortunately I was out the door to catch an early train, otherwise I wouldn't have made it."

"Well, I'm afraid you won't find much relief in here," said Irene.

"What do you mean?" asked Cathy.

"Jean's dead," Edith blurted out, before any of the rest of us could soften the blow.

"Dead?" Rachel gasped. "How is that possible?"

"She was murdered," said Edith, her doe eyes growing even wider. "Evelyne found her."

Rachel whipped around to face me, clearly horrified.

I held up my hands. "I happened to be in the wrong place at the right time."

"That's awful. Poor Jean," said Rachel.

"Yes," Cathy murmured as she stared at her hands. "Poor Jean."

I frowned, wondering at the subdued nature of her reaction. However, before I could ponder it any further, Miss Wilkes swept in wearing a light blue blouse underneath a somber gray suit and looking as though she'd slept a full night and was ready to face the day. She clapped her hands and the room fell silent.

"Ladies, I know that it has been a trying night," she said. "However, we must all remain vigilant and continue to do our very important work."

"Copying documents and taking memos?" Irene muttered.

Miss Wilkes rounded on her. "Doing the work of keeping this office ticking over and taking care of those who serve the prime minister and his cabinet, Miss Travers. If you do not see the value of that, I suggest that you seek employment elsewhere."

Irene straightened. "I apologize, Miss Wilkes. I didn't mean to suggest that I don't want this job."

"I am willing to attribute any dissatisfaction this morning to the very tragic news of yesterday afternoon and the nighttime air raid. However, if any of you are uncertain that you wish to continue working in this office, you are free to leave." Miss Wilkes paused, adding a sense of drama to the entire speech that I felt Moira would have appreciated.

"Very well," she resumed. "I am happy to report that I have already made inquiries about a girl coming in to take Miss Plinkton's desk. She will start on Wednesday."

Anne raised her hand. "Will she be on the day shift, Miss Wilkes?"

I could see Miss Wilkes struggle not to roll her eyes. "She will be for the time being so that we may train her, just as you were, Miss Paxton. Then I will assess where her strengths can best be used." Anne raised her hand again and Miss Wilkes added, "That may be on any shift I see fit. This is not a social club, ladies. Do you think that Mr. Churchill's ministers complain when they have to work?"

I suspected some of them did, actually, but I didn't want to diminish Miss Wilkes's point.

The door to the typing pool opened, and Lieutenant MacIntyre, who had escorted me from the crime scene, poked his head in. Giggles rippled around me as he shot my fellow typists a smile.

"Yes?" asked Miss Wilkes, clearly exasperated by his interruption of her speech.

"If you please, Miss Wilkes, Sergeant Maxwell asks if Miss Bainbridge can please join him in the interrogation room," he said.

Patricia went nearly as white as her jumper. "Me?"

"Yes, Miss," said Lieutenant MacIntyre, addressing Patricia.

"But I'm supposed to go home. It's my day off," Patricia protested.

"You may leave as soon as your interview is completed, Miss Bainbridge," said Miss Wilkes. "The same goes for you, Miss Tierney."

Edith nodded while Patricia looked as though she was about to protest again, but then seemed to think better of it. She shuffled out of the room with her head down, her stacked brown heels scraping against the floor, looking for all the world as though she would rather be anywhere else.

As soon as the door was shut, Cathy put her hand up.

"Yes, Miss Ingersol?" asked Miss Wilkes.

"Will the inspectors be asking to speak to all of us?" asked Cathy. "Even those of us who weren't working yesterday?"

"I suspect we will find out soon enough. In the meantime, I would suggest that you turn your attention to the work at hand," said Miss Wilkes.

The women on the day shift all snapped to it, keys almost immediately beginning to thunk away while the night shift girls slipped away to the canteen for breakfast. I had no doubt that they would hurry to the Dock as quickly as they could for a much-needed rest. In all likelihood, they wouldn't have much more luck than we had at sleeping, but at least it seemed unlikely they would have to contend with the air raid siren or bombs falling while they were trying to rest.

I reached for a piece of paper and the carbon papers that we used to make duplicates and was just feeding them into my typewriter when the typing pool's telephone rang. I was half-conscious as I began to type that Miss Wilkes picked it up, but my attention was focused on writing up a memo from some higher-up or another at the Royal Navy that was full of long strings of technical jargon. I'd been warned on my second day for missing a number off the name of a Fleet Air Arm plane, and I was not going to make the same mistake again.

I was squinting hard at the page in front of me when Miss Wilkes's gardenia perfume wafted around me and her shadow fell across my desk.

"Miss Redfern, I trust that you are proficient in shorthand?" she asked.

I thought of all of the practice I'd done over the last two weeks. "Yes, Miss Wilkes."

It was only partially a lie. I was confident that I could take decent shorthand so long as no one spoke too quickly.

"Good. Mr. Pearson from the Ministry of War has just requested a typist to take minutes for a meeting he is leading and then type them up," she said. "Miss Plinkton regularly helped him, but . . . If you do well, it will be a great help. Miss Plinkton was our most requested stenographer."

I highly doubted that anyone would say that I was a good replacement for someone skilled at stenography, but I nodded nonetheless. "I understand, Miss Wilkes."

Miss Wilkes glanced at her watch. "Mr. Pearson expects you in fifteen minutes."

I gathered up my notepad and my pencil, and made my way out of the door.

TWELVE

I glanced down at the piece of paper Miss Wilkes had scribbled the meeting room's number on and frowned as I hurried along. I stopped when I saw Mr. Rance, the Office of Works official who made a habit of posting the weather report every day.

"Good morning, Mr. Rance," I said as he slid in a card that read "Clear."

"Good morning, Miss Redfern. It's going to be a beautiful one today," he said with a smile, as though London hadn't just been heavily bombed.

"Let's hope so, Mr. Rance. I don't suppose you could tell me where Room 45 is?"

"Just follow this corridor halfway down and take the first right. It will be on your left about two doors down," he said.

"Thank you very much."

He smiled. "It takes a few shifts to find your sea legs down here."

"It does indeed," I agreed.

As I rounded the first right, I spotted a woman ahead of me in a white jumper, brown skirt, and matching heels walking swiftly out of a room. I frowned, certain it was Patricia scurrying away, but before I could call out to her, Maxwell and Plaice emerged from the same room.

"Gentlemen," I said, stopping with my hands folded over my notepad in front of me.

"Good morning, Miss Redfern," said Sergeant Maxwell. "I trust you're well."

"Have you made any progress in your case?" I asked.

The pair exchanged a look.

"We have a number of leads we are chasing down," said Sergeant Maxwell.

"I imagine that you searched Jean's bunk in the Dock yesterday evening."

"Corporal Plaice did an initial examination of Miss Plinkton's things, and they were removed to be looked at further," said Sergeant Maxwell. "And before you ask, we also sent someone to her home this morning."

"Did she live at home or with a flatmate?" I asked.

"Miss Redfern, I am beginning to wonder whether you have forgotten that we are the inspectors and you are a suspect," said Sergeant Maxwell.

It took everything in me not to snort. "A suspect?"

Corporal Plaice flipped back a page in his infernal notebook, and asked, "Is it true that you only started working in the cabinet war rooms last Monday, Miss Redfern?"

"Yes," I said.

"How often did you speak to the deceased?" Sergeant Maxwell asked.

"Outside of the standard introductions? Once. And since I'm certain that it will come up in your interviews, I didn't have a particularly positive impression of Jean. She went out of her way to try to humiliate me in front of my new colleagues."

"Why is that?" he asked.

"I wasn't a secretary before the war. She decided that I was unqualified for my job before she saw any evidence of my work."

"How is it that you have this job if you don't have the skills for it?" he asked.

I crossed my arms. "I didn't say I don't have the skills, Sergeant Maxwell."

"Then how did you find yourself in the cabinet war rooms?" he asked.

I simply stared at him, having no intention of disclosing how I had been recruited.

"Very well. If it becomes necessary, there are ways of finding these things out," Sergeant Maxwell said.

"Then I'm sure, if it is necessary, you will. What did you discover among Jean's things?" I asked again.

"Miss Redfern, I understand that a murder investigation is all very exciting, but I promise you that we know how to do our jobs. We're trained professionals," said Sergeant Maxwell.

"It is just—"

"Excuse me."

We all turned to find Mr. Poole heading toward us with a clutch of files under his arm. The inspectors and I parted like the proverbial Red Sea, and as Mr. Poole passed by I could have sworn there was a slight upward turn to his lips.

As soon as he was gone, Sergeant Maxwell put his hands up, as though to placate me.

"We've seen this time and time again, Miss Redfern. Murder holds a curious fascination for many people, especially women. They all think they can solve one, if only they came across one. When a murder does land on their doorstep, they fancy themselves amateur detectives."

"If there are that many unsuspecting women stumbling across that many unsolved murders, I have serious concerns about the lack of reporting in this country's newspapers," I said.

That earned me a heavy sigh. "I can assure you, that 'women's intuition' or whatever the ladies' magazines are calling it these days has no place in an investigation."

Any last grains of respect I had for the inspectors dissolved like sugar in water.

"'Women's intuition'? That's why you think I'm interested in who might have killed a woman I worked with?" I asked.

"I can tell you that, if you had the experience I do, you would know that the simplest solution is often the right one in these cases," said Sergeant Maxwell.

"What does that mean?" I asked.

"The manner in which Miss Plinkton was killed indicates that this was most likely a crime of passion," Corporal Plaice piped up.

"An intimate murder?" I asked with a raised brow. It was precisely what I had suggested during my interrogation.

"It's likely that she was killed by a jealous lover," said Sergeant Maxwell.

All of this felt far too familiar. In the aftermath of my mother's death, a police detective had done a cursory investigation that only served to confirm his initial impressions. No matter that I told him *Maman* was careful with her medication, he'd taken one look at the beautiful Lady Redfern dead in her blush satin negligee surrounded by the opulence of our luxurious hotel suite and decided that her death was due to the carelessness of a spoiled, indulged woman who didn't know any better.

Every instinct had screamed at me that he was wrong, but I had been thirteen and powerless to push back against the detective. Grieving and lost, I'd been ignored, and so my mother's death had been brushed aside with hardly an investigation.

Maman deserved better, and so did Jean.

"What if Jean wasn't killed by a lover? Have you considered that possibility?" I asked.

"Now, now. There's no need to become uppity," said Sergeant Maxwell.

Uppity. I'd show them uppity. . . .

But when I looked at these two men who were so convinced that they knew more than me, I knew that arguing with them would be futile.

"I suppose, then, that I should say goodbye, gentlemen," I said.

"Miss Redfern," Sergeant Maxwell called after me as I walked away. "We all have our jobs during this war. Let us do ours."

———

As soon as I was out of sight of Maxwell and Plaice, I snuck a glance at my watch. The night shift girls had only just gone off to the canteen for their breakfast before heading to bed. The Dock should be empty. With six minutes before I needed to be in Mr. Pearson's meeting, I should have been on my way. However, I didn't think the Dock was likely to be empty again that day, and I wanted a look at the bunk Jean was so protective over.

I doubled back on myself until I reached the top of the stairs to the Dock. There, I paused to listen. I couldn't hear anything that sounded like voices, so I padded down as quietly as I could.

I held my breath when I reached the bottom of the stairs and peered around the corner. It was empty. I made quick work of checking the row of bunk beds to see if anyone was sleeping.

Nothing.

I set my notepad and pencil to the side and approached Jean's bed. It looked like a completely ordinary, empty bunk. Still, there must have been *some* reason she was so particular about it.

I lifted the pillow and mattress, unsurprised when I found nothing underneath them. Working quickly, I ran my hands around the edge of the bed frame, wincing as a splinter from the rough wood caught my hand. A pinprick of blood appeared. I popped my finger into my mouth to suck on it and resumed my work.

With my free hand, I checked the mattress, pressing on it as I went. Nothing. Chewing my lip, I looked at the piped edge of the mattress, but there were no zips or buttons. I was about to move on when I noticed that some of the navy stripes of the mattress ticking were slightly out of alignment. It might not have caught my eye in the same way before the war, but with the government's campaign to "make do and mend" I was more than a little acquainted with Mrs. Jenkins's heavy iron Singer and my sewing basket. Not being a particularly accomplished seamstress, I had struggled to match the patterns on a chevron top I'd made a few months ago, the stripes causing me a headache Mrs. Jenkins had to help me unpick.

I pulled at each side of the mattress seam and squinted. The tiny bit of thread now exposed was pure white up until a point. Then it turned cream. Someone had unpicked a piece of the mattress ticking and restitched it again.

I reached up to the bunk above where I'd left my things to grab my pencil. Sticking the sharpened end in the seam, I worked it back and forth until I heard the telltale pop of a weak stitch. Carefully, I eased the mattress pieces apart and looked inside.

At first I saw nothing except for inexpensive mattress foam. However, when I ripped a little farther, there was a piece of cream cloth that shouldn't have been there. Excited, I worked the cloth out. It was made of the sort of muslin a dressmaker would use for a toile, and when I pressed it, it crinkled.

Quickly, I unwrapped the bundle. Two pieces of paper fell out. The first one was a list:

DNARYSHGOAEYS
BEATKFROJ?
ELRYRHDDHEL
UHJPNSIRGHYGMJPRL
QHKLEMHARKOEAY
QRHLKMYJLRHKMY

The string of letters made no sense to me. I shook my head and lifted the other piece of paper. It was small and typed:

You ruined my life, you bloody whore.

A chill ran down my spine. Was Jean the ruiner or the ruined? The sender or the recipient?

I flipped it over, but there was nothing on the back.

Out of the corner of my eye, I saw something scurry away. I looked up just in time to see a mouse disappear under a doorway.

"Ugh." Shuddering, I rewrapped the two scraps of paper and slid down. It was nothing to nip over to my bunk to slide the papers into the most secure place I could think of and then collect my things for the meeting.

THIRTEEN

Back on the main level of the CWR, I hurried down the corridor, sending up a little prayer of thanks when I reached the door of the room I was meant to report to. My watch said I was already two minutes late. I hoped that Mr. Pearson wasn't a strict sort. Taking a deep breath, I patted my hair, knocked, and walked in.

Six men swiveled in their chairs to stare at me from their seats around a long, rectangular table. At the head sat the man I presumed was Mr. Pearson, his hands folded in front of him on the table. Two down from him on his right sat Mr. Poole.

"Yes?" Mr. Pearson asked.

I fought a blush as I held up my notepad. "I've been sent by Miss Wilkes to take notes."

"You're late," he said, looking back down at his file.

"I'm new," I said by way of explanation. "I became lost."

He grunted and indicated to a seat at a small table in the corner. I slid into place and opened my notebook, just catching Mr. Poole's curious gaze as I sat poised, pencil in hand.

"As I was saying," Mr. Pearson began, and I tried to let my thoughts recede and simply transcribe.

While I was on my secretarial course, I had been scolded by an instructor for thinking too much while taking shorthand. I'd shot back that I would be able to do a better job if I paid attention to what was being said. She hadn't liked that answer one bit, and she had forced me to stay behind for an extra session of shorthand every day for a week, making me transcribe as she read aloud from a telephone directory to prove a point.

Now, I was grateful for both my former instructor's strictness and the muscle memory built up in that secretarial course. Even as my pencil flew across the page, all I could think about was the list and the scrap of letter now nestled in my book. It was the clearing of a throat that brought my attention back to the meeting. I jerked a little in my seat when I found all of the men staring at me.

"Could you please read that back, Miss Redfern?" asked Mr. Pearson.

I glanced down at the paper, certain for one horrible moment that I had been transcribing gibberish, but sure enough there were the pencil scratches of shorthand flowing across the page.

"'It is the recommendation of this joint committee of the Ministry of War and the Ministry of Information that a strict ban be placed on the reporting of specific casualty or damage numbers after the events of the evening of the seventh of September. We also recommend to the minister that, in the case of future air raids over London, this ban stands,'" I read out.

"Thank you, Miss Redfern," said Mr. Pearson even as Mr. Poole dipped his head to hide what I suspected very much was a smirk.

Who was this Mr. Poole, who always seemed to be lurking just in the corner of my field of vision? And what had he been doing around the sunlamp room that led him to find me first? For all I knew, he could have been the killer himself.

I shuddered at the thought. Had Hercule Poirot, Lord Peter Wimsey, or Detective Chief-Inspector Roderick Alleyn ever felt the same unsettled sense when they realized that they might be in the presence of a killer? Probably not, for they were all men, and no man I'd ever met had displayed that level of natural common sense.

They were also, admittedly, all fictional.

"If we are agreed, gentlemen," said Mr. Pearson, looking around the table, "then I believe we all have a great deal of work to do."

The men all rose. I did the same and moved to try to follow them out of the room, but Mr. Pearson put his hand up.

"Miss Redfern, a moment of your time, please," he said.

I couldn't help feeling like a schoolgirl called to the headmistress's study to answer for some transgression. Mr. Poole, who was the last out of the room, cast a look back at me, his brow furrowed even as he closed the door.

"Miss Redfern," Mr. Pearson started as soon as we were alone. "In light of you being new to the CWR, I am willing to overlook the fact that you were late to a meeting."

"Thank you, Sir," I said.

He studied me a moment and then sniffed, sending his bottle-brush mustache twitching on his face. It was brown but flecked with red and gray, making him seem older than I expected he probably was. It was a ridiculous thing—the sort of affectation someone who fancied himself a man of empire would have worn in the last century. I was tempted to tell him to shave it off.

"I realize that it can be difficult coming into a new place of work, but a girl like yourself must be especially vigilant," he said.

"Sir?"

" 'The Parisian Orphan'? I recognized your name." He gave me a little smile. "I can understand why having such a notorious family might leave you in a difficult situation."

"What difficult situation would that be?" I asked.

"Some people can be less understanding than others. If your colleagues were to learn who you are and what happened to your mother . . ."

I narrowed my eyes. "I've already told my fellow typists. Given that you're clearly aware of who I am, I imagine that it is no great secret."

He looked a little taken aback. "And that doesn't bother you?"

"I've had rather more on my mind in the last day," I said.

"Ah yes. I understand you were the one who found Miss Plinkton's body. How horrible for you. You must have been terrified."

He reached out, and one of his hands landed on my upper arm. Then he squeezed. If he'd meant it to be a comfort, he was far off the mark.

Fortunately, the door opened. I stepped away as Mr. Poole stuck his head in.

"I am sorry to interrupt," Mr. Poole said, his eyes flashing to Mr. Pearson's hand as it fell back to the man's side.

"I was just telling Miss Redfern that I might request her assistance again," said Mr. Pearson, clearing his throat.

"I'm sure you were," said Mr. Poole, his tone as dry as a good champagne and masking the concern in his expression as he studied me.

"The loss of Miss Plinkton as well is a very great one," said Mr. Pearson.

My interest was immediately piqued. I seemed to have found someone who actually liked Jean.

"I'm afraid I couldn't say," I said. "I didn't know her well."

"She was a good secretary—far too good to be stuck in the typing pool. No offense, of course," he said.

"Not at all," I said, although I suspected he never would have been able to last one day working at the brisk clip Miss Wilkes expected from her typists.

"I never worked closely enough with Miss Plinkton to assess her talents," said Mr. Poole, neatly bringing Mr. Pearson back to Jean.

"She was sharp and intelligent. Detail-oriented too. Those are a rare combination of traits in anyone in my experience." Mr. Pearson looked a little wistful. "Perhaps if I had requested her assistance rather than Miss Travers, she would still be alive."

"Miss Travers?" I asked with interest. If I was to play amateur detective to Maxwell and Plaice's professionals, I would have to establish the alibis of every likely suspect and Irene was as good a person to start with as any. There was, of course, also the larger task ahead of finding out which of the CWR's dozens of employees were actual suspects and who had simply been going about with their jobs. I didn't know how I was going to eliminate all of them, but I trusted that I would come up with a plan as I went.

"Yes, she took notes on changes to a report that Mr. Faylen and I were working on," Mr. Pearson said.

"When was this?" asked Mr. Poole.

"Just before two o'clock," said Mr. Pearson. "It is unfortunate. If not for that trick of fate, Miss Plinkton might not have been in that room at that time. She might still be alive."

"What a tragedy indeed," I said. "I can't imagine who would have done such a horrible thing."

"It is clearly the work of a madman," said Mr. Pearson firmly.

"A madman who works in the CWR, where we all undergo background checks?" asked Mr. Poole.

Mr. Pearson shook his head. "Miss Redfern, what must you think about this place when only a few days into your employment there has been a murder."

"Oh, well . . ." I floundered at the concern that now seemed to lace Mr. Pearson's voice.

"If you need any assistance at all, you must come to me," he insisted.

Mr. Poole cleared his throat. "Miss Redfern, I wonder if you had had the chance to finish the memo I gave you yesterday."

I frowned. Mr. Poole hadn't given me a memo. But when I opened my mouth, he inched his chin down a fraction of an inch and I realized that he was providing me with an elegant exit.

"I was just checking it over before I left the typing pool. If you will walk back with me, it won't take two minutes to finish," I said.

Mr. Poole gave me a tight smile and then nodded to Mr. Pearson. "If you're done here, of course, Pearson."

Mr. Pearson made a gesture as though to say "go ahead," and I scurried out of the door.

In the corridor, I fell into step next to Mr. Poole. "Thank you, I—"

He nodded to a pair of men ahead of us. "Not here, Miss Redfern."

FOURTEEN

We were almost to the canteen when Mr. Poole pulled out a key, unlocked an unmarked door, and held it open. Inside stood a small table and two chairs. In front of one of the chairs, there was a stack of files with a pen resting on top. Nothing else.

When I turned to Mr. Poole, he wore a grim expression.

"Miss Redfern, I know that you have suffered a great shock, but I hope that I don't have to warn you to be careful," he said.

I crossed my arms. "I can't imagine what you mean."

"Pearson? Comforting you?" he prompted as though I was an idiot.

"If you think I in any way encouraged or welcomed Mr. Pearson's attention, you have vastly underestimated my character. Not that it would have been any of your business in the first place."

He sucked in a breath as though trying to compose himself. "I apologize, Miss Redfern. I was only thinking of your own best interest. I'm sure you will find this out on your own, but the CWR can be a very small environment in which to work. Rumors can be powerful things," he said.

I cocked my head. "There is nothing but rumor floating around at the moment. Everyone is speculating about Jean's murder."

"I'm aware."

"Have you been in to speak to the inspectors yet?" I asked.

"I have. They are, as far as I can tell, useless."

"They hardly asked me anything except why you were the one who released me from the sunlamp room."

He gave a little snort. "Well, that's an easy enough answer. It's because you were making an unholy racket banging on the door."

"You would have too if you had been trapped with a body," I shot back.

He tilted his head to concede this point.

"Actually, Mr. Poole, I have wondered what you were doing there myself. There aren't any offices in use down that way."

"I was on my way to meet someone," he said.

"Who?" I asked.

"Why were you late to Mr. Pearson's meeting?" he countered. "It is only a few minutes' walk from where I saw you speaking to the investigators to the meeting room."

We stood there, arms crossed, staring at each other for a moment. Finally, I said, "I'll answer if you do."

"I was on special business for the minister," he said.

"Meeting someone you refuse to name?"

"And where were you this morning?" he shot back, ignoring me.

"I was in the Dock."

"What were you doing down there?"

"I thought I had snagged my stocking. Since new ones are so difficult to find these days, I wanted to fix any damage I may have caused." If he wasn't going to tell me the entire truth, neither was I going to confide in him.

"And was your stocking snagged?" he asked. Asked by another man, there might have been something lurid about that question. However, he simply sounded suspicious.

"No. Fortunately I hadn't caught it after all," I said.

"That is lucky indeed. I do have a few other questions," he said, rounding the table to lift the pen and open the top file. From halfway across the small room, I could see my name at the top and I could just make out the line "Date of birth."

"Is that my personnel file?" I asked, taking a step forward.

He looked up at me. "It is."

"Why do you have my file?" I asked, my heart beating a little faster in a way it hadn't when Mr. Pearson revealed what he knew about my past.

"I've been doing a bit of reading up on you."

"Why?" I asked.

His finger skimmed down the page before stopping. "Miss Redfern, am I correct in thinking that before the war you worked in an advertising agency?"

"I did."

"Did you ever work with any German or Austrian members of staff?" he asked.

I swallowed. This conversation had veered out of my hands, and I didn't like it one bit. "No, not that I'm aware."

"Are you acquainted with any German or Austrian people? Perhaps from your school days," he said.

I frowned. "There was a German girl a couple years ahead of me. I think her name was Marie." He made a note. "What are you writing down?"

"Have you been in touch with this Marie recently?" he asked, ignoring me.

"Why are you asking me these things? What is it that you're accusing me of?"

He looked up. "Are you aware that sensitive information discussed in the cabinet war rooms has recently made its way into German hands?"

"I've heard the women in the typing pool talking about something appearing on one of Lord Haw-Haw's broadcasts," I said. "But surely you don't think I had anything to do with that. I only just began working here."

"Our intelligence service believes that there is a concerted effort to ferry information out of this office and into the hands of the enemy. They believe that the Germans may have managed to secure employment for a plant, and that this is a sophisticated operation," he said.

"You think there's a mole working in the CWR?" I asked, hardly believing what he was saying.

"Essentially yes."

"And you think that I had something to do with that," I said, giving voice to all of the implications behind his words.

"You were late from a meeting at a time when most of night shift from the typing pool is in the canteen having breakfast. If you were in the Dock, you could have secreted information away to smuggle out of the CWR either when you go up top for some air or when you leave at the end of your shift." He looked up at me. "You understand that I have to examine all of the possibilities."

I sat back in my chair, arms folded. "Should I say that I had nothing to do with the leak of any information? Or would that even matter?"

"It certainly wouldn't be a bad place to start."

"All right, I had nothing to do with it. I take my oath to this government very seriously."

A pause stretched out between us. Finally, he asked, "What were you really doing in the Dock?"

My first instinct was to clam up, but then a greater, overriding feeling struck me. I didn't trust this man, but I remembered the look on his face when he'd found me in the sunlamp room with Jean's body. He hadn't assumed I was about to faint or would collapse in a weeping heap. He'd left me in charge.

Granted, I'd only been in charge of a dead body, but a woman should display a degree of grace in these matters.

"I went to examine the bunk where Jean Plinkton always stayed," I said.

His brows popped halfway up his forehead. "I beg your pardon?"

"One of the first things I was told when I joined the typing pool was that I could take any bunk in the Dock but one. That was Jean's bunk. I wanted to see why she always insisted on it."

"Surely the inspectors had already done that," he said.

"They had. In fact, all of her belongings had been removed when I arrived."

"Then what was the purpose—?"

"I found something."

He stared at me. "You found something."

"Yes. Two pieces of paper wrapped in a bundle of cloth."

"Where?" he asked.

"Inside the mattress."

"But surely that should have been found upon inspection," he said.

"Apparently the investigators—good as I'm sure they can be at some aspects of their jobs—are not particularly gifted seamstresses. I'm much more of a knitter myself, but I've had to construct and mend a few garments since this war broke out. I know a repaired seam when I see one, even if it is well done."

He stared at me a moment and then opened his mouth. Then he closed it again. Finally, he said, "Two pieces of paper, you say?"

"Yes. One was a list written in some sort of code. I will admit that I don't have the first clue how to decipher it. The other was a typed note," I said.

"What sort of note?" he asked.

"A threatening one."

"Miss Redfern, I'm going to need to see that note and the list."

I smiled. "I would be happy to show you, Mr. Poole, on one condition."

The man had the audacity to look bemused. "Considering that you are withholding what might be vital evidence in a murder case, I'm not entirely sure that you have a leg to stand on, but do go on."

"I will show you the letter and the code, but in return I want to join you in your investigation."

"My what?"

"Come now, Mr. Poole. I'm not foolish enough to think that you're asking questions about German associates of CWR staff for no reason."

He grunted.

"And," I said, planting my hands on the table to lean across it, "I do not think it's too much of a stretch to guess that if you're asking about Jean's murder, you believe that it may very well have something to do with your leak."

FIFTEEN

Mr. Poole's expression gave nothing away as he took his seat.

"Think about it," I said, mirroring him by sinking into the chair opposite.

"I am, and I'm not sure I like it," he said.

"It's too much of a coincidence that Jean was murdered at the same time information is being leaked out of the CWR," I pressed on. "She probably knew something that she shouldn't and she was killed for it."

"That is wild speculation, but it is possible that you aren't entirely misguided," he conceded.

I grinned, prompting him to shake his head.

"I'm going to need to see the coded note, Miss Redfern," he said.

"Do you think that, if you reiterate your request in several different ways, I'll eventually forget myself and agree without you conceding something in return?" I asked.

He rubbed his forehead. "I thought it was worth a try."

"Mr. Poole, if you fear I would be a detriment to your investigation, I can assure you that you are very mistaken. I would be an asset, and I suspect if you gave it a moment's thought you would realize how right I am. Just look at how well we interrogated Mr. Pearson together!"

"Was that an interrogation?" he asked.

"It was the beginnings of one, was it not?" I challenged.

"First of all, I am not authorized to bring anyone on to assist with my investigation."

"I've signed the Official Secrets Act, just like you. I type up Top Secret documents every day. I have access to some of the most sensitive information that any Briton can hold in this war. I've already begun investigating Jean's murder. And I've found things out that the inspectors don't know," I said triumphantly.

"You found a couple of pieces of paper. That is all," he said.

"It isn't all," I argued.

He raised a brow.

"I've also begun to establish the alibis of several people—"

"Your fellow typists?" he asked.

"They are suspects, aren't they?" I asked. Everyone was a suspect, but those who worked closely with Jean even more than most.

"What have you found out so far?" he asked.

"That there is at least one guard who can be persuaded to fib about whether one has gone up top or not," I said.

He stared at me blankly.

"If he is willing to lie about whether a woman left the CWR while she's meant to be on shift, I wonder if it's that much of a leap to also persuade him to overlook security checks as well," I said.

"You think that's how someone might be ferrying sensitive information out of the CWR?" he asked.

I shrugged. "It's possible."

"You said one guard? What is his name?" he asked.

I crossed my hands in front of me, despite knowing full well that I had no idea. "Mr. Poole, I'm sure that you will understand that I don't feel comfortable disclosing that piece of information unless I have your reassurance that we are working together to catch Jean's murderer and your mole."

His eyes narrowed, and I almost thought he would protest again. Instead he asked, "How do you know that I'm not the murderer?"

"I suppose I could ask you the same thing. What if I'm simply playing at investigating Jean's death to throw suspicion off of me?" I asked.

A tiny smile tugged at the right corner of his mouth, and I knew I had him. "When you present it like that, I suppose we would simply have to trust one another. If we do work together."

"I suppose we would."

"Let's say, hypothetically, that I bring you on to my investigation. How do you propose we go about this partnership?" he asked.

"I'm going to hazard a guess that since I haven't heard any gossip about it yet, your investigation isn't common knowledge," I said.

"The powers that be thought it best if I worked undercover so that I didn't draw suspicion. However, they have decided that time has come to an end. I will endeavor to be as discreet as possible, but I've been instructed to begin questioning suspects in a more direct manner."

"Then may I suggest that for a brief period of time you put in a request to have me assigned to you as a secretary?" I asked.

"Won't that make you unpopular with the other women? I've always had the impression that there's a hierarchy dividing those who also sub in as secretaries and those who don't," he said.

It would. Some of them would secretly hate it, especially Anne, who seemed Hell-bent on abandoning the night shift. However, that was a problem I would have to address after the important business of finding a murderer and a mole was done.

"I will manage the other women. I think it would be best if I'm seen to assist you for part of the day while continuing to work as a typist. Maintaining access to the typing pool is important. I'm still unpicking everything I've learned about Jean so far," I said.

He nodded. "I can make sure the request is for a few hours of your time each day. That should give you enough flexibility to assist me while also keeping a hand in."

"Thank you," I said.

"Right." He sucked in a breath. "What I'm about to say cannot leave this room."

"I suspect I'm bound by the same rules as you," I reminded him.

"This goes even higher than the Official Secrets Act. Some of the information that has been smuggled out was marked Top Secret. Other pieces are meant for ministers' eyes only. If you are privy to it, you cannot speak to anyone about it, no matter who asks," he warned.

"I understand."

"By now you no doubt will have realized that I am not actually an assistant secretary to the minister of information—or at least that's not exclusively my role. I work for a branch of the Joint Intelligence Services, which is tasked with stopping leaks of vital information into enemy hands. A few months ago, the intelligence services intercepted a Top Secret document—part of a report—listing some of the suspected German allies we have had under surveillance here in London.

It was passed to one of our plants in the field, and we were able to trace the connection back to the CWR. That's where the trail went cold.

"After a further review of intelligence information, we've identified three other instances where sensitive information may have been leaked. One was a potentially explosive report on dissent among the Admiralty about Operation Catapult," he said.

"What is Operation Catapult?" I asked.

"The order to scuttle French naval ships to prevent them from falling into German hands. Churchill decided it was vital for the war," he said, his voice somber.

"He ordered the destruction of allied ships?" I asked.

He gave a sharp nod. "When France fell, difficult decisions were made. The other pieces of information were about the number of RAF planes in service and qualified pilots trained. That sort of intelligence in the wrong hands could be devastating."

"And it fell into the wrong hands," I said, understanding now the gravity of what he was telling me.

"Yes. We don't know how the information is making its way out of this office, and we don't know who is behind it," he said.

"Is there any pattern to what is being leaked? Is there any single department that seems to be to blame?" I asked.

He shook his head. "It has been random. That is part of what has frustrated our efforts so far."

"How do you know that there is just one mole then? There could be multiple leaks," I said.

"Security measures have been tightened since I arrived in June. It's improbable enough that one person would be able to smuggle out sensitive materials, let alone two or three."

"How can you be sure?"

He pinched the bridge of his nose. "I suppose that, if we are speaking purely hypothetically, there could be more than one person, but I don't want to even entertain the thought."

"If we discount what could be legitimate theories, we will only make it more difficult for ourselves." I'm sure I'd read some detective or another say that at some point in a novel.

Mr. Poole sighed, so I hurried to ask, "And you have also been asking yourself if Jean fits into this?"

"The thought had crossed my mind that the two cases are connected, as you said. However, if the mole was looking to keep their real intentions secret for as long as possible, inviting the inevitable investigation that would follow a murder isn't really the way to do it," he said.

"That is, assuming that you think the investigators are competent," I said, earning another little smile. "So, what do you propose we do first?"

"Miss Redfern, I've laid my proverbial cards on the table. Now it's your turn," he said.

I hesitated. Something told me to keep Grove House to myself. I wanted to investigate it, to search out what its meaning might be. If I found something significant, I would tell him.

"I've been gathering little bits of information here and there. I want to establish who was where in the window of time when Jean was killed," I said.

"When do you think that was?" he asked.

"I last saw her at two o'clock. She announced that she was going on a delivery. I believe she relished her time outside of the typing pool.

"Miss Wilkes sent me to the sunlamp room at a quarter to three, but I went to the Dock to pick up a book in case there was a queue," I said.

"Which book?" he asked.

"*Busman's Honeymoon*."

He pulled a face.

"You aren't one of those boring people who dismisses detective novels outright simply because they're popular, are you?" I asked.

"No, but I prefer the Americans," he said.

"The Americans!" I cried. "All of that hard-boiled stuff about statues of birds?"

"Do you mean *The Maltese Falcon*? It is already a classic of the genre. Dashiell Hammett is a genius," he said.

"I'm not saying that the man doesn't have talent, but there's no elegance to the crime in those books," I said.

"You discovered a body with a knife protruding from its throat, and you're worried about elegance?" he asked.

"In my fiction, yes," I said, sounding rather more prim than I liked. "Now where were we? Oh yes. The time of the murder. I expect I reached the Dock at ten to three and the sunlamp room about ten minutes later. That gives a timeline of almost an hour when Jean could have been killed."

"I imagine it takes time for a person to die after being stabbed in the throat," he said.

I couldn't help touching my own throat, but still I nodded. "At least a few minutes for the loss of blood to take effect, I would think."

"Did she have whatever she was meant to be delivering with her?" he asked.

"I wondered the same thing at the time. I couldn't find anything on or near her body. There were no files, no notebook, nothing."

"So either she made the delivery and then went to the sunlamp room, or the killer took the files," he said.

"Exactly."

"Why did she take a detour to the sunlamp room instead of going back to her desk? Was she meeting someone?" he asked.

"Mr. Poole, I believe we are singing from the same hymn sheet," I said with a bright smile.

Mr. Poole huffed, which I decided to take as a sign of agreement. Then he pulled out a clean sheet of paper. "The first thing we should do is draw up a list of your suspects and see if they correspond with my suspects."

"And figure out where everyone was between two and three yesterday afternoon," I added.

"Don't forget, the killer stayed around long enough to lock you in," he said.

I shivered. "I'm not likely to ever forget that."

I held my hand out for his pen. He passed it across the table to me and then pulled out a blank sheet of paper from under the pile of files.

"Right now, everyone in the CWR could be a suspect," I said, scribbling down notes. "It isn't a foolproof methodology, but I think the best thing to do is to focus first on those most likely to have had some issue with Jean and begin to eliminate names. Here are the names of the women working yesterday."

On the paper, I wrote down:

Miss Wilkes
Edith Tierney—Day shift
Caroline Adams—Day shift
Patricia Bainbridge—Day shift
Irene Travers—Day shift

Betty Lewison—Night shift
Joy Hawkins—Night shift
Jill Osman—Night shift
Joanna Gilbert—Night shift
Claire Boyd—Night shift
Anne Paxton—Night shift

"We'll also need to speak to the men," I said, scribbling down names before pushing the paper back to him.

"The men?"

I folded my hands on the table and leaned forward. "Clerks, deputies, secretaries, perhaps even the ministers who often came into contact with Jean."

"You want to speak to ministers?" he asked.

"Well, if their movements can't be accounted for . . ."

"Have you seen a minister walking around the CWR?" he asked.

"Yes. I passed the War Secretary on Wednesday." I'd seen the rather distinguished Anthony Eden in many photographs, but I had been surprised at how slight he seemed in person. His mustache, however, was a sight to behold both in and out of print.

"And did you notice all of the people around him? Those briefing him and those clinging to his coattails, wanting a moment of his time?" he asked. "How could Anthony Eden or any of the other ministers slip away while in the CWR and murder someone undetected?"

I chewed on my bottom lip. That was a fair point. "Well, what about those who don't run around with an entourage? People like you?"

"Thank you for reminding me I'm not important enough to merit a staff," he quipped, but by the way he said it I could tell he didn't mind. From underneath my file, he pulled out a list. "Here are the names of the people I plan to speak to."

I read down the list quickly:

Sir Alexander Halson
Lawrence Pearson
Harold Faylen
Archibald Conley
Grahame Morgan

"I recognize a few of these names. Obviously Mr. Pearson, and Mr. Faylen is back and forth to the typing pool so often that you'd think he might request a desk there. I've also done some typing for Mr. Conley," I said.

"All of these men have been present in meetings where the information leaked to the Germans has been discussed or they have written memos that have included that information. Are any of them on your list?" he asked.

"I know that Jean was a favorite of Mr. Pearson. And Mr. Conley and Mr. Faylen would have interacted with her quite a bit. I would add the Royal Marine I mentioned earlier," I said.

"The one turning a blind eye?" he asked.

I nodded.

"Damned fool." He stopped himself. "I beg your pardon, Miss Redfern."

"He is a damned fool," I said. "And I think, under the circumstances, you can call me Evelyne."

Out of all of the things I'd said that morning, *that* seemed to be the one that shocked Mr. Poole the most.

"It would be best if we keep things strictly professional, don't you think, Miss Redfern?" he managed to choke out.

I rolled my eyes. "Leave it to me to find out the name of the Royal Marine."

"I thought you said you didn't feel comfortable disclosing his name," he said.

I shifted in my seat. "I did."

"Implying you already know who he is," he continued.

"Fine, I don't know his name exactly, but I know how to find it out. I promise."

He closed his eyes. If I didn't know better, I might have said the man was trying to hold back his frustration.

"How will you do that?" he asked.

"I have my methods," I said, being intentionally cryptic. I fixed my attention back on the paper in front of us. "I think this is a good start."

"I'll find out if all of them were in the building on the day of the murder," he said, making another note before looking up. "Now, Miss Redfern, I think it's time to show me that code."

SIXTEEN

T he papers are in my bunk in the Dock," I said in a low voice as Mr. Poole fell into step beside me after we left his makeshift interrogation room.

"Are they secure?" he asked, sounding positively scandalized by the thought of me letting them out of my sight.

I scowled. As though I would let sensitive documents that might be linked to a murder case lay about in the open where anyone could get to them. "Don't worry. They're in a place no one will ever think to look."

A commotion ahead of us in the corridor pulled my attention back, and I frowned as I saw a column of men in gray suits and military uniforms round the corner ahead of us.

"What is . . ."

I trailed off because, in the center of the scrum, with his pugnacious face screwed up in thought and an unlit cigar clamped in his hand, strode forth Winston Churchill.

Other people in the corridor stopped what they were doing to stare at the prime minister as he barreled forth. I remembered all of us sitting around the wireless at Mrs. Jenkins's in June to listen to the BBC presenter read out passages of Mr. Churchill's speech to Parliament when he promised that we would fight on the beaches and on the landing grounds and we would never surrender. Even after a long day of work, the words sent shivers dancing down my spine, and we'd all looked at each other—half terrified with worry that we were about to be invaded and half invigorated with the idea that our nation would not be brought down by the Germans.

Now he was a mere few feet from me.

"See?" Mr. Poole whispered. "Surrounded by people."

I shot him a look, glancing back in time to see the PM give a fast, almost imperceptible nod our way as he passed.

"What was that?" I hissed under my breath.

"What was what?"

"Why did the PM nod at you?"

"He didn't nod at me," said Mr. Poole, beginning to stride down the corridor again.

Tall as I was, I still had to scramble to keep up with him. "He absolutely did. I know a nod of acknowledgment when I see one."

"He probably remembers me from one meeting or another," said Mr. Poole, his voice too tight to be casual.

It seemed that I wasn't the only one who was withholding some information. However, since Mr. Poole seemed unlikely to elaborate, I let it go for the moment.

At the top of the stairs to the Dock, I paused. "Wait here. I'll fetch the letters."

"I could come down—"

"No, you absolutely can't. First of all, you aren't allowed. And second of all, I know for a fact that there are women sleeping down there. Unless you wish to alert the entire CWR to our investigation because you set a bunch of women off screaming, you'll need to wait right here," I said.

Mr. Poole crossed his arms but didn't protest again, so I took that as a signal that I could proceed. I hurried down the stairs and rounded the corner, stopping with a gasp when I saw a rat sitting in the middle of the passageway next to my sleeping colleagues. It stood up on its hind legs, nose twitching.

"Who's that?" the groggy voice of one of the women on the night shift asked from one of the bunks.

"Nothing. Sorry. I'm just fetching something," I said, easing forward. The rat scurried away.

The woman whom I'd woken muttered something and snuggled deeper into her bed.

I walked on the balls of my feet to keep my heels from clicking against the concrete. Luckily, the bunk underneath mine was empty. I hauled myself up, unlocked my cubby, and dug into my things.

I hadn't been lying when I'd told Mr. Poole that I'd hidden the letters in a place no one would think to look. I slipped a hand under my spare shirts and pulled out the little canvas pouch where I kept my belt and sanitary cloths. It was an old boarding school trick, hiding things you wanted no one else to find in and among your truly unmentionables. I drew out the palm-sized notebook I'd stashed the clues in. It and an accompanying silver pencil were regular Christmas gifts from Aunt Amelia because "a lady never knows when she might need to record her enemies' misdeeds," which seemed strangely appropriate for investigating a murder.

Before joining forces with Mr. Poole, I hadn't been sure how I would manage holding on to the papers. There was nowhere permanent to put them. The bunks and cubbies changed hands with each shift change, and our desks were checked daily. The guards on the staircases examined our handbags and cases whenever we left, sometimes requesting we turn out our pockets. Occasionally, Miss Wilkes would perform spot checks of our things after a shift so I couldn't risk keeping them with my clothes long-term. However, if Mr. Poole was tasked with investigating this leak, he should be able to subvert the rules in the name of solving his case.

I hesitated, the papers in my hand. Could I trust him? Was it wise to take that sort of leap of faith?

No.

Maybe?

As a woman in the typing pool, I could melt into the background of many places in the CWR without attracting notice, but only up until a point. What I couldn't very well do was march up to a clerk or an assistant secretary and demand that he give me the time of day, let alone his alibi. No matter how I examined the situation, it seemed that I needed the power of Mr. Poole's investigation to ask the questions that I needed to know the answers to. I needed an ally.

Back upstairs, Mr. Poole's gaze immediately fixed on my hand, a grin morphing his features in a way that made me wonder what he was like outside of the staid seriousness of his work. It was a question I wasn't sure I wanted to know the answer to.

"Let's go back to the room and have a look," he said.

I n the makeshift interrogation room, I laid the two bits of paper from Jean's mattress on the table in front of me. The paper crinkled a little under my fingers. I held my breath.

"This is it?" Mr. Poole asked after a long moment.

"What were you expecting?" I asked.

"Something a little more"—he waved a hand—"substantial."

"I apologize for not finding a written, signed, and witnessed confession instead."

He sighed and picked up the threat first, his forefinger running over the edge of the slip of paper.

"It sounds as though Jean made someone very angry," he said.

"Or she was angry herself, wrote a note, and then thought twice about sending it," I said.

"If that was the case, why keep it?" he asked.

I shrugged. Mr. Poole made a *humph* noise and turned his attention to the code.

"Do you know much about codes?" I asked hopefully.

His brow crinkled. "A little. Have you tried to crack it?"

I shook my head. "I wouldn't know the first thing about how."

He pulled his pen and paper closer to him. "I'll admit that this isn't my area of expertise, but I understand a little bit of the principles. 'E' is the most common letter in the English language, so in theory it should be one of the most common letters."

"It's unfortunate that it looks like a list rather than a series of sentences," I said, peering around his right arm.

"Why do you say that?"

"I imagine, if they were sentences, there would be short words that would be easier to identify," I said. "Things like 'a,' 'as,' 'of,' 'me,' 'you.'"

"But none of these are spaced out into words," he said.

"What about double letters then?" I asked.

"Here." He pointed to the third row of lettering with a grouping of two letters: DD.

We both stared at it for a few moments. Then I hazarded a glance in his direction. "This is going to prove difficult, isn't it?"

He set down his pen and scrubbed a hand across his chin. "I suspect that our energies might be better used in another way."

"We can't simply neglect the code," I said.

"We won't. I know a place that we can send it. They might be able to do something with it," he said.

"Letting someone else in?" I asked. "Are you sure that's wise?"

"This place has some of the very brightest someones you'll ever meet, and they're all playing by the same rules that we are," he said in a rather cryptic manner.

"How long do you think that will take?" I asked.

He shrugged. "It could be a snap. It could take a very long time indeed."

"I'd like to keep a copy of it. That list was important enough that she hid it away. It has to mean something," I said.

He gestured to the pen and paper, and I stooped to scribble the random jumble of letters out. Unsurprisingly, writing them did nothing to clarify things for me. When I looked up, I noticed him jotting down the code in a notebook as well.

"Where will you hide the list and the threat?" he asked.

It appeared that Mr. Poole might not be as helpful on that front as I had hoped.

"I haven't figured that one out yet," I said.

"If you're caught smuggling things out—"

"I will have to do my best not to be caught," I said with more gusto than I actually felt. I hoped that my connection with Mr. Fletcher might protect me, but I didn't even really know what the man did in the government apart from recruit unsuspecting family friends for clandestine war work.

"Right." Mr. Poole straightened and clapped his hands together. "I think it's time that we start."

"Start?" I asked.

"Questioning our suspects. Isn't that what you wanted to be a part of?" he asked.

"Absolutely."

"Good. Then why don't you go fetch the first person?" he asked.

"Why me?"

"Because I'm going to phone Miss Wilkes and explain to her that I'll be needing your assistance today," he said.

"I'll have to return to the typing pool at some point to type up Mr. Pearson's meeting minutes," I pointed out.

He nodded. "We'll start small. One suspect." He ran his finger down the list but then stopped. "I'd like to speak to your Royal Marine."

"*My* Royal Marine? My, you must think I operate quickly. I've only been at the CWR for five days," I said.

"I meant the one you mentioned earlier. Who is covering for girls who sneak out without questions?"

"I see," I said.

"If that man is willing to lie about whether he's seen girls go up top or not, who knows what he's willing to do," said Mr. Poole.

I nodded. It was sound logic. "Give me a few minutes, and I suspect I'll be able to find out who we're looking for."

SEVENTEEN

As soon as I walked through the typing pool door, Miss Wilkes hurried over.

"Miss Redfern, what is this about you working for Mr. Poole? He just telephoned," she asked in a hushed voice.

"He has need of some help with a project." When I saw the look of pain on her face, I added, "It's for the minister."

"But who is going to cover your work here?" she asked, wringing her hands. "We're stretched enough as it is with Miss Plinkton's . . . departure."

I composed my face into what I hoped was an expression of reassuring sympathy. I didn't like seeing this previously unflappable, controlled woman distressed, but I suppose she was dealing with a murder and a staff shortage all at once.

"Miss Wilkes, I promise that every moment I am not working with Mr. Poole, I will be here," I said.

"I don't know. I simply don't know . . ." she muttered, wringing her hands. "It has been so difficult, this awful business."

"It is terrible," I agreed.

"And to think that if she hadn't insisted on going on that delivery, she might still be alive," the older woman said.

"Insisted on going? I thought that you would have been the one to send her."

Miss Wilkes shook her head. "Oh, no. You see, Miss Plinkton was very much in demand to lend extra support to several departments, and given that she had been working at Number 10 since before the war, she practically had her own schedule. It wasn't ideal, but there is a war on and needs must."

Her own bunk, her own schedule. Was there anything that Jean hadn't made sure she was an exception for?

"Did she say whether she was planning to meet anyone after her delivery?" I asked.

"No," said Miss Wilkes.

"And do you remember anyone else being away from the typing pool at that time?" I asked.

Miss Wilkes screwed up her brow. "Miss Bainbridge was out on a delivery, and Miss Travers was taking notes for a meeting. You were going for sunlamp treatment. Other than that, all were present and accounted for. Why do you ask?"

I made a mental note to speak to both Patricia and Irene about their alibis.

"Oh, just my own curiosity. The timing is so tragic, as you said," I said.

"Miss Wilkes!" called Cathy from behind us. "Miss Wilkes, I'm sorry but I can't understand a word of these handwritten notes."

Miss Wilkes sucked in a breath. "Just a moment, Miss Ingersol." She lowered her voice. "No one ever can read anyone in Air Raid Precautions' handwriting. Miss Redfern, if you could please tell Mr. Poole that we really are shorthanded and to make economical use of your time, I would be very grateful."

"Of course. I'll just collect a few things from my desk," I said.

I watched Miss Wilkes glide toward Cathy, and then hurried to my desk. I could feel the other women's eyes watching me as I failed to uncover my typewriter.

With Miss Wilkes still engaged with Cathy, I caught Irene's eye.

"Did something happen after your meeting?" she asked in a hurried whisper.

"I've been seconded to a special project. It's going to take me away from the typing pool for a period of time every day," I said.

"Well, you do operate quickly, don't you?"

The frost in her tone took me aback. "I don't know what you mean."

Irene flipped her dark hair over her shoulder before placing her hands back on her typewriter. "I know you're new, but a word of advice: don't assume that the other girls and I will all be happy to pick up your work like we did for Jean."

"I'm simply doing my job, just like any of the rest of the women here."

"I hope you enjoy your time with Mr. Pearson," she said, turning back to her typewriter.

My brow crinkled. "Mr. Pearson? I won't be working with Mr. Pearson."

Irene stilled, then turned around. "You won't?"

"No. I'll be working with Mr. Poole. I did some typing for him on Wednesday, so I suppose he thought of me," I fibbed.

Irene blushed. "Oh. Well, that's all right then."

"Why is Mr. Poole all right but not Mr. Pearson?" I asked.

Her blush deepened and she dropped her voice even lower. "I shouldn't have said anything. It's just, Mr. Pearson has a bit of a reputation."

"You're the second person today who's warned me away from him. I promise I have no interest in the man," I said.

Irene let out a breath of relief. "I'm glad to hear it. I didn't want you mixed up with any of that. Miss Wilkes is very strict."

Across the room, I could hear Miss Wilkes wrapping up with Edith.

"Listen, Irene. You told me about a Royal Marine," I said, gathering up my things.

"There are a lot of Royal Marines here," she said.

"You know the one that I mean."

She stared at me.

"The one who will look the other way when—"

"Not here!" she hissed, glancing about her. "Later. We can talk later."

Then she gave me her back again, making it clear that this conversation was done.

Damn. Perhaps I hadn't chosen the right time to ask—a quiet place where Irene was less concerned about being overheard might have been better—but I'd wanted to report back to Mr. Poole when I returned. It felt important, proof that I could bring something useful to our odd little team. However, if Irene wouldn't talk to me in the typing pool, I would simply have to figure out another way to extract the name.

"Miss Wilkes, I need to take this duplicate to Mr. Dean's office. It was due a quarter hour ago," I heard Rachel say behind me as I pulled another pencil from my desk drawer and then locked it all up.

I waved goodbye to Miss Wilkes and the rest of the ladies. Then I pushed open the typing pool door and almost walked straight into Rachel.

"Evelyne," she breathed, holding a buff envelope close to her chest. "I hope you don't mind, but I overheard you speaking to Irene."

"Did you?" I asked, raising a brow.

Rachel looked down, her cheeks pinking. "I know I shouldn't listen, but it's just that I sit so close to you both . . ."

"It's all right," I said.

"Don't let Irene bother you. She's nice enough most of the time, but she can be territorial when it comes to work," said Rachel.

"I thought that was what people said about Jean."

"It's both of them, really. They were always vying for attention, trying to make sure that they had all of the prime assignments. I think they both liked being the top girl, and I suspect that Irene assumed she would automatically be after Jean died. Now you've been requested as support and have a special project."

"That would explain it, thank you. I thought it odd because Irene's been nothing but friendly with me since I arrived," I said.

"She really is very good like that." Rachel opened her mouth again but then seemed to think better of it.

"Is something the matter?" I asked.

"Not the matter, no," she said slowly. "It's just that I also overheard you asking about a Royal Marine."

"Yes, Irene mentioned that one of them can be helpful if you forget your pass or need to slip outside for some air while you're on shift when you're not necessarily supposed to," I said carefully.

Rachel's eye lit up. "Oh, that would be Jonathan."

"Jonathan?" I asked, a little surprised at the familiarity. The typists all used each other's Christian names, but all of the men were always referred to as Mr. So And So or Lieutenant Whoever He Is.

"Lieutenant Jonathan MacIntyre. All the girls are sweet on him. He's one of the nice ones."

"Really?" I asked, remembering the Royal Marine who had escorted me to the canteen. With a close crop of blond curls, I suppose

he was better-looking than most men in the CWR—and younger too—
but I didn't think he was particularly special. Rachel, however, must
have disagreed with me because she was positively beaming.

"Well, he's kind, which is more than can be said of most," she
said. "Some of them are so snobbish, it feels as though they look right
through you."

"Do you know when Lieutenant MacIntyre might next be on duty?"
I asked.

"He's guarding Staircase 14 now. I passed him on my way in this
morning," said Rachel.

I thanked her and hurried along the corridor back to Mr. Poole's
makeshift interrogation room.

"Did you find out who he is?" he asked as soon as I burst in.

"Yes, and he's on duty now," I said.

"Then shall we take our questions on the road?" he asked as he
stood.

"I think, Mr. Poole, that would be for the best."

———

Lieutenant Jonathan MacIntyre?" I asked as I approached Staircase 14 with Mr. Poole in tow.

"Can I help you, Miss?" Lieutenant MacIntyre asked.

"I'm Miss Redfern. This is my associate, Mr. Poole," I said, ignoring
Mr. Poole's choked cough at being described as such. "You were so
helpful to me yesterday, I wondered if you could answer some questions I had."

"Can't leave my post, Miss," he said, giving me an apologetic smile.
"Not without an order from my commanding officer."

"That's all right, Lieutenant. We would be happy to speak to you
right here," I said with a smile. "I wanted to ask you about the murder."

I watched his Adam's apple bob with a swallow. "It's a horrible
thing that happened."

"I didn't realize when we spoke yesterday that you knew Miss
Plinkton," I said.

"I know all of the typing pool girls," the lieutenant said. "You're a
hard bunch to miss."

"Is that so?" Mr. Poole asked.

"Standing guard all day, you come to look forward to seeing anyone really. You learn their names when you check their passes. Learn who has a kind word for you," Lieutenant MacIntyre said.

"Did you know Miss Plinkton well?" I asked.

Lieutenant MacIntyre shook his head. "Not well. I saw her from time to time in the corridors and the canteen, like most of the girls in the typing pool and the switchboard."

"Where were you on duty between two and three o'clock yesterday?" I asked.

He frowned. "I've gone over all of this with the inspectors, same as all of the other guards on duty."

"We're simply double-checking the timeline that's emerged from the inspectors' questioning," I lied.

"Respectfully, aren't you a typist, Miss Redfern?" Lieutenant MacIntyre asked.

Mr. Poole stepped forward. "Lieutenant MacIntyre, as you are aware, this is a very serious investigation—"

"All right, all right." The young man rubbed his forehead as though suddenly exhausted. "Normally I'm posted here, but sometimes on Saturdays, they move me. I was on the other side of the complex—Staircase 15—where you found me and told me to alert the military police, Sir," Lieutenant MacIntyre finished, nodding to Mr. Poole.

"Why were you on Staircase 15?" I asked.

"Because I do what I'm told," Lieutenant MacIntyre said. "I get orders to stand here, I stand here. My commanding officer tells me to go somewhere else, I go somewhere else. I'm a Royal Marine, Miss."

I lifted both of my hands in what I hoped was a placating gesture. "I understand. Did anyone try to take the staircase you were guarding during that time?" I thought it unlikely that anyone had run by him, blood dripping from their hands and wearing a hand-painted sign around their neck that read "I'm the killer," but someone had to ask the question.

"So many people pass, it's impossible to keep track of all of them," he said as three men in the gray suits of civilians walked by, proving his point.

"Do you think it's possible that someone from the outside could have slipped by you or one of the other guards either to enter or to exit the CWR?" I asked.

He scoffed. "No. Even if they did make it past one of us, there are other guards on the upper floors they'd need to go by. Someone would have demanded they see their pass at some point. If they refused, security protocols would have been triggered."

"What if someone who does work here didn't want anyone to know that they'd left the CWR?" I asked.

Again he shook his head. "Impossible, Miss."

"That's not what I've heard," I said. Lieutenant MacIntyre suddenly became very still, so I pressed on. "I've heard that sometimes, you'll help a woman hide the fact that she wasn't on premises if she wants a moment to herself. Perhaps you'll even let her pass without checking her bag."

"I don't know what you're—"

"We have witnesses who are willing to swear that what Miss Redfern says is true," said Mr. Poole. Apparently I wasn't the only one prepared to fib on the fly.

Lieutenant MacIntyre's face fell. "It's not such a big thing, is it? I mean, we're really meant to be keeping people from getting in, not preventing them from leaving."

I could almost feel sorry for the man, especially when Mr. Poole said, through what I suspected were gritted teeth, "You realize that this is a huge breach of security, Lieutenant."

"It was just a few of the girls. They work so hard and they just want a break without telling their supervisors. It isn't natural for women to be working like that," Lieutenant MacIntyre protested.

Which is precisely when the lieutenant lost me.

"Who have you looked the other way for?" I asked.

He shook his head.

"Lieutenant MacIntyre, this will be far worse for you if you don't tell us," I warned.

The man looked up at the ceiling, as though weighing every single way that us being in possession of this bit of information could be used against him. He sighed.

"Rachel, Irene, and Helen, the switchboard operator. Charlotte when she still worked here. They've all asked me to let them through but not to say that I saw them if anyone asks," he said.

"And Miss Plinkton?" Mr. Poole asked.

I could see Lieutenant MacIntyre swallow. "And Miss Plinkton."

"How often?" I asked at the same time that Mr. Poole asked, "Was there a pattern to when?"

"Well, I couldn't really say. There are so many people with so many different shifts . . ." Lieutenant MacIntyre trailed off.

"How often did Jean ask you to pretend you hadn't seen her?" I asked again.

Lieutenant MacIntyre cringed, no doubt dreading how bad whatever was about to come out of his mouth would sound. "Every fifth night."

Mr. Poole and I exchanged a look. If typists worked in three-day shifts with two days off in between, that meant that one night every shift Jean was sneaking out of the CWR.

"Please don't tell my commanding officer," said Lieutenant MacIntyre. "I was only trying to be nice."

"Did you have any other relationship with Miss Plinkton?" I asked.

"Relationship?" He shook his head. "I hardly knew the woman."

"Then why did you help her lie about her whereabouts?" I asked.

Any bravado seemed to drain from the man, leaving him looking like a lost schoolboy. "I just thought I was doing a nice thing."

I suspected what he was actually trying to do was charm the women he worked with, but instead of accusing him, I lifted my chin. "That is all for now, Lieutenant MacIntyre, but I suspect we'll be speaking to you again soon."

EIGHTEEN

By the time we finished with Lieutenant MacIntyre, it was impossible to ignore the incredibly unladylike growls coming from my stomach. Mr. Poole was enough of a gentleman not to comment, but instead suggested that we reconvene after lunch.

I don't know where Mr. Poole chose to have his repast, but I went straight to the canteen. It wasn't the food or even the steady supply of tea that drew me there. It was the gossip.

As soon as word got out about Mr. Poole and my investigation, I knew that it would become more difficult to convince even the women of the typing pool to speak to me without raising their suspicions. It was vital, therefore, that I try to establish alibis as early as possible.

As I rounded the door in the canteen, I found I was in luck. Caroline, Rachel, Cathy, and Irene all sat together at a four-seat table. I bought a liver paste sandwich and a cup of tea for my lunch, and began to make my way over, catching Cathy's eye as I approached.

"Join us," she called.

Irene, I noticed, had the good grace to look a little sheepish as Rachel and Cathy squeezed in to make room for me.

"You've been gone for ages," said Cathy.

"I had to take some shorthand earlier," I said by way of apology.

"Look at you, already becoming a favorite," Cathy teased, but I didn't sense any jealousy there.

"All of us are valuable to the CWR in our own way," said Caroline primly.

Irene lifted her head. "Leave Evelyne alone. She's still learning how things work around here."

I knew an olive branch when I saw one, and I also knew that they weren't often offered so I should take it while I could. I smiled at Irene. "Thanks, but really, don't mind me. Besides, all I can really think about is how horrible this business with Jean's murder must be for all of you."

"Is it true that you found the body?" Cathy asked breathlessly, her eyes a little wide.

"Miss Wilkes stepped out for a half hour while you were gone this morning, so we were able to properly fill Rachel and Cathy in," said Irene.

"Even though we were supposed to be working and not talking," said Caroline. But then she turned to me, naked curiosity replacing her usually severe expression. "I can't imagine how awful that was for you, Evelyne."

"It was horrible, but perhaps in a different way than if it had been any of you. You all knew her for so much longer than I did," I said.

Irene gave a soft snort, Caroline looked away, and Rachel and Cathy suddenly seemed remarkably preoccupied with their sand-wiches.

After a moment, Irene cleared her throat. "The people I feel really bad for are Edith and Patricia. Can you imagine going home knowing that you wouldn't be able to find out what's happened with the mur-der investigation for two entire days?"

"At least they're safe," said Cathy. "It's you we should be worried about, Evelyne."

"Me?" I asked in surprise.

"What if the killer thinks that you know something?" asked Cathy.

"How thoughtful of you to mention that, Cathy," said Irene with a dry tone. "Anyway, I'm sure Evelyne is fine. First of all, she hasn't worked here that long, and second, I'm certain we're all safe."

"Why do you say that?" I asked. I happened to agree with her—mostly—but I was curious as to her logic.

"Because I don't think it's accidental that Jean was the one who ended up murdered," said Irene.

"You can't say that sort of thing about the dead!" Cathy cried, crossing herself.

"It isn't as though, by dying, Jean's suddenly absolved of all her flaws," said Irene. "She was a rotter."

"She wasn't a rotter," hissed Caroline.

Irene pointed at her. "Are you forgetting the time that she told everyone that you stuff tissue in your brassiere?"

Caroline blushed to the roots of her auburn hair.

"And what about you, Cathy? She had all sorts of horrible things to say about you because you're Catholic," said Irene.

Cathy inhaled sharply.

"Rachel, remember the clerk you liked? Do you remember how she took it upon herself to flirt with him once she saw you both having a cup of tea at Lyons Corner House?" Irene asked.

"I'd rather not think about that," said Rachel softly.

"And what did she do to you?" I asked, realizing quickly that Irene was at risk of plunging this entire lunch into an emotional tailspin.

Irene laughed. "Oh, that's easy. She thought I was loose."

"Irene," Cathy admonished.

"It's laughable really. The pot calling the kettle black and all that. If the rumors are to be believed," said Irene.

"What sort of rumors?" I asked.

"Oh, take your pick. I've heard that she was the mistress of one of the higher-ups at RAF bomber command," said Irene.

"I heard someone say that she's really the illegitimate daughter of an earl," said Caroline, who, despite all of her stern propriety, perked up at the prospect of a good bit of gossip just like the rest of us.

"I heard that she was engaged to Michael Redgrave, but he wanted her to come with him to Hollywood and she refused to leave London," said Cathy in a rush.

"She wished," said Irene with a snort.

"That does seem very unlikely," I agreed.

"The truth is that none of us really knew all that much about Jean," Irene said. "She was very cagey, even though she wasn't above rummaging through other people's dirty laundry."

"Do you think she might have made anyone angry enough to kill her?" I asked.

My question was met with a chorus of nos, but they didn't sound all that convincing.

"What if she asked the wrong sort of questions?" I asked. What if, in nosing around in other people's business, she'd found out who leaked the information out of the CWR?

"Jean was mean and high-handed, she wasn't stupid. Her greatest concern was always herself," said Irene.

I sat back with my cup of tea, letting that sink in.

"I imagine we'll know more once the inspectors are done investigating," said Caroline.

"Have you all spoken to them?" I asked.

"Yes. They asked me all sorts of questions about where I was and what I was doing at the time they think Jean was killed," said Irene.

"What were you doing?" asked Cathy before I could ask.

Irene leveled her a look. "I was taking shorthand in a meeting."

"Who with?" I asked.

"Mr. Pearson and Mr. Faylen," said Irene.

"What about you?" I asked Caroline.

"Edith and I were in the typing pool," she said.

"I suppose that it must have been a comfort knowing that Edith and Miss Wilkes could confirm your alibis," I said.

"Yes . . ."

The way that Caroline drew out the word made me stop, but Cathy had already piped up, "I suppose in a way it's a good thing I was off duty that day. All I had to do was say I was at home and give the names of some of the people who might have seen me."

"I did that as well," said Rachel.

"Who was on nights that day?" Irene asked.

"Betty, Anne, Joanna, Joy, Claire, and Jill," Caroline rattled off, listing them in the order their desks were placed around the typing pool.

"Well, Joanna's alibi will be easy to confirm. She snores like a wildebeest," said Irene.

I made a mental note to catch Betty on our shift change and see if she could give me details of where and when she saw the other women in the Dock the previous night.

"All of this talk of murder, I think I need a cigarette. I'm going up top. Does anyone want to come with me?" Rachel asked, pushing away from the table.

"I don't smoke, but I'll come," said Cathy, collecting her handbag and her gas mask to follow Rachel.

"I should go as well. I need to speak to Miss Wilkes about something," said Caroline before hurrying off.

As soon as we were alone, Irene said, "I've been working with Cathy for months now, and she refuses to admit that she sneaks cigarettes every chance she can."

"Why doesn't she just come out and say that she smokes?" I asked.

Irene waved her hand. "Something about her mother thinking it's common. How her mother would ever find out, I don't know."

"Sometimes we tell stories about ourselves that suit us best," I said.

Irene smiled tightly. "Isn't that the truth? Actually, I'm glad to have a moment with you. I wanted to apologize."

"Oh?" I asked.

"I'm sorry for snapping at you earlier today. I didn't mean to make it seem as though I was . . . oh I don't know."

"Jealous?"

"Concerned," she corrected. Irene picked up her cup of tea and threw back the dregs before answering. "Look, all of us are trained to take shorthand and we help out when requested by various departments who are pinched for secretaries. However, there are some typists who seem to be requested again and again by certain men on staff, and maybe it isn't just because of their stenography skills."

"From how Mr. Pearson spoke about her, I take it Jean was one of those?"

Irene tilted her head in acknowledgment.

"She was gorgeous. Do you think there was something between them?" I asked.

Irene let out a long breath. "Between Jean and Mr. Pearson? I think Jean wished."

"Why is that?" I asked.

"He's high up in a department. That makes him important. All of those things the other girls said about Michael Redgrave and all of that? They ring true because at her core Jean liked lording things over other people. She liked the power," said Irene.

"Do you know if she had any relationships with men in or out of work?" I asked.

Irene shook her head. "We weren't exactly friends, so it wasn't as though she was about to tell me all about her most recent date."

"No, I suppose not," I said.

"Look, I didn't like Jean. I'm not going to pretend that I did. But I also hate seeing a woman dragged through the mud when she can't defend herself. It isn't fair," she said.

"No," I said, thinking about *Maman* and how her reputation had been torn apart once she no longer had the protection of her marriage.

"Anyway, all I really meant to do was apologize. I thought it best to warn you away from Mr. Pearson. I truly am sorry if it came out the wrong way," said Irene.

"I've been thinking about that, actually. Wouldn't a reputation for chasing secretaries or typists put Mr. Pearson's position in jeopardy if he was caught?" I asked.

"In that regard, the CWR is exactly the same as every other place I've ever worked. Men set the rules and break them, and in the end it's the women they seduce who find themselves punished," said Irene.

I covered Irene's hand with my own and gave it a squeeze. "I promise you that you don't have to worry about that with me."

I had a murder to solve and a job to keep and Mr. Fletcher to report to. Besides, I'd seen what becoming involved with a man could do to a woman. Despite all that he'd done to her, *Maman* had loved my father until her dying day.

I started to draw back, but Irene caught my hand. "Evelyne, I'm serious. You never know who you might meet here. Be careful and don't lose your head. Girls have been fired over less."

"Like Charlotte?" I asked.

Irene looked surprised. "Charlotte? What about her?"

"Everyone speaks of her with such hushed tones. I assumed something happened."

Irene shook her head. "Charlotte was everyone's favorite. There was no one more intelligent, beautiful, or fun. Naturally, Jean hated her, and that made the rest of us adore her even more. Then, one day, she quit.

"She had a brother in the Royal Navy, so I sometimes wondered if she joined the WRNS, but I didn't think the navy—or any of the women's auxiliary services—were for her. Maybe she met a man," Irene mused.

"Could it simply be that she moved to another government department and couldn't talk about it? We're all bound by that sort of secrecy," I said.

Irene shrugged. "Your guess is as good as mine. Now, I should probably go back to work. Not all of us are lucky enough to escape Miss Wilkes today."

Before she could stand, however, I stopped her. "Irene, just one more thing."

"Yes?"

"I know we haven't known each other long, but if you ever need to speak to someone about . . . anything. I know you didn't have the chance to see your friend yesterday night. If you want to talk about it . . ."

Irene's lips twisted into something of a smile. "You're sweet. I'm glad Jean never got her claws into you."

I felt a little pang of guilt. I wasn't sweet at all. I was curious and determined to find a killer.

NINETEEN

I let Irene go ahead of me while I tidied away my plate and cup. I was due to return to Mr. Poole's poky little room in ten minutes, but there was something I needed to do first.

I went to the Dock for my handbag. Slinging it and my gas mask over my arm, I made my way to Staircase 15, where a Royal Marine I didn't recognize checked my pass and then my bag before I started the long climb out of the CWR and into the light.

Out on Horse Guards, I blinked in the bright sunlight and then hurried around the corner to the red telephone booth I'd passed on my way in to work what felt like ages ago. I couldn't believe that it had only been a day and a half since I'd waved goodbye to Moira, still sleepy in her bed, and descended into the prime minister's bunker.

I pushed open the booth's door, picked up the receiver, and fed a coin into the telephone. The line connected with a crackle.

"Hello, number please?" the switchboard operator asked in a bored voice.

"Fleet 1537," I said.

"Thank you."

I waited for a moment, and she came back on the line. "Connecting you now."

"*London Evening Examiner*, how may I direct your call?" asked the newspaper's switchboard.

"Miss Jocelyn Green, please," I said.

"Hold, please."

I tapped my foot impatiently, aware that I would likely be late meeting Mr. Poole.

All of the sudden, a familiar voice filled the line. "Jocelyn Green speaking."

"Jocelyn, it's Evelyne Redfern."

"What's the matter? Is everything all right?" my fellow Bina Gardens lodger asked.

"Everything's fine. Or rather it isn't, but it isn't Moira or any of the rest of the girls at Mrs. Jenkins's. I'm calling to ask you a favor, but I can't tell you exactly what it's for."

Jocelyn paused before finally saying, "This is intriguing."

I took a deep breath. I knew Jocelyn a little—one didn't run into a woman in the queue for the bath every morning and not know *something* about her—but I was particularly aware in that moment that the journalist and I weren't close. It was Moira who had met her on a photo shoot. It was Moira who had convinced her to join the joyful chaos of Mrs. Jenkins's boardinghouse. And, although always pleasant enough, it was Moira whom Jocelyn was easiest with.

Still, I suspected she was my best chance at finding out whatever had happened to the mysterious Charlotte.

"I'm trying to find a woman named Charlotte Deeley. She was a typist working in the civil service for a time, but she was either fired or quit earlier this year and no one's heard from her since."

Even over the line I could hear the scratch of a pen on paper as Jocelyn noted everything down. "Can you tell me which department she worked for?"

"I'm afraid not."

"Do you have anything else for me to go on?"

"She would have been unmarried while she was working. Likely London-based. I imagine she would have been around my age, but of course I can't say for sure," I admitted.

"You certainly don't make things easy, do you? No matter, I'll have our researchers see what they come up with. Where should I telephone?" she asked.

"You can leave the message with Moira if I'm not home."

"That's right. You have a new job that takes you away from us for a few days at a time. Very intriguing indeed. One day you'll have to tell me everything," she said.

"Perhaps over a glass of something strong—if we can find it."

Jocelyn laughed. "If worse comes to worst, you can come to the newsroom. I know where my editor keeps his emergency Scotch."

"Won't that be you doing me another favor?" I asked with a grin.

"Call it making up for lost time. We've lived across the hall from each other for months, and we've barely sat down together outside of breakfasts at Mrs. Jenkins's."

"We'll remedy that the next time we're off work at the same time," I said firmly.

"Right then. I'd better go find this Charlotte of yours. Speak soon."

B ack in the CWR, I reversed my route, thinking to drop my things. It should have taken only a moment, but when I arrived in the Dock, I found my bunk occupied.

Caroline slipped down, her heels clicking on the floor as she landed. "I thought you would never come back."

"And that necessitated sitting on my bed?" I asked, pushing a little more disapproval into my voice than I actually felt. Caroline, while undoubtedly good at her job, could be more than a little high-handed.

"Sorry. It's just that I wanted to speak to you about—"

"Some of us are trying to sleep!" called a woman down the row.

I put up a finger to ask Caroline to stop, stowed my bag, and then hurried up the stairs again. Just outside of the Dock's entrance, I stopped with my hands on my hips.

"I apologize," Caroline immediately said. "I'm a bit of a worrywart, and sometimes I can sound as though I can't mind my own business. It's just—I wonder . . ."

I let my features soften, hoping it made me look more approachable. "Is there something on your mind?"

She bit her lip and then nodded. "Earlier you asked about who was in the typing pool with me during the time when Jean was killed. The inspectors asked the same questions but—that is—I may not have been entirely accurate in what I told them."

I stared at her. "Did you tell them that Edith was there when she wasn't?"

"Oh, no. Nothing like that," she said in a rush. "Miss Wilkes, Edith, and I were in the typing pool yesterday afternoon."

"Then what's the matter?" I asked.

Caroline twisted her hands in front of her. "Miss Wilkes wasn't there the entire time."

"Miss Wilkes? Are you certain?" I asked.

Caroline nodded miserably. "She was gone for about twenty minutes."

"When did she leave?" I asked.

"Not long after you. Maybe five minutes?"

"Where did she go?" I asked.

"I don't know," said Caroline, "but she does this from time to time when things are very quiet. She'll leave me in charge of the typing pool, and she'll slip off for a few minutes without any explanation."

"Do you think that she was in the powder room?" I asked.

Caroline blushed but shook her head. "When she returned, she rushed in and stuffed her handbag into her desk drawer."

"When she leaves like that, how long is she usually gone?" I asked.

"Maybe fifteen minutes. Sometimes thirty," said Caroline.

"And you didn't tell the inspectors this?" I asked.

"No. I just . . . Miss Wilkes has been so very good to me. She thinks that I have potential, that maybe I could run a typing pool in another department before too long. I hated to say anything that might cast suspicion on her when I'm positive she had nothing to do with Jean's death."

I blew out a long breath. "You need to talk to them and tell them that you were mistaken."

"But Miss Wilkes—"

"If they haven't already, they're going to find out from Edith or a guard or someone who spotted Miss Wilkes outside of the typing pool. If they discover you withheld information, you could end up in real trouble."

Caroline grabbed my arm. "But if it isn't relevant—"

"You don't know that," I said.

"It isn't relevant," said Caroline more firmly. "Miss Wilkes would never hurt anyone."

"That may be the case—and Miss Wilkes might have a perfectly reasonable explanation for what she was doing between those times— but you need to give another statement."

Caroline blinked back what looked very much like tears. "You won't tell the other girls that I lied, will you? I know they don't like me very much because Miss Wilkes deputizes me from time to time."

I smiled. "None of them ever need to know."

"Thank you," she whispered before fleeing down the corridor.

As I walked back to Mr. Poole's room, I made a note to move Miss Wilkes up my list of suspects.

TWENTY

I rushed back to our makeshift interrogation room, but before I could inform Mr. Poole of what I'd learned over lunch, a knock sounded on the door.

"Are you ready?" asked Mr. Poole.

I slid into my seat next to him and then nodded.

Mr. Poole rose and opened the door. "Come in, Mr. Morgan."

Grahame Morgan, a short man with an unruly head of salt-and-pepper hair, shuffled in. "I hope this won't take long. I have some work to do ahead of the minister's meeting this afternoon."

"I understand," said Mr. Poole. "This is Miss Redfern. She'll be taking notes."

I raised my brow, knowing that I had no intention of only taking notes.

"How do you do, Miss Redfern?" asked Mr. Morgan, unbuttoning the jacket that managed to both bag around his shoulders and stretch across his stomach.

"How do you do," I responded.

"Right," said Mr. Poole, settling down. "As you may be aware from recent meetings, we are concerned that there has been not only a series of dangerous security breaches originating in the CWR, but also that that information has been handed over to the Germans."

"A very distressing situation," Mr. Morgan muttered. "Very distressing indeed."

"I have been asked to make inquiries among the staff," said Mr. Poole.

"Of course. I'm happy to help however I can," said Mr. Morgan.

"Have you noticed any unusual activity among any of your colleagues?" asked Mr. Poole, giving a nod to the notebook on the table between the two of us. I stared at him as though not understanding his meaning.

Mr. Morgan frowned. "No, not as such. It's such a distressing time, especially with all of the bombings yesterday night."

"Quite," said Mr. Poole, stifling a sigh and grabbing the notebook himself. "Outside of the events of yesterday, though, have you seen anything else that might cause concern? It may even be something very small, such as a colleague skirting the new security rules or being a bit too loose-lipped in the pub."

"I don't frequent pubs, Mr. Poole," said Mr. Morgan, sounding more than a little horrified.

"It was meant only to be illustrative, Mr. Morgan," said Mr. Poole.

That seemed to placate Mr. Morgan because he screwed up his face as though deep in thought. "I don't think so. No."

"Mr. Morgan," I cut in, even as I felt Mr. Poole turn to look at me, "did you know Miss Jean Plinkton?"

"The young lady who was murdered?" he asked sorrowfully. "A sad thing, very sad indeed."

"Yes, it was," I said.

"I'm sorry to say that I did not know her except by sight. She was in several meetings I attended. I expect she also did some of my typing," Mr. Morgan said.

"I'm sure she did," I said.

Mr. Morgan's eyes softened. "It must be very hard for you ladies in the typing pool."

"Thank you. We are bearing it as best we can," I said. "Do you happen to recall where you were yesterday afternoon between the hours of two and three o'clock?"

He brightened. "I was in my office for most of that time. I was working on a report for the minister about— Well, I suppose I'm not really meant to say outside of the department."

"You may speak freely in front of Miss Redfern. The minister is aware of her presence in these meetings"—Mr. Poole's eyes slid over to me—"if not her propensity to ask questions."

I'd have to speak to him about the sarcasm behind that last sentence afterward.

Mr. Morgan, however, didn't seem to notice because he said, "Well, in that case, I was working on a report around the idea of disinformation. That is what we can put out into the wider public to confuse the enemy. It's a fascinating subject, really—"

"Mr. Morgan," I cut him off with a smile before he could merrily skip down a rabbit hole, "do you share your office with anyone? I'm afraid I'm not yet acquainted with where you sit in the CWR."

"Before the war I had my own little space, but there isn't much of that down here," he said with a chuckle.

"So there would have been people around who would have seen you working?" I asked.

"Yes. That is, no. Not at that time. Mr. Conley is usually present, but he stepped away around a half past two," he said.

Conley was one of the names on Mr. Poole's list.

"Do you know why?" I asked.

Mr. Morgan shook his head. "He might have said, but I didn't hear. Sometimes when I'm working away I become a little too absorbed. My wife likes to think that it probably comes from my childhood building models. They're intricate things, models. They need attention and focus."

I gave him another smile. "It sounds as though you're well suited for that sort of hobby."

"I like to think so, if you'll forgive a little boasting," he said.

"Of course. And did you have any luck delivering your report?" I asked.

"Yes," he said, sitting up a little straighter with pride. "It was on the assistant secretary's desk at five to three, thirty-five minutes before he expected it. Oh, now that I think about it, I did meet Mr. Conley in the corridor outside our office as I was returning to my desk."

"Did you both resume working then?" I asked.

"We did," said Mr. Morgan. "That is, I did until I went to the canteen to fetch a cup of tea at four o'clock. Even in war, one must observe teatime."

"Mr. Morgan, no doubt before you began to work in the civil service, you went through something of a vetting process?" asked Mr. Poole, looking up from his notes.

"Oh yes, it was very extensive. I had to answer all sorts of questions about where I was from, where I've lived, my education, things of that nature," said Mr. Morgan.

"And if the vetting process were to occur now, what would we find?" Mr. Poole asked.

"It would be much the same. My wife and I live a fairly quiet life. No children, unfortunately. We were not blessed that way, but we have a good little life all our own," he said with a smile.

"Do you have any connection to any German, Austrian, or Italian nationals?" Mr. Poole asked.

"Why, I don't think so. I did go on a walking holiday to the Black Forest in 1926. My wife and I do enjoy walking," he said.

"Do you still have any contact with anyone you met on that trip?" I asked.

"Oh, no," said Mr. Morgan. "We keep mainly to ourselves."

Mr. Poole inclined his head slightly in my direction. I did the same, and he turned back to Mr. Morgan.

"Thank you for answering our questions. You can go now," said Mr. Poole.

"Oh, I do hope that this was helpful," said Mr. Morgan.

I reassured him with a smile. "Very."

I watched as he scrambled up and made for the door. When it was shut, Mr. Poole shifted in his seat to face me.

"Did you have a chance to ask everything you wanted?" he asked, crossing his arms.

"I beg your pardon?" I asked.

"I know that I agreed that you could be present for these interviews, however it really would be best if I asked the majority of the questions."

"And what do you expect me to do?" I asked, mirroring his crossed arms.

"I thought you would take notes," he said, waving his hand toward the notepad.

"Mr. Poole, I am an intelligent woman, and if you would think about it for a moment, you would realize what an asset I can be to your investigation. However, make no mistake: I will not work with someone who does not wish me to be a full partner. It will only slow down my own inquiries.

"I fully intend to speak up in these meetings when there is a question I need answers to. If you are not comfortable with that, you may find yourself another partner and another way to access the confidences of the women in the typing pool and any other women of the CWR you might wish to speak to."

He stared at me for a long moment and then sighed. "My apologies, Miss Redfern."

"Thank you," I said with a nod. "Is there anything significant in Mr. Morgan's personnel file?"

He reached for the folder on the top of his stack and flipped it open. "Grahame Morgan. Graduated from Durham University before joining the civil service at twenty-two. Married twenty-three years. His house is paid off, and at the latest check last year there are no records of outstanding debts against his name." He glanced up at me. "It is common practice to check into the financial background of civil servants in case of instances of bribery."

"Very sensible," I said.

"A team will look into his background again, but I doubt they'll find anything more. I don't think he's the mole," he said.

"Or the murderer."

"You believe his alibi even though he was alone?" he asked.

"And was proud as punch that his report was on the minister's desk at five minutes to three."

Mr. Poole closed Mr. Morgan's file and shuffled through the rest of the stack. "In that case, shall we speak to Mr. Archibald Conley?" he asked.

"The absent officemate," I said. "Perhaps he will prove a little more promising."

"Perhaps."

———————

Mr. Conley was everything that Mr. Morgan was not. A tall man with sandy hair, striking cheekbones, and an elegant, straight nose, he was dressed in a single-breasted suit that had obviously been well tailored. While Mr. Morgan had been jolly, ennui seemed to roll off Mr. Conley like waves of perfume.

I remembered him from his visits to the typing pool and, looking at him seated across the table from me, I wondered that none of my fellow typists had fixated on him rather than Lieutenant MacIntyre.

"I tried to join the Royal Navy at the start of the war, but the doctor found that I had a heart condition," Mr. Conley was explaining after Mr. Poole had asked him about how he came about his job in the CWR. "It's an old family trait, I'm afraid, but a disappointment nonetheless. Ironically, I've ended up a little closer to the action than my brother did. As far as I can tell, he's been patrolling the Atlantic for a year with hardly a U-boat sighting."

"You are aware, I imagine, of the recent breaches of information in this office?" Mr. Poole asked.

"Bloody inconvenient things." He glanced over at me. "My apologies."

I lifted my chin. "Not at all. It is bloody inconvenient."

Mr. Conley looked at me with something akin to bemusement. "I won't pretend to be one of those do-gooders like Morgan who live for the work. I know there's a war on, but I would give anything for the old days of cricket on the green, punts on the river, and boater hats. I was at Oxford, you see, when war broke out."

"Have you seen anything during your time here that you would consider unusual or alarming?" asked Mr. Poole.

"Other than what passes for pudding in the canteen?" Mr. Conley asked.

"Mr. Conley, I ask you to take this matter seriously," said Mr. Poole.

Mr. Conley leaned back in his chair. "No. I haven't seen anything unusual. I haven't smuggled anything out of the building and sold it to the highest German bidder either, if you want to ask that."

"Jokes like that could land you in a great deal of trouble," Mr. Poole warned.

"Mr. Conley," I interjected. "I understand that this is all a bit of a bore. If you would only help us, we can all go back to the business at hand."

When he didn't fire back a retort, I assumed I had his attention. "What we want to know is whether you believe anyone in this building might be capable of betraying this country."

Mr. Conley sniffed. "No. I might not particularly like my colleagues, but I don't believe them capable of doing that. Most of the men here are, at their core, gentlemen."

"Thank you," I said.

"Do you have a great deal of interaction with the women of the typing pool?" Mr. Poole asked.

"I do not outside of requesting typing," said Mr. Conley.

"Were you acquainted with Miss Jean Plinkton?" Mr. Poole asked.

Mr. Conley shook his head. "Not any more than any of the other girls. I try to stay away from that lot. Present company excluded, of course, Miss . . . what did you say your name was?"

"Redfern, and thank you," I said, my tone dry. "Why is it that you don't associate with them?"

The man reached into his jacket pocket and pulled out a silver cigarette case that was down to its last two. "Do you mind?" he asked me. I shook my head and watched as he stuck a cigarette in his mouth and then patted his pockets for a light. He struck a match to light his cigarette and then blew a stream of smoke up to the ceiling.

"I find that it's best to keep to my own company," he finally said. "My colleagues are colleagues. My friends are outside of this building. It's neater that way. Not that I've ever really found much appeal in the personalities of those I work with."

I was beginning to understand the mystery of why the handsome Mr. Conley was not a typing pool favorite.

"Where were you yesterday afternoon between two and three o'clock?" asked Mr. Poole.

"I imagine I was at my desk," said Mr. Conley.

"Mr. Morgan believes that you were not," I said.

Mr. Conley tilted his head to consider this before saying, "Oh yes, yesterday I took a few minutes to nip out and pick up a few things from the tobacconist."

"Do you know when that was?" I asked.

"About half past two, I suspect. I'm not much of a clock watcher," he said with a tight smile.

"Do you recall when you returned?" Mr. Poole asked.

"I really don't know. I might have lingered a little bit. I don't know anyone who enjoys being stuck down in this bunker for days on end. I take a walk most afternoons, and Saturday was no different," said Mr. Conley.

"Did you come across anyone on the stairs as you left or came back for your walk?" I asked.

"That older woman who runs all of you girls. What's her name?" he asked.

"Miss Wilkes," I supplied.

He pointed at me, his cigarette burning in his fingers. "That's the one. She was coming up as I was going down. I remember because I almost bumped into her, and she looked as though she was about to bite my head off."

That was another person saying that Miss Wilkes was not in the typing pool for at least part of the window in which the murder could have happened. It was possible that it was entirely innocent, but I would need to speak with her nonetheless.

"Do you recall seeing anyone else?" I asked.

"I ran into Morgan outside our office. He was nattering on about some memo or another he'd just left with the minister's secretary," said Conley.

There was a slight pause before Mr. Poole said, "Miss Redfern? Any other questions?"

I couldn't help the little smile tugging at my lips. He was learning.

"That will be all, Mr. Conley," said Mr. Poole. "Thank you very much."

TWENTY-ONE

With two interrogations done, Mr. Poole had a meeting that he could not miss, so I returned to the typing pool. Miss Wilkes was not there when I arrived, so I sat down at my neglected typewriter.

I finished typing up the notes for Mr. Pearson's meeting in triplicate, and then edged away from my desk, placing my hands on the small of my back to stretch. There was no denying that my body was feeling the effects of sleeping on the Dock's lumpy mattresses. My eyes, not to be outdone, felt as though I'd stood at the end of Brighton Pier with the wind blowing sand straight at me. I wanted sleep—hours of it—and preferably in my own bed, if it was still standing.

In the bright light of day, people had begun to report the extent of the damage across the capital city. I learned that a clerk from the Map Room had been darting in and out all day to give updates on which areas were reporting damage since no one at the CWR could go back home until their shifts were done. I watched the door open and heard the collective intake of breath as the girls waited to find out whether any of the major roads he rattled off would be in their neighborhoods. A good deal of the bombing was focused on the East End, but that was not by any means the only place devastated by the Luftwaffe's air raid. High-explosive bombs had been mixed in with incendiary ones, whose purpose was to start fires that could rip through densely packed neighborhoods. Places ranging widely, from working-class

Kennington south of the river to the posh environs of Belgravia, had seen bombing and that meant that no one was safe.

It only made things more tense that, apparently, periodic calls had been made to the typing pool throughout the day, asking Miss Wilkes to send another of us to Maxwell and Plaice for questioning.

"Who else do you think they're speaking to?" I heard Rachel ask Cathy, whose desk was next to hers, in a half-whisper.

"I heard from Mr. Worthing that they interviewed him and Mr. Faylen this morning," said Cathy. "Did you hear that someone said Jean used to go to the pub with some of the men?"

"The pub? With whom?" asked Rachel, clearly taken aback. "I never thought she'd deign to do that."

Cathy nodded. "The way she talked, it seemed as though the Dorchester was far more her speed."

"Cathy and Rachel," snapped Caroline. "If you can find the time to gossip instead of work, I assume that means that you do not have enough to keep you occupied. Is that correct?"

I could practically hear Cathy and Rachel roll their eyes, and I caught Irene's raised brows even as Miss Wilkes pushed through the door, the dull tan fabric of her skirt belling out around her knees.

"Ladies, your attention please." Miss Wilkes waited while we all swiveled to face her. "As I mentioned before, a new typist will be joining us. Her name is Georgiana Gregory, and she will begin on Thursday. Until then, I will ask you all to please work twice as hard to make sure that all work is taken care of.

"I am also going to ask some of you to help take over some of Miss Plinkton's responsibilities on the day shift. As you all know, Miss Redfern will be supporting Mr. Poole temporarily. That means that Miss Travers, you will likely be fielding more requests for note taking. I will be asking Miss Bainbridge to do the same when she returns on Tuesday.

"I will also need someone to take over Miss Plinkton's responsibilities in collecting and destroying documents as part of our daily security protocol," Miss Wilkes finished.

Irene raised her pencil. "I'll do it. I've done it a time or two before when Jean was ill, and I know the procedure, not to mention where the incinerators are. That's half the battle."

"Thank you, Miss Travers," said Miss Wilkes.

The telephone rang, and Miss Wilkes picked it up. She nodded, and said, "I'll send her right over." Then she put down the phone.

"Miss Travers, the inspectors would like to see you now," said Miss Wilkes.

Irene stood and flung on her little claret jacket with a bit of flare. "Wish me luck, ladies."

"This is not a stage, Miss Travers. There is no need for dramatic entrances and exits," said Miss Wilkes.

That drew a laugh even from Caroline, and Irene stuck her tongue out at Miss Wilkes's back as soon as our supervisor turned away.

"Miss Wilkes," I said, seizing my moment when I had the chance, "I wonder if I might speak to you about something."

She frowned. "Is it entirely necessary, Miss Redfern? I'm very busy."

"It's rather a delicate matter," I said.

Miss Wilkes gave me a hard stare, but then lifted her chin. "Will the corridor do?"

"It will," I said.

As I had yesterday when Miss Wilkes had quizzed me about finding Jean, I followed her outside. Only this time, when we were safely out of earshot of the other women, I was the one who started the conversation.

"Something came up as part of my questioning with Mr. Poole," I said.

"He hasn't done or said anything too forward, I hope," she asked, studying me.

"No, nothing of the sort," I hurried to reassure her. "He has asked me to find out where the women from the typing pool were during Jean's murder."

Miss Wilkes's hand flew to her neck. "But I was told that he was investigating a question of a leak of information."

"He is looking into both."

"I see. Well, I suppose you may speak to the other ladies about where they were when that unfortunate incident happened," she said.

"Thank you, Miss Wilkes. However, I must ask, were you in the typing pool between two and three o'clock yesterday?" I asked.

"You may recall that I was here with you. I'm always here unless I'm called away for some reason," said Miss Wilkes.

"And after you sent me for my sunlamp treatment?" I asked.

Miss Wilkes's hesitation was brief enough that, if I hadn't been looking for it, I might not have caught it. "I may have stepped out for a moment."

"May I ask where you went and why?" I asked her.

She looked away. "I cannot say."

"Miss Wilkes, I promise, only Mr. Poole need know what we discuss here."

Miss Wilkes sighed, the downward turn of her mouth and the strain at the corners of her eyes suddenly making her look tired.

"I was placing a telephone call," said Miss Wilkes. "It was personal, so I was upstairs to the booth around the corner."

That would explain why Mr. Conley had crossed Miss Wilkes on Staircase 15. "That must have taken you some time," I said.

"If you mean to imply—"

"It's not my intention to imply anything or to be impertinent. I am only trying to establish a timeline of what happened yesterday, at Mr. Poole's behest," I said.

She pressed a hand to her forehead. "I do apologize. I find the entire matter rather distressing."

I had the impression that she wasn't speaking exclusively about the murder.

"My mother is a very sick woman, Miss Redfern. Once, I was able to leave during the day for work and care for her in the evenings. However, she declined rapidly after Mr. Chamberlain's declaration of war. It was the stress, you see.

"Mamma cannot be left on her own overnight these days. When I am on shift, a woman named Mrs. Holland comes in to help tend to her needs and stay in the house. Friday night, when I telephoned home on my way to fetch supper, Mrs. Holland told me that Mamma had not settled that day and was refusing to eat. Given that it was quiet in the typing pool yesterday afternoon, I went to call and check on Mamma," Miss Wilkes finished.

"That must be very difficult," I said.

Miss Wilkes squeezed her eyes shut as though gathering her strength. "Yes, well, we all must make sacrifices during these times."

"Still," I said.

I could see the moment that the official, workplace Miss Wilkes slid back into place. She opened her eyes, her lips set in a thin line.

"Since I'm sure it will be your next question, I don't know what time it was exactly when I left. However, I do remember that I took Staircase 15. I'm sure that one of the guards who was on duty can confirm that he saw me," she said.

She'd passed Lieutenant MacIntyre then.

"When did you return?" I asked.

"I was at my desk by ten past three."

"Do you recall seeing anyone else during that time?" I asked.

"Mr. Conley nearly ran me down on the stairs. He hardly stopped to apologize either," she said.

That was two confirmations of Miss Wilkes heading back into the CWR near the time of the murder but on the opposite side of the building from the sunlamp treatment room. That also provided a neat corroboration of Mr. Conley's alibi. It wasn't impossible for either of them to have quickly made their way from the sunlamp room to Staircase 15 after the murder, but it seemed unlikely.

"Thank you, Miss Wilkes. Just two more questions, if I may," I said.

Miss Wilkes crossed her arms over her chest but didn't say anything, which I took as permission to continue.

"What was your relationship with Jean like?" I asked.

"Miss Plinkton," Miss Wilkes started, emphasizing the formality of her address, "was a very hard worker in her own way."

"But how did you feel about her personally?" I pressed.

"When you manage a staff, it isn't necessary to have a convivial relationship with all of them. In fact, sometimes it is detrimental," she said. "I had no objection to Miss Plinkton's work. That is enough."

"Do you know of any reason that someone would have wanted to harm Jean?" I asked.

"I believe that Miss Plinkton sometimes played games that only she understood the rules to."

"What do you mean?" I asked.

"She did things to amuse herself. She liked to know things about people. To find out what their weak points were. As I said, it was a game to her.

"Now, I believe, Miss Redfern, that it is time for both of us to return to work," Miss Wilkes said, leaving me standing in the corridor, mulling over whether Jean's games had been dangerous enough to get her killed.

———

I kept my head down through the rest of the afternoon, and when the night shift typists arrived, I briefed a slightly perturbed Betty about the change in my working situation, and then tidied my notes and things into one of the locked boxes due for the incinerator. Irene, who was loading the other box onto the cart, gave me a resigned grimace.

"I'll need to let out the seams on my sleeves if I do this for too long," she said.

"Why did you volunteer then?" I asked with a laugh.

"Miss Wilkes was going to assign me the job anyway," she said, dropping her voice so that the other women couldn't hear. "Why give her the satisfaction of thinking she's gotten one over on me?"

"Here." I helped her load both of the boxes onto the cart. Both of us sighed with relief when the work was done.

"You'll have a task pushing that cart," I said.

"At least I have two days off," said Irene.

"Do you have plans for your weekend?" I asked, holding the door open for her.

Irene pulled a face as she pushed the cart through the door. "A weekend isn't a weekend when it falls on a Monday and a Tuesday. But I do have a date tonight."

"Your gentleman?" I asked.

"Yes." She practically preened.

"What will it be then? A romantic dinner? Drinks at the Ritz bar? Or maybe a trip to the theater is in the cards," I teased.

Irene's face fell a little bit. "Oh, nothing like that."

"What's the matter?" I asked.

Irene stopped and glanced either way, but the only people in the corridor ahead of us were a pair of RAF officers. "I hope you don't mind me saying, but I know you grew up in France and . . . well, there's the matter of your parents."

She watched me closely, as though trying to gauge my reaction.

"Don't worry. When your family is written about in international newspapers, you do learn to expect people's curiosity," I said.

"It doesn't bother you, people thinking they know all manner of things about you?" she asked, clearly a little surprised.

"I find that preempting people's judgment has the delightful effect of disarming them. If you are unashamed, they don't know what to make of you," I said.

"Is that why you told all of us on your first day about being 'The Parisian Orphan' and how your father is Sir Reginald Redfern?" she asked.

"Precisely."

"And what about your mother? All of the things that people wrote about her . . ."

I made myself look Irene in the eye, not giving away any of the pain of thinking about how unfairly the press had labeled my darling mother. "*Maman* loved me. No matter what those journalists wrote about her, I wouldn't have changed her for the world."

Irene worried the gold bracelet on her left wrist. "I don't suppose I should be telling you this, but somehow I feel as though you'll understand."

"Your secret is safe with me," I promised.

"The truth of the matter is, the man I'm meeting tonight? Well, he's married," she said, quickly adding, "You'll understand why I can't say anything to the other women here. They would judge me harshly, but I feel that you must understand, having such an unconventional mother. . . ."

I didn't have the heart to point out that my mother, unconventional as she had been, had been a married woman and what Irene was doing . . . well, that was a far riskier than *Maman* had ever played. Society was not generally forgiving to unmarried women who got themselves into trouble.

"Oh, it does feel good to tell someone," Irene said with a little laugh. "I've had that bottled up in me for a month now."

"Isn't there anyone you can talk to outside of the CWR?" I asked.

She shook her head. "My parents died. I was an only child. I have no family."

"What about the rooms you live in?" I asked.

"It's just my landlady and we don't rub on well. She's always threatening to throw me out when I put one foot out of line, so you see, I really don't have anyone I can speak to," she said.

She was alone. I knew what it was to essentially have no family except Aunt Amelia, but I had Moira. I had the other girls at Mrs. Jenkins's. I had people around me, some of whom loved me dearly.

"Just promise me you'll be careful with this man," I said.

She reached out and squeezed my hand. "I will. Now, I should go destroy these things before the air raid siren sounds and I'm stuck here."

As I had my heart set on a temporary escape from the CWR, I said my goodbyes. However, I was only a few feet away when a thought struck me. I stopped and called out, "Irene, how did you know the newspapers called me 'The Parisian Orphan'?"

She looked surprised. "I recognized it from the stories at the time."

"Really?" Irene was maybe a year or two older than me, no more. Most of the people who remembered these days were at least ten years my senior.

"Redfern is a fairly unusual name, and my mother thought your father was rather dashing," she admitted with a blush.

"Everyone does," I said with a snort.

She gave me a little wave and began once again to make her way to the incinerators. As I watched her round a corner, out of sight, I couldn't help but think that Irene must have a very good memory indeed.

TWENTY-TWO

F inally free from my duties, I retrieved my handbag, discreetly
slipped my notebook into the top of my right stocking, and, for
the second time that day, made the long walk to the telephone
booth around the corner from the CWR.

It took a few rings before a very harried Mrs. Jenkins answered.
"Jenkins residence."

"Hello, Mrs. Jenkins," I said.

"Oh, Miss Redfern. There's been ever so much commotion today.
Miss Fein just had some terrible news about her man," my landlady
said in a rush.

"Oh no." Joan was a tiny scrap of a woman who worked in a bookshop and hardly said a word to anyone. We'd all been amazed when,
the day after war was declared, she'd come home sporting a chip dia-
mond engagement ring and telling us that she'd soon be Mrs. Walters
once her fiancé could find enough leave from the RAF to marry her.
That was more than a year ago, prompting some of the rest of us living at the house on Bina Gardens to wonder whether there was any
Flight Lieutenant Walters at all.

"I need to go console the poor thing. Who would you like to speak
to?" she asked.

"Is Moira in?"

"Miss Mangan!" I heard her call. "Miss Redfern is on the telephone
for you."

There were a few clunks and clatters on the line as Mrs. Jenkins put the receiver down, and a few moments later Moira picked up. "Evie."

"What's happened to Joan's fiancé?" I asked. "He wasn't shot down, was he?"

Moira snorted. "Shot down? Try left her for another woman."

"What?"

"He showed up about an hour ago with a blonde who could be Mae West's sister and introduced her as the new Mrs. Walters. Joan burst into tears, and she's locked herself in the first floor loo. The third floor one is out of commission, so we're all trying everything we can think of to lure her out."

"Oh, Lord," I muttered.

"Apparently the new Mrs. Walters is a barmaid at a local pub near his RAF base," she said. "She actually seems lovely and is completely mortified at the whole scene. Apparently the flight lieutenant told her that they were going to visit his sister."

"Men," I said.

"I couldn't agree more. By the way, there's a message here for you from Jocelyn. Do you have your notebook to hand?" asked Moira.

With a glance to my right and left, I extracted my small notebook from my stocking top. "Go ahead."

"She said to tell you that there are a number of Charlotte Deeleys in London alone, but the one who best fits the age you gave her lives in Finsbury Park."

"She found Charlotte?" I asked, duly impressed. I had expected it to take Jocelyn's newspaper researchers days to find the missing woman—if this proved to be the right one.

"I guess," said Moira. "She said the address you're looking for is 100 Ennis Road. She also said to remind you of that drink."

"If you see her tonight, tell her it'll be two drinks and they will be on me, I promise," I said.

"Who is Charlotte Deeley?" Moira asked right as a scream erupted somewhere near her.

"I'll have to explain later." Or at least explain as much as I could.

"There's also a message from your Aunt Amelia here," Moira continued, unfazed by the chaos in the background. "She says that she's in town and you're expected for luncheon at her club on Tuesday."

I groaned. I had a murder on my hands, a mole in the center of government, and an appointment with Mr. Fletcher on Tuesday where I would have to attempt to explain all of this. I didn't have time for luncheon with Aunt Amelia.

"She didn't sound angry or annoyed this time," Moira said, trying to be helpful.

"At least there's that," I muttered.

There was a muffled string of words in the distance on Moira's end.

"Oh, Lord. Marjorie says that Joan made a break for it, locked herself in her room, and is now chucking things out of the window into the road. Mrs. Jenkins is beside herself," said Moira.

"Go. I'll be home tomorrow evening, and we'll talk more," I said.

The line went dead, and I hung up the telephone with a laugh. Sorry as I felt for poor Joan, I almost wished that I was at home seeing the circus unfold. However, I had more than enough to keep my mind occupied as it was.

I slipped my notebook back in its hiding place and was pushing out of the telephone booth when, out of the corner of my eye, I caught a glimpse of gray suit jacket and a second later found myself confronted with a scowling David Poole.

"Miss Redfern."

"Hello. I thought you were in meetings for the rest of the day," I said.

"It's evening," he said.

"So it is. I was just on my way to find myself a spot of supper."

"Via a telephone booth?" he asked.

"I was telephoning home to check to see if there were any messages for me," I said.

"Would that message happen to have anything to do with a Charlotte who once worked with our colleagues?" he asked, carefully modulating his language so as not to reveal anything about our place of work.

"Were you eavesdropping?" I accused.

He folded his arms.

"You were, weren't you! You're my partner. You're meant to trust me," I said.

"Couldn't I say the same about you?"

Well, he had me there, but I wasn't about to admit that.

"What did you find out?" he finally asked, breaking our stalemate.

I rocked back on my heels, studying him. "If I tell you, I want something in return."

"What would that be?" he asked.

"Your promise that we do things together as equals in this investigation. No more telling people I'm there to take notes."

"I apologize. I didn't mean any offense, but I've obviously caused it."

"Thank you," I said.

"I've never had a partner before."

"Neither have I."

"There might be growing pains," he warned.

"For both of us," I agreed.

"All right," he said.

I glanced right and left. "I discreetly asked a friend with good contacts to pull a list of Charlotte Deeleys living in London. Charlotte used to work as a typist, but she quit a few months ago under mysterious circumstances. One of the Charlottes my friend found is the right age. She's in Finsbury Park."

Mr. Poole pushed up his jacket cuff and checked his watch. "At this time of day, it'll take us an hour to get there."

"I have my bus map right here," I said, diving into my handbag once again, but a hand on my elbow stopped me.

"I'll drive."

I stared up at him in disbelief. "You have a car?"

He nodded.

"And petrol for it?" The petrol ration had been in place since almost the first day of the war.

He gave me a small smile. "Consider a generous petrol allowance a perk of having me for a partner."

"Well then, partner. Lead the way."

———

Mr. Poole maneuvered his black Morris through traffic across the city as quickly as he could. Twice we were diverted because of bomb debris, and once we turned into a road where a crew was working to shore up the facade of a collapsing building. Each time, he set his jaw and reversed the car out of a now dead-end street, finding another route.

"Did you grow up here?" I asked after the third time we'd turned around.

He shot me a look as he swerved around a stray brick in the road. "No, but I know London well."

That was as much as I was going to get from him, apparently, because he fell into silence for the rest of the drive.

When Mr. Poole pulled up to the curb of the address Jocelyn had given me, he killed the ignition and we climbed out of the car. It was the neat little brick Victorian with whitewashed trim that you see all over London. The blackout curtains were drawn back in the bow window, showing a pair of gauze curtains in their place. One of them twitched.

"Why don't you let me lead the conversation this time?" I suggested, waiting to see if he would balk at the idea.

After a moment's pause, he said, "All right. Partner."

Mr. Poole unlatched the low wooden fence and let me go ahead to the front door. There were pots that I imagine once held flowers but now had the last of the summer lettuces and herbs growing in them.

I leaned on the doorbell, and almost immediately a brunette with a large beauty spot on her right cheek opened the door. She wore a light blue dress with black piping at the collar and sleeves, and her hair was held back in a snood.

"Can I help you?" she asked.

"We're looking for Charlotte Deeley," I said.

The woman's mouth twisted as she looked between the two of us. "It's Holmes now."

"Mrs. Holmes, my name is David Poole, and this is my colleague Miss Redfern. Would you mind if we asked you a few questions?"

She crossed her arms, looking him up and down. "About what?"

"I believe we have a mutual friend. Patricia Bainbridge?" I asked, remembering what everyone had said about how close Charlotte and Patricia had been. "Patricia and I work together."

Immediately Charlotte's confident defiance melted away. "You'd better come in."

She led us to the front room with the bow window, the heels of her black shoes clicking between the polished pine boards and rugs. Moving boxes stood on either side of a coal fireplace framed with burgundy and mustard art tiles and a wooden mantel topped with a large gilded mirror. The rest of the furniture was relatively modest except for a wireless in a rosewood cabinet, which stood next to the sofa.

"Would you like any tea?" asked Charlotte, sounding very much as though making us tea was the last thing in the world she wished to be doing.

Not a woman to go without supper by choice, I was desperate for any sustenance, so I accepted for both Mr. Poole and myself. While she went off to the kitchen, I peered at the framed photographs on the mantel. There was one of Charlotte on what I assumed was her wedding day from the spray of flowers she held in one hand, the other hanging on to the arm of a man in an army uniform. Another showed Charlotte and a woman who looked so like her she must have been her sister. The rest of the photographs were all of a little girl, cherubic cheeks and golden hair, at different stages of her life. There she was with Charlotte at the seaside. Another, younger photograph showed Charlotte holding up the girl as a baby dressed in a knit matinee jacket.

I nodded toward them, and Mr. Poole frowned. "What?" he mouthed, but before I could respond Charlotte returned with the tea tray.

"I'm sorry there isn't much to give you by way of food. I won't be able to brave the queues until Monday morning," she said. "We'll leave the tea to steep for a moment, if you don't mind."

Knowing that probably meant that the leaves had been carefully saved and reused from her afternoon cuppa, I didn't mind at all. Weak tea is an affront to good taste.

"Am I to understand that congratulations are in order?" I asked, gesturing to the photograph of our hostess as a bride.

"Yes," breathed Charlotte, her eyes fixed on the photograph. "William and I were married two weeks ago while he was on leave. He's in the army."

"You must be very happy," I said.

I thought I saw the woman's lip wobble. "Yes. Meeting William changed my life. He went back to his unit last week."

"That must be very difficult," I said.

She gave a stiff nod. "It isn't easy, but it's no more than many women are dealing with these days. I've been keeping busy by unpacking his things. This was my grandmother's house, and she kindly left it to me when she passed."

"Mrs. Holmes, you must be very busy, so I won't take up too much of your time. Mr. Poole and I understand the conditions that would have been placed upon you when you were working, however, I can reassure you that you can speak freely to us," I said.

"What did you say your name was?" she asked.

I produced my CWR pass. "Evelyne Redfern."

She took the pass, examined it back and front, and then returned it to me. "It was drilled into us never to speak about work."

"I can reassure you that you're safe talking to us," said Mr. Poole.

"We are investigating several crimes that have taken place in the CWR," I said.

She jerked back. "Crimes? I would have thought that would be the most secure place in the world."

"Unfortunately, that's proven not to be the case," said Mr. Poole.

"Over the last few months, there have been a series of leaks that we believe have placed vital information into German hands," I said.

"I remember rumors before I left," Charlotte murmured.

"And then, yesterday, Jean Plinkton was murdered," I said.

Charlotte was quiet a moment before saying, "Thank you, Miss Redfern. Sometimes you wonder if horrible people will ever get their comeuppance. I suppose now I have my answer."

"We gathered that Jean wasn't the most popular person at the CWR," I said.

A flash of fury crossed Charlotte's face. "That would be an understatement."

"Can you tell us more?" I asked.

"She was horrible—a bully at best and evil at worst," she bit out. "I was in the typing pool at the Home Office before I was transferred over to the CWR. I was so excited to be in the thick of things. My brother was in one of the first waves called up after war was declared, and I've hardly seen him since. I finally felt as though I was contributing something to the war effort that might really matter. Do you understand?" she asked.

I nodded, remembering my own sense of relief and higher purpose when I walked through the CWR's doors. I could sense that that was the place where everything happened, and that in and of itself had been exciting.

"I've always managed to be friendly with all of the women I've worked with, ever since my secretarial course before the war," Charlotte continued. "But Jean was different. It was as though the moment we both arrived in the CWR typing pool, she was watching me. At first she was pleasant enough, but it never felt entirely genuine. She would ask me a few too many questions about my life but never offer up anything about hers. It felt as though she was mining me for facts and storing them away for later.

"I stayed away from her as much as possible. At first I hardly thought about it because I became friends with the other women. It almost felt inevitable working and living in such close proximity to one another."

"I understand," I said.

"Then one day—" Charlotte dropped her head, cutting her own sentence short. "I'm sorry, I can't."

"Mrs. Holmes, what is wrong?" I asked.

Her eyes slid up to Mr. Poole. "I'm sorry, I can't."

I twisted on the sofa. "Mr. Poole, could you . . . ?"

He didn't protest. Instead, he simply picked up his hat and said, "I'll wait in the car."

TWENTY-THREE

Charlotte and I sat in silence until the door shut behind Mr. Poole's retreating back. Then she let out a long breath. "I shouldn't have made him go."

"Oh, he'll be fine," I said. "Before we go any further, do you need any tea?"

She shook her head with a laugh. "It's awful stuff when it's been reused, but what can you do? No, I need to say what I have to say all in one go. I think that's for the best."

"Whenever you're ready," I said.

Charlotte closed her eyes. "Like I told you, I tried to stay away from Jean. She could be nice enough when she wanted to be, but then she would turn around and snipe at you in a way that made you feel two inches tall. Then, one day at the start of June, she caught me when I went up top after my shift for a cigarette. It was as good an excuse as any for some fresh air. You know how claustrophobic it can be in that place."

"I do," I said.

"I tried to fob her off, but she wouldn't leave me alone. She told me that I'd want to hear what she had to say, and then she pulled an envelope out of her handbag. I recognized it immediately. It was a letter from my sister. I'd run into my postman on the way out the door before my shift, and I thought it would be safe enough to bring it to the Dock in my handbag. Jean must have gone through my things when I was in the typing pool and she was out."

"What was in the letter?" I asked.

Charlotte reached into her pocket and pulled out a crumpled packet of cigarettes. She shook one out and, with trembling hands, lit it using a heavy metal lighter shaped like a shell that rested on the coffee table. She blew out a shaky stream of smoke.

"My sister, she writes to me every month." She took another draw on her cigarette and then fixed her eyes on me. "To tell me about my daughter."

"The little girl in the photographs," I said, nodding to the mantel.

"Her name is Harriet, and she's the dearest thing in the world to me. I've never been able to talk about her. Not until I met William.

"You see, when I was sixteen, a man took advantage of me. He was a neighbor—a good ten years older than me. He told me that he loved me and—well, you know that tired, old story. When I found out that I was pregnant with Harriet, he was long gone. I heard that he died at Dunkirk. Good riddance.

"You can imagine that I couldn't exactly go around telling everyone that I was an unmarried woman about to have a child. I went to stay with my sister, and when I had Harriet she took her on. Harriet thinks that I'm her aunt. One day, when she's older, I'll tell her the truth. William has already said that he wants to adopt her, to give her a better father than she might have had."

"That is very good of him," I said.

"I suppose you think I'm rather stupid and gullible," she said.

"I think that you were barely a child yourself, and you did what you needed to do."

She ashed her cigarette. "Thank you. Many people wouldn't be so generous."

"So Jean found out that you had a child by snooping around in your things?" I prompted.

"And then she tried to blackmail me."

I stilled. "What did she say exactly?"

"She told me that I was hers now to do her bidding, and if I didn't do as she said, she would tell Miss Wilkes about Harriet. She was going to ruin me."

"What did she want you to do?"

"I don't know," Charlotte said with a shake of her head. "I went to Miss Wilkes the following morning and quit. I told Miss Wilkes that the stress of working in the CWR was all too much for me. That my nerves were on a knife's edge. The last thing they want is a girl who is going to crack up. It's too risky."

"You didn't tell anyone that Jean had threatened you?" I asked.

Charlotte shook her head. "If I'd done that, Miss Wilkes would have asked what sort of hold Jean had over me."

If she alerted anyone to the blackmail attempt, Charlotte would have been forced to tell everyone about her daughter and experience all of the shame she'd tried so hard to avoid.

She looked at me imploringly. "I only just managed to get my old job back at the Home Office by convincing them that I'd had enough rest for my nerves. I've even managed to persuade them that I should be allowed to stay on now that I'm married because they're desperate for experienced typists who know how the place runs. But if anyone learns why I'd left the CWR . . ."

I sat back against the sofa, thinking.

"When was the last time you were in the CWR?" I asked.

"They take everything from you as soon as you quit. I lost my pass, all of my privileges. I haven't stepped foot in there since June," said Charlotte.

"And do you have any idea of who might have killed Jean?" I asked.

Charlotte shook her head. "I wish I could tell you—I really wish I could—but I haven't seen a soul from that place in months."

"Thank you, Mrs. Holmes. This has been very helpful," I said.

We both rose, but just before she was about to open the sitting room door, I stopped.

"What about Patricia?" I asked.

"What about her?" Charlotte asked.

"Everyone said that you were close. It strikes me as rather odd that two women who were such good friends haven't been in touch."

Charlotte worried her lip. "Patricia was a good friend, but we didn't always see eye to eye."

"Did you have an argument?" I asked.

"Please, Miss Redfern. Please understand . . ."

"Did you tell Patricia about Harriet?" I pressed.

"No, although I realize now that I could have."

"What do you mean?" I asked.

Charlotte bit her lip. "Nothing."

"Does Patricia have secrets of her own?" I asked.

I could see her fighting with her judgment, and I silently willed her to tell me what she knew. Instead, she shook her head and hugged her arms to her chest. "I'm sorry. I can't."

"If Patricia hasn't done anything wrong—"

"Patricia would never hurt anyone. Even Jean," Charlotte insisted.

I held my hands out to placate her. "If Patricia is innocent, I promise that no harm will come to her."

Charlotte's mouth twisted. "Don't make promises that you can't keep."

"Really, I can help," I pressed.

My hostess gestured to the sitting room door. "I think it's time for you to leave."

"Of course. I'll see myself out."

Charlotte lifted her chin. "That would be best."

TWENTY-FOUR

I could feel Charlotte watching me from the bow window as I walked to the car.

Mr. Poole hopped out of the driver's seat and walked around to open the passenger door for me, leaning in to ask, "How did it go?"

"Inside," I murmured.

He didn't protest, instead waiting for me to settle myself before closing my door and climbing back in.

"Do you think we could find a restaurant? I'm feeling peckish," I said.

"What did Mrs. Holmes tell you?" he asked.

"Food first. I can't think on an empty stomach."

With a huff, he turned the key in the ignition and started down the road.

"Will you at least tell me whether you found anything useful?" he asked as he reached the bottom of Ennis Road and made a right turn.

"Oh, I found out a number of useful things," I said.

I could see him struggling not to demand right then and there that I tell him everything, but instead he wisely drove on until we came across a café a short distance away on Stroud Green Road. Mr. Poole hustled me inside.

As soon as I had a rather meager-looking sandwich in front of me, he leaned in and said, "Tell me what happened."

I took a bite of my sandwich, chewing thoughtfully before swallowing.

"I need to ask you something, Mr. Poole."

"Miss Redfern . . ."

"If there is information that is not relevant to either of our investigations, will you promise you will not mention it to anyone else?"

He looked thoroughly unimpressed. "Even in a court of law?"

"I don't know what the protocols are for a court trail when it pertains to a murder in our sort of workplace, but yes. I'm asking you to keep information that could be harmful to someone else and doesn't pertain to our case out of any public or private record," I said.

After a moment he said, "Fine."

"Good. First, I don't think Charlotte is our killer, although I suspect that's not a surprise to you. There's the matter of her no longer having a pass and, if she had made it into the CWR, it's easy to imagine she would have been recognized by someone almost instantly. However, she did provide a potential motivation for our murderer."

"What is that?"

"Jean tried to blackmail her."

"How?" he asked.

"By threatening to tell people that she has an illegitimate daughter whom she is currently passing off as her niece."

He slumped back against his chair. "An illegitimate daughter?"

"You can imagine what would have happened if it became widely known that Charlotte was an unmarried mother," I said.

"She would have lost her job and never been able to work in the civil service again," he said.

I nodded before swallowing another bite. "And I doubt she would have been able to find a job of that caliber anywhere without a reference."

Mr. Poole let out a long breath. "What did Jean want her to do?"

"According to Charlotte, she didn't stay around long enough to ask. She called Jean's bluff and quit the CWR.

"Everyone in the typing pool warned me that I should be careful around Jean. No one would be specific about why, but Miss Wilkes did say that Jean liked to dig around and find things out about people. I think that, whatever Jean's plan was, she was gathering information on her colleagues in order to twist them to her own purposes," I said.

He raised a brow. "And her purposes could have been to ferry information out of the office?"

"Jean could be your mole."

"What would Jean gain from blackmailing Charlotte?" he asked before stopping himself. "I'm beginning to wonder . . ."

"What is it?" I asked, neatly finishing my sandwich and reaching for my cup of tea.

"It's something you said to me earlier. You suggested that there could be more than one mole. What if Jean was the source of the leak, but in blackmailing Charlotte she was trying to build a wall between herself and the information she was passing along?" he asked in a low voice so as not to be overheard.

I leaned in. "Drawing attention away from herself? That would be clever."

"I've been looking for a pattern in what we know has been leaked. Some if it comes from the Ministry of Information meetings, some of it from the Home Office, the War Secretary, and so on."

"I assumed as much because the list of your suspects isn't limited to one department," I said.

He nodded. "I couldn't figure out what the pattern was. There are overlaps, but I haven't been able to identify one single meeting where all of the men I've put on that list were with each other at the same time. Reports and memos pass through so many hands as they're compiled."

"Not everything was included in typed documents, and not every meeting had a secretary or typist taking notes," I said, understanding him.

"And there's reason to believe that one of the leaks came from a series of telephone calls that were never documented. I've been struggling to find the thread connecting all of the leaks."

"But the thread could be Jean," I finished for him. "It stands to reason that if she did try to blackmail Charlotte, unsuccessfully, she might have had more luck with other colleagues. Maybe she wasn't just looking for help carrying information out, but she was also using people to gather information. She could have cultivated a whole network of informants who were under her thumb, too scared to say no."

He nodded. "It would explain why different departments have been involved, different personnel."

"So we might not be looking for one mole, but one or two or a dozen informants. And, retaliation against blackmail might be the reason someone murdered Jean." I leaned back against my chair heavily. "We're right back where we started."

"Without a murderer or a mole," he agreed.

"And with an entire office full of suspects.

He sighed. "Also, if it all comes back to Jean, we don't know how she was passing off information, and who her contact with the Germans was."

I played with the handle of my plain white teacup, thinking. After a moment, I asked, "Shall we review our list of suspects?"

"It couldn't hurt," said Mr. Poole.

"Right. Mr. Morgan says that he was at his desk during the time of the murder."

"He was seen when he dropped off the memo," Mr. Poole said. "I asked around this afternoon."

"So we can reasonably eliminate Mr. Morgan."

"What do you think about Conley?" he asked.

"As a person or a murder suspect?"

Mr. Poole shot me a look.

"I spoke to Miss Wilkes. She had initially said that she was in the typing pool the entire time, but one of the women told me she stepped out. When I confronted her about it, she admitted that she went aboveground to place a call to check on her ailing mother. She said that she passed Mr. Conley on the stairs while returning to work."

"That puts him in the vicinity of Staircase 15 around when he said that he was gone. That means he's unlikely to be the murderer. However, he could still be our mole," he said.

"If he is, it would be for the money. He doesn't strike me as much of a joiner or the type who would be motivated by political passions."

Mr. Conley didn't seem the kind to be passionate about anything except maybe himself.

"I'd like to see if either Mr. Conley or Miss Wilkes could have made it from the stairs to the sunlamp treatment room and back within our time frame," I said, reaching beneath the table to pull out Aunt Amelia's notebook.

"Do I want to know where you've been hiding that notebook?" Mr. Poole asked.

"No," I said, opening the book to begin taking notes. "Right, we know that the last time I saw Jean was at two o'clock. Mr. Conley said that he was away from his desk for about a half hour, and Mr. Morgan says that they met each other in the corridor just outside their office at three o'clock after Mr. Morgan delivered his report. That would mean Mr. Conley left his desk around half past two."

"What about your Miss Wilkes?" asked Mr. Poole.

"Caroline said that she remembers Miss Wilkes leaving for approximately twenty minutes. Miss Wilkes told me that she returned at ten minutes past three, which would mean she probably left the typing pool around ten minutes to three. Since she crosses with Mr. Conley on the staircase, we'll put her as exiting the CWR around five to." I looked up from my notebook. "Jean didn't have the papers she was meant to deliver with her, so that means either she successfully made the drop-off—which no one has been able to confirm for us yet—or the killer took the papers with them. What is the likelihood that a killer would linger at a crime scene longer than necessary?"

"Probably slim to none," he said.

I nodded. "I discovered Jean's body around five minutes to three, at which time the killer turned off the lights, shut the door, and locked me in." I looked up at Mr. Poole. "I don't think either Mr. Conley or Miss Wilkes could have done it."

"Tell me why," he said, picking up his sandwich for the first time since we'd sat down and taking a bite.

"Well, Mr. Conley is easy. He was seen descending the stairs and then five minutes later he met Mr. Morgan in the corridor. Both he and Mr. Morgan said they worked in silence until four o'clock, when Mr. Morgan went to the canteen for tea.

"In the case of Miss Wilkes, she would have had to double back on herself without being seen, kill Jean, and then go back up the stairs in order to lend credibility to her story before returning to the typing pool. She might have been able to slip by a more careless guard like MacIntyre once, but twice? It seems improbable," I said.

"It does, so long as you believe that the murder occurred just before you arrived," said Mr. Poole.

"There was still blood dripping onto the floor when I found her," I said, shivering.

Mr. Poole tilted his head in acknowledgment before taking a sip of tea. "Right. Well, if that's the case, that would revise the murder window to, say, five minutes."

"Meaning that we need to find someone who is unaccounted for between approximately five to three and three o'clock yesterday," I said.

"Who would that be?" he asked.

I set my notebook down with a sigh. "I don't know."

Mr. Poole dabbed his mouth and threw down his napkin. "Well, we won't find the answer in Finsbury Park. Come on, I'll run you back."

I stood and realized that the man sitting at the table next to us was staring at us, wide-eyed and a little green around the gills.

"Sorry about that," I said with a grimace before following Mr. Poole out.

"Those things you were talking about . . ." The man trailed off.

"We're writing a film. Enjoy your supper!" I called as I hurried to follow Mr. Poole outside.

We were on the pavement, the door closed behind us, when Mr. Poole and I exchanged a look and burst out laughing.

———

It was nearly nine o'clock when I finally staggered back into work, exhausted. Wailing Wally had sounded while Mr. Poole was driving us back to the CWR, warning us of another air raid, but we were so close to the building that we accelerated and hoped for the best. Fortunately, we arrived in one piece and said our good nights at the bottom of the stairs.

As soon as I showed my face in the Dock, I was set on by my colleagues.

"Where have you been?" Rachel demanded with unbridled curiosity.

"Out," I said.

"Did I see you drive by in Mr. Poole's car earlier?" asked Cathy, rolling over on her bunk onto her stomach, her chin nestled against her hands.

I froze, glancing from woman to woman. The way their eyes shone—the glint of gossip alight in all of them—immediately set me on the defensive.

"What were you doing in his car?" asked Caroline.

"It has to do with some work that I'm helping him with. I'm afraid that's all I can say," I said.

"He is rather dreamy, isn't he?" sighed Rachel.

This was exactly the sort of thing Irene had warned me against, and I regretted that her shift end meant she wasn't there to defend me.

"He is a colleague," I said firmly.

"All right then," said Cathy, rather too slyly for my taste. "If you say so."

"Anyway, we have more important things to worry about," said Caroline, "like whether there will be another night of bombing. This air raid siren has me worried."

"The Germans wouldn't dare. The anti-aircraft guns will keep them away," said Cathy.

Caroline crossed her arms. "Like they did yesterday? I'm not saying they don't help, but you saw for yourself what happened."

"What do you think, Evelyne?" asked Rachel.

I dropped my handbag on my bunk and tugged down my case. "I think I'd better ready myself for bed in case it's a long night."

TWENTY-FIVE

I t was, I'm sorry to report, an abysmal night.

The German bombers were merciless. I knew that aboveground our fighters and anti-aircraft gunners were firing away, trying their damnedest to shoot down the Luftwaffe planes that seemed intent on destroying this beautiful city. Still, throughout the night, the vibrations from the explosions far too close to our bunker rattled the ground underneath us, jerking girls awake with cries. At some point, I managed to fall asleep, only to be awoken by the soft crying of one of my colleagues.

When finally the all clear sounded in the morning, I leaped out of bed. I desperately needed out. I couldn't quite explain it—maybe it was spending a second night under all of that concrete with bombs raining down, wondering whether it really was as safe as everyone reassured me it was—but my entire body craved light and air.

I had to check in with Miss Wilkes in the typing pool before Mr. Poole expected me at half past nine, so I needed to be quick. I managed to make my way through the queue for the showers at lightning speed before going back to the Dock to throw on clothes and grab my pass. I had twenty minutes, and I was going to use every moment of it.

I showed my pass to the Royal Marine at the bottom of the stair, turned out my pockets, and went through the tedium of letting him rifle through my handbag, and began the climb up, up closer to the light. When finally I passed out of the doorway of the New Public

Offices onto the road, I breathed out a sigh of relief, trying to ignore the acrid stench of hundreds of house fires set off by the incendiary bombs. I hurried down the steps, across Horse Guards, and into the entrance to St. James's Park. People streamed out around me, leaving the air raid shelter there to go to work or back to their homes, if either of those stood in the morning light. Children raced along the path while parents sporting dark circles under their eyes hauled bundles of bedding and clothes. A few of my fellow readers had books tucked under their arms. Everyone looked in need of a bath, as hearty a breakfast as their ration books would allow, and eight hours of uninterrupted sleep.

I made my way to a wooden park bench a little way up the crushed lime path and away from the scrum to sit down. I took another deep breath.

A cigarette lighter snapped. "I can't stand being down there for too long either."

Lucy, my fellow typist who worked the swing shift and had been off for the past two days, sat one bench over. Taking a long draw on her cigarette, she sighed, hauled herself up, and then dropped herself on the bench next to me.

"Do you smoke?" she asked, pulling her pink cloth coat closer around her against the early autumn morning chill.

"No," I said. "I tried when I was in school, but I never managed to do it without sending myself into a coughing fit."

She stared at her cigarette. "I tell myself that it calms my nerves, but sometimes I think I only smoke so that I can have an excuse to come out here on breaks."

"Don't you start in a few minutes?" I asked, tipping my wrist to read my watch.

"Yes. Three long days in the typing pool while all of this happens around us," she said, waving her hand across the park. "My family home was bombed yesterday."

"Oh, Lucy, I'm so sorry," I said.

She shook her head. "Mum and I were in the shelter down the road in Pimlico. When we came back to the house, it was nothing but a pile of rubble."

"You shouldn't be at work," I said. "Surely Miss Wilkes would understand."

That earned me another shake of the head. "It's the only place I have to go right now. I managed to convince Mum to go stay with my aunt in Hampshire. Dad works on the railways so he's a reserved occupation. He's been gone for two weeks working somewhere he can't talk about. I told Mum I'd write to him at the address he left so he knows what happened. I don't want him to come home and find the house gone."

"Where will you stay once your shift is over?" I asked.

"I have no idea."

"I could ask my landlady if there's room in my boardinghouse. It's a bit of a squeeze, but I'm sure she wouldn't say no given the circumstances."

Lucy looked surprised. "You'd do that for me? You don't know me."

I leaned across the gap between us to nudge her with my shoulder. "We work together, don't we?"

She let out a long breath. "There are some people who don't think that's much in the way of a bond."

I frowned. "What do you mean?"

Lucy flicked at the end of her cigarette with her thumbnail. "I hate going in knowing that I'm going to have to see Jean. Work on the same shift as her. She's the worst kind of bully."

I swallowed. "I'm sorry I have to be the one who tells you this, Lucy, but Jean is dead."

She stared at me. "Bombed?"

"She was murdered."

Lucy dropped her cigarette and had to scramble to standing, slapping at her coat to keep it from igniting. "What do you mean murdered? How? Are you certain?"

I lowered my voice when a child buzzed past us, his arms spread wide like a Spitfire. "I'm positive."

"I don't know what to say." Lucy retrieved her cigarette only to hold it with trembling fingers. "She was a mean one, but I never would have wanted to see her hurt."

We sat on the bench for a moment, London still waking up around us, before Lucy spoke again.

"I suppose that means that someone will be asking us questions, won't they?" she asked.

"There are two inspectors from the military police here. They've been calling all of us in to answer questions. I imagine they'll want to speak to you today."

She took a shaky draw on her cigarette. "They'll want to know about Sunday morning then."

I stilled. "What happened on Sunday morning?"

"I was sitting on a bench on the other side of the park when I spotted Patricia and that Royal Marine Rachel has a soft spot for, Lieutenant MacIntyre, talking. Well, arguing really."

"What were they arguing about?" I asked.

"I didn't hear all of it. They were walking and stopped a few feet away from me for a minute or two." Lucy paused. "I did hear him ask her what she'd done."

"What she'd done?" I repeated.

"Yes. Then he said, 'I knew you were angry, but I didn't think that you would ever do *that*.'"

"And what did she say?" I asked.

"She claimed she didn't do anything. He laughed at that—you know the kind of laugh that people give when they don't believe a word coming out of your mouth?" Lucy asked.

"I'm familiar with it," I said.

"Well, then she said something like, 'Maybe it *was* you. If I had reason to do it, so do you, and they might actually believe *me*,'" Lucy said, imitating Patricia's cut-glass upper crust tones perfectly. "Then he said, 'You have just as much to lose as I do. Just think about Charlotte.'"

"Charlotte? Are you sure?" I asked.

She shrugged. "That's what I heard."

I thought about how Charlotte had spoken to me freely about Harriet but clammed up the moment I tried to press her on Patricia's secrets. Now it seemed as though I was going to have to speak to Patricia as soon as I could.

"What else?"

"That was it. She sort of stormed off, and he followed her. If they said any more, I didn't hear it," Lucy said.

I sat back, absorbing what she'd told me. The snippet of conversation certainly sounded suspicious, but I didn't want to jump to any conclusions too quickly. They could have been talking about Jean's murder or something else entirely.

The sound of Lucy grinding her cigarette underfoot brought my attention back to the park bench.

"I should go if I don't want to be late," she said. "Good thing is, I don't have much to store in the Dock before our shift starts."

I rose as well, but before we headed for the entrance, a thought struck me. "Lucy, if your shift starts today, what were you doing in the park yesterday?"

She ducked her head as though embarrassed. "Well, Pimlico's not very far from here, is it?"

When I raised a brow, she elaborated. "When I first started working here, I was terrified of making a mistake. I'm not as . . . posh as some of the other typists."

I had noticed that her accent, no matter the polish she'd obviously worked to layer on top of it, still had a hint of the working-class London about it.

"I worked hard on my secretarial course. I know that I deserve to be here, but sometimes I can't help feeling like everyone's watching me as though I'm one mistake away from being given the sack. I used to work myself up into such a tizzy.

"Charlotte stumbled across me one day when I was in a spare room. She took the time to take me aboveground and walk around the park with me. It calmed me right down. Now, I come here for a walk on most of my days off. It's a nice place for a sit and a think."

"Were you here on Saturday as well?" I asked.

She looked startled. "Saturday? Yes. I was here in the afternoon."

"Do you know what time?" I asked.

"I don't wear a watch when I'm not working," Lucy said.

"Did you see anyone you recognized then?" I asked.

"No, I don't think so. I came with a book and read for a little bit. Then I went home to cook dinner with Mum, only those Nazis started dropping bombs on us." She glanced down at her wrist, where she now did wear a watch. "I really should go now."

I needed to go back to my shift too, but I hung back a moment and let her scurry ahead of me for the entrance to the New Public Offices.

Two things were increasingly clear: I needed to speak to Patricia, and Lieutenant MacIntyre hadn't been entirely forthcoming when last we'd spoke.

TWENTY-SIX

Back in the CWR, I took the corridor at a clip. If Mr. Poole had an issue with my lateness, I would tell him that I had a more pressing matter I needed to attend to.

I could tell that, even in the few days that I'd worked at the CWR, change was afoot. Since Saturday's bombings, the corridors, which had struck me as being busy hives of activity before, had become pseudo-offices with all manner of secretaries and clerks jammed into alcoves or next to huge wooden filing cabinets. There was hardly room to turn without bumping into someone in some areas, and everyone wore a slightly strained, haunted look. The last two days of bombings had shredded all of our nerves.

I should probably have been more affected. However, other than my low-level, constant worry about Moira, Jocelyn, and the other women at Mrs. Jenkins's, my mind was focused. I needed to find Jean's killer and Mr. Poole's mole.

I found Lieutenant MacIntyre not on Staircase 15, where he'd been stationed Saturday and Sunday, but standing guard at the entrance to the cabinet room, where the prime minister convened his ministers.

As soon as he saw me, Lieutenant MacIntyre swallowed.

"Miss Redfern," he said as I came to a stop in front of him.

"Good morning, Lieutenant MacIntyre."

"You can call me Jonathan. Some of the other girls do," he said with an easy smile.

I placed my hands on my hips. "Lieutenant MacIntyre, I have a few more questions."

He glanced around. "This really isn't the best time—"

"Is there a cabinet meeting underway?" I asked.

"No, but—"

"Excellent. That means you are standing here without any occupation."

"I'm really not meant to be speaking to anyone while I'm guarding."

"I'm sure there are all sorts of things that you are or are not supposed to do when you aren't on duty. Aren't there?"

He stiffened. "At least make it quick."

"Have you spoken to the inspectors yet, Lieutenant MacIntyre?" I asked.

"I told you yesterday that I had."

"And did you speak to anyone else in anticipation of that interview?"

"I don't know what you mean," he said.

"Perhaps you spoke to someone about what you were going to say to the inspectors," I suggested.

"No. Why would I have done that?"

"Or maybe you took the time to accuse someone of what they might or might not have done," I said.

He blanched.

"An eyewitness says that they saw you in St. James's Park, speaking to Patricia in a very agitated manner yesterday morning after the typing pool's shift change," I said.

He nodded.

"Before or after she gave her statement?" I asked.

He swallowed. "It was before."

"Why?"

"All I was meant to do was escort her to the inspectors, but Patricia told me that we had to talk. She demanded that we go to the park," he said.

"What did she want to talk about?" I asked.

He grimaced. "She was worried about the inspectors and the questions they were going to ask."

"Why?"

"If the average person realized what had happened in the prime minister's own offices . . ."

"What did Patricia have to worry about?" I asked.

"If you were told so much about our conversation, shouldn't you know?" he challenged.

"I want to hear it from you," I shot back. "I would think that you would want to explain your own side."

That brand of logic seemed to convince him because he relented. "She was hysterical—not because she was unhappy someone had killed Jean but because she knew that the inspectors were going to ask everyone questions, and she didn't want that."

"Why would she be worried?" I asked.

"You come to know people down here because you all live so close to one another. Most are nice enough, even friendly. Not her. I must see her three or four times a week, and she's never done more than give me her pass to check."

"Being a private person—or even an unfriendly one—doesn't explain why she would want to speak to you so urgently."

"Maybe I was the first person she came across."

That reasoning didn't make any sense, especially not with what Lucy had told me. However, I didn't want to show my hand too quickly.

"What else did you talk about?" I asked.

"She thought I might be able to help her persuade the inspectors not to talk to her. I started to become suspicious, and I asked her what she'd done."

"Just like that?" I asked.

He nodded.

"What did you mean by that?" I asked.

"I thought it was suspicious that she was so intent on skirting the investigators' questions. Why not simply speak to them and have it over with?"

"How did she answer?" I asked.

"She said she didn't do anything."

A man walked by and shot us an odd look. As soon as the interloper was gone, Lieutenant MacIntyre leaned in, his voice a harsh whisper. "You can't be here."

"Tell me about the rest of the conversation, and I'll go. What happened next?" I asked.

"Nothing. We went back inside."

I leaned back, studying him. "That's not what my eyewitness says. They recall that Patricia said you both had reason to do it because you both had things to lose."

"I didn't—"

"Think very carefully about whether you want to continue lying to me, Lieutenant MacIntyre, especially when everything I've told you so far has been true."

That made him hesitate, and I could see him weighing up whether it was worth trying again to fool me.

"Patricia caught me looking the other way for Jean a couple of times late at night," he said.

"Why would you do that?" I asked.

He opened his mouth and then shut it. Finally he said, "I did it as a favor."

"Did Jean ever pressure you into it? Perhaps she threatened you?"

He looked away. "Like I told you, I was just being friendly. Don't we all need a bit of kindness in this war?"

"I doubt your superiors would see it that way."

His shoulders slumped. "They'd court-martial me."

"I'm going to ask you again. Did Jean ever threaten you?"

"She approached me one day and told me that she knew I was letting girls out and was willing to lie about their whereabouts. She also accused me of being lax checking pockets and bags. If I didn't do the same for her and swear up and down I'd never seen her leaving at night, she would report me for dereliction of duty," he said.

I nodded. As I thought, Jean's threatening influence stretched further than just targeting Charlotte.

"So that's what Patricia meant when she said that if she had a reason to do it, so did you. What about you?" I asked.

"What about me?"

"What did you know about Patricia and Jean that Patricia might not want to come out?" I asked.

"They were just words. She had me backed in a corner."

"I don't believe you," I pushed.

"Really, it was nothing."

"Lieutenant MacIntyre," I said sharply.

He winced. "I knew that Patricia hated Jean, but I don't think she would actually kill her. Patricia is a lot of things, but she's not a murderer."

"Why did Patricia hate Jean?" I asked.

"They were like oil and water, those two. That's all."

"Why do you think that was?" I asked.

"Some women just don't get along, do they?"

In many ways, my life can easily be split into two parts—before *Maman* died and after. Before that horrible day, I'd been the beloved child happily doted on by an adoring mother. Even with all of the parties, the gentlemen, the distractions, I knew that I was the only one whom *Maman* truly loved unconditionally. I was the cherished daughter.

After *Maman* died and my father sent me off to boarding school, everything changed. No longer was I the center of anyone's world. Instead, I was just one child in a sea of children. It had been jarring at first. Amid all of those other girls, I didn't instinctively know how to fit in, so I studied the behavior and the relationships of those around me until I became more than proficient. When I moved to London, I went from one world of women to another in the boardinghouse on Bina Gardens, learning more about the relationships between grown women.

I didn't believe for one moment that the root of Jean and Patricia's animosity was simply a clash of personalities with no other catalyst. Women are not irrational creatures. If we dislike someone, there is generally a reason for it.

Lieutenant MacIntyre was lying to me.

"Is there nothing that you can think of that might have caused your suspicion of Patricia? The person I spoke to said that you said, 'I knew you were angry, but I didn't think that you would ever do *that*.'"

His head jerked up as I repeated Lucy's memory line for line. But still he shook his head.

"What about Charlotte?" I asked.

His already pale face went even whiter. "I don't know what you're talking about."

"My witness swears that you mentioned Charlotte. I assume that's Charlotte Deeley, who used to be a part of the typing pool."

"Yes, that's her name."

"Tell me about her."

A door nearby banged open, and Lieutenant MacIntyre straightened to attention. "That is something you'll have to ask Patricia yourself, Miss."

"My witness says you said, 'You have just as much to lose as I do. Just think about Charlotte.' What did you mean with that threat?"

"It wasn't a threat. It was a reminder. Now, you need to leave."

I could sense him closing off to me even as I stood there. Instead of pushing against a closed door, I stepped back.

"Thank you, Lieutenant MacIntyre. If you remember anything else, please do let me know."

TWENTY-SEVEN

I have so much to tell you about," I said as I pushed through the door to the interrogation room.

Mr. Poole looked up from the stack of files sitting in front of him and then glanced at his watch. "Can it wait? Faylen is due in any moment now."

I pursed my lips, but nodded.

Mr. Poole handed me an open file as I slid into my seat and prepared to turn my mind to the interrogations at hand.

"Thank you," I said, not failing to notice the fact that since our talk he was making an effort to treat me more like a partner and less like a secretary he could order around. "I've had my run-ins with Mr. Faylen already. He's not a favorite of the typing pool."

"No?" asked Mr. Poole.

"He's demanding and discourteous. He doesn't have much regard for deadlines or the urgency of other people's documents. He seems to think that it's acceptable to charge up to Miss Wilkes and take her to task because something he handed in late has not yet been done," I said, recalling my first encounter with Mr. Faylen the moment I stepped foot into the CWR.

"In my limited experience of office politics, I would imagine that does very little to make a veteran like Miss Wilkes move faster," said Mr. Poole.

"You would be correct."

I quickly cast my eye over Mr. Faylen's file. Harold Faylen was fifty-four years old and born in Surrey, where he still resided. He had a wife, three children, and a thoroughly conventional life.

"He doesn't seem particularly extraordinary," I said.

"I believe you'll find that the civil service is full of unextraordinary men who are bolstered by a few bright stars," said Mr. Poole.

"Is there anything interesting in any of those files?" I asked, gesturing to the stack at his hand.

"Other than yours?" he asked archly.

"Yes, well, most of that has nothing to do with me and a great deal to do with my parents. I've hardly done anything extraordinary in my life," I said.

He gave me a look I couldn't quite read. "I wouldn't be so certain about that."

I wanted to ask him what he meant, but the door to the room swung open.

"Faylen," Mr. Poole said, half rising out of his chair.

"What is this about, Poole? You know that I have work to be doing," barked Mr. Faylen.

"Please, take a seat," said Mr. Poole, gesturing to the chair in front of us.

"The minister—"

"Both Eden and Cooper know that you're here, speaking to us. In fact, they have the PM's support in authorizing this investigation," said Mr. Poole.

That stopped me short. Winston Churchill knew what it was we were doing?

Mr. Faylen looked as though he was about to protest again that he was too busy to speak to us, but instead he sat with a grumble. "Investigation? Which one? The entire place has gone to Hell in a handbasket."

He did not, I noticed, apologize to me for saying "Hell." In fact, the man hardly seemed to notice I was there.

"Miss Redfern and I would like to ask you some questions," said Mr. Poole, as though noting Mr. Faylen's lack of acknowledgment.

That brought Mr. Faylen's attention to me. "Aren't you a typist?"

"I am," I said.

His eyes narrowed at that. "What are you playing at here, Poole?"

"As you know, there have been a series of leaks out of this office."

"Nothing to do with me," said Mr. Faylen, sniffing and leaning back in his chair.

"Actually"—Mr. Poole slid the file I'd been examining toward him—"two of the items did cross your desk, so to speak. One was a line from a memo you wrote about supply chain issues for the army, and one was as a consultant in a meeting with the Ministry of Information on the public messaging around women's recruitment."

Mr. Faylen immediately sat forward. "That's preposterous. Many people saw that memo and attended that meeting."

Mr. Poole pulled out a sheet of paper. "The meeting was attended by you, Mr. Morgan, and Mr. Penwright."

"There was a secretary there as well," Mr. Faylen said.

"Was it Miss Plinkton?" I asked.

His eyes cut to me. "No. It was another one. I think her name is Travis."

"Irene Travers?" I asked. "Dark hair? Shorter than me?"

"That's the one," he said.

"What about the memo?" I asked.

"What about it?" he shot back.

"Did Miss Plinkton type up the memo that was about the supply chain issues?" I asked.

"No. It was the other blond one. I don't know her name."

"Patricia Bainbridge?" I asked.

"I don't know their names. They're just typists," he snapped.

I decided right then and there that, when I finished with my work that day, I would make sure that Mr. Faylen's life was made all the more difficult by the women whom he called "just typists."

"Faylen, have you seen anyone acting suspiciously in the CWR?" asked Mr. Poole.

"No one would be stupid enough. They'd be shot on sight," he said, his face still a revolting shade of puce.

"And where were you between the hours of two and three o'clock on Saturday?" I asked, not letting on that Mr. Poole and I had narrowed the window down to a mere five minutes.

"I was with Pearson and one of the secretaries," he said. "The one you first mentioned."

"Miss Travers," I supplied.

"Her. We were going over drafts of a joint-department policy document and Pearson thought it would be helpful having her there to make sure that the annotations were correctly noted on the final document," he said.

"Which room was this?" I asked.

"Seventy," he said.

A room clear across the CWR from where the sunlamps had been set up in Room 56. Even if he had stepped out to use the facilities, it would have been unlikely that he could have slipped out, killed Jean, locked me in, and made it back fast enough so as not to raise suspicion with Mr. Pearson and Irene. Still, it was worth a try.

"Did you leave at any time during that hour?" I asked.

"No."

"Did anyone else leave the room?" Mr. Poole asked.

"No. I really don't know what else I can tell you that I haven't already disclosed to the inspectors. All of this business has nothing to do with me," said Mr. Faylen.

"What did you think of Jean Plinkton?" I asked.

He waved his hand dismissively. "She was a typist and secretary."

"But you worked together. Surely you must have some opinion on her," I said.

"Miss Redfern, was it? I am a busy man. My work here keeps me from home most of the week, so you can imagine that I endeavor not to embroil myself in staff politics or fraternization of any sort. Now, if you'll excuse me," said Mr. Faylen, standing abruptly.

He charged out of the room, leaving behind him a wake of silence to replace his frenetic energy.

As soon as the door shut, I let out a long breath. "What a charming man."

"In my short experience working around Faylen, that was one of his better moods," said Mr. Poole.

"Good Lord."

"My thoughts exactly," he agreed.

If Mr. Faylen was all chaos and frustration, Mr. Pearson was a study in calm.

"I suppose it's inevitable that my name would be connected with some of those pieces of information leaked," Mr. Pearson said, a pipe settled in his hand.

"Why is that?" asked Mr. Poole.

"I am an assistant secretary. I'm often the one sitting in interdepartmental meetings and overseeing policy recommendations when the minister cannot be in attendance. A great deal crosses my desk," he said, casting a smile at me.

"I see," said Mr. Poole, sounding not at all convinced by the argument of the man's importance.

"I suppose you would like me to defend myself and tell you why I am not the one who has been leaking things to the Germans," he said.

"It wouldn't be a poor place to start," said Mr. Poole.

"You can only take my word for it until you find some concrete evidence to the contrary," said Mr. Pearson. "However, I can assure you that it wasn't me. I fought against the Hun in the last war. I was captured and held as a prisoner of war for two hundred and seventy-two days. Two hundred and seventy-two. That sort of time away changes a man.

"And then there is the practical side. I was one of the men who recommended that we increase the security protocols around these offices. We were too lax. Perhaps it was because we grew too quickly out of necessity, or maybe it was naïveté on the part of my predecessor and those like him. Who is to say?"

"Do you have any idea how the information might be making its way out of this office?" I asked.

"Miss Redfern, when you have worked here for longer, you will realize that people have an incredible capacity to both follow the rules and break others at the same time. They can hold the idea that they are doing the right thing in their mind while also acting on the wrong thing," he said.

I thought that, given Mr. Pearson's reputation for enjoying the company of secretaries and typists, this was rather rich. However, I leaned over the table just a little bit as though I was hanging on to his every word. "It's been a shock. In just one week of working here I've learned that there is a mole, and then there was that horrible murder."

"A ghastly thing. I cannot stop thinking about how you must have been frightened half to death finding Miss Plinkton's body," said Mr. Pearson, the concern lacing his voice with honey.

"I was. I keep thinking about how it might have been me," I fibbed.

"I was given to understand that the inspectors think that Miss

Plinkton might have been killed out of jealousy either from a lover or a rival," Mr. Pearson said.

So Maxwell and Plaice had added rival to their working theory. I had to admit, I couldn't wholeheartedly dismiss it knowing how disliked Jean had been—even more so with blackmail at the core of her motives.

"You told me earlier that Miss Plinkton was an asset to the CWR," I said.

"She was sharp and intelligent. Detail-oriented too. Those are a rare combination of traits in anyone in my experience. She was a good secretary as well as a good typist," said Mr. Pearson.

"Where were you during the time she was killed?" asked Mr. Poole.

Mr. Pearson frowned. "What time do they believe that was?"

"Between two and three o'clock," Mr. Poole said.

"Ah, yes. I was in a meeting with Mr. Faylen. We were discussing a policy document with recommendations for additional recruitment campaigns. We are hoping to bring more women into the war effort," he said, smiling at me again in that way that made my skin crawl. "Not all women are as aware as you are, Miss Redfern, that doing their bit can include taking a job."

"There are quite a few campaigns asking us to free up a man to fight," I said.

"And yet more women are needed every day. It is incredible how much of the burden just one hundred women signing up can relieve. We are seriously considering conscription for women," he said.

"Were you and Faylen alone?" Mr. Poole asked.

"No. Miss Travers took notes. She had already typed up the draft documents, and I thought it would be easier for her to annotate them for the final copies," he said.

"Why did you not request Miss Plinkton? It seems as though she was a favorite of yours," said Mr. Poole.

"Because when we first started working on the drafts, Miss Plinkton was engaged with other work. If not for that trick of fate, she might still be alive," said Mr. Pearson.

"That must weigh heavily on you," I said.

When Mr. Pearson turned his eyes to me, I could see the depths of sadness there. "Trust me, Miss Redfern, not an hour has gone by that I have not thought that very thing."

TWENTY-EIGHT

We had a few more questions for Mr. Pearson about his movements on the day of the murder, but the interview was over soon enough.

"What do you think?" I asked Mr. Poole when we were alone.

He rubbed the back of his neck. "I think that we're no closer than we were when we started."

"I disagree. We have alibis for the murder for most of the men on your list except . . ."

"Sir Alexander Halson," he said. "Undersecretary of State for War. I already checked with his private secretary, and he wasn't in the building during the time of the murder."

"But he could still be a suspect in your case," I said.

Mr. Poole sighed. "If a man that high up in the government is a mole, we're in very deep trouble indeed."

I couldn't agree more.

"I've requested time with Sir Alexander tomorrow morning at half past nine," said Mr. Poole.

"Tomorrow is my day off," I said.

"I will do my very best to limp along without you," said Mr. Poole rather more dryly than I thought necessary. "Now what was this about having news when you first arrived?"

I recounted my story of running into Lucy in the park and then interrogating Lieutenant MacIntyre for the second time. After I finished, Mr. Poole simply stared at me.

"What?" I asked

Slowly he shook his head. "First Charlotte Deeley, now these two. How is it that people simply tell you things?"

I grinned. "I must have an honest face."

That earned me a snort. "Do you believe what Lieutenant Mac-Intyre told you?"

I tilted my head. "I believe that Jean threatened to report him, and I believe that there was ill will between Jean and Patricia. However, I don't believe that the source of that animosity was simply a clash of personalities."

"What do you think it could be?" he asked.

"I don't know," I said honestly. "Patricia's and my shifts don't overlap again until Thursday."

Truth be told, I was torn about my shift ending. I wanted to continue to investigate at the CWR, but I was itching to try to find the mysterious Grove House. And then there was the little matter of making my first report to Mr. Fletcher.

"I could speak to her before that if you like," offered Mr. Poole.

I hesitated. "I don't know if that would be a good idea. Patricia keeps to herself. I have the sense that she's very private. I worry that if you interrogate her, she might clam up. At least she knows me."

Mr. Poole tilted his head. "Suit yourself. I have plenty to do while you're gone."

"Like what?"

He sighed, appearing suddenly tired. "I'm going through every communication that Jean Plinkton worked on—or at least those we can trace back to her. If she had informants—and I think we must operate as though that theory is correct—I want to find them. They're as culpable as she was."

I winced in sympathy. The CWR produced an incredible amount of paperwork every day that whipped around from department to department, touching all sorts of hands. You never would guess, coming down here, that the nation was on a paper ration.

"Hopefully that will bring you a little closer to understanding the scope of what she was doing here," I said.

He grunted. "What about your case?"

I pulled out the list of names that we'd drawn up the morning before and that I'd transcribed into my notebook. "Some of the girls are easy to eliminate. I've managed to confirm that all of the typists on the night shift were in the Dock asleep at the time of the murder."

I picked up a pen and crossed out Betty, Joy, Jill, Joanna, Claire, and Anne.

"Sir Alexander was off-site," said Mr. Poole, "and Faylen and Pearson were both in a meeting."

"With Irene taking shorthand for them," I said, crossing off their names. "And Edith and Caroline confirmed each other's presence in the typing pool."

He nodded. "So what does that leave us with?"

I showed him the list.

Miss Wilkes
~~Edith Tierney—Day shift~~
~~Caroline Adams—Day shift~~
Patricia Bainbridge—Day shift
~~Irene Travers—Day shift~~
~~Betty Lewison—Night shift~~
~~Joy Hawkins—Night shift~~
~~Jill Osman—Night shift~~
~~Joanna Gilbert—Night shift~~
~~Claire Boyd—Night shift~~
~~Anne Paxton—Night shift~~
~~Sir Alexander Halson~~
~~Lawrence Pearson~~
~~Harold Faylen~~
Archibald Conley
Grahame Morgan
Lieutenant Jonathan MacIntyre

"Conley and Morgan both have alibis that check out," said Mr. Poole.

I struck their names as well.

"We know that Miss Wilkes stepped out of the typing pool and, she says, went up to use the telephone booth on the road," said Mr. Poole.

"But we agreed that it seems improbable that she had the time to murder Jean," I argued.

"Improbable but not impossible," agreed Mr. Poole.

"I suppose the same can be said for Lieutenant MacIntyre. He could have left his post, and it isn't as though he has the most stellar record when it comes to his duties. However, the chances of him sneaking away undetected and then making it back in time to be spotted by both Miss Wilkes and Mr. Conley seem . . ."

"Unlikely," said Mr. Poole.

I crossed off their names as well, leaving only Patricia Bainbridge at the top.

"It's a rather thin list," I said.

"It only takes one person to commit a murder," Mr. Pool reminded me.

"Of course, there's also the possibility that it is someone we haven't thought of. Or that someone is lying," I said.

Before Mr. Poole could respond, there was a loud knock. We both looked up as the door swung open, revealing Maxwell and Plaice. They did not look at all pleased.

"Miss Redfern, we would like a word," Sergeant Maxwell practically growled.

"A word with me?" I asked.

"Yes," he said.

"Of course. What can I do to help?"

Sergeant Maxwell's glare flicked to Mr. Poole. "Alone, if you would."

Mr. Poole squared up to the inspectors. "I'm sure that whatever you have to say to Miss Redfern, you can say in front of me."

"With all due respect, sir, this is a private matter about an aspect of Miss Redfern's work. It has nothing to do with you," said Sergeant Maxwell.

"If that's the case, I think it has very much to do with me. Miss Redfern is working with me now," Mr. Poole said.

Corporal Plaice frowned. "You're a typist."

"Yesterday, I was temporarily reassigned to support Mr. Poole," I said for what felt like the tenth time that day.

"Miss Redfern is being far too modest. She is not supporting, she is an integral part of my project, so, you see, any complaints about her work are also my concern."

I could practically hear Sergeant Maxwell's teeth grinding from where I sat.

"Very well," the man finally said, stepping fully into the room so that the door shut behind him and his partner. "Miss Redfern, it has come to our attention that you have been questioning some of the women in the typing pool about their whereabouts during the estimated time of Miss Plinkton's murder. We must ask you to stop as you are confusing our investigation."

"I don't see how asking a few simple questions could be confusing your investigation," I said.

"Nevertheless, I must insist," said Sergeant Maxwell.

"Well, that is going to be very difficult, because I insist that Miss Redfern continue," said Mr. Poole. I could have sworn there was a note of glee in his voice, but his expression remained sober as a judge's.

Sergeant Maxwell stepped forward. "Mr. Poole—"

"At the minister's bequest, I am investigating the leak of information out of the cabinet war rooms and into German hands. During the course of my investigation, with the vital help of Miss Redfern, I have come to believe that there may be a connection between the murder of Jean Plinkton and a possible mole working within these walls. Miss Redfern and I have been pursuing that line of inquiry," said Mr. Poole.

Sergeant Maxwell's expression grew smug. "Mr. Poole, I appreciate that this all must be new to you, but let me tell you about murder. Whoever killed Miss Plinkton did it in a moment of passion. It was a violent act, not a calculated one. It was either an act of jealousy or revenge."

"Nonetheless, I wouldn't wish to leave any stone unturned," said Mr. Poole.

Sergeant Maxwell's eyes narrowed, and then he looked at me. "What have you found?"

"You just told me to stop investigating because my investigation wasn't valid. Now you want me to tell you what I've discovered?" I scoffed.

"What's this?" asked Corporal Plaice, rather undermining my efforts to stand up to his superior as he bent down to peer down at my notebook page covered in names and strikethroughs.

"We were just discussing alibis," I said.

Corporal Plaice flipped open his notebook. "Miss Wilkes was in the typing pool at the time of the murder. Why is her name on here?"

"Because she left the typing pool to make a telephone call above-ground," I said.

The inspectors exchanged a look.

"She didn't tell us that," said Sergeant Maxwell.

"She says she was calling the woman who nurses her ailing mother to check on her," I said.

Both men sniffed, but Corporal Plaice made a mark in his note-book.

"And what about Lieutenant MacIntyre?" asked Sergeant Maxwell.

"He was on duty at the time of the murder," I said.

"There were many Royal Marines on duty. Why aren't their names on this list?" he asked.

"Because as far as I know, Jean hadn't threatened them," I said.

"Why would Miss Plinkton threaten Lieutenant MacIntyre?" he asked.

"Because Jean knew that he would sometimes let women ascend to the ground level without performing the necessary security checks as well as being willing to lie if asked whether he had seen a woman pass by," I said.

Sergeant Maxwell looked positively apoplectic.

"Is there anything else you've found?" asked Sergeant Maxwell.

"No," said Mr. Poole before I could mention anything about the code or the threatening note. Not that I was planning to.

"Now it's your turn. What can you tell us about your investigation?" I asked.

Sergeant Maxwell crossed his arms. "This is not a game of barter."

"No one thinks this is a game, sergeant. A woman lost her life, and anything that any of us can do to help find her killer is invaluable," I said, hoping I didn't sound too sanctimonious given that I hadn't yet revealed Jean's history as a blackmailer.

"Do you have any particular suspects in mind?" Mr. Poole asked.

"We can't say," said Sergeant Maxwell, so fast that I knew they were floundering.

"What about the search of Jean's bunk? Did you find anything?" I asked.

Sergeant Maxwell gave a sigh. "Why do I suspect that you will not stop asking questions until we tell you something?"

I beamed at him. He was learning.

Sergeant Maxwell flicked a finger, and Corporal Plaice begrudgingly began to read from his notebook.

"The search recovered one suitcase, brown; one skirt, navy; two silk blouses, light blue and cream; one nightdress; one dressing gown; one pair of nylon stockings; two sets of ladies' undergarments; one case of cosmetics including powder, mascara, and lipstick; one wash bag with soap, flannel, toothbrush, and tooth powder; one silk scarf of light blue, navy, and cream; a tin of pins; one copy of *Rebecca* by Daphne du Maurier; one handbag containing a comb, lipstick, house key, and purse with thirteen shillings in it."

It all sounded completely normal for a woman in the Dock.

"Was there an address book?" I asked as both Mr. Poole and I finished scribbling down the items. Apparently Corporal Plaice's incessant note taking was catching.

"No," said Corporal Plaice, flipping the book shut.

"And there was no indication anything was missing from Jean's things?" I asked.

"No," said Sergeant Maxwell.

"What about the murder weapon?" I asked.

Sergeant Maxwell nodded, and Corporal Plaice sighed and opened his book again. "A short, flat, thin knife with a blade that folded in on its handle, thrust with great force from above at an approximately forty-five-degree angle."

"Do you know how someone could have smuggled a knife into the CWR?" I asked.

"We are looking into that," said Sergeant Maxwell, meaning they didn't have a clue.

My eyes slid to Mr. Poole, who gave me an imperceptible shake of the head. I heard his silent message loud and clear. *That's enough for now.*

"We understand that you are looking into a series of leaks from this office. If you find anything in the course of your own investigation that might be pertinent to our murder case, you would be wise to tell us," Sergeant Maxwell warned Mr. Poole.

Mr. Poole crossed his arms over his chest. "So long as it doesn't jeopardize my ability to stop those leaks, I would be happy to comply. You see, my orders to protect my investigation at all costs come from the highest level."

"And I have an obligation as an officer of the law to catch Miss Plinkton's killer and see this case to its natural close," said the sergeant.

"I understand," said Mr. Poole, giving nothing more away.

A silent standoff positively pulsing with masculine tension ensued until I broke in.

"Well, this has been illuminating, gentlemen. Now, if you'll please excuse us, Mr. Poole and I have work to do," I said.

"Miss Redfern, it would be advisable that you keep your activities limited to the scope of Mr. Poole's investigation. We must insist that you do not poke your nose into matters of interest to the military police if you yourself wish to remain working at the CWR," said Sergeant Maxwell. Then he nodded. "Poole."

When the door closed behind the inspectors, leaving Mr. Poole alone with me, I let out a long breath. "Well, that was eventful. Thank you for standing up for me."

"I wasn't standing up for you. I was simply protecting a valuable asset to my investigation."

"Oh, what woman doesn't like being called an asset," I quipped.

Mr. Poole frowned. "Shall we resume our work?"

"Absolutely. What do we do next?"

"Go over the personnel files. Perhaps there's something we missed," he said, hauling up half of the files on the table in front of us.

I stuck out my hand. "Let's find out."

TWENTY-NINE

The rest of Monday crept by with Mr. Poole and me swapping files to read over the little metal table. I learned far more about my colleagues than I expected, but most of it was decidedly mundane. Finally, when my eyes burned from reading the small type densely covering those pages, I announced I was going to fetch us a couple of cups of tea. Mr. Poole hardly looked up from his folder.

Murder investigation or not, I had to admit as I dragged myself through the corridors, that I was ready for a couple of days away from the CWR. I had talked to so many people and learned so many things it was almost overwhelming. Still, there was much to be done, the chief task being figuring out what on earth "Grove House SW" was.

Unfortunately, I would have to put off my search for Grove House because of an unavoidably busy start to my weekend. In the morning, I was due to give Mr. Fletcher my first report, and then I had to answer Aunt Amelia's summons for luncheon.

I suppose I could have telephoned her and protested that I was far too busy to dine with her, but I knew that she would persist until I relented, and I would find myself in exactly the same situation I started in.

I stuck my hand in my skirt pocket, my fingers brushing a few loose shillings, when a thought stopped me. Perhaps, if I was clever, I could give myself a head start on finding Grove House.

Up the stairs of the CWR I went until I burst out onto the road. It was blissfully sunny for an early evening in September, and the air raid siren hadn't yet sounded.

In the telephone booth, I pushed my coins into the slot and asked for Fleet 1537 as I had the day before. This time, Jocelyn came on the other line with remarkable speed.

"Evelyne, this is twice in two days, and I haven't even seen you at home," she said.

"I know. I'm due back this evening. Look, I'm very sorry to do this, but I have another favor to ask."

"Another?"

"I'm trying to find a place called Grove House. I have a partial postal code: 'SW,'" I said.

"It's a fairly common name. There are likely to be several in Southwest London alone," said Jocelyn. "Evelyne, I need to ask why you want to know."

"I really can't say much," I hedged.

"If you're in trouble—"

"No, it's nothing like that."

"I handle sensitive information every day as part of my job," she reassured me.

This was far more sensitive than she knew, but I couldn't actually say that. Still, Jocelyn was helping me and I decided she deserved to know what little I could tell her.

I took a deep breath. "Someone was murdered at my place of work."

I heard Jocelyn check her gasp. "Murdered? When was this?"

"Saturday," I said.

"I haven't heard of any reported murders on Saturday—unless you count the bloody Germans trying to flatten London." When I remained silent, she said, "I'm not certain I can help you. You see, if I don't have a story, I don't eat. It's rather cutthroat in the offices of the *London Evening Examiner*—even more so given that I'm a woman."

"Even with the war on?" I asked.

"Even with the war on," said Jocelyn. "The young men might have gone off to fight, but the retired reporters have also come out of the woodwork. It's in their blood. Staying at home while all of this action is going on would be unnatural to them."

"What if I told you that I'm investigating because it was a woman who was murdered—someone relatively low in the office pecking order—and I don't think that the men who are charged with catching her killer are exploring every possibility?" I asked.

I could hear the click of a lighter and then Jocelyn drawing on a cigarette. "Go on," she finally said.

"They've convinced themselves that this was a crime of jealousy or passion, and I'm not so certain of that. I think there is more here than meets the eye," I continued.

"So these men aren't taking the murder of a secretary or some such woman seriously, and you want to investigate it yourself," she said.

"Yes, but I don't have the resources that they do. One of my few leads is the name Grove House, but I don't know how to go about finding it short of slogging through telephone books in the library."

"Give me twenty-four hours. I'll find you your addresses."

I smiled. "Add another favor to my tab. So long as it won't land me in prison."

Jocelyn laughed. "Then, I think we have a deal."

———

I was nearly to the doors of the New Public Offices when I spotted Mr. Poole, leaning against a low wall on the pavement with an evening newspaper open in front of him. He wore a gray hat with a black band at an angle that made him look a bit like a film star, not that I would ever give him the satisfaction of knowing that.

"Were you waiting for me?" I asked, coming to a stop in front of him.

He folded his newspaper, his movements slow and deliberate. "I had a sneaking suspicion that you might come up for air."

"Why?"

"Do you want to go back to reading files?" he asked.

I pulled a face.

"Then shall we have an early supper?" he asked, gesturing with his newspaper down the road. "I have a feeling you'd like to discuss the case—and perhaps whatever took you to the telephone booth—as much as I do."

"How did you know I was—?" I shook my head. "Never mind. I don't want to even ask. I'm afraid I don't have my handbag or my ration book."

He grinned. "Then it's good that I know a place that will be happy to serve you if you run them coupons later tonight when you leave work."

We crossed the road to Storey's Gate and then turned on Tothill Street, where Mr. Poole steered me into a small Cypriot restaurant. When he was greeted like an old friend by a waiter with the grooves of age carved deep on either side of his mouth, I sent Mr. Poole a look. "How often are you here?" I asked.

"Far too often," was all he said.

We settled down in our seats and the waiter appeared, holding a bottle in his hand and looking rather expectant.

"Would you care for wine, Mr. Poole?" the waiter asked.

Mr. Poole raise his brows, and I nodded.

As the waiter poured the wine, I couldn't help thinking that, if circumstances had been different, this might have felt strangely like a date. However, there was a murder, a mole, and rather a lot of begrudging but growing professional respect between the two of us to keep this safely in the realm of business.

"Is there a menu?" I asked as the waiter glided away, having dispensed his wine.

"Things are rather limited with rationing so I usually just let them bring me whatever is looking most promising that day. I hope you don't mind," he said.

I shook my head. "Not at all. I'm pleased I don't have a family to try to cook for with all of the restrictions that are in place."

"What do you normally do for food?" he asked.

"You mean when I'm not eating in the canteen? Mrs. Jenkins collects ration books from all of the girls in my boardinghouse. She does the shopping for us and makes sure we at least have a square breakfast in us before we head out into the world."

He grunted, and I wondered if that felt rather familiar to him.

I realized, sitting across the table from Mr. Poole, that I knew nothing about this man. Oh, certain things were obvious. He was intelligent enough to realize what an asset I could be to him, and that spoke to him having some sense. He also, in certain lights and with an unbiased eye, could pass for conventionally handsome.

In a way.

If a girl were looking for that sort of thing.

I took a sip of wine and then refocused on the matter at hand.

"What is turning around in that mind of yours?" he asked.

"What makes you think that I have anything on my mind?" I shot back.

He didn't answer, instead sitting back and giving me a look.

"Fine," I said. "I've been thinking about gossip."

"Gossip?" he asked.

"Gossip can be a very powerful thing, especially when there are no men around to interrupt it. Reputations built and destroyed. Information shared and spread. The typing pool thrives on gossip—and not because it's a group of women. Rather, we see everything that comes through the office, and yet people often forget we're there because they think all we do is type," I said.

"Then let us gossip." He paused. "I'll start. How likely do you think it is that a woman serving in the civil service—even in a more senior role—might be able to afford full-time care for an ailing relative?"

"You're thinking about Miss Wilkes?" I asked.

He nodded.

I considered this, taking into account my own modest salary. "I would imagine that would be unlikely. We aren't paid particularly well."

"I've been thinking about who Jean might have had contact with and who might have weaknesses that she could exploit. What if Jean found out about Miss Wilkes's mother?" he asked.

"A sick relative isn't like an illegitimate child," I said.

"But the cost of hiring a full-time carer . . ."

"What you're suggesting wouldn't be blackmail, it would be bribery," I said in a low voice.

"We have to consider every possibility," he said.

I chewed my bottom lip, mulling it over. "I don't know. Miss Wilkes is such a stickler for the rules."

"Even rule followers have weaknesses," he pointed out.

"How would Jean have afforded to bribe Miss Wilkes?" I asked.

"That I haven't figured out yet," he admitted.

The waiter came out with a platter of food. There was a bit of what I thought smelled like lamb, as well as a fairly generous helping of vegetables, and a small amount of a white, semi-hard cheese I didn't recognize. I could imagine that, if we hadn't been in the middle of a war, it might have been piled high with roasted meats, cheese, and bread. However, everything smelled delicious and looked excellent.

I eagerly picked up my knife and fork as we began to help ourselves from the platter.

"I've been thinking about what Mr. Faylen said earlier about keeping his work and home lives separate," I said.

"Yes?"

"One of the girls in the typing pool mentioned that Jean used to go to the pub with some of the men we work with."

"Including Faylen?" he asked, surprised.

I closed my eyes, trying to remember if their names had been connected specifically or it was more a string of speculation. "I can't be certain. So much has happened in the last two days."

"Well, if it is true, Faylen certainly failed to mention that in his interview."

"He certainly did, which means he either forgot—"

"Unlikely," Mr. Poole interjected.

"Or he is lying. Why would Mr. Faylen lie about having a connection to Jean if he doesn't have anything to hide?" I asked.

"Perhaps because he's a married man and Miss Plinkton was an attractive, unmarried woman," he said.

"You think they might have been having an affair?" I asked.

"Maybe."

"Mr. Faylen said that his work at the CWR keeps him away from home," I said.

"So it does with many people. That doesn't mean that they're all having affairs," he said.

"True," I conceded. "What about you?"

"What about me?" he asked, touching a napkin to his lips.

"Did you find out anything else?" I asked.

"Apparently I'm not as fast an operator as you are," he said with a little smile. "I did manage to contact that colleague who might be able to help us with the code. I told him that it's urgent."

"I wonder if he'll be able to crack it," I mused.

"If anyone can, he will," he said.

I hoped that he was right.

THIRTY

I made it home that night before the air raid siren sounded, which I was eternally grateful for because I was desperate to see Moira.

I knew that I wasn't supposed to speak about the CWR or anything that happened inside its walls, but as soon as I opened the door to our shared bedroom to find my roommate wrapped in a green and silver silk gown with a powder puff in hand, I couldn't have been happier.

"Going out or coming in?" I asked.

"Hello, darling," she said, touching the puff to her nose with delicate pats. "Coming in. I'm only dressed like this because I had a photoshoot and they let me keep the gown. It will be helpful if the clothing ration rumors ever become true. Have they let you out of wherever you go these days?"

"For two whole days," I said as I dropped my case and flopped down on my bed, my hat, coat, and shoes still on. This breach of decorum prompted Moira to spin around, an alarmed look on her face.

"What's happened?" she asked.

"I don't even know where to begin," I said.

"You weren't bombed, were you? It hasn't been terrible around here yet, but . . ."

I shook my head, not caring that I was probably mussing up my brushed curls against the duvet. "There was a murder."

Moira blinked and then slowly rose. "Darling, you haven't been reading too many of those awful murder mysteries, have you?"

I shoved myself to sitting. "There *was* a murder. A real one. One of the women I work with was killed in a spare room in our building. I found the body."

"You found the body?"

I turned to find Jocelyn, all long legs and Katharine Hepburn grace, in a chocolate brown suit with a navy hat set at a jaunty angle, leaning against our doorjamb.

"You didn't tell me that over the telephone," Jocelyn continued.

"Hello, Jocelyn dear. Why don't you come in?" Moira called out. "Evelyne was just telling me the most positively ghastly story. Are you all right, Evie darling?"

I shrugged. "Yes? I think. I want to figure out who did it."

"Well, of course you do. This is what you've been reading for your entire life," said Moira, sitting down on the edge of my bed.

"You don't think I'm being foolish?" I asked.

"Far from it," she said. "I think that if anyone is equipped to investigate a murder, it's you. Frankly, I'm surprised you don't dream the things with how much you read."

I did actually, but I felt as though admitting that would only make her worry more.

"Jocelyn's been kind in helping me."

Jocelyne perched herself on the edge of Moira's bed. "The ladies of the newspaper's library are doing their work as we speak."

"And one of my colleagues is helping. Well, he's not really a colleague, but we work in the offices together," I said.

Moira immediately perked up. "Does this man have a name?"

"David Poole."

"David Poole. A good, solid name. Is he handsome?" asked Moira.

"He's not terrible to look at," I admitted.

Jocelyn snorted while Moira cackled, "Evelyne Redfern!"

"What?"

"From you that's practically a ringing endorsement," she said. "You've never been even remotely that positive about any of the men I've introduced you to."

"That is because most of the men you introduce me to are in love with you."

Moira tsked her tongue. "That is absurd."

"The fact that you believe that is one of my favorite things about you," I said with a laugh.

"Evelyne's right," said Jocelyn.

"Oh, stop being ridiculous, both of you. Now," said Moira, "tell us everything you can about this murder case just in case the air raid siren sounds. In a shelter, there are too many other people around to talk properly."

———

We did, as it happens, end up sheltering that evening. When we and what felt like half of the rest of London emerged Tuesday morning, more than a little disheveled, I made straight for the bath at Mrs. Jenkins's to fix myself up. I had a meeting with Mr. Fletcher first thing, and I was not going to start a day featuring Aunt Amelia feeling frantic.

I considered taking the bus to Mr. Fletcher's office, but all of my fellow boarders warned me off. Too many buses were being rerouted for closed roads—some filled with craters and debris where high-explosive bombs had fallen and others smoking with the smoldering reminders of fires set by incendiary bombs. It was easier to go by foot, the sharp, overwhelming smell of destruction becoming unsettlingly normal the farther I walked.

I passed by several teams of men removing rubble from piles of what had once been buildings. In one instance, there was a green van with a bright red cross painted on one side that was doing roaring business in handing out tea and blankets. It was parked close to the rope set up to keep passersby away, and I heard a woman say to another, "That's an entire family gone because they stayed in bed rather than going down the road to shelter."

"'orrible, innit?" responded the other woman before she sipped the tea in her tin mug.

I swallowed hard and hurried on. I had my own assignment to do, and I couldn't stop at every devastated place. There were far too many of them.

Gosfield Street was mercifully untouched. I leaned heavily on the buzzer for Mr. Fletcher's office and waited for an answer. It was Mr. Fletcher's secretary, Miss Summers, who opened the door and set me up with a cup of tea to wait.

My employer arrived a couple moments after I took my first grateful sip of tea, looking as perfectly pressed and polished as the first time I saw him at the Ritz.

"Ah, Miss Redfern. I was glad when Miss Summers reminded me that today would be the first of our reports together. I take it that you have had sufficient time to settle in to your new role?" Mr. Fletcher asked, from the chair opposite me.

"There's been a murder," I blurted out. "A typist. She was killed on Saturday."

"Yes, and I understand that you found her body," he said, picking up his delicate China cup and lifting it to his lips.

I stared at him. "You know?"

Mr. Fletcher smiled as though he was privy to a secret only he knew. "Information of that nature has a tendency of making its way around to me. I take it that you are not too disturbed?"

"It was ghastly," I said, recalling Moira's words from the previous evening, "but I'm fine. I continued to work for the rest of my shift."

He inclined his head. "Good. And what is it that you have found for me in your first two shifts in our prime minister's bunker?"

"Well, I'm not entirely certain of what it is that you're looking for if a body isn't shocking to you—"

"Have no doubt, your observations are valuable, Miss Redfern. Even the smallest ones," he reassured me.

I considered where to start. "Well then, the entire place runs in a very efficient manner, but I suspect that isn't the entire story."

"Go on," he said.

"I know we're all meant to be working as one for the war effort and all of that—and in some ways we are—but there are certainly people who seem to be inclined to take liberties," I said, thinking about Jean, Miss Wilkes, Irene, and Lieutenant MacIntyre, and who knew who else.

"And then there are the rumors that there is a mole in our midst," I said.

Mr. Fletcher leaned forward, as though I'd finally properly caught his attention. "Is that right? How did you hear about that?"

"Everyone was up in arms the other day because somehow information that was meant to be Top Secret made it onto Lord Haw-Haw's broadcast. However, I discovered that this isn't the first time that something like this has happened. Now there are worries that the Germans must have learned about it from inside the cabinet war rooms. They're checking everyone's bag as they leave the building, and all of the typists have to lock up or burn their notes and shorthand once they are finished with them. Oh, and there's a rumor that we might all be forced to write in code, but no one seems to actually have any credible information about that one, so I doubt that it's true."

I'd heard two of the night shift girls fretting over that one during the handover, but when I'd asked Caroline about it she'd dismissed my words with a laugh.

"Miss Redfern, let me ask you this. Do you think any of your colleagues in the typing pool could actually be capable of obtaining information, smuggling it out, and sending it to Berlin?" he asked.

I drew in a breath. "I think that's precisely what the murdered woman did—or tried to do. I don't really know the details yet."

"Why do you say that?" he asked.

"Jean Plinkton—that's the victim—tried to blackmail a colleague named Charlotte. I think Jean might have been angling to force Charlotte into helping her smuggle information out of the CWR, but Charlotte quit instead of capitulating."

"A woman of principle," said Mr. Fletcher.

"I'm working to confirm that was Jean's plan and also identify anyone else who might have been vulnerable enough that Jean might have tried to exploit them."

"These are people who have been carefully vetted by government officials," said Mr. Fletcher.

"I think Jean had a talent for finding out things that people would rather not be made public. I suspect that there is something in someone's background that was missed."

"Do you believe that, even though Jean Plinkton is dead, there is still a leak in the CWR?" he asked.

"I don't know. If we can get a better picture of Jean's actions and motivations, we might be able to uncover how she or a contact passed along information to the Germans."

"Hypothetically, of course," he said, reminding me that all of this was still speculation.

"Yes, sir."

"If Jean Plinkton was behind the leaks, why do you think she did it?" he asked.

"Money seems to be the most likely motivation. That or a sense of loyalty to Germany and the Nazi cause."

My stomach churned at the thought of that.

"There is also, of course, the question of how Jean Plinkton was sneaking information out of the building," he said. "I presume she could have simply remembered anything simple, but more complicated documents would have proved a challenge.

"Rules have been put into place to try to keep documents in the CWR, but I suspect that if someone is truly determined and clever, they might be able to evade suspicion. After all, they aren't checking the tops of our stockings yet."

Mr. Fletcher cleared his throat.

"I beg your pardon, Mr. Fletcher," I hurried to say.

"Not at all. We must think like the enemy in these times, and often the enemy doesn't display the decorum that one might hope," he said. "You've had a very fruitful first two shifts, Miss Redfern. Consider me impressed."

"Thank you." I hesitated and then added, "I should say that I have had some assistance. There is someone internally investigating the mole. He has been posing as a member of the Ministry of Information. We have discussed both this case and the murder case."

Mr. Fletcher seemed to study me, giving me ample time to wonder whether I'd made a mistake in taking Mr. Poole into my confidence. Whether I was supposed to be doing it all on my own. Except I didn't know what "it" was exactly.

"Is that right? May I ask who this person is?" he asked.

"His name is David Poole. He has been in the CWR for a few months now. I believe that he was encouraged to keep the investigation a secret and try to root out the mole without causing a fuss, but he has reached the point where he needs to take a more direct approach."

"And he has confided in you the way you have in him, this Mr. Poole?" Mr. Fletcher asked.

"In a way. He has brought me onto his investigation under the guise of being his temporary secretary. It means that I can question people who outrank me and gather information I might not otherwise have access to. I thought it might be useful in my work for you as well," I finished.

"And you trust him?" he asked.

"I have no reason to believe that he is untrustworthy, but I haven't told him about your assignment. I don't know his character well enough to trust him," I said carefully.

"That is a very wise policy during a time of war," he said.

"Thank you."

"Very good, Miss Redfern," he said, setting his cup of tea down. I felt certain that he intended for me to rise and leave him then, but I stayed perched on the edge of my seat.

"Is what I've told you today the sort of thing you wanted to know, Mr. Fletcher?" I asked.

He gave me a little smile. "I am happy for you to continue as you have been. I will see you again next week."

I was nearly out the door when he stopped me, saying, "Oh, Miss Redfern. Have you had any word from your father?"

Nerves fluttered faintly in my stomach. This was the second time that he'd asked me about whether I knew of the whereabouts of my father. Both times he'd attempted a degree of casualness that fit as well as an ill-tailored suit.

"No, I haven't, although that is not usual. My father is not what one would normally call the *paterfamilias*," I said.

"It is a shame that not every man is as well suited to the role as one might wish," he said generously.

"I believe it is less a question of suitability and more one of desire to assume responsibility for anything. Sir Reginald has never been known for his magnanimity."

That elicited a snort from my employer. "I remember from Oxford."

"You knew my father at Oxford?" I asked, realizing that I really did have no idea what Mr. Fletcher's connection to my family was other than the fact that I remembered him as one of the cast of characters who seemed to waltz through *Maman* and my father's 8th Arrondissement flat in the endless stream of parties they were always throwing even as their marriage fell apart.

"Indeed I did. We were at Balliol together before he was sent down for violating too many of the college rules," said Mr. Fletcher. "I believe the last straw was when he tried to break into the Master's Lodgings, convinced they were his own."

"Was he drunk?" I asked rather archly.

"He was," said Mr. Fletcher. "I didn't see him for many years until I bumped into your charming mother at a party in Paris."

I gave him a little smile. "It would appear you know more about him than I do, Mr. Fletcher. However, I'm to lunch with my aunt today. She might have had word from him. I can ask if you like."

"Please do. I'd be very curious to find out what your Aunt Amelia says."

I was halfway down Gosfield Street when I realized I'd never mentioned that it was Aunt Amelia I was meeting.

THIRTY-ONE

I will say one thing for Aunt Amelia, she never does anything by halves when it comes to food and drink.

We were seated at the secluded balcony table overlooking the dining room at the Burke Club, where she had long been a member, a cup of coffee sitting within easy reach after an excellent three-course lunch paired with three wines that almost made me forget that I had my ration book in my handbag.

"It's a miracle that Winchell, the steward here, has been able to keep the kitchen properly stocked," Aunt Amelia was saying as she stirred her coffee. "I can't abide any of the substitutes. Mrs. Jessup tried to serve me some of that horrible Horlicks the other day. I almost walked right out of her drawing room. She is very much Down in my book."

I took a sip of my own coffee, reveling in the clean, bitter taste of it. I decided that if listening to my aunt talk about which of her many varied friends were Up or Down—the point system known only to Aunt Amelia but by which she measured everyone—meant drinking real coffee rather than Horlicks, it was a price worth paying.

"Aunt, when was the last time you had word from Sir Reginald?" I asked.

Aunt Amelia's brows shot up. "Evelyne, please tell me that you're not beginning to show an interest in that bore."

"He is my father," I said, although it hardly sounded convincing even to my own ears.

"I hope you're not beginning to become sentimental," she sniffed.

"Hardly, Aunt," I reassured her.

"Well, if you must know, I had a letter from Reggie about six months ago," said Aunt Amelia.

"Really?" I asked, intrigued.

"He was writing to me from Mexico," she said.

"Mexico?" I asked. "I thought he hated his time in Mexico."

My parents had spent their honeymoon touring Central America, with *Maman* showing a never-again-displayed enthusiasm for the sort of trekking through unspoiled jungle and hunting down ancient ruins that had first made my father famous.

Never again, ma chérie. *I am meant for hot water and champagne, not dirt and mosquitos,* she had sworn to me each time she told me a bedtime story about discovering a burial chamber that hadn't been opened in centuries or flying so high over the canopy of the rain forest that even the birds couldn't reach their little plane.

"No, darling, that was Costa Rica. He couldn't stand the monkeys. Your mother loved them, apparently," Aunt Amelia said.

"What is he doing in Mexico?" I asked.

She waved a hand. "Running amok and then writing about it in some terribly daring fashion that the newspapers simply goggle up, no doubt. All of this courting the press simply wasn't done in my day. A woman was meant to appear in the *Times* three times: when she was born, when she was married, and when she died. I don't see why the same rule shouldn't apply to men."

"What else did he say in his letter?" I asked.

Aunt Amelia glanced from side to side and then leaned over the table. "He asked for money. Apparently he had some debts he left behind in Argentina. Or was it El Salvador? I can't remember."

"Money?" I asked, surprised. "But I thought that his books were selling so well."

My aunt sat back, a smug expression on her face. "And when was the last time he published a book?"

"I don't know," I said.

"I do. It was *For the Love of Adventure* in 1935. Horrible, tawdry thing that it was," she said. "I sent him a letter telling him that if he wanted to write about that awful Dubois woman he met in Belgium, he would be exposing the entire Redfern name to shame, but did he listen to me? He did not. He's never known what is good for him."

I suspected that the problem actually lay in the fact that my father never cared what was good for anyone else, but I knew not to interrupt my aunt when she was working up a head of steam.

"No, you can trust me, your father will have spent all of the money his publisher gave him as an advance in 1934 for a book that came out in 1935. He lets money slip through his hands like water, that man. And the books aren't selling nearly as well as they once did. The royalty checks are shocking," said Aunt Amelia.

"Is he . . . well, do you know what he's been doing for money since then?" I asked.

"No," she sniffed. "I might have been able to tell you once. I used to receive all of his communications from his publisher, and I came up to London once a quarter to do all of his banking for him at Coutts."

"That's very generous of you," I said.

"I should hope you think so. I was the one authorized to write the checks for your fees at Ethelbrook. In fact, sometimes it was left to me to cover the costs of your schooling from my own accounts when Reggie was short—and he was often short, Evelyne."

"What?" My aunt had never told me before that she'd been the one putting me through school some terms.

"Why do you think I was so happy that you went off to Edinburgh for university and actually did something with your education?" asked Aunt Amelia. "At least the investment was worth it."

For once in my life, I was speechless. I hadn't really thought about it before, but my aunt had been unusually unperturbed by my decision to go to university, especially given that so many of the girls at Ethelbrook had gone off to the debutante balls of the London Season. She certainly hadn't pressured me to continue my education, but neither had she stopped me—and that really was the more extraordinary thing.

"I'm sorry, Aunt. I hadn't realized," I said.

She squinted at me. "You're not going to begin blubbering, are you?"

"Certainly not," I said, sitting up straight in my chair to show I could display the sort of stiff upper lip demanded of the British gentility in general and a Redfern in particular. "However, I've been laboring for far too long under a misapprehension that my father was at all involved in my life."

"Evelyne, darling. Let me offer you a bit of advice. I've found that it's far better to rely on yourself than anyone else, but if you must rely on someone else, let it be an older woman who has seen something of the world. It's preferable if she is a widow of some means, like myself. You'll find that we've usually tasted enough freedom to realize what it is to actually enjoy our lives." Aunt Amelia grinned. "And we usually have heaps of money so we can do what we will."

I wondered how strong the wine we'd had with lunch had been for my aunt to speak so candidly about money in public—although admittedly no one could hear us up on the balcony.

"Now, enough of Bolivia or Argentina or wherever your father is this month. You have managed through an entire lunch to evade my questions about what you are doing with your life," said Aunt Amelia.

"I've taken a job with the civil service," I said.

"A reliably solid sort of profession. What do they have you doing there?" she asked.

"I'm a typist."

"A typist? But you were a copywriter at that poky little advertisement agency you worked at. Why don't they have you writing for the Ministry of Information or some such job?" asked Aunt Amelia.

"We all go where we're needed," I said.

Aunt Amelia narrowed her eyes. "You're not telling me everything."

"I beg your pardon?"

"I've known you your whole life, Evelyne. If you think that you can lie to me, you are sorely mistaken."

"I . . ."

Something like understanding dawned over my aunt's face. "Oh, I see. Never mind, those of us who did our bit during the last war understand."

I frowned. "I thought you spent the Great War rolling bandages."

Aunt Amelia's answer to that was simply to raise her eyebrows. "If you happen to cross paths with him, remember me to Major-General Sir Vernon Kell."

"Aunt Amelia," I said slowly, recalling the name from one of the memos I had typed, "how do you know the former director of the Security Service?"

"Oh, darling," said Aunt Amelia with a broad smile, "I'm certain that you will figure that one out for yourself. After all, it's always been my belief that you received the lion's share of the brains in this family. It's good to see you putting them to use."

S lightly tipsy, I braved the bus on my way back from the Burke Club to Bina Gardens, arriving just in time to cross paths with Jocelyn.

"Oh, Evelyne. I'm glad I caught you." She opened up her brown leather satchel and pulled out a scrap of paper.

"Grove House?" I asked excitedly as I opened the paper to find a list.

"There are four locations called Grove House with a Southwest London postal code. Grove House on Roehampton Lane, one on Cedars Road in Battersea, another on Conifer Gardens in Streatham, and the last is on Ritherdon Road in Tooting," she said.

I threw my arms around her. "Thank you, thank you, thank you, Jocelyn!"

She laughed, gently pushing me off and discreetly ignoring my slightly inebriated state. "If only my editors were that enthusiastic when I delivered news. Are you certain that you can't tell me any more details? I might be able to help further."

"I'm sorry, I really can't, but as soon as the war is over, I'll give you the entire story," I promised.

"That's good enough for me. I'm off to the night shift," she said.

"Good luck and watch the skies."

"I will!" she called over her shoulder.

With a smile on my face, I trooped upstairs to my room, Jocelyn's paper in hand, only to find Moira yawning, still wearing a pair of the men's pajamas she favored.

"How was Aunt Amelia?" she asked as soon as I was in the door.

"Enlightening. Did you know that she paid my fees for Ethelbrook?"

"She did?" Moira asked, sounding as stunned as I felt. "But you always said that she virtually ignored you on your school holidays."

"I know, but I'm beginning to wonder . . ."

Apparently there was much I didn't know about my aunt from her quiet generosity to what she'd done during the last war.

"Perhaps I've incorrectly judged her," I said.

"That woman who says everyone's Up or Down? I wouldn't be surprised if she's rewritten her will fourteen times given all of the things she seems to take as a personal affront," said Moira.

My friend wasn't wrong, but I couldn't shake the feeling that my aunt was a more complicated woman than I'd previously given her credit for.

"Anyway, how was your meeting this morning that you can't talk about with the person I'm supposed to pretend you weren't meeting?" she asked.

"Uneventful," I replied, a half-truth.

Now that I'd had some time to think about our conversation, I couldn't help feeling more than a bit frustrated with Mr. Fletcher. He'd seemed interested in the news of a mole, but he hadn't exactly jumped up and yelled "Eureka!" Instead, he'd walked me calmly and coolly through what amounted to a thought exercise.

If only he would give me *something* of a clue as to what he wanted me to look for in the CWR—some real guidance—I might be able to give him a report of substance rather than simply guessing.

"What about you? I thought you had a job today," I said to Moira.

She shook her head. "I telephoned ahead because of the bombing, and I found out that the location where we were meant to film has been hit, so they're scrambling to find another."

I shuddered at the thought that, if Moira had been at work and there had been a day air raid, she might not be having this conversation with me.

"Do be careful out there," I said.

Moira fixed me with a look. "All of London's a target, darling." But then she softened her tone, adding, "I will do my best if you promise to do the same."

"I promise," I said.

Moira stretched her arms over her head, gave one last yawn, and then asked, "What are we doing tomorrow?"

"We?" I asked with a smile.

"You've been locked away wherever it is you work now, and I've hardly seen you. Ergo, we should spend the day together. What shall we do?" she repeated.

I held up Jocelyn's list of Grove House addresses. "I'm going investigating."

"Well, then I'm coming with you," Moira announced. "I may not be as handsome as this Daniel Poole—"

"David," I corrected her.

"But a detective needs a sidekick," she finished.

"Trust me, I'd much rather you were my sidekick," I said, refusing to give her the satisfaction of knowing that I had wondered several times that day how Mr. Poole's half of our investigations had progressed during my day off.

"I don't believe that for a second," she teased.

I held up the paper and arched a brow. "All of these places are south of the river."

Moira, who had never lost her lifelong Central London snobbery, groaned.

"Come on, it will be fun," I said.

She pulled a face.

"I'll buy you lunch," I added.

My friend's expression melted into a smile. "Deal."

I laughed. "Now, if you'll please excuse me, I'm going to need at least two hours of knitting and reading to recover from seeing my aunt."

Moira laughed. "Oh, darling, don't be silly. You'll need at least four hours for that."

THIRTY-TWO

Y ou didn't tell me that being your sidekick involved waking up quite so early," Moira grumbled as we disembarked from the bus to Roehampton the following morning.

"A detective never rests while there is a case to be solved," I said.

"Fine, but I want something sweet with my luncheon as well," Moira grumbled.

"I'll see what my ration book can stretch to."

The Grove House on Roehampton Lane was the first location on Jocelyn's list, so I decided that was as good a place to start as any. It was also the address that would take us the farthest from Bina Gardens, so I thought that it would be best to eliminate it from my inquiries early.

Now, on the pavement at the junction between Upper Richmond Road and Roehampton Lane, Moira put her hands on her hips and looked around us.

"This is a busy road," she said, the edge of her blond pageboy lifting in the breeze.

"And longer than I expected," I murmured.

Now that we were here, I silently wished that I had a little bit more to go on than just the name of the road and neighborhood. However, Jocelyn hadn't provided me with a proper address. In fairness, in London, where the streets had sprung up out of old villages that each had their own nomenclature, the names of roads changed so rapidly that it normally wouldn't be a problem. Roehampton Lane, however, was a main road and therefore its own challenge.

"We'll walk down and find it," I said, with more conviction than I felt, locking my arm through my friend's.

As we walked south, away from the bus stop at Upper Richmond Road, a huge green space stretched out to the right of us. A discreet sign at a drive told me that it was Roehampton Club.

"I wonder what that is," I said, trying to peer through some of the vegetation shielding the land.

"It's a golf club. They play polo there too," said Moira. When I gave her a look, she added, "A few of Papa's friends were members. We went once or twice."

"So you have been south of the river after all," I teased her.

"Not by choice," she said with a sniff.

A little farther down, the land along the road opened up again. To our left appeared a hospital.

"Could that be it?" Moira asked.

"I don't think so. It distinctly said 'Grove House.' Not 'Hospital.'"

"Excuse me!" Moira called out to a man ahead of us, transforming into the picture of an innocent, lost young lady whom no one would deny directions. When he turned we saw that the lower part of his left arm was missing and the sleeve of his jacket was pinned up and out of the way.

"Looking for Queen Mary's?" he asked, his voice carrying a thick Yorkshire accent.

"No, I'm afraid we aren't," said Moira sweetly.

"Ah, I thought you might be visiting someone. The hospital moved a few years ago, but those who had kin in the first war remember it. Although, I suppose you're both too young to have visited all those years ago."

"We're actually looking for Grove House," I said.

"Oh you mean the college." He looked us both up and down from the tops of our hats to the toes of our polished shoes. "Lucky students who will have you two for teachers. Keep going down this road until you reach the next left. If you cross Clarence Lane, you've gone too far."

He tipped his flat cap to us, whistling to himself a little as he went.

"Teachers?" Moira asked.

I shrugged. "Let's go find out."

We took the directions the gentleman had given us and found ourselves walking down a long drive. A large white house rose up above us. A few women, conservatively dressed, milled about. One or two held books in their arms, like schoolgirls.

I walked up to a pair of young women, put on a smile, and gave them a little wave. "Hello, I'm looking for Grove House."

"You've found it," said a small, bird-like girl with her hair pulled up on top of her head like a Gibson Girl from the start of the century.

"This building?" I asked.

"That's right," said the girl's much taller companion. Both were similarly dressed in straight skirts and hand-knitted wool jumpers.

"And what exactly is it?" Moira asked.

"Froebel College," said the Gibson Girl with a giggle.

"A teaching college. You really should know where you are if you want to enroll," said the tall girl

I gave them both a tight smile. "Yes, I believe we would like to enroll. You wouldn't happen to know who we would see about that, would you?"

The tall girl twisted to point to the entryway of the white building. "If you just go inside and speak to Miss Reynolds at the desk, she'll help you."

I nodded my thanks and Moira and I hurried away.

"We're not really going to enroll, are we? I don't think my complexion could stand the strain of teaching," Moira whispered as we approached the big white house.

"Of course not. Can you imagine us as teachers? But I do want to ask them some questions," I said in a low voice.

"Like whether the woman who died was a student?" she asked.

"Precisely," I said. I didn't know what else to do. I had four places all called Grove House located in Southwest London and Jean's name. That was all. I didn't know what I was meant to be looking for, but I had a sneaking suspicion that if I saw it, I would know it.

At least that's what I told myself as we walked through the front door of Grove House.

A delicate-looking woman with flaxen hair pulled severely back from her face who sat behind a desk lifted her head and greeted us with a smile. I felt it was safe to assume that this was Miss Reynolds.

"Can I help you?" she asked.

"We would like to inquire about the possibility of enrolling," I said.

"How delightful!" cried Miss Reynolds. Then her face fell. "I'm afraid, however, you're rather late. The term for new students is already fully enrolled."

"Oh, that's all right," said Moira, stepping forward. "My sister and I are interested in next term."

Miss Reynolds brightened. "A very good idea. One can never think too far ahead about these things, can one?"

"Certainly not," said Moira with a smile.

"And there is such a need for teachers these days," said Miss Reynolds.

"Which is precisely what inspired us. We'd like to be useful," I said.

"Oh, that is a very noble thought indeed," said Miss Reynolds, who, by now, was positively beaming. I almost felt guilty about my lies, but I knew that they were for a purpose all their own.

"Is there someone whom we might speak to about the school? You see, there is a teaching college that is closer to our home, but the reputation of Froebel College is such that we're quite torn," I said.

Miss Reynolds was up like a shot. "You'll want to speak to Miss Mortimer. She is our head of school, and she knows everything about Froebel College. If you'll just take a seat, I'll see if she's available. I won't be a moment."

THIRTY-THREE

As soon as Miss Reynolds had bustled down the corridor, leaving us to perch on a pair of hard wooden seats facing her desk, I leaned over to Moira. "Sisters?"

"I thought we needed a credible reason to be here together," she whispered back.

"You could have said that we were friends. Or even flatmates. Both of those things would be true and far more likely given that you look as though you could play a Greek goddess in a film, and the best I could hope for is your lanky, mousy friend," I said.

"You are neither mousy nor lanky, Evelyne Redfern. You look like the heroine in a Brontë novel," she said.

"Don't they all die in the end?" I asked.

"Not all of them. At least I don't think they do. I've only ever read *Jane Eyre*. What a depressing book. Anyway, where is your taste for daring? Your sense of adventure?" Moira asked.

"Investigating a murder isn't enough adventure for you? Now you need to go making up stories about who we are?" I asked in a whisper.

"I thought it would be something that a detective in one of those novels you're always reading might do," she said.

"I suppose." Only most detectives seemed to announce themselves the moment they appeared on the page. However, they were proper detectives, not a determined young woman straight out of the typing pool, so I suppose that did make a difference.

Miss Reynolds appeared a moment later with a considerably older woman trailing behind her. This woman wore rose-colored skirts that fell to the floor with a pearl gray cardigan buttoned to her neck, and she leaned lightly on a polished wooden walking stick topped with a carved doe's head.

Moira and I stood immediately, no doubt compelled by the same sensation of being called in front of our headmistress at school.

The older woman stopped, her cane braced before her with both hands. "Welcome, ladies. I am Miss Mortimer. Miss Reynolds tells me that you have come to inquire about places at Froebel College."

"Yes," I said. "We're very keen to learn more about the curriculum."

Miss Mortimer nodded. "If you will come with me. We will be more comfortable in my office."

She turned and began to make her way back down the corridor. Moira and I fell into line behind her.

Miss Mortimer's sitting room was exactly what I would have imagined from this woman, decorated in heavy pink brocade curtains with gold trim and matching upholstered furniture. Lace antimacassars covered the backs of all of the chairs and the faint scent of rose potpourri hung rather cloyingly in the air. There was a delicate desk with carved legs—the only concession that this room existed as a place for work—that held a tidy stack of papers to the left and a pen and ink holder on the right.

Miss Mortimer indicated that we should sit and sank down herself. "Now, Miss . . ."

"Redfern and Mangan," said Moira.

Miss Mortimer frowned. "I thought Miss Reynolds said you were sisters."

Moira froze next to me so, stifling a sigh, I said, "My father tragically died just after I was born, and my mother remarried."

"That does explain the difference in your coloring," said Miss Mortimer.

I suppressed the urge to shoot Moira a look.

"Miss Reynolds tells me that you would like to be teachers," said Miss Mortimer.

"We are very seriously considering it," I said, resting my gloved hands on my knee and sitting up a little straighter. I was oddly happy that I had worn my best shoes that day. I felt as though Miss Mortimer would notice such things.

"Teaching is a noble profession, and never more so than during a time of war," said Miss Mortimer. "It is teachers who helped evacuate their students to the countryside, keeping their children calm on their train rides away from home. Some of those teachers even made the sacrifice to stay and teach in requisitioned homes. They provide stability to those children. And then there are those who choose to stay in the cities, risking the very bombings that are plaguing us now.

"Teaching is also a profession that requires attention to detail. May I ask why it is that you are inquiring about enrolling just as the term starts and not before it when the possibility of open seats was far more likely?" Miss Mortimer asked.

I had no interest in becoming a teacher, and yet my cheeks flushed anyway.

"We've been caring for our ailing father," Moira piped up before I could answer. "My ailing father, that is. Evelyne's stepfather."

Sisters and now an ailing father? I was going to have to have a very stern conversation with my friend about the best lies having a modicum of the truth at their core.

"I see," said Miss Mortimer. "I hope that he is better."

"He is," I said, before Moira could kill off my poor imaginary stepfather.

"I am glad. May I ask how you learned about Froebel College?" asked Miss Mortimer.

"A friend," I answered at the same time that Moira said, "A friend's sister."

I glared at Moira. "She was a student here."

Miss Mortimer looked between us with a raised brow. "It sounds as though she was a very good friend. What was her name?"

"Jean Plinkton," I said.

"Plinkton? I don't recall a Plinkton ever enrolling here in the thirty-five years I have worked at the college," said Miss Mortimer.

Moira gave a little laugh. "Surely you don't recall every woman who has been a student in thirty-five years."

Miss Mortimer's brow inched ever closer to her steel gray hair. "What age would you guess your Miss Jean Plinkton to be? That is, if you do not know off the top of your head already, you being so very close."

"In her early twenties," I said.

"I could consult our records, but I can assure you that no one of that name has ever enrolled here in my time. I have an excellent memory, and it is a distinctive name."

Miss Mortimer stood, leaning on her cane but no less commanding for it. "Now, if you will excuse me, ladies, I have a class to observe."

"But our enrollment," Moira began to protest.

Miss Mortimer gave us a withering stare. "If I thought for one moment that either of you was actually interested in teaching, I would stay and speak to you more about our philosophy and our curriculum. Good morning, ladies."

Silently, Moira and I rose and walked out of the head of school's office. We said a subdued goodbye to a cheery Miss Reynolds. As soon as we were out in the open, we looked at each other and burst out laughing.

"Is that how being a detective is supposed to go?" she asked me.

"Oh, I don't know. Hercule Poirot never seems to find himself shamed by a stern older woman," I said. Then again, I was certain he always had his story straight with Captain Hastings before speaking to a witness. If I'd learned nothing else that day, it was that I would have to brief Moira better next time.

"Do you think that this was the place you were searching for?" she asked.

I looked about at the distinguished, stark white facade and the women milling about. "I don't think so. Something doesn't feel like it fits."

"Right. Then where to next?" Moira asked.

I took out the piece of paper where I'd scribbled Jocelyn's instructions. "The next on the list is in Battersea. That isn't too far from here."

"It's also not particularly close," Moira pointed out.

"Giving up on me already?" I asked.

Moira laughed. "Absolutely not. I'm your sidekick like . . . what's his name from Sherlock Holmes?"

"Watson," I supplied.

"That's the one," said Moira. "I'll come with you, but first I want that lunch you promised me."

After Moira had practically cleaned out my ration book and my purse at a little French restaurant we found nestled into a row of shops on Upper Richmond Road in Roehampton, we hopped back on the bus and headed east to Battersea. My friend was, annoyingly, absolutely correct that Battersea was not particularly close to our first destination, and once we finally arrived on Cedars Road it was well into the afternoon and exhaustion was setting in.

"Bloody hill," I muttered as we both leaned into the steep incline that my hazy knowledge of South London told me would deposit us into Clapham Common if we continued to climb.

"If I die, tell James that I love him," she groaned.

"I thought Robert was courting you out these days," I said.

"That was two weeks ago. Before I met James," she said. "I know that you're away three days at a time, but do try to keep up, darling."

I would have rolled my eyes, but I spotted a carved sign reading "Grove House" half obscured by wildly creeping ivy.

"There it is," I said, pointing to the big redbrick building set back from the road and flanked on three sides by a four-foot brick wall. The house looked as though it might have once been grand, but at some point it had clearly been allowed to fall into a not-so-distinguished state of near neglect. Weeds grew up between cracks in the path and paint peeled off the windowsills and the front door, which had no doubt once been white but now was tinted a light gray from smoke and time. Grove House was an eyesore in the middle of an otherwise perfectly respectable row of homes.

When I went up to the door, I found that there was a line of names next to corresponding doorbells.

"It's been broken up into flats," I called out to Moira.

"Do you see anyone's name you recognize?" she asked.

I peered at the hand-inked labels, some incredibly faded. None of the names looked familiar. Just for good measure, I rang each bell in succession, but either no one was home or everyone was very reluctant to come to the door.

Defeated, I hurried back down the path to Moira where she stood waiting at the low-slung brick wall that separated the property from the pavement.

"Nothing?" she asked.

"Nothing."

"Oh well. Let's head home before it becomes dark," she said, looking at the sky as she pulled the collar of her coat a little higher around her neck. "I hate the thought of being caught out somewhere I don't know when Wailing Wally sounds."

I groaned. "Can't they give us one night off from the bombing?"

Moira sighed. "I wish, darling. I wish."

THIRTY-FOUR

I would never have admitted it to Moira, but I was practically buzzing with excitement the following morning by the time I was due back in the CWR for my third shift. Our investigations into the first two Grove Houses had been helpful—and even a bit of fun if not fruitful. However, I had a very important conversation ahead of me that morning.

I headed straight to the Dock to claim a bunk and stow my things. Edith and Caroline, who were partway through their three days, waved me sleepy hellos as they made their way back from the showers.

"How is it up top?" asked Edith with a yawn.

"Bad," I said honestly. "My bus had to turn around three times this morning because it couldn't get through all of the regular roads."

"I've been telephoning Mum and Dad every break. It's costing me a fortune, but I can't stand not knowing what's going on," said Edith. She glanced at her watch. "Speaking of which, I think I'll try them now before the shift starts. Was Horse Guards open as usual?"

"Yes," I said.

"I might do the same," said Caroline, twisting her hands.

We said goodbye and I set about locking my things away. I was just finishing when Patricia came down the stairs, her pink dressing gown wrapped tight around her. Her hair was bundled up in a turban, and there was still steam edging her glasses.

"Good morning," I said.

"Good morning," she mumbled.

"Patricia, do you have a moment?" I asked.

She looked up sharply. "Why?"

If I hadn't already known her reputation for being taciturn and a bit sharp, I might have been taken aback. Instead, I simply folded my arms one on top of the other and waited.

"That is, what can I help you with?" she asked, as though she realized how harsh she sounded.

"Have the inspectors spoken to you yet about Jean?" I asked.

"They did. I told them I don't know anything," she said, adjusting her glasses.

"But Patricia, that isn't true, is it?"

She stared at me.

"I know about your argument with Lieutenant MacIntyre in the park," I continued.

Without warning, Patricia sank down onto her bunk and dropped her head into her hands.

That, I will admit, did take me aback. Not entirely knowing what to do, I edged over and cautiously sat on the bottom bunk next to her.

"It's all right. Whatever it is, it's going to be all right," I said.

"No, it's not," she sobbed.

"What's the matter? Would you like to tell me?"

She raised her now blotchy face, her expression wretched. "I can't."

"If something is weighing on you, perhaps it will be better to share your burden," I said.

"People say that, but it's never actually true, is it?" she asked.

"It is true," I told her with a firm nod. "When I was younger, I was sent off to boarding school. I hated it. I was miserable."

"Why didn't you write to your parents to ask them to let you come home?" she asked, her sobbing lightening just a little bit.

"Because my mother had died, and my father had no interest in having me around. I used to cry myself to sleep every night in the dormitory until one day a girl walked up to me and asked me why I was crying so much. She told me that it would feel better if I had it out once and for all. She also promised that if we talked about it one time, we never had to talk about it again."

"What did you do?" she asked.

"I talked to her, and we became best friends. We still live together to this day," I said.

Immediately Patricia began to sob again, this time pressing her face against my light blue jumper.

Goodness, I thought, and set about rubbing her back. Irene rounded the corner, and stopped. I shook my head, and she crept forward to grab her clothing, then fled.

When finally Patricia's sobs began to subside again, she pulled away. "Oh, I'm sorry. You're all wet."

"That's all right," I said.

She pulled a handkerchief out of her dressing gown pocket and began dabbing at her eyes. "I'm acting like a fool, I know."

"Not a fool, but the fact of the matter is that you're going to have to speak to someone about what happened in the park because someone saw you. The investigators know that you and Lieutenant MacIntyre rowed, and that means they also know you lied."

"It wasn't a row. Not really," she said.

"Then tell me what happened. Help me understand."

She swiped haphazardly at her tears again. "After Jean was— After Jean died, I was so worried. I know that Lieutenant MacIntyre hated her, and I thought that he might have . . . well, you know."

"Why did he hate Jean?" I asked.

"Because Jean threatened to report him for dereliction of duty," she said.

I nodded slowly. "How do you know that?"

"Charlotte told me."

"Why would Charlotte know?" I asked.

"He told her. He was in love with her," said Patricia miserably.

That revelation caught me by surprise.

"Charlotte's such a friendly person, I think he was drawn to her. He used to follow us to the pub when he was off duty, and he would corner her for hours," Patricia continued. "It wasn't as though Charlotte was toying with him or anything. She just has a way about her. So many people fall in love with her when they meet her, but she hardly notices."

"Did Charlotte reciprocate his feelings?" I asked.

Patricia shook her head. "No."

"You're certain?"

"I was her best friend. I should know. She told me that the two of them didn't see eye-to-eye about some very important things."

"Do you know what those were?" I asked.

Patricia shook her head. "Anyway, after I found out Jean died, I wasn't thinking straight. I hated her so much, but I never would have wanted her to die because of it."

"Why did you hate Jean?" I asked.

"Because Jean is the reason that Charlotte left the CWR!" said Patricia fiercely. "It was a completely normal day. Jean was off somewhere, shirking her typing like she always did. Charlotte got up for a break. When she came back, red-faced and obviously upset, I tried to ask her what was the matter, but she told me that we would talk about it later.

"That was the last day of my shift, and I couldn't catch her before I left. When I came back in to work, Miss Wilkes told me Charlotte had quit."

"Did Miss Wilkes say anything else?" I asked.

Patricia dabbed at her eyes with the edge of her dressing gown. "No. I thought Charlotte maybe would have left a note or something, but it was like she had never worked here. They erased her completely."

"Have you seen Charlotte since she left the CWR?" I asked.

Patricia looked up at me, devastation clearly written on her face. "No."

"Did she never give you an address or a telephone exchange?" I asked, feeling horrible that I knew that, less than ten miles away, Charlotte was living a new life as Mrs. Holmes.

"We worked together. We didn't need to speak on the telephone," said Patricia.

I must have looked skeptical, because she grabbed my hand. "We were *best* friends."

"I believe you," I said. "But even when you are close with someone, you can fall out. Or you can do something that the other doesn't understand."

Patricia sniffled.

"Patricia," I said as a thought struck me. "Why do you blame Jean for Charlotte quitting?"

"What?" she asked.

"You said that Jean was off somewhere when Charlotte left. Then Charlotte returned, upset. Why do you think that Jean was the one who made Charlotte upset?" I asked.

Patricia bit her lip. "When I found out that Charlotte had quit.

I . . . I may not have composed myself particularly well. I cried a lot. I couldn't help it, even though I knew that it angered Miss Wilkes.

"Sometimes it became too much, thinking about Charlotte not being here any longer. I sometimes would take deliveries just so I could find a quiet room for a moment. Jean found me in an alcove on one of the less used corridors about a week after Charlotte left. She said that if I knew the things she did about Charlotte, I wouldn't think so highly of my friend. I became angry, and I called Jean some names that I'm not proud of. Lieutenant MacIntyre was walking by when it happened, and I nearly ran into him as I stormed off.

"You have to understand. I don't have any family. I hardly do anything except work. I've never seen Charlotte again, and it's horrible."

I would be lying if I said that I didn't feel for Patricia in that moment. She was lonely. She had lost her best friend through no fault of her own. What if it had been Moira and me in that same situation?

"I'm so sorry, Patricia."

"Thank you." She swiped at her tears again.

"I have to ask, where were you on Saturday between two and three o'clock?" I asked.

Her shoulders stiffened. "I heard that you've been poking around in other people's business. Jean did that too."

"I promise, I'm not Jean. But I do want to figure out what happened to her," I said.

"Even though she was an awful person?" Patricia asked.

"No one deserves to die the way she did," I said quietly. "She should have justice, just like anyone else."

Patricia sat for a moment, staring at her hands. Then she said, "I told Sergeant Maxwell that I left the typing pool around ten past two. I went to deliver a memo to Mr. Dean's secretary, Miss Upson. Her typewriter was acting up, so I helped her rethread the ribbon and also clean it. After that, I went to wash my hands, and I ended up speaking to a clerk who had questions about a report I'd typed. By the time I made it back in the typing pool, it was nearly three."

"Thank you," I said.

She stood, and I watched her compose herself, that aloof mask that held everyone at an arm's length sliding back into place. "I need to dress and report for my shift."

She grabbed her clothes and hurried away.

I sat for a moment on her bunk, processing everything I had just heard. I believed Patricia's story, but something about it felt off. I couldn't put my finger on it, except to say that to leave your close friend behind with hardly a word felt so . . . cruel.

THIRTY-FIVE

After speaking to Patricia I went straight to the room I shared with Mr. Poole only to find the door locked. With a frown, I navigated my way to Mr. Poole's desk with the rest of the Ministry of Information staff, but none of the clerks in the nearby rooms had seen him.

A bit disappointed, I made my way back to the typing pool where Miss Wilkes introduced me to the new girl, Georgina, who wore the same slightly overwhelmed look that I'm sure I had on my first day. Then Miss Wilkes immediately set me to work on a large stack of documents to duplicate. Patricia, I noticed, kept her eyes resolutely on her typewriter as I sat down.

At lunchtime, Irene, Caroline, Edith, and I took Georgina to the canteen with us for a sandwich and a chat. I couldn't help noticing Irene glance around every few minutes, her mind clearly on something else. On our way out of the canteen, I fell into step with her and asked, "Is everything all right?"

"Of course. Why wouldn't it be?" she asked quickly.

"You seemed distracted at lunch."

For a moment I thought she might confide in me, but instead she laughed and waved a hand. "It's just this shift. I've one more day and then I have a Saturday and a Sunday off. A real weekend. Can you believe it?"

"That is cause for celebration. Are you going to see your fellow?"

I thought I saw a shadow pass over her eyes, but then she grinned wide. "I am. He's taking me out."

"Is that right? Where are you going?"

"Somewhere very special," she said, playing coy.

"Well, I hope you have fun," I said.

Irene fluffed her hair. "Oh, I will. I should give credit to you, actually."

"To me?"

"When you asked if we had plans the other day, it made me think. Well," she dropped her voice, "we've been staying in so much at a little place he has, but I told him that he has to take me out like he did when we first started courting."

"I see," I said, not entirely sure how I felt about being the inspiration for rekindling the passion in an affair, but happy at least that Irene seemed excited.

After lunch, the door to Mr. Poole's room was still locked. A huge assignment hit the typing pool at half past two, and I hardly had time to think about where my erstwhile partner might be. I wanted to tell him that I'd spoken to Patricia, but I also couldn't shake the feeling that something about that conversation had felt off. I needed to speak to Charlotte, but there was no chance of slipping away with all of us typing away frantically as clerks hovered along the walls and watched us eagerly.

"Goodness, is it always this busy?" asked Georgina when a clerk practically ripped a page from her hands, ink still wet.

"Not always, but days like this are becoming more and more common," said Caroline.

"It's all of the bombings. Reports are coming in at all hours now," said Edith.

"It's running my wrists into the ground," said Irene, stretching her hands.

"Do you think that typing too much can make your knuckles larger?" asked Edith, staring at her hands.

"Don't be silly," I said. "You have perfectly lovely knuckles."

"Look at them." Edith held her hands up. "I'm convinced they're growing."

We all swung around in our chairs to stare at Edith's hands until Miss Wilkes walked into the room looking peaky.

"Miss Wilkes, is everything all right?" Caroline asked.

"I'm fine, I'm fine," the older woman said, touching her hand to her temple. "I am concerned, however, that I see a distinct lack of typing."

Immediately, hands flew to keyboards.

Miss Wilkes stopped by my desk and leaned down. In a whisper, she said, "Miss Redfern, that matter that I spoke to you about the other day, have you told anyone else about it?"

I studied her worried face. "Mr. Poole and I did speak to the inspectors about it in the context of both investigations."

She closed her eyes but then nodded. "I suppose you had to."

I twisted farther around in my chair. "They didn't accuse you of anything, did they?"

"No, no. Nothing like that. However, I am being asked to produce my bank book. They have it in their heads that I wouldn't be able to pay for my mother's care. They would be right too, under normal circumstances," said Miss Wilkes.

"May I ask . . ."

Miss Wilkes glanced around once more to make sure no one was listening and leaned in even closer. "I was engaged once." I tried to school the shock off my face while she continued in a hurried whisper. "He was a young man of considerable means, and he had no family to speak of. He was killed on the Somme, and I found out after the war that he had provided for me in his will. I never felt right about using that money until Mama needed help."

I touched the older woman's hand. "I'm so very sorry, Miss Wilkes. I can imagine it was difficult speaking about that."

She shook her head. "I should have disclosed the entire situation earlier, but at least it seems to have cleared me of suspicion. Now I'm hopeful that this is the last time I ever have to speak of it in the CWR."

"The last time?" I asked.

"Miss Plinkton found out about Mama's situation a few weeks ago. I've never understood how she learned about it, but she did," said Miss Wilkes.

"Did she . . . say anything in particular to you?" I asked.

Miss Wilkes puffed out a laugh. "The silly thing seemed to think that I was in"—she lowered her voice even further so that it was hardly distinguishable above the dull of the modified typewriter keys—"financial difficulty. She implied that she could help."

"What did you say to that?" I asked.

"I told her that I was perfectly capable of arranging my own affairs and that she should mind her own business. She didn't like that very much."

"Did she approach you again?" I asked.

"No. I think she received my message loud and clear. Anyway, now all that is done," said Miss Wilkes, straightening the edge of her jacket. "I believe you have rather a lot of duplication to do, Miss Redfern."

"Yes, Miss Wilkes."

As she turned to leave, I placed my hands on the keyboard once again, but I didn't begin typing straightaway. Miss Wilkes had confirmed my suspicions that Jean's scheme to gather information had stretched beyond Charlotte. I felt, for the first time since I'd spoken to Charlotte, as though the pieces were actually beginning to come together.

———

The afternoon of typing with no relief in the form of a conference with Mr. Poole left me exhausted. However, as soon as Betty took over my desk for the night, I was out of the CWR like a shot. I had too many things I needed to do before the near inevitability of the air raid siren sounded later. It was strange how governed by the blasted thing we'd all become, almost as though nightly air raids were a normal part of London life when for months Wailing Wally had signaled nothing but false alarms.

Aboveground, I made a beeline for the now-familiar telephone booth on Horse Guards. I waited impatiently for a dark-suited man wearing a bowler hat and an umbrella hooked over his arm to finish his call and then, the moment it was free, I pushed inside.

It took the switchboard a moment to connect me to Mrs. William Holmes's exchange, but I was rewarded when Charlotte picked up on the second ring.

"Mrs. Holmes, it's Evelyne Redfern."

I heard a sharp intake of breath on the other end of the line. "Miss Redfern, please understand. Last week I spoke about things that . . . are difficult. I don't wish to—"

"Just a moment of your time, please. I'm not calling about Jean. Or at least not really," I said.

She sighed. "What is it you want?"

"It's about Patricia."

Charlotte went so quiet that I couldn't be entirely certain the connection hadn't cut out until she finally asked, "What about Patricia?"

"I spoke to her today," I started. "She misses you."

Another pause. "I miss her too, but I can't."

"She was adamant that you had nothing to do with Jean's death," I said.

"I didn't," she insisted.

"I know that, but I thought you should know that Patricia was ready to defend you to the end."

"That's Patricia, loyal to a fault," said Charlotte, the warmth in her voice unmistakable.

"I think she misses her friend," I said. "I have a best friend and I know that if something happened that put us at odds, I'd like to think that we could find a way back to one another."

"It's impossible," said Charlotte, but I could hear the waver in her voice.

"Did Patricia do something?" I asked.

"I . . . I can't."

"You trusted me with Harriet. Can you trust me with this too?" I asked.

Finally, Charlotte let out a long sigh. "You promise that no harm will come to Patricia?"

"If what you tell me has nothing to do with my investigation, then yes, I can promise that."

"Jean didn't just threaten me with Harriet. She also tried to use Patricia against me," she said.

"How did she do that?"

Charlotte sighed. "Apparently Jean thought that Patricia was in love with me."

"Oh."

It wasn't as though I hadn't heard about two women falling in love—I went to a girls' school for heaven's sake—but I hadn't expected it. However, the more I thought about it, the more it made sense. The grief Patricia felt over Charlotte leaving the CWR went beyond what most friends would feel for one another. And, if Charlotte hadn't reciprocated those feelings . . .

"She never had any evidence," Charlotte hurried to add. "She was just casting about. And anyway, I quit before Jean could do anything about it."

"Do you know if Jean threatened Patricia as well?" I asked.

"No," Charlotte said quietly. "At least I don't think so."

"But you quit and left Patricia behind without any explanation," I said.

"You have to understand, my daughter . . ."

"Even if Patricia did have romantic feelings for you, she was your best friend."

"I—I know," she said, her voice breaking. "I left without telling her how to find me because I was afraid. I was afraid for Harriet and my job and . . . I suppose I was afraid for Patricia as well. But I miss her so much."

"You could tell her that," I said.

"But what if Jean was right?" Charlotte asked.

"Does it matter? You could have spoken to Patricia rather than simply leaving her behind. Jean might have been wrong—"

"She wasn't. I knew. I think I always knew, but I didn't feel that way," said Charlotte.

"Then you could have spoken to your friend and told her that."

"I don't know," Charlotte whispered. "It might change things between us."

"It might, but it might not. Whether you're right or wrong about Patricia, both of you hate the way your friendship ended. Perhaps you can save it, but you won't know until you ask her yourself."

"You won't tell anyone, will you?" asked Charlotte. "Patricia hasn't hurt anyone. She wouldn't. I promise."

"I won't tell anyone, Mrs. Holmes. I promise."

"Thank you," she breathed. "How does she seem?"

"You should ask her yourself. I could find her address for you."

She sucked in a breath. "I'll think about it."

"Do. This life is too short to lose a good friend."

I gave Charlotte my own details so that she could contact me and then hung up the receiver, thinking how much I wished that Moira was there to give me a hug and tell me, "Everything's all right with us, darling." Instead, I would have to content myself with an early supper and the Dock.

I was just turning when a familiar figure caught my eye. I squinted through the dirty glass of the telephone booth's door. Mr. Faylen, shoulders hunched and the usual fury etched onto his face, was walking with great speed. At the stop up the road, he hailed an approaching bus and stepped on.

I hesitated for a moment, wondering where a man who lived out of town was going in such a hurry on a bus bound for North London.

"What would a detective do if they spotted a suspect acting suspicious?" I muttered to myself.

Then I pushed out of the telephone booth and raced to catch the bus.

THIRTY-SIX

I don't, as a rule, love pubs. I blame this on Moira. She has much more particular taste than I do, and she loves nothing more than a drink at the Ritz or the Dorchester—Claridge's if she really must. She carts me along often enough that I too have acquired a taste for the finer things. If *Maman* started my education in Paris, Moira facilitated its completion in London.

That is why, when I saw Mr. Faylen hop off the bus and make a beeline for the door of the Bishop's Hat off Camden High Street, I sighed. I had come this far, only just making the departing bus and praying that he hadn't seen me as I'd paid my fare. I knew I had to follow him into this pub, but I didn't relish the thought of the glass of sticky sherry from a bottle that had been opened for who knows how long that surely awaited me. However, needs must and all that.

I saw through the Bishop's Hat's big plateglass window that Mr. Faylen turned into the bar, which presented more than a little bit of a problem for me. As a woman, I would be confined to the lounge— the only space where ladies would be served. Still, perhaps he was meeting a woman and would change sides at some point. Either way, I waited a good minute and then followed, peeling off through the door to the lounge as I went.

The space was filled with women and men, and I had to angle my way between the tables in order to finally find a free one in the back corner. As soon as I sat down, I scanned the room for Mr. Faylen.

"Waiting for your fellow, are you?"

I turned to find a rake-thin woman with peroxide hair and a knowing grin, who had spoken to me.

"Not quite," I said.

"I know how it is," she said, swinging her knees around under her table so that she faced me square on. "You give them one inch and they take a mile."

"I'm afraid I don't know what you mean," I said.

"The ponies. That's what mine does. He pretends that he likes a little flutter from time to time. No harm in that, except it isn't just from time to time, is it? He's in here every week. At least," she said.

Understanding dawned on me.

"If I can be candid," I said, leaning in, "I followed mine here."

Sometimes I really can take a moment to catch on, but I can pick up a thread and run with it like the best of them.

"Wanted to see what he was getting up to, did you?" she asked with a laugh. "Well, at least it isn't another woman. I used to see a lot of that when I was a barmaid."

"How does it work?" I asked, looking around me.

She shrugged. "Same as any other place, although I don't suppose you've seen much of that. You don't sound like you spend much time in places like this.

"In the bar, there'll be a bookie set up at a table, usually near the back. He takes slips and cash and then, when the results of the races come in, he'll pay out anyone whose day it's been," she explained.

"What happens if someone can't pay?" I asked.

She looked thoughtful. "I doubt there are too many of those. Bookies don't usually go around offering lines of credit, but I suppose if they thought someone was good for the money, they might come to an arrangement."

I nodded. "Is your husband good at gambling?"

"He wins about as much as he loses, which I suppose means he is. Most men don't become rich from playing the ponies, but plenty of them try." She nodded at something behind me. "Looks like yours hasn't had a good day of it at all."

I spun around in my chair, expecting to find Mr. Faylen bearing down on me. Instead I saw Mr. Poole pushing through the crowd and looking distinctly displeased.

"Darling," I said with a little wave as soon as Mr. Poole had stormed close enough to be within earshot, "have you had any luck?"

The question put a hitch in his step, and he frowned as he stopped in front of me. "I beg your pardon?"

"I'm sorry that I followed you here, but I just had to know what you were up to. You know me. Always curious," I said with a silly little laugh that grated on my own ears. "My friend—I'm sorry, I don't know your name."

"Margot," she said, watching with amusement.

"How do you do, Margot? I'm Evelyne and this is David, my fiancé," I said.

"Hasn't he bought you a ring yet, love?" asked Margot.

"Would you like to explain?" I asked, blinking up at David expectantly.

His jaw worked, but he managed to mumble, "I'm having my mother's ring resized for her."

"The mother's ring? Well, that's all right then," said Margot, suitably impressed.

"David, darling, Margot has just been explaining to me how things work. I wish you had told me. I would never have been so jealous," I said.

Mr. Poole pulled out the chair across from me and squeezed into it as best he could, looking somewhat dazed and defeated—the perfect cornered fiancé. "I apologize, darling."

I beamed at him. "You're completely forgiven, my love."

"You probably should fetch the lady a drink, don't you think?" asked Margot.

Hauling himself up out of his newly occupied seat with an "of course," Mr. Poole shot me one last look before retreating from whence he came.

"Oh, and here's my one, right on cue. It looks like it's been one of his losing days," said Margot, gathering up her coat and taking one last drink from the glass in front of her. "He'll be in a mood until he comes back next week."

"Goodbye, Margot. It was lovely meeting you," I said with a genuine smile.

She gave me a once-over, shook her head, and then laughed. "You have a good night, pet."

I watched her walk off to collect a glum-looking man in a brown sack suit holding his hat in his hands. She patted him on the shoulder and then steered him out of the lounge.

Mr. Poole returned with our drinks and then slumped into the chair opposite me. It was easier to access now that Margot had vacated her table.

"Are you going to tell me what that was all about?" he asked.

"I was gathering information," I said.

"About a cheap North London pub?"

I took a sip of the half pint of lager he'd put in front of me. "A cheap North London pub that Mr. Faylen is currently in."

Mr. Poole's head whipped around. "He's here?"

"He's in the other part. The part I can't go into," I said, pulling a face. I took another sip of beer. "This isn't half bad."

"I'm glad you approve," he said.

"I approve that it isn't sherry. Men always think that's what women want to drink, and I hate the stuff."

"So do I," he said. "Explain to me again how you know that Mr. Faylen is here."

"I followed him. I was making a telephone call in the booth at the end of the road when I spotted him tearing over to a bus stop." A thought struck me. "Were you on the same bus?"

"I saw you running like a mad woman for a bus and jumped into a taxi," he said.

I cringed sympathetically. "I'm sorry for the expense, it's just Mr. Faylen looked like he was in such a hurry—and such a mood—that I thought it would be wise to see where he was going. When he entered the bar, I came in here thinking that if he showed his face on this side I could at least see who he was with."

Mr. Poole sucked in a long breath as though trying to calm himself. "And what was your plan if he saw you, a single woman who is technically on her shift right now, drinking alone in a pub lounge?"

I shrugged. "I'm sure that I would have come up with something."

"Evelyne . . ."

I grinned at the fact that I'd irritated him enough to use my Christian name.

"Anyway, that isn't important. Would you like to know what I discovered?" I asked, leaning forward across the sticky table and then thinking better of it.

"I'm not sure that I could stop you from telling me if I tried."

I ignored his unnecessarily sardonic tone. "According to Margot, this pub has a bookie who sets up shop in the corner of the bar."

"Fascinating," he said, sipping his beer before taking a closer look at the glass. "You're right. This actually is good."

"Right. Here's my theory. We know that money might be a reason that someone might be"—I glanced around—"borrowing things from work. What if—hypothetically—Mr. Faylen comes to this pub to place bets on the horses. It's a long way away from work, and since he's paying with cash, it won't be noticed either by his wife or by his employer. Only he loses. He continues placing bets, assuming that his luck will turn around. It doesn't, and he becomes desperate. He needs to find more money to fund his gambling, but because of where he works, he knows that he can't exactly take too much money out of his bank or someone might notice. Perhaps, because he seems affluent, he is extended a line of credit by his bookie."

"If he did that, his debt's probably risen well beyond his means. Hypothetically," said Mr. Poole.

I leaned in close, my hands cupping my lager. "Precisely. Margot seemed to think that it is unusual for a bookie to extend credit, but I'm willing to guess that if a bookie saw a man like Mr. Faylen, he'd assume Mr. Faylen would be motivated to find the money to pay down his debts or risk social shame. I can't imagine that bookies are particularly understanding when people place bets that they can't cover."

"No, they aren't generally known for their compassion, and neither are the firms that run them," he said.

"The firms?"

"Gangsters," he clarified.

"I thought that was just in films or those awful American books you like so much," I said.

"One day you'll learn I'm right about those books," he said.

"Unlikely. Back to Mr. Faylen, what if he begins to feel the pressure to pay off these debts? What if, surrounded by all sorts of valuable pieces of information at work, he realizes that an interested party might want to buy them? Let's say he sells a few pieces. It isn't quite enough to pay off his debt—or perhaps he goes back and gambles all over again."

"It is a common problem," Mr. Poole said.

"He continues to sell information because he thinks it's his only way out. It escalates. His contacts want more from him. Now he's caught in a web and he can't stop." I sat back. "What if he's your man?"

He studied me for a long beat and then scrunched up his nose. "That is a lot of what-ifs. And how does Jean fit into all of this?"

"Remember the gossip about Jean going to a pub? She could have been his contact, or she could have been helping him. Either way, I suspect this was their meeting place," I said.

"That's a reasonable hypothesis," muttered Mr. Poole.

"It's clever, that's what it is."

"And do you think he was the one who killed her?" he asked.

"He might be."

"Why?" he asked. "He has to have a reason for doing it."

"Maybe she wanted a larger cut than he was willing to part with, or he wanted out and thought the only way he could stop all of this was with Jean dead. She could even have been threatening to expose him like she did with Charlotte. We don't know, but I think it's worth asking him about, don't you?"

"Right, we need to speak to Mr. Faylen again," said Mr. Poole, pushing back from our little table. "I'm going to check the bar. You meet me outside."

We threaded our way through the pub before peeling off to our respective destinations. Outside, the light was lavender tinged. It might have been romantic once, but now people hurried along faster than ever. Night had come to mean death and destruction.

The pub door flew open, and Mr. Poole stormed out. "He's gone."

"Gone?" I asked.

"He must have slipped away while we were talking."

"Come on, we might be able to catch up with him again," I said, tugging on his arm.

Mr. Poole opened his mouth to say something, but a mechanical scream of an air raid siren split the air.

I groaned. "Not now."

"We need to go back to work," he said, steering me in the direction of the CWR.

"Do you think we have enough time to make it?" I asked, hurrying beside him and struggling not to be separated as people dashed for the public air raid shelters. We were all the way across London, and many of the bus drivers had taken to stopping their buses mid-route and running for cover.

"I don't know," said Mr. Poole, his jaw set.

"Should we just go into the first shelter we see?" I asked.

"You're meant to be in the Dock. Don't you think people will ask questions about where you were?" he asked.

"They already have. After we went to Charlotte's, everyone wanted to know where I'd gone with you," I said.

"With me?" he asked.

"One of the ladies saw us drive off. We're the best gossip in the CWR at the moment. Well, except for the murder."

"People shouldn't gossip about things they don't understand. You could lose your job," he gritted out.

The thought of simultaneously disappointing Mr. Fletcher and not solving Jean's murder hit me harder than I thought it would. These last two weeks I'd felt more purposeful than I had in a long time—perhaps my entire life. I *liked* what I was doing, not just being a part of the CWR but the investigation with Mr. Poole. It felt as though I was part of something bigger—something that mattered.

"Let's try to make it back on foot," I said, picking up my pace and praying that the Luftwaffe would hold off on peppering London with whatever wretched devices they had planned for us until we made it to safety.

THIRTY-SEVEN

W e were near the Covent Garden Tube Station when we heard the first bomb fall. Mr. Poole and I looked at each other even as we kept walking at a clip.

"I think we need to risk my reputation and find a shelter," I said.

"You're sure?" he asked.

Another series of explosions, this time all in a row, sounded through the night. I peered up at the not yet fully dark sky and nodded. "Neither of us is worth anything to work or this investigation if we're dead."

"I think there's one around this corner." He reached over and squeezed my hand. "We're going to be fine."

I nodded again and hoped that he was right.

At the very least, he was correct about the shelter. The white painted "Public Shelter" sign marked with an arrow appeared as we turned onto the next road. I could see a queue of latecomers anxiously shuffling forward down the pavement toward the door. Mr. Poole pulled us into their number, and we were nearly to the front when an explosion shook the ground. I stumbled, catching myself half on the brick wall and half against his chest. His arm went around me to steady us both.

"I have you. It's okay, I have you," he said.

I pushed myself back to standing and straightened my beret. "Thank you."

The queue moved forward again, and I breathed a sigh of relief for at least being inside.

We were, I knew from the scene around us, woefully underprepared. Families had brought bundles of linens and cases filled with belongings to keep their minds occupied during the long night. A little girl with big dark eyes and tight brown curls clutched a well-loved stuffed bunny as she stared at me. I gave her a little wave, and she ducked her head while her mother smiled tightly and smoothed the child's hair back from her forehead.

"I think the best we can hope for is a spot of wall to lean against," he said.

"So long as we're safe, I'm not planning to complain to management," I told him, and followed him to a corner where the crowd of Londoners was thinner.

"This will have to do," he said.

Mr. Poole shucked off his trench coat and laid it on the floor for us to sit on. I settled in next to him, aware of our arms pressing against one another. Perhaps I should have moved away, but I couldn't quite make myself care. The adrenaline pumping through my veins from our dash after the air raid siren was beginning to subside, and I craved the comfort of someone else's presence.

We sat in silence for a few minutes, watching the stragglers set themselves up across the shelter floor. A woman with three little ones was pulling bundles of wax-wrapped food from a basket. She unscrewed the top of a flask, and I could see steam rising up from it.

"We should have had dinner," I said.

"Pubs like the Bishop's Hat don't serve food," he pointed out.

"No, but we could have grabbed something on the walk back. What I mostly want right now, however, is a cup of tea."

Mr. Poole leaned over. "I don't suppose you have any food in that handbag of yours, do you?"

I unsnapped the top and peered in, knowing that I didn't. "I have a coin purse, comb, my pass, and a book."

"Which book?" he asked.

I pulled out Anthony Berkeley's *The Poisoned Chocolates Case*.

He pulled a face. "More evidence that you are still clinging to the incorrect notion that we produce better detective fiction than the Americans."

"If you're not careful, Mr. Poole, I might start to call your loyalty to king and country into question," I said with a laugh.

"Do you think the Americans will ever join us?" he asked.

The sharp change in conversation drew my attention. "I don't know. If the newspapers can be believed, it seems as though some people in America are determined never to be involved in another war. Would that we had the luxury of such a choice."

"Roosevelt has started sending us arms and other things," he said.

"But that's hardly showing up with troops, is it?" I asked.

He scrubbed a hand over his chin. "I suppose not. After Dunkirk, it does rather feel as though we're alone."

It was the first time that I'd ever heard him express an opinion about the war, and it struck me that his was hardly the "Keep Calm and Carry On" message that the Ministry of Information was trying to tout.

I knew that we couldn't talk about work or the case we were on with all of these people around. It would be too much of a risk and, if the wrong person overheard, it could be just as devastating as the leaks that Mr. Poole was trying to stop.

"What did you do before the war?" I asked.

He glanced at me. "I was a buyer for a wine distributor, believe it or not."

"A wine buyer? And you ordered lager?"

He made a face. "I wouldn't risk the wine in a pub."

"Sage advice."

"I loved my job. My father wanted me to be a barrister, like he is. I went to Oxford and left with a mediocre degree but a great appreciation for wine. I moved to London and managed to talk my way into the business.

"I used to spend every harvest season in France. I would travel all over, from Champagne to Burgundy. I took a few trips to Italy over the years, Germany, even Slovenia."

I immediately switched into French. "How good is your French, Mr. Poole?"

He gave me a small smile. "Not as good as yours, apparently. You sound like a native."

"That would be my mother's influence," I said. "She insisted I was raised in France, even if my father won the argument that I should be born on British soil."

He sighed and said in English, "I hope very much to go back to

France one day once this war is over. I know it won't be the same, but there are people I left behind . . ." He cleared his throat. "Anyway, it feels like a very long time ago."

"My job before the war wasn't nearly as glamorous as yours," I said, offering him a change of subject. "I was in an advertising agency, although you already know that."

"I do."

"It hardly seems fair that you've seen my file and I haven't seen yours," I said.

"There isn't much to tell."

"Oh, I doubt that very much. At this point, any information about you would be a revelation," I said.

He frowned. "What do you mean?"

I shrugged. "I just know very little about you. The wine buying, for instance. And I don't even know if David Poole is your real name."

He gave a laugh. "Why wouldn't it be my real name?"

"I don't know. Perhaps you felt the need to change it for your . . . project," I said, waving a hand around as I looked for the right word to substitute for "investigation."

"I can't lay exclusive claim to it—my father was also a David—but I promise that David Poole is the name on my birth certificate," he said.

A blast rattled the ground under us, pulling cries from many of those around us. Even I let out a little gasp. I hugged my stomach, wishing that I was back in the confines of the Dock. At least there, I felt safe from everything except the rats and the stench.

"It's going to be okay," said Mr. Poole.

Another blast shook us, this one closer. The lights flickered, and I held my breath until they became steady once again.

"I haven't been in an air raid in a shelter where the bombs have been this close," I admitted.

"It's going to be okay," he repeated.

I nodded, but I had my doubts.

"Tell me where you've sheltered when you haven't been on shift," he said.

I swallowed past the fear rising in my throat. "Mr. Rutter owns the large house across the road from Mrs. Jenkins, my landlady. He has a cellar that he outfitted with benches and electric lights. He's even stored foldable card tables down there for people who want to play games. He's sweet on Mrs. Jenkins, so all of us troop over there every time the siren sounds.

"It isn't too bad actually. I know that some people have it a lot worse in terms of damp and flooding and things like that. Instead, we have mugs of very weak tea Mr. Rutter makes on an old camping stove and Juliet from the third floor snoring every night. In that regard, it's rather like the Dock, actually.

"What about you?" I asked, realizing that it wasn't just Mr. Poole's life before the war that I didn't know anything about.

"I go home to a bachelor flat when I'm not working. There's a cellar there too," he said.

"I take it that means that there is no Mrs. Poole?" I ventured.

A shadow crossed his eyes. "Not any longer."

I moved carefully because I wasn't entirely sure that he would be pleased about my familiarity, but I set a hand on his forearm. "I'm sorry."

"Thank you. But what about yourself?"

"I'm unmarried, of course. Women can't work in our office if they aren't."

"And there's no boyfriend or fiancé sending you letters from wherever he's posted?" he asked.

I gave a snort. "Hardly. I am what my best friend, Moira, likes to call 'independently inclined.' Others simply call it being bloody-minded. It is not, I'm reliably informed, a quality that most men look for in a woman."

"That's their loss then." He studied me. "You know, I wouldn't have taken you for the kind who minded what other people think."

"I don't, really."

Maman had never minded. All she'd wanted to do was live a good, happy life. Some might think her a contradiction, a woman who lived for parties as much as she adored her daughter, but to me it made sense. She wanted to soak up as much life as she could. Even Paris had seemed too small to contain her.

I missed her desperately.

"Good." He shifted to settle against the wall a little more comfortably. "Now, I suppose you'd better take that book of yours out. Who knows how long the light will last."

"I beg your pardon?" I asked, shaking my head to clear my mind.

"If you hold it between us, we can probably manage to read the thing at the same time," he said.

"Mr. Poole, are you telling me that you actually want to read a British-authored detective novel?"

"Needs must. And perhaps it's time to dispense with Mr. and Miss. What do you think?" he asked.

I grinned. "I think that I really hope you read as fast as I do, David."

THIRTY-EIGHT

I'd like to pretend that I am the sort of woman who awakens gracefully with dew drops on her lashes or some such romantic nonsense. In reality, I am awful in the mornings before I have a chance to have either a bath or a cup of tea. Preferably both, if I'm being honest.

You can imagine my confusion then when I awoke the next morning in an unfamiliar space, surrounded by dozens of other people, and my face smashed into my colleague's arm.

"Good morning," said David, looking down at me.

I jerked away, blinking rapidly in the electric light. The book we'd been reading slid off my lap and onto the floor.

"What time is it?" I asked, pushing my rumpled hair back out of my face.

"Half past five. We're just waiting for the all clear," he said, gentleman enough not to mention whether or not his arm had gone dead from my resting on it.

I groaned. I knew that my back would likely make me pay for sleeping half upright on the hard ground all night. And if that wasn't enough, I was also going to face all sorts of questions when I returned to the Dock.

"I feel as though I could sleep another ten hours," I said.

"A cup of tea will set you right. We have a big day ahead of us," he said cheerfully.

I squinted at him. "You would be one of those unbearable people who actually enjoys the mornings."

"Pipe down over there!" came a shout from a few feet away. "Some of us are still trying to get a bit of kip!"

Roughly a quarter of an hour later we heard the all clear and people began to rise from their makeshift beds to make their way out into the world. David and I were some of the first out of the shelter, arriving at the CWR by half past six.

We stopped at the bottom of the stairs.

"Have a shower and something to eat and then meet me at half past eight. I'll ask Faylen to come speak to us. I don't want to tip him off too early," said David.

I did not have to be told twice to go to the canteen. I was starving and in desperate need of caffeine.

After breakfast, I slipped into the queue for the showers. I was just coming out, fresh and feeling at least a little more awake, when I ran into Irene. She grinned at me and leaned in. "Your bed was empty all of yesterday night. Where were you?"

"Stuck in an air raid shelter near Covent Garden," I grumped.

Her expression changed. "Are you all right?"

"I'm fine. Just a bit stiff and tired," I said.

"What you need is a bit of fun. Tomorrow night," said Irene.

I frowned in confusion. "What about it?"

"The two of us are going out. It's Saturday! We'll have a night on the town. Dinner, dancing, the works," said Irene with a grin.

"I don't know . . ."

She looped her arm through mine and started toward the Dock. "I won't take no for an answer. We're both off at the same time. That only happens every once in a while."

The last thing I wanted to think about was dressing up to go out dancing, but Irene looked so happy about the idea that I simply nodded. "All right then."

"Oh good! You leave everything to me. I'll make all the arrangements," said Irene. "I knew that we were going to be the best of friends from the first day I saw you in the CWR."

Now, I already have a best friend. It wasn't as though I was opposed to the idea of having more friends, but something about Irene's declaration felt strange to me. A little too eager.

I shook my head. The sleep deprivation was muddling my thinking. Maybe I needed a second cup of tea that morning . . .

"Irene, I meant to ask you something," I said, stopping at the top of the Dock's stairs. "Did the inspectors ask you where you were when Jean was killed?"

Irene frowned. "I told you, remember? I was with Mr. Pearson and Mr. Faylen. They wanted me to put the final touches on a report that was due that day."

"Oh, silly me. Of course you did," I said with a laugh. "I just thought I overheard someone saying that they'd seen Mr. Faylen in the corridor during that time."

"I doubt it, although he did show up last," she said.

"That must have been it. There's been so much going on," I said.

Irene rubbed my arm. "I don't blame you for being a little confused. You must have slept horribly in that shelter."

I sucked in a breath, thinking about waking up pressed against David's arm. "You have no idea."

———

At half past eight, I was seated across the table from Mr. Faylen, David at my side.

"I really don't have time for this. I'm meant to be in a meeting first thing," Mr. Faylen said, smoothing down the front of his navy suit. He no longer wore the agitated expression that had prompted me to hop that bus yesterday evening, but I could tell by the way that he kept fiddling with his clothes that he wasn't entirely comfortable.

"Your colleagues will understand, I'm sure," said David.

"Mr. Faylen, we have a few more questions for you," I started.

"I've already spoken to both of you and to Maxwell and Plaice. I don't know what more I can tell you," he said, drumming his fingers on the table.

I smiled. "Perhaps you can tell me about the Bishop's Hat."

His fingers stopped moving. "The what?"

"The Camden Town pub that you go to in order to meet your bookie," I said.

"I don't know what you're talking about," he said.

"I think you do," said David.

"I wouldn't bother denying it if I was you. We saw you there, Mr. Faylen," I added.

Mr. Faylen looked between the two of us like a trapped animal.

"This is what we think has been happening," I continued. "You like gambling—perhaps it isn't a like so much as a compulsion—but either way, you go to the Bishop's Hat to meet your bookie. You place bets. My guess is that, at some point, your betting becomes out of hand, because you start looking around for a way to pay off your debts. You can't drain your bank account, because what would your family live on, and if anyone in this office were to find out, you would be fired because of the possibility that your debt could be used to turn you into an enemy agent.

"Then you realize that you work in a place where some of the most sensitive information in this war is being handled every single day. That could be sold to help pay down your debts. You make contact with a German agent. The more information you feed them, the more money you make. You're in so deep that you can't stop.

"I also think that Jean Plinkton was connected to your plan somehow. Perhaps she was your intermediary with your German contact, or maybe it was her idea all along and she approached you. Either way, she would go to the Bishop's Hat well away from the CWR to meet you. When she either decided you were no longer useful to her, or she became a threat to maintaining this double life you've been leading, you killed her."

"No," whispered Mr. Faylen, fear clear in his eyes. "No, that's not what happened."

"Then what did happen?" asked David.

"I . . . I have gambled a little. I won so much when I started—beginner's luck maybe. But recently I haven't been so fortunate. I do have debts, but I don't have a German contact. You have that all wrong," he protested, mopping sweat from his brow with his handkerchief.

"Then set my story straight," I said.

He puffed out his ruddy cheeks as though steeling himself for what he was about to tell us.

"A few months ago, Miss Plinkton approached me in the Bishop's Hat," he started. "She made it seem as though it was chance that we were both there, but I know now that she must have followed me there. Stupid of me not to see it at the time, really. She was so easy to talk to. Such a pretty woman. I'd just lost quite a bit of money and I was feeling low and lonely. I couldn't tell my wife what was happening, so I told Miss Plinkton.

"I woke up the next morning, terrified that she would tell someone at work. Instead, the next time I was at the Bishop's Hat, so was she. She sat down across from me in the ladies' lounge and told me that she wanted to help me. She could secure me cash if I did favors for her."

"What sort of favors?" I asked.

He swallowed but then lifted his chin. "She wanted information about what I was working on. She would pay well if I brought her things that were useful."

"What kinds of things?" David asked.

"She wanted to know what memos were being drafted and what policies I had been briefed on. Big, small, at first it didn't seem to matter. I was to write them down when I left the CWR and take them to the Bishop's Hat. There is a telephone booth. Under the telephone table, an envelope of cash would be taped up. I would take out the cash, leave the information, and that was it," said Mr. Faylen.

"Did you ever ask her what she was doing with this information?" I asked.

Mr. Faylen squirmed in his chair, all of the bluster and barking he usually displayed gone. "No."

"You work for the Ministry of War. You were fully aware that you are not meant to let anything leave the CWR. You are not meant to speak about it, write about it, even dream about what you hear or read here. Even your wife and children can't know what you do," said David, his voice rising.

"I didn't think it would do any harm. They were just little things until . . ."

"Until what?" I asked, putting a hand on David's shoulder to try to calm him. It would do us no good if Mr. Faylen stopped talking when he was so close to a confession.

Mr. Faylen dipped his head. "A few months ago, I happened to hear some information that our troops were going to cease operations in Norway. I thought it would be safe enough. It should have been obvious to anyone paying attention that we were drawing down troops. I didn't think it mattered that much."

"That was information about troop movements," said David, his voice a deadly whisper. "That's treason."

"I didn't do it!" protested Mr. Faylen. "In fact, I didn't go to the Bishop's Hat that week. The next day, Miss Plinkton cornered me and demanded to know what had happened. I told her that I didn't want anything to do with this any longer and she threatened me. She said just what you did—that what I was doing was treason—and she would turn me in if I stopped feeding her information."

"Is that why you killed her?" I asked.

"I didn't kill her!" he cried, his eyes bulging out as his face went an even brighter shade of red.

"Mr. Faylen, you have to see this from our perspective. Miss Plinkton threatened your life, your livelihood, your family. Who has a better motivation than you?" asked David.

"It wasn't me," he insisted.

"Where were you when she was killed?" I asked.

Mr. Faylen looked down, and I knew that his alibi was a lie.

"I left the CWR to use the telephone booth. I rang my bookie. My wife's birthday was last Tuesday, and I knew that I needed to be home or there would be Hell to pay. I was trying to arrange things so that I could pay him at a later date," he said.

"So you lied about your alibi? You were not actually with Mr. Pearson and Miss Travers?" I asked.

"I was there for a little while and then I made an excuse, saying I had left a supporting document on my desk," he stumbled to say. "You have to believe me. I did not kill Jean."

There was a knock on the door, and Maxwell and Plaice entered. They nodded to David and me and then Sergeant Maxwell said, "Harold Faylen, you are being arrested on suspicion of treason and murder."

"I didn't do it!" Mr. Faylen cried, trying to yank himself free when the two inspectors hauled him up. "I didn't do it!"

"I suggest that you keep quiet then," said Sergeant Maxwell. "Besides, you'll have a long time to think about things where you're going. Corporal?"

Corporal Plaice clipped a set of handcuffs on the man's wrists and steered him out of the room, leaving Sergeant Maxwell with David and me.

"Miss Redfern, I owe you an apology," Sergeant Maxwell started.

I raised a brow.

"I understand from Mr. Poole here that you have been integral in uncovering this traitor. Clearly I underestimated you, although I suggest that in the future you leave the policing to the professionals," he said.

I gave him a thin smile. "Thank you for your suggestion."

I had no intention of even considering it.

Sergeant Maxwell nodded. "Poole." Then he left.

"Well, your first murder case solved and your first mole uncovered. How do you feel?" David asked.

I stared at the open door. "I don't know."

"It's a bit anti-climactic in the end, isn't it?" he asked.

"I suppose it is," I agreed. But that wasn't it. A man might be in handcuffs, but I couldn't help the feeling that we'd missed something—another puzzle piece—and I needed to figure out what it was before I could be satisfied.

THIRTY-NINE

The strange thing about solving a murder is that, once it is over, life returns to normal. Rarely did the writers that I read detail *that* aspect of a detective's life. Instead, they focus only on the glamour of the case.

Naturally, rumors of Mr. Faylen's arrest spread through the CWR like proverbial wildfire. By lunchtime, the canteen was unusually full and, had she been on shift, I suspected even Patricia would have sat with the women from the typing pool so that she didn't miss out on one bit of information.

"I heard that he tried to run and it took three Royal Marines to stop him," said Cathy breathlessly.

"It was two Royal Marines and that handsome Mr. Poole," said Rachel with great authority.

"Ladies," Caroline admonished them, "that is enough. And it was the investigators who did it."

Rachel turned to me. "You were there, weren't you?"

I simply nodded, not entirely sure that I wanted the depth of my participation in apprehending Mr. Faylen on display right at that moment.

"What happened?" Rachel asked.

"Oh, leave her alone," said Irene sharply. When everyone's attention turned to her, she sank back in her seat a bit. "I just think it's awful. Mr. Faylen selling secrets. Someone *we* worked with."

"I never would have thought he would be the kind," said Cathy.

"Everyone has a price," said Irene.

"I couldn't be bought," said Caroline with her chin in the air.

Irene turned her sharp, dark eyes on her. "Yes, you could. Maybe not with money, but if someone dug deep enough, they could find the one thing that would make you lie, cheat, and steal because *everyone* has a price."

"Irene, I only meant—"

Irene stood up abruptly, cutting Caroline off. "I'm sorry, I just— It's all very distressing."

She turned and rushed out of the canteen. We all sat there for a moment until I said, "I'll just go check on her."

I found Irene in one of the alcoves by the typing pool. She was breathing deeply, clearly trying to calm herself.

"Are you all right?" I asked.

She gave me a watery smile. "I shouldn't have lost my temper. Sometimes I just can't stand the hypocrisy of people. Mr. Faylen has a family. He has a life and people who care about him outside of the CWR, and we're all sitting there ready to rip him to shreds. I'm sure that whatever he did, he did it for a reason."

A thought struck me then, so obvious that it was incredible I hadn't seen it before. "Irene, is Mr. Faylen your lover?"

She stared at me and then burst out laughing.

"Oh, Evelyne! Oh, I needed that. Thank you," she said, wiping away tears from the corners of her eyes. "No, I'd never let Mr. Faylen near me with a ten-foot pole.

"Look, I've booked us a table at Café de Paris for tomorrow night. My treat. We'll have dinner and then dance with whomever we like. It will be just the thing to shake all of this gloom off, don't you think?" Irene asked.

She looked at me with such hope in her eyes, I could hardly say no.

———

The following evening, after a long, uneventful end to my shift at the CWR, I hurried home to ready myself for Irene's evening out.

Moira waved me a hello on her way out the door, dressed in my rose bias-cut silk evening gown.

"Where are you going?" I asked, my front door key still in my hand.

"James is taking me out to the theater. We might end up at Café de Paris later, if you'd like to come along."

"Actually I'll already be there," I said.

Moira looked taken aback. "Are you going out with a gentleman and not telling me, Evelyne Redfern?"

I pulled a face. "No, it's one of the women I work with."

"Then I will see you there." She gave me a little wave and turned for the door but couldn't resist tossing over her shoulder one final opinion. "If you wear the black and gold, put your hair up in a roll at the back of your neck. It always looks best that way."

M oira was right, as she so often is. With my hair off of my neck, the dress's deep back V looked stunning.

I threw my mother's arctic fox wrap over my shoulders and hurried out of the door just in time to catch the bus and make it to Café de Paris in time for Irene's dinner booking.

She met me, her chocolate eyes glowing brightly in the electric lights illuminating the lobby.

"I'm so glad you've come," she said, gripping my arm. "I've spent half the day getting ready."

She swayed a bit, and I raised a brow. "Did you have a drink before you came?"

She giggled. "Just one or two. What good is a night out if you can't have *fun*?"

Before I could answer, we were being whisked away to our table by a maître d' in a perfectly cut dinner jacket. I thought he would lead us to one of the more intimate small tables for two on either side of the room, but instead he steered us toward a floor-side table where two RAF pilots rose as we approached.

"Evelyne Redfern, meet Squadron Leaders Mitchell and Beckett," she said proudly.

"How do you do?" I asked, assessing the two men and wondering where on earth Irene had dug up a pair of squadron leaders, neither of whom, I noticed, was wearing a wedding band.

"Gentlemen, Evelyne is my very good friend from work, so I expect you to be utterly charming to her," said Irene.

Mitchell grinned. "We will certainly do our best, Miss Travers."

"Oh, none of that. Call me Irene," she laughed. "We're friends here, aren't we?"

Despite my reservations, the men proved to be the perfect dinner companions. Irene clearly had her sights set on Mitchell, which left Beckett to me. The squadron leader did all the proper things, asking me about my job but not probing with more questions after I told him I was a secretary in a dreary building in Whitehall, forever filing paper. It turned out that Beckett had an easy laugh and a way with a story and, if I hadn't been so distracted, I might have actually enjoyed his company. However, I couldn't help keeping an eye on Irene the entire time. She drank everything placed in front of her, and the longer the night went on the more animated she became.

When finally the dancing started in earnest, Beckett dutifully led me on to the dance floor. We were halfway through a foxtrot when he said, "You're worried about your friend."

"I am," I admitted. "I think she's had more to drink than she realizes."

He gave me a look that told me he suspected that Irene had drunk exactly as much as she'd planned, but instead he said, "Would you like me to make an excuse to pull Mitchell aside so that you two can have a few minutes together?"

I smiled at him. "That would be wonderful, thank you."

He was as good as his word too. After the song was over, he intercepted Mitchell as he and Irene made their way back to our table.

"I heard a rumor that there are bottles of Bollinger '28 stored away somewhere on the premises. Let's see if we can convince the maître d' to open some for these lovely ladies," Beckett said, clapping his friend on the shoulder.

Whether Mitchell bought the excuse to leave Irene and me alone or not, he went along with it, and soon I was seated at the table again with my pink-cheeked, glassy-eyed colleague.

"Didn't I do well in finding those two?" she asked.

"They're certainly perfect gentlemen," I said.

She tossed back an inch of champagne that remained in the glass in front of her. "It's good to be reminded from time to time what it's like to be treated like a lady."

"Irene," I said, pressing a hand to her arm to stop her from making inroads on my glass, "what's the matter?"

"I don't know what you mean," she said. "I'm having a good time."

"Are you certain? Because it seems to me that you're chasing after Squadron Leader Mitchell when I know that you already have a gentleman. Did you two have a fight?"

"Yes." Irene's face crumpled. "Yes, and I don't know what to do about it."

"Is it something you can fix when you're clearheaded in the morning?" I asked.

"I don't know!" she wailed. "It's impossible!"

I glanced around, wondering if anyone would notice the woman sobbing into her evening gloves, but the music drowned her out and all eyes were on the dance floor anyway. "Perhaps it's for the best."

"What do you mean?" she asked fiercely.

"You did say that your fellow is married," I said.

"He doesn't care about his wife. Not really."

"Irene," I said softly.

Irene's eyes filled with tears. "I know. I know. I sound like every other mistress who ever was. I promise it didn't start like that."

"When did you start seeing each other?" I asked.

"Oh, it's been months now. I swear I just thought it would all be a bit of fun to help with everything awful in the world, but now . . ." She gave a miserable, shaky sigh. "He was so charming at first. He told me how beautiful I was, how he couldn't stop thinking about me. He kept asking me to dinner. 'Just dinner,' he said. But it wasn't just dinner. Of course it wasn't.

"I refuse to feel bad about that, though. It was so romantic, and I really think he was head-over-heels for me. You can't fake that. He would send flowers to my room, and take me out for these long, wonderful walks along the Embankment at night. But in the last few weeks, things have changed."

"How have they changed?" I asked as the band struck up a new song.

She sucked in a breath. "His wife became suspicious at the beginning of the summer, so he let a flat away from Central London where we could meet. At first, I thought it was all very daring, but the reality is it's a horrible, cramped little place with nothing but a bed and a gas ring in it. The only place he'll ever take me to now is a grotty pub called the White Horse Tavern across the way. He says that there's too much of a risk that we might be seen and he wants to save my reputation. He worries that his wife will divorce him and I'll be labeled as an adulteress in court and lose my job.

"Oh, I don't know, Evelyne. What am I doing? The only present he's ever given me was this bracelet," she said, holding out her arm to show me the gold bangle she always wore. "Oh, and a book about a horrible man who marries a woman he probably really hates and keeps her locked up in a house where she doesn't know anyone. It's hardly the gift you give the woman you claim is your shining star."

A book sounded like a fine present to me, but I suppose to each her own.

"If he makes you this unhappy, why don't you leave him?" I asked.

Fear crept into Irene's expression. "I can't do that," she whispered over the blast of the brass section.

"Why not?" I pressed.

"I just can't." She gripped my hand. "Evelyne, you must promise me that you won't tell anyone about this. And don't ask me again why I won't leave. I can't bear to talk about it."

I opened my mouth to protest, but Mitchell stepped into my field of view.

"We are happy to report that we have secured the best champagne in the house, ladies, and it's on its way," he promised.

Behind his friend, Beckett mouthed an apology to me.

Irene quickly pressed at the outer corners of her eyes, eliminating any trace of the tears she'd just spilled. Then she pasted a bright smile on her face and turned to face the RAF man. "I think that's just the thing! Dance with me, will you?"

Mitchell swept her away on the dance floor, and I knew that I would find out no more from Irene that evening.

FORTY

"E vie."

I groaned and tried to roll away from my name.

"Evie!" Moira insisted, shaking me from my half-slumber.

"Oh God." I pressed the heel of my hand to my forehead. A headache pulsed there, at the base of my neck, everywhere really. My mouth felt as though someone had stuffed it with cotton wool, and my stomach was more churned up than the English Channel.

I was, undeniably, hungover.

"Moira, I am dying," I announced.

"You aren't dying, darling. You just drank too much champagne. It's a good thing you didn't wake Mrs. Jenkins up elephanting up the stairs yesterday night. Or rather this morning," she said. "Anyway, it's time you were out of bed."

"I don't want to," I grumbled, petulant as a child.

Out of my half-cracked eye I could see her plant her hands on her hips. "I don't care if you want to or not, you're going to wake up because there's a man here asking for you."

"A man?" I asked, hoping that I hadn't done something stupid like promise to marry Squadron Leader Beckett after he gallantly pulled my high heel out of a deep crack in the pavement I'd accidentally stepped into last night. Thanks to Beckett and Mitchell's liberation of the Café de Paris's best champagne, the details of the night were rather hazy.

"A man. Tall, dark, and handsome," said Moira.

"Who?"

My friend arched her brow. "Rather interestingly, he says his name is David Poole."

I bolted up in bed and then groaned at how the sudden movement simultaneously made my head pound and the earth shift off its axis.

"Apply pressure, darling!" Moira cried in encouragement.

I pressed a palm to my right temple. "What is he doing here?"

"Why don't you go downstairs and find out?" she suggested. I began to slide out of bed, so Moira helpfully added, "You might want to pull some more appropriate clothes on."

I looked down and realized I'd fallen asleep in the black and gold dress, the tulle probably pressing a horrible honeycomb pattern into my skin by now. "The drinks at the Café de Paris are lethal."

"Only if you consume them in volume," she remarked as I flung open the wardrobe door, nearly pulling the thing off its hinges.

"I didn't see you there yesterday, did I?" I asked.

She shook her head. "James and I had an argument after the theater."

"What about?" I asked, peeling off my dress and slip and pulling on fresh undergarments.

"He objects to the idea of a woman working after she's married," said Moira.

"What a beast. Did you tell him of your plan to make it big in films and then move to Hollywood when this wretched war is over?" I asked without a bit of irony. I knew that many people had aspirations for stardom, but I truly believed that Moira had the talent and the tenacity for it. The fact that she looked like the very manifestation of the goddess Diana didn't hurt.

"He said that he thought that would be all well and good before I was married, but then I should be focusing on our children," she said. "I told him it was rather presumptuous to think that I would be having any children with him."

"You're better off without him," I told her, yanking a pale yellow dress over my head. On went a cardigan as I stuffed my feet into shoes. I ran a comb over my half-mashed curls and then hooked them into a snood.

"How do I look?" I asked.

Moira frowned and reached over to her bedside table to pluck up a gold tube of lipstick. She tossed it to me. "Pale as a ghost. If you put this on, at least it will look intentional."

I twisted up the bloodred lipstick, slicked it on, and realized she was right as she so often was. It distracted from the fact that I looked as though I'd come in with the milk delivery.

"Right. I'm going down," I announced.

"Godspeed, darling," she said, opening up one of the copies of *PhotoPlay* that an American cousin sent her every few months.

I rattled down the stairs to the ground floor and walked into the back sitting room Mrs. Jenkins allowed us to use for guests. David was sitting, coat and hat across his lap, fending off the attentions of Marjorie and Clara from the first floor.

"Mr. Poole," I said, shooting the other two girls a glare. "I'm so sorry to have kept you waiting."

He stood, and Marjorie and Clara both scowled but gave their excuses before slinking off. I couldn't blame them really. Men under the age of sixty were in short supply around London these days.

"Why are you in my boardinghouse?" I asked as soon as we were alone—with the door open because Mrs. Jenkins likes to remind us that she runs a respectable home for ladies.

"There's been another leak," he said.

"What?"

"There's been another leak," he repeated.

"Could it have been information that Mr. Faylen passed on before his arrest but only just made it over to Germany?" I asked.

The grim line of his mouth told me everything I needed to know before he even said, "It was information that only came through the office on Friday afternoon, hours after Mr. Faylen was arrested."

I sank down onto the sofa and muttered, "I was right."

"Right about what, Evelyne?" he asked.

I lifted my head. "Something about Mr. Faylen's arrest felt . . . incomplete."

"He admitted to handing secrets off to Jean in exchange for money," he said.

"But why would he confess to smuggling information out of work but not admit to killing Jean? He's already committed treason. If he were to be found guilty, he would hang regardless."

"You think that there's something we missed?" he asked.

"We looked for the simplest answer, found it, and stopped. But what if this case is much more complicated than we ever anticipated?" I asked.

"What do you mean?"

"Jean must have been working in concert with someone else." I looked up at him. "David, what if the killer and the mole are both still active and all we've done is scratch the surface of these cases?"

He let out a long breath. "Then we need to re-examine everyone, and fast."

"There have been two teams of investigators on this case for days. Whoever it is will be cocky enough that they think they won't be caught even after Mr. Faylen has been arrested. I think we need new information."

"We've already interviewed everyone. Maxwell and Plaice have interviewed everyone. They were just as satisfied with the arrest yesterday as I was," he pointed out.

"Then we need to take another approach."

"Who?" he asked.

"Not who. Where." I stood up. "Give me two minutes to grab my handbag and my coat."

"Evelyne, where are we going?" he asked.

I did my best to pull myself up to my full height and don some of the dignity I'd lost in my hungover state.

"There is something I have to tell you," I said.

"What?" he asked.

"I've been pursuing another line of inquiry, and I believe that it may have just become our last hope of solving this case," I said.

"What line of inquiry?" he asked.

"Do you have your car with you?" I asked, ignoring his question.

"Yes, but Evelyne—"

"Stay here," I ordered him, skirting around the door to fetch my things from my room.

To David's credit, he didn't move.

FORTY-ONE

David's car was parked at the bottom of the road. We climbed in, and as soon as the doors were shut and no one could hear us, he asked, "Where do you want to go?"

Instead, I reached into my handbag, pulled out my list of Grove House locations from inside my notebook, and passed it to him.

He stared at the paper with a furrowed brow. "You want me to drive to Southwest London?"

"Before the inspectors came, when you left me with Jean's body, I saw a bloodstained scrap of paper trapped under her. On it was written 'Grove House SW' in light red pencil. I suspect that by the time Maxwell and Plaice managed to examine Jean's body, the blood had marred the writing. I don't think the inspectors know anything about it," I confessed.

David stared at the list of addresses for a good, long while. "Evelyne . . ."

"I know," I said.

"You could be thrown in prison for withholding evidence from an active investigation."

"I know."

"What were you thinking?" he asked, his voice raising now.

I put my hand on my hip, which admittedly lost a bit of its effect given that I was seated. "I think that the real question that we must concern ourselves with is what are we going to do about it now?"

With a low grumble, he reached over and popped open the car's glove compartment to extract an *A to Z*. "Do I want to know how you found these addresses?"

"No," I said honestly.

"I thought so. Have you visited any of these yet?"

"Yes. The Roehampton and Battersea addresses. One was a teaching college and the other was a house that's been broken up into flats. I didn't find anything I thought was relevant at either of them."

He flipped to the back of the map book and then, finding the entry he was looking for, thumbed ahead in the pages. Then he shoved the *A to Z* at me.

"Hold that. I might need directions. I don't know my way around south of the river as well as I do north," he said, turning over the ignition once again.

I peered down at the map. "We're going to Conifer Gardens in Streatham?"

"Yes," he said.

"Excellent," I said, rather pleased with myself, all in all.

Before he drove off, however, David turned in his seat again to look me square on. "Evelyne, is there anything else relevant to the case that you think I should know?"

I shook my head.

I knew too much about too many things, but I still couldn't put the pieces together, sorting out what mattered to our two investigations. I was grasping at straws, hoping that something on this list Jocelyn had given me would give me a sign that I was on the right path.

"Good," he said. "Then let's hope that Grove House in Streatham has some answers."

———

It is incredible how, even during a war with petrol rationing, it can be impossible to find a parking space in some London neighborhoods.

After a quick drive down Conifer Gardens with no success, David managed to park the car two roads over. It was a short walk back to the tree-lined street. No bombs had fallen here, which I'm certain the residents must have been grateful for, and as a result it was pleasantly quiet. With an old man with a cane and a woman pushing a pram the only people out for a walk, I could almost imagine that the war wasn't on.

"Here it is," said David, stopping in front of a short block of flats. "Grove House, 1882" was sunk into the concrete block framed by brickwork above the door. It looked as though the building was spread over three stories plus a set of basement windows that likely once were for servants but now probably made up flats all their own.

I took in the chipped white paint on the front door and the cracked tiles that made up the single step up to the ground floor. "It doesn't look like much, does it?"

"It's modest at best," he agreed.

"I'm going to see if I recognize any names," I said.

We both marched up the short front path to the door where the bells for the flats all sat in a neat row. There were eight buttons, two flats per floor with two units on the lower ground floor, as I'd guessed.

"Carter, Smythe, Wells," David began to read off. When he finished the list he looked at me. "Anything?"

I shook my head.

"What now?" he asked.

"We ring the bells and ask if anyone knows a woman named Jean Plinkton," I said.

I leaned on the first one and then stepped back to wait.

"The building needs a little bit of care, but it's not a bad road, is it?" David asked, peering around at the collection of two-story houses that lined either side of Grove House. "I suppose it depends on how you feel about having a pub on the corner, though."

"A pub?" I asked.

He pointed over my shoulder in the opposite direction from where we'd come. I could just see the edge of a redbrick pub with "Real Ales" painted in yellow on a black sign that matched the top of the wooden window frames.

My pulse quickened. I didn't want my instincts to be right, but in that moment I knew. I ran down the garden path and back out into the road. A tree rose up, blocking my view of the pub from the pavement.

"Evelyne, where are you going?" shouted David after me.

I ignored him until the pub's sign came into full view and I skidded to a stop.

It was of a knight sitting on the back of a noble steed that reared up on two legs, and painted above the illustration in bold letters was the name: "White Horse Tavern."

My stomach sank.

David stopped next to me. "Evelyne."

"How long do you think it will take us to return to the CWR?" I asked. "No, wait. Irene is still off work today."

"Irene Travers?" he asked.

"Yes. We need to find out where she lives. Right now."

Despite how friendly Irene had been to me when I'd arrived at the CWR, I knew very little about her life outside of the bunker. Then again, I knew very little about anyone's life in the real world. We were merely people who had been thrown together by a war we were all just trying to survive.

"There was a telephone booth on the main road near where we left the car. Give me a few minutes, and I can find that out," David said. "But Evelyne, why do we need to find Irene?"

"Because, last night Irene Travers told me that she was having an affair with a married man. Only it's not going as well as it once was. The only place he takes her these days is a horrible pub—"

"Called the White Horse Tavern," he finished for me.

"I think that Jean found out, and she was blackmailing Irene."

"But that doesn't explain why we had a leak yesterday after Mr. Faylen was arrested," said David. "Unless Jean and Irene teamed up to ferry information out of the CWR."

"Irene hated Jean. She made that very clear when she was showing me around the office on my first day."

"Maybe Irene turned on Jean . . ."

"Which would give her more than enough motive to kill," I said.

David set his jaw. "There's a telephone booth back by the car. Let's go."

FORTY-TWO

I paced outside of the telephone booth as David placed first one and then another call. When he hung up for a second time and pushed the glass door open, he announced, "I have the address."

"Where does she live?" I asked.

"A room in Parsons Green. Purser's Cross Road," he said.

We rushed back to the car, and David navigated our way north across Wandsworth Bridge. Finally, we crossed into Parsons Green. Big white houses surrounded the picturesque, sleepy green, but we passed those places and turned onto a small road of short, squat terraced houses.

"It's number 14," said David, peering out of the car window.

"There." I pointed to a small black door in the middle of the row.

David swung the car into park, and I was out almost as soon as the engine was off. There was no doorbell, so I knocked loudly.

No one answered.

I knocked again, harder and more insistent this time.

"Hold your horses, will you!" came a muffled shout from behind the door, which a moment later swung open.

A woman, shaped much like the houses on the road, filled the door. She wore a calico housecoat and slippers, but her hair was immaculately marcelled in a style that had gone out with the Charleston. Her scarlet lips twisted down in a frown as she raked her eyes over me and then David.

"Hello, we're looking for Irene Travers," I said.

The woman crossed her arms. "What has she done then?"

"Are you her mother?" David asked.

The woman barked a laugh. "Her mother? That's a good one. I'm her landlady, Mrs. Millicen." The woman's eyes flicked back to David. "Normally I don't allow men to visit."

"We need to speak to Miss Travers on a matter of great importance," I pushed. "I promise, we will be brief."

After a moment, the woman jerked her head in the direction of the stairs. "All right then. Two flights up and the door on your right. I can't promise what kind of state you'll find her in though. She came back at five o'clock in the morning, stumbling around. It's a wonder the entire neighborhood didn't wake up. This will be her last week here, I can tell you that. This is a respectable house."

We started to make our way up, even as the landlady shouted, "Respectable!"

The door we'd been instructed to approach was firmly shut to the world despite the fact that it was already nearly one o'clock.

I knocked.

"Not now, Mrs. Millicen," came a groan from the other side.

I tried the handle. It popped open, revealing a darkened room with all of the blackout curtains still drawn.

"Irene, I'm coming in," I said.

The figure in the bed popped up and then moaned. "Evelyne? What are you doing here?"

Behind me David flicked on the light.

Irene threw an arm over her eyes. "Oh! Turn that off, won't you?"

The illuminated room was a tip. Clothing spewed out of the wardrobe and onto the floor, her rayon dressing gown I recognized from the Dock haphazardly draped over the foot of the bed and stacks of magazines covering every surface. At least there was a lone book sitting on the nightstand, stoneware tea mugs abandoned all around it.

"Irene, we need to speak to you," I said.

"We?" Irene uncovered her face. "Mr. Poole! What are you doing here? You can't be here. Mrs. Millicen will throw me out."

"It sounds as though she's already prepared to do that," he said, looking around.

Irene fell back onto the pillows. "She threatens that every week, but every week she has me back. She wants the rent, and she's too lazy to let to anyone else. Not that anyone else would put up with her."

"Irene, we need to speak to you about Jean," I said.

"Why? Mr. Faylen was arrested," she said.

"Irene, I know about the blackmail," I said.

Her face paled. "What do you mean?"

"We know that Jean was blackmailing Mr. Faylen, procuring information from the CWR and passing it along to the Germans. We think that you were involved," I said.

"That's ridiculous," said Irene, her hands twisting in her bedsheets.

"Did Jean find out about your affair and threaten to use that against you? Is that why you hated her so much? Is that why you killed her?" I asked.

She stared at me for a beat, and then, to my surprise, began to laugh. "You think *that* is what happened? Oh, Evelyne, you have it all wrong."

"We know for a fact that Jean was threatening people in the CWR and—"

"Jean wasn't blackmailing me. She was my competition," she said, cutting me off.

"Your competition?" I asked.

She rolled her eyes. "Jean was having an affair too, with the same man, right under my nose."

Suddenly, things began to make sense. Irene's hatred of Jean. The competition I'd seen in her eyes when I'd returned from my first meeting acting as a stenographer.

"It's Mr. Pearson. You were both having an affair with Mr. Pearson," I said slowly.

"You should really win a prize for that one," said Irene. "All of this time, and no one else figured it out. It took me long enough to put two and two together about him and Jean, but I did in the end."

"He would request Jean for meetings so that it wouldn't seem strange for them to be seen together," I said. "He did the same with you."

"He used our different shifts to keep us apart. It worked for a time too. Of course, it wasn't just in the office. He'd find ways to see us outside of work as well," she said.

"Grove House in Streatham," David said.

Her expression became guarded, as though she'd only just remembered he was there. "No one knows about that place. He lets it under another name."

"Did he take Jean to Grove House too?" I asked, ignoring her question.

Irene sniffed. "Yes."

"Irene, you told me yesterday night that you can't leave him. Why?" I asked, cautiously taking a seat on the edge of her bed.

Her defiance melted into devastation. "I just can't," she whispered.

"This is important. If he has something that he's holding over you, perhaps we can help," I urged.

She shook her head. "I just— That is—" Irene's shoulders sagged. "Photographs."

"Photographs?" I asked.

She nodded miserably. "He persuaded me to let him take pictures. When I was . . . well, you know."

"Nude?" I asked.

She bit her lip. "He promised me that they were only for him, so that he could look at them when we were apart. As soon as he had them though, he began to change. He didn't call me to assist him as often and then when we did see each other all of the romance was gone. He would hardly look at me after we'd—after we'd made love."

"When was this?" David asked.

"About two weeks before Jean's murder," said Irene. "I suspected he might have another woman on the go, so I followed him. We were supposed to meet at Grove House, but last minute he told me that he couldn't make it. Only he'd acted so strangely that I decided to wait there and see if he showed up. I saw him walk up to the building's door. There was a woman with him, but I couldn't make out her face. I waited around all evening until they came out again. That's when I saw Jean," she said.

"Did she know that you'd seen her?" I asked.

"I don't think so. She never mentioned anything until I confronted her."

"When was this?" David asked.

"About a week before Evelyne started work," she said.

"What did you say to her?" I asked.

"I asked her how long she'd been seeing Lawrence. She told me that it had been months, and she'd known about me the entire time. She said they were laughing about it behind my back," said Irene, tears beginning to threaten to spill over. "She didn't even sound upset. She was smug."

"Smug?" I asked.

She nodded. "She told me that I didn't matter. He would always come back to her. I thought that was rich coming from a woman having an affair with a married man. I can see now that he wouldn't have left his wife for either of us."

No. A man like Lawrence Pearson would have continued on with his life, his wife at home and his mistresses elsewhere. I'd seen my own father do it to *Maman* until *Maman* decided enough was enough—no matter how much she loved him.

"What did you do after you talked to Jean?" I asked.

"Nothing. I didn't do anything. I knew he wouldn't choose me. And I couldn't leave him. Those photographs . . ."

"Did you send Jean a note threatening her?" I asked. "And another with 'Grove House' written on it?"

Irene's eyes went wide. "How did you know about those?"

"They were found among Jean's things," I said.

Irene didn't speak.

"Where were you really on the afternoon when Jean was killed?" David asked.

"And don't tell me that you were with Mr. Faylen," I warned.

Irene opened her mouth and then shut it again. When finally she spoke, she said, "I did leave a note for Jean among her things in the Dock earlier that week, but I didn't kill her. I swear."

"Where were you last Saturday between two and three o'clock?" I asked. "The truth this time."

Irene lifted her head and set her jaw. "I was with Mr. Pearson. I think you can imagine that we were not editing a document."

David cleared his throat behind me, but I leaned in to grab Irene's hand. As I did, my eyes slid over to the book sitting on her bedside table.

"Irene, I want you to listen to me very carefully," I said quickly. "Did Jean or Mr. Pearson ever ask you to do anything that breaks security protocols?"

"Like what?" she asked.

"Remove anything from the CWR? Or tell him information from meetings you've been in or typing you've done?" I asked.

She stood up abruptly, the sheets falling away from her to reveal a peach-colored slip trimmed in tattered lace. "I can't believe you would ask me that. I would never do that."

She gestured so widely that she knocked one of the tea mugs, sending it teetering dangerously on the edge of her bedside table. I jolted forward to catch it, just as she did, my hand bumping the book and revealing the title. *Rebecca*.

Irene met my eyes, fear creeping into them.

"Irene," I murmured. "What else did he make you do? If you tell us, we might be able to help."

She jerked away from me, wrapping her arms around her midsection, and whispered, "I think that it's time for you to leave."

She turned away from us, her shoulders beginning to shake.

"We'll leave you a telephone number where we can be reached. If you change your mind," I said, turning to David. Without me having to ask, he produced his notebook and pencil and scribbled down a Whitehall exchange. He placed it on top of the book, and we retreated.

As soon as David and I were out of the room and heading down the stairs, he whispered, "Something isn't right here."

"I know," I whispered back. "I'll tell you everything, but not here."

FORTY-THREE

As soon as we were in the car, David asked, "What is it?"

"Did you notice the book on her bedside table?" I asked. "It was a copy of *Rebecca*, covered in tea mugs." I shook my head. "Horrible treatment for a book."

"Isn't that the book that the inspectors found in Jean's things?" he asked, turning out onto the main road.

"Yes. Stop here," I ordered. As soon as he pulled up to the curb, I opened the door and climbed out, stopping only to lean down and say, "I need you to stay here for a few minutes. Watch the road. If Irene comes out, follow her."

"Where will you be?" he asked.

"I'm going to the bookshop," I called, slamming the door behind me.

I hurried across the roads as quickly as a woman in low heels could to the bookshop I'd spotted on the green as we drove into Parsons Green. A small bell on the top of the door dinged to announce my arrival, and a short man with a few strands of gray hair stretching over his shining pate looked up from the book he was reading behind the counter.

"Hello, Madam. May I help you?" he asked.

"I'm looking for a copy of *Rebecca*," I said, trying to keep from gasping after my near sprint that constituted the most vigorous exercise I'd had in months.

"Ah, I'm always pleased to meet a fellow reader who knows exactly what she wishes to purchase, although of course there is a great deal of charm in browsing." He slid off his stool and rounded the counter to approach a bank of shelves marked "Fiction" with a little handwritten sign. "Yes, we have Miss du Maurier's novel here."

He pulled the book off the shelf—the same edition as Irene had. "Would you like me to hold it for you while you look around?"

"I'm afraid I'm already late coming back from luncheon," I lied.

"Of course, of course, my dear," he said.

I waited with barely contained impatience as he wrapped the book in brown paper and twine and then collected my money.

"Thank you!" I called out, promising myself that if I was ever in Parsons Green again, I would stop off at this little bookshop to give it the time and attention it deserved.

It started to rain on my way back to the car. I had no umbrella, and I'd foolishly left the house without my hat. By the time I wrenched open the door to David's car, I'm certain that I looked a state, but I hardly cared.

"I have it," I said, holding the book up triumphantly before tearing off the paper.

"What is this all about?" he asked.

"When I went dancing with Irene, she drank too much and began to tell me things she probably shouldn't have. She said that the man who she was having an affair with has only ever given her two things: a bracelet and a book. She described it to me as a book about a man who marries a woman and keeps her locked away in a house.

"I knew it sounded familiar. *Jane Eyre* has the most famous wife locked away in a house, but that isn't really how someone who has read *Jane Eyre* would describe the story. They'd mention the attic. Instead, I think Irene was speaking about a much more modern book." I held up the edition of *Rebecca*. "I think Mr. Pearson gave her a copy of *Rebecca*, just like he gave one to Jean."

"But what's the significance of *Rebecca*?"

I smiled in triumph. "I think that the list I found hidden in Jean's mattress is a book code."

"Evelyne," said David slowly, "I think you might be a genius."

"I'm so glad you've finally realized it," I said, pulling my notebook out of my handbag to flick through the pages.

"I'm also beginning to think that you're in danger of beginning to rival Corporal Plaice in your reliance on your notebook," he said.

I shot him a look. "What do you know about book codes?"

"The book acts as a key. I believe it usually requires not only the correct edition of the book but also the page on which the code starts," he said.

"So the question remains, if you were Lawrence Pearson, what page would you choose?"

I closed my eyes, thinking back to our conversation with Mr. Pearson. He was a proud man, egotistical. The sort who was confident enough that he could have affairs with two women who worked in the same typing pool. He would have chosen something significant to himself.

My eyes flew open and I flipped through *Rebecca* until I reached page 272. "Let's try this."

"Why that page?" he asked.

"Mr. Pearson told us that he was held in a prisoner-of-war camp during the last war for two hundred and seventy-two days. He was very particular about it."

"Here, give me that," said David, gesturing to my notebook and pencil. I passed them to him, and he wrote down the alphabet on a clean page.

"The first letter on this page is 'L.'" He wrote an "A" under the "L." "Then it's an 'A' so that becomes 'B.' 'R' becomes 'C,'" he murmured, carrying on until he had the vowels and most of the alphabet. Then he pulled out his own notebook and flipped to the page where he'd written down the code. Methodically, he penciled in the corresponding letters:

IDHBCGPDTEBMGP

"That can't be right," he said.

I stared down at the book. If it wasn't letters and where they sat sequentially perhaps . . .

"What happens if you try the first letter of each line of text?" I asked.

David scribbled the letters down as I read them out.

"I think that's enough," he announced when I was two pages in.

This time, as he began to write down the corresponding letters to Jean's code, words appeared:

faylengambling
wilkesdebt?

ireneaffair
cathygermanmother
patricialesbian
pearsontreason

"Bloody Hell," David breathed out.

"It's a blackmail list," I said.

He frowned. "Why is Pearson on that list if he's the one who gave her the book and presumably taught her the code?"

"I think Mr. Pearson recruited Jean, just like he recruited Irene. He gave them the books and told them what to do, gathering information and encoding it to pass along to him," I said.

"Why recruit two of them?" David asked.

"Maybe he was hedging his bets if one or the other of them refused or was transferred to another department. Or maybe he was just greedy. Either way, he used shifts and clandestine meetings to give himself cover for the affairs and to allow them to meet him."

"So what changed?" he asked.

"Irene and Jean both found out about their respective affairs, remember?"

"So what? Jean confronts Pearson about it, and he kills her for it?" asked David.

"It's plausible," I said.

David began to shake his head. "It still doesn't account for all of the leaks. Pearson, Jean, Irene, and Faylen would have had to be at every meeting that leaked information came from. That's too many departments, even if they'd managed to blackmail every person on that list."

"At some point, all of that information except phone calls one of those men was privy to would have passed through the typing pool. Just think about how often we're asked to type up notes or memos or even attend meetings to cover for secretaries. There is so much there."

"But the security protocols mean that everything is destroyed," he said.

A thought dawned on me. We'd been so blind—all of us. "Someone on every shift is in charge of incinerating notes, duplicate copies, and typewriter ribbons. Irene volunteered to take up the task after Jean was killed, even though lugging the boxes around is hard work and it holds you back from going home promptly. I think Irene was positioning herself to have access to the same information Jean had when she was alive. That's how they continued to know so much."

"What about the coded list?" he asked.

I sat back in my seat, my brow scrunched up in thought. "Jean must have realized that Pearson felt she could be replaced—not just as his girlfriend but in his blackmail business. What if she decided to strike out on her own? That's an even stronger motive to kill Jean than her threatening to leave him."

"If she left him, he has Irene waiting in the wings. But if she cut into his business . . ." I could see the muscle in David's jaw working. Finally, he said, "We need to find Pearson."

I was about to respond when a flash of green caught my eye. Irene, dressed in a green coat and matching hat, emerged from the end of her road and turned toward the shops.

"There she is," I said.

With a grunt, David turned over the ignition and put the car into gear just as she stuck her hand out and a taxi glided up to her. She gave the driver her instructions, opened the door, and slid inside. David, to his credit, managed to ease his way into traffic two car lengths behind her.

"Do you think I should keep my head down?" I asked.

He glanced at me. "Why?"

"In case she spots us," I said.

"If she spots us, I'm not doing my job properly," he said, not protesting when a blue Morris barged in front of us.

"Where do you think she's going?" he asked.

"To the one place where she and Pearson can meet in private. Grove House."

FORTY-FOUR

When Irene's taxi crossed the river at Wandsworth Bridge, I could almost feel smug. She was going back to Streatham, on her way to meet with Pearson. I knew it.

"Why wouldn't she simply telephone him to tell him what she knows?" David asked as he battled through traffic to keep Irene's taxi in our sights.

"Maybe they're worried about what might be overheard. You never know if the switchboard operator is listening in," I said.

We followed the taxi as it wound its way along the edge of Wandsworth Common and turned left on Trinity Crescent in Tooting. When we crossed Tooting Common, I worried that we might lose her when a lorry pulled out ahead of us, but David managed to maneuver around it. Finally, when the taxi turned onto Conifer Gardens, David drove a little beyond Grove House and parked.

We were out of the car just in time to see the tail of Irene's green coat disappear into the front door.

"Do you think he's inside?" I asked.

David peered up at the windows. Two of them one story up were cracked, but the blackout curtains were firmly shut against the light, although the rain had subsided and blue sky peeked through the clouds.

"I don't know," he said.

I watched him stride forward to rattle the front door, but it didn't give.

"We could ring the neighbors' bells," he said.

"If Mr. Pearson hears several bells going off in quick succession, it could tip him off," I said.

We both stepped back from the front door to stare at the building.

After a moment, I looked David up and down. "How tall are you?"

"I'm six foot one. Why do you ask?" His tone was unmistakably suspicious.

"Perfect. Can you give me a boost?"

"You want me to boost you . . . where exactly?" he asked.

"Just onto your shoulders. That flat is the only one that has the blackout curtains drawn, even if the windows are open. If that's them, I might be able to hear something."

David sighed but went down on one knee next to the wall, bracing his hands against the brick. I tipped my shoes off with my toe and then stepped first on his knee and then onto his shoulder. I wobbled a bit, catching myself against the wall.

"Steady on," he gritted out.

"Sorry." Cautiously I placed my other foot on his other shoulder. "There."

Slowly, David stood to straighten, his hands bracing my legs while I tried my best to steady myself. On top of his shoulders, there was still a good gap between the windowsill and my ear, but I could hear the faint sound of sobbing coming from what sounded like another room.

"Can you sidestep to the other window?" I whispered down to David.

He grunted, but he managed inch by inch to crab walk his way closer to the other open window.

"—hadn't been so careless," I heard a man roar.

"I'm sorry, Lawrence!" wept a woman I immediately recognized as Irene.

"You've put everything in jeopardy now. Do you know what they'll do to me if they find out? What they'll do to *you*?"

"I haven't done anything! Not really!" Irene cried.

"They won't believe that. Not when I've spoken to them. I'll tell them it was you who killed Jean. You who smuggled out the information. I've destroyed the codes. Nothing traces me back to my contacts. My hands are clean," said Pearson.

"I have the book. I'll tell them what you forced me to do on Friday.

The people in the White Horse will recognize me. I swear I'll make them see it!" Irene threatened.

There was a soft silence, and then, very low, I heard him say, "Perhaps you're right. It would be foolish to risk them being able to connect the two of us."

"Lawrence . . . Lawrence, what are you—"

A choking sound cut Irene short. I heard a crash.

"Down!" I shouted to David. "Down!"

He managed to lower halfway to kneeling before the momentum of all of our weight wobbling around sent both of us tumbling to the ground. I landed in a heap on my hand, my wrist burning in a bright shot of pain. I rolled to sitting while he grunted and tested his shoulder.

"We need to find a way inside. I think he's choking her," I urged.

David was up to his feet in a split second, hauling me up by my good wrist. We rushed to the front door and, before I could suggest anything, he had his jacket off and was wrapping his elbow in it. It took a few blows, but the pane of glass making up one of the windows next to the door shattered, and he flicked the lock open.

"Stay here," he said.

"Not bloody likely!"

He growled, but then he grabbed me by the hand and pulled me inside.

We attacked the stairs, him taking them three at a time for my two. There were two doors off the landing.

"This one," I said, steering us toward what I guessed would be the unit at the front of the building.

David tried the doorknob. It was locked.

He put his shoulder down, slamming his body once, twice, three times against the door. The lock exploded in a shower of long wooden splinters. In the middle of the room, Mr. Pearson stood, bearing down on Irene, his hands wrapped around her neck. Her eyes were already rolling back in her head, her face turning blue as she scrabbled at his hands.

"Pearson, let her go!" David ordered.

The fury in Pearson's eyes made him look like a madman.

"Let her go!" David repeated.

Sense seemed to strike Pearson, and his grip on Irene's neck loosened. She tore herself away, falling to the floor coughing. I rushed forward, dropping to her side.

"Breathe, just breathe as steady as you can," I said as she gasped for air.

"I caught her. I caught the woman who murdered Jean," Mr. Pearson said, edging away from Irene. "She's raving mad."

"Pearson, we know. Evelyne figured it all out," said David.

Mr. Pearson backed away from him still, his eyes darting to the door. I shot to my feet, leaving Irene to block the door. I didn't imagine that I was the most imposing figure, but he would have to knock me down to get out and that would at least slow him down a bit.

"We know that you're the mole," I said. "We know that you've been selling information, probably to someone you met while you were a prisoner of war."

Fear flickered in his eyes, and I knew that I'd guessed right.

"You tried to keep your hands clean so that nothing would point to you, so you seduced Jean and recruited her to do your dirty work," I said. "She gathered information for you and passed it along in coded messages. She helped you figure out who could be blackmailed.

"Mr. Faylen was the perfect target, wasn't he? If anyone found out about his gambling debts, he would have been out of civil service. His life would have been ruined. You probably told Jean to tell him that she could cut him in, give him money to help pay things off. That convinced him in the end, didn't it?"

Mr. Pearson inched back until he was flush against the windows.

"It was all working so well," I said. "You had Jean, you had Mr. Faylen. I'll wager you thought you were especially intelligent having Irene waiting in the wings if Jean ever turned on you. You even gave Irene the same book to use as a cipher—*Rebecca*—if she ever needed it. What was it? Page 272?"

"You don't know what you're talking about," snarled Mr. Pearson.

"You bastard. You bastard! You told me that I was the only one," Irene managed to croak out from her damaged throat before rounding on me. "He told me that, if I loved him, I would do these things for *us*. That it was his wife who had all of the money, and we needed to sell secrets so that we could start a life together."

"There was another leak of information on Friday after Faylen was caught," said David.

Irene threw her hand up, her finger pointing straight at Pearson. "He made me do it even though I said that everyone would know because Mr. Faylen had been arrested. But he didn't care. He wanted the money."

"You simpering, pathetic little bitch!" Pearson roared. "You had to go and tell Jean, didn't you? You ruined everything!"

"Jean realized that whatever you'd said to her, Mr. Pearson, you were prepared to betray her, so she decided to do exactly what you'd done to her," I said. "Except she didn't take on another lover to do her work for her. She set herself up in the blackmail business all on her own. It was risky, but my guess is the profits would be higher.

"What happened? Did you let the name of your German contact slip? Let her seduce it out of you?" I asked.

"She followed me," he spat. "She found the drop and replaced my message with one of her own. She offered my buyer more for less."

"And so you killed her," I said.

I could practically hear Pearson grinding his teeth from where I stood.

"You set up a meeting telling her—what? That you wanted to reconcile? That if you teamed up properly this time you could make even more money?" I asked.

"She'd told me we needed to talk because someone knew about Grove House. Someone had slipped her a note with just the name of the building where we met and the postal code. She said it meant that we were both compromised," he gritted out.

"I followed you, you bastard," Irene hissed. "I left her that note and another too. I wanted her to know that I *knew*. I wanted her to feel the way she made the rest of us feel—like someone had something over her."

Pearson's eyes cut to Irene, so I enlightened him.

"Irene confronted Jean about two weeks before you killed her," I said. "When you didn't do anything, Jean must have realized that you didn't know that Irene knew you weren't being faithful to her. Maybe she thought that she could use that as more leverage against you. Maybe she didn't care anymore.

"It doesn't really matter though because, Irene or no Irene, Jean still presented a problem. She was cutting into your business. When she wanted to meet, you suggested the sunlamp room. It was quiet and away from most of the offices. You even had the perfect alibi in Mr. Faylen and Irene—people already under your thumb who had to lie for you if you told them to.

"I think that when you arrived, Jean was already there. She told you someone knew about Grove House because they'd left her a note. Maybe she even mentioned the threats. You let her think that you were worried about what it could mean for you. Then, when she looked away, you stabbed her in the throat. You probably thought you could steal her files to see if she had anything written down that could implicate you, only I came along at the wrong time. You heard me at the door so you grabbed what you could, not realizing that Jean had fallen on the note about Grove House and hidden it from view. You stood behind the partition, and then blacked out the lights and locked me in."

"You were supposed to be scared off, not become some fucking amateur woman detective!" he roared.

"That's enough," David said. "Lawrence Pearson, I am arresting you for the murder of Jean Plinkton and for treason to your country."

A slow, sinister smile spread over Mr. Pearson's face as he edged back a fraction of an inch.

"Try to catch me!" he snarled.

"David!" I shouted.

But I was too late. Mr. Pearson was out of the window. For a second, silence hung tense in the air, broken with the sound of a sickening thud.

"Oh my God!" I cried as I rushed to the window.

I could feel David pressed against me, peering over my shoulder. On the ground, Mr. Pearson squirmed, his leg and arm skewed out at strange angles. One of his shoes had fallen a few feet away. We watched him try to struggle up, but he flopped back down again.

"Telephone the police," instructed David. "And watch Irene."

"Where are you going?" I asked.

"To make sure he can't make a run for it," he said.

I watched him go, and then turned to Irene, who had gone completely pale.

"You're going to be okay," I said, crouching down to her.

She gripped my hand, and looked up at me, eyes shining with tears. In a wrecked voice, she asked, "Is it over?"

"It is."

She collapsed to the floor, her shoulders sobbing.

FORTY-FIVE

After Mr. Pearson threw himself from the window in an attempt to escape, a veritable army of people arrived at Grove House. First there were the police officers who handcuffed him to an ambulance bed to be carted off to the nearest hospital. Then there were the detectives who came in with their fingerprinting kits, cameras, measuring tapes, and notepads. Someone had the idea to call a doctor to examine Irene's throat even as a female officer sat with her to make sure she didn't run away before she could be taken to jail.

Eventually the inevitable happened, and Maxwell and Plaice walked through the door.

"You," they said as soon as they saw me.

"Me," I said wearily. "Shout all you like. It won't change the fact that I've delivered you a murderer and uncovered a network of blackmail and treason with the help of Mr. Poole. Really, you should be thanking me."

Sergeant Maxwell, face beetroot red, looked as though he was about to argue when David stepped into place next to me. "I wouldn't, gentlemen."

Sergeant Maxwell clamped his jaw shut and then nodded. "Tell us what you know."

We related the entire story to them, and I found a good amount of satisfaction in the way that their jaws slackened as they came to understand the extent to which Mr. Pearson had managed to infiltrate the inner workings of the cabinet war rooms.

"Right," Sergeant Maxwell finally said. "I'll start filling out the paperwork."

"There is one thing I've wondered about," I said. "If Irene and Jean coded messages and passed them along to Pearson while they were in the CWR, how did he reliably smuggle them out?"

David cleared his throat. "His shoes. Or his right shoe to be specific. There was a false heel, which could hold small scraps of paper. Or a short, flat, thin knife like the one used to kill Jean." He glanced at me. "It partially opened on impact, so I had a look at it before the police arrived."

Sergeant Maxwell blew out a long stream of air. "Right. Miss Redfern, I hope you will understand when I say that I hope we never cross paths again."

I tilted my head in acknowledgment, and Sergeant Maxwell stormed off with Corporal Plaice hurrying after him.

A constable took that moment to approach David and me with two very well-timed mugs of tea. "I took the liberty of guessing a cuppa might be appreciated, Miss. Sir."

"Thank you," I said, gratefully accepting the mug. The tea was strong and sweet, just the thing that I'd read Red Cross trucks were serving to bombing victims for the shock.

David and I both took sips of our tea, watching another constable packing up his kit.

"How is your wrist?" he asked.

I flexed it, wincing a bit. "Never better. How is your shoulder?"

"Strangely, it feels as though a woman's stood on it."

I nudged him. "Oh stop it."

He laughed.

"I suppose now that your case is solved, you'll be heading back to wherever it is that you were working before," I said.

He raised a brow. "The Ministry of Information, you mean."

"I've never thought you were with the MOI. Not really."

He merely smiled. "What about you?"

I shrugged. "I don't really know. I suppose I'll be back in the typing pool. It will seem very quiet now that all of this is settled."

"Don't you have another day off?" he asked.

I nodded. "I'm meant to be back on Tuesday."

"Take some time to relax then. Read one of those cozy mysteries of yours," he teased.

"One day you'll see the value of them," I promised him, smiling against the edge of my mug.

"Perhaps," was all he said.

I don't see the point in a detective lying in their own narrative, so I will admit now that I wasn't entirely honest with David. I would not be free to laze about all day in bed, recovering from my adventures— much though I might want to.

Instead, I fell into bed Sunday evening after hours of paperwork and police procedures, only to drag myself up for the battle that was the queue for the bath first thing Monday morning. I had one last duty to perform before I could have a proper rest. I needed to give Mr. Fletcher my report.

I wasn't entirely certain how I was going to open my meeting that morning.

"How are you, sir? Oh, I'm so glad. Did you know, I caught a murderer yesterday? Also, if you were worried about a mole in the CWR, I managed to snag him and his accomplice too. What luck!"

That didn't feel like quite the right tone to convey the gravity of what had happened that weekend, but I didn't have any better plans when I rang the bell to Mr. Fletcher's office.

Miss Summers led me up the stairs, but she stopped at her desk. "If you'd like to see yourself in, I'll fetch the tea," she said in her sweet voice.

"Thank you," I said, grasping the door handle.

When I entered, however, I found that Mr. Fletcher was not alone. Mrs. White, in another gray jacket and skirt, sat on the edge of the sofa.

"Ah, Miss Redfern," said Mr. Fletcher, rising from his seat. Mrs. White simply stared at me.

"Good morning," I said.

"I hear that you have had an eventful week," he said.

I raised a brow. "If you already know what happened, I'm concerned that I've become redundant."

He waved a hand to brush away the idea. "Come, come. There is nothing better than hearing it from the source."

I glanced at Mrs. White, very aware that she still hadn't said anything.

"Please, do tell us," Mr. Fletcher encouraged me.

And so I did. I launched into the whole story, from the murder to the investigation to the realization of how the many pieces fit together. When I was done, Mr. Fletcher looked pleased and Mrs. White's expression was unchanged.

"It sounds as though you and this Mr. Poole make a formidable team," he said.

"We worked well together, despite a few bumps and misunderstanding at the start," I said.

"That is good to hear, Miss Redfern," said Mrs. White.

"Is it?" I asked, surprised that she'd spoken.

"It is indeed. I would hate to hear that you'd given me a poor review."

I whipped around to see David walk through the door, buttoning the middle button of his single-breasted gray suit. He took a seat on the sofa opposite me as though it was the most natural thing in the world that he would be there.

"You—you know Mr. Fletcher?" I managed to stammer out.

He tipped his head, clearly fighting back a smile.

"I'm sorry to have kept you in the dark, Miss Redfern. Mr. Poole has been an agent of mine for some time—since before the war. I like to keep his role very quiet. The fewer who know about him the better," said Mr. Fletcher.

"What is your role exactly?" I asked, squinting at David.

"Mr. Poole is a member of the Special Investigations Unit. It is a joint effort between the Security Service and the Secret Intelligence Service, with a smattering of the Special Operations Executive thrown in for good measure. Officially, we do not exist. Unofficially, the prime minister sees us as a vital piece of stopping some of the most dangerous threats to this country," said Mr. Fletcher.

"Mrs. White," he continued, "is Mr. Poole's handler. She manages his cases and he maintains contact with her during an operation."

"I am impressed with your work, Miss Redfern," said Mrs. White in a tone that I could have been forgiven for calling begrudging.

"Thank you," I said.

"You are still very green and rough around the edges, but you do show potential. Possibly," she said.

It wasn't exactly the most effusive compliment I'd ever received, but I would take it.

"Mr. Poole, how did you find working with Miss Redfern?" asked Mr. Fletcher.

David straightened in his seat, the very official veneer I'd seen crack over the past few days firmly back in place.

"Miss Redfern has good natural instinct, although I believe that she sometimes is willing to go haring off in a way that shows an alarming disregard for her own personal safety," David said.

I almost disagreed, but then I remembered that I'd gone crashing through the door of a flat with a known murderer inside, strictly against the orders of a man who turned out to be a trained agent, and shut my mouth again.

"I believe with the correct training, she could be an asset to this department," he finished.

"Interesting," said Mr. Fletcher. "Mrs. White?"

"There would be value in having another woman in the SIU," said Mrs. White cautiously. "There are some jobs that simply cannot be done by a man."

"Miss Redfern, what do you say to that?" Mr. Fletcher asked.

All eyes fixed on me. "I'm not entirely certain what the question is," I said.

"Now that you've had a taste for the unofficial, would you care to officially work for our little clandestine corner of the world?" he asked.

"It will be dangerous," warned Mrs. White. "I won't lie to you and pretend that your life may not be in peril on every operation."

I couldn't imagine Mrs. White lying to anyone, so I nodded.

"And you will need to go through the official training with the SOE. All agents do, although we can fast-track some of your work given your relevant experience in the field." Mr. Fletcher's expression softened. "You may wish to take some time to think about this. There is a great deal that you will sacrifice by living the life of an agent."

"Would I be able to maintain my residence in London?" I asked.

Mrs. White glanced at Mr. Fletcher. "Yes, but you may find that the demands of the work may take you all over Britain—even Europe."

"Evelyne, you should know what you're getting yourself into. This life . . ." David trailed off. "It isn't an easy one. You can't trust anyone with who you are or what you do. Not even your closest friends and family."

In that moment I thought of Moira and—surprisingly—Aunt Amelia. I'd spent the past few weeks evading questions about where I worked, but could I live an entirely separate life that they knew nothing about?

"There's also the matter of your father," Mr. Fletcher started to say, but then the telephone on his desk rang, making all of us look up. He gave a smile. "Another conversation for another time, perhaps."

Mr. Fletcher rose to answer the telephone. "Hello . . . Ah, that's very good of you, sir . . . Yes, she's here . . . Yes, one moment." He held the receiver out to me. "It's for you."

With a frown, I stood and took the receiver from him. "Hello?"

"Miss Redfern, I presume." Even over the telephone, the booming, stately tone of Winston Churchill's voice was unmistakable.

"Sir," I managed to get out.

"Fletcher tells me that you were one of the pair who caught the mole in my cabinet war rooms," he said.

"Yes, sir," I said, staring at David in bewilderment. He mouthed, "What?" which didn't help matters at all.

"Good work. Then I trust that you'll be joining him. This war will be won on the battlefield, but it will also be won with information and disinformation. We need to be on the right side of that fight, Miss Redfern."

"Yes, prime minister," I murmured as the line clicked and went dead.

Mr. Fletcher peered at me over the top of his glasses. "Well, Miss Redfern?"

I stared at the receiver in my hand. "I want to join."

Even without a telephone call from the prime minister, that would have been my answer. I'd had a taste for detection, and I wanted more.

"Evelyne," said David softly, "you'll have to give up the CWR."

"If you were in my position, would you give any further thought as to whether you said yes?" I asked.

He shook his head.

I squared up to Mrs. White from across the sofa. "I want to join," I repeated.

Mrs. White gave me a rare smile. It was not an entirely pleasant experience.

"Good, Miss Redfern," said Mr. Fletcher. "Once you are trained, you will be paired with Mr. Poole to receive further field training."

"Wait," said David quickly. "Evelyne did very well in the field this time, but she's still a novice. Surely some less complex missions would be a better start."

"We worked together perfectly well," I insisted.

"The work that I do—"

"Will benefit from Miss Redfern's assistance, I have no doubt, Mr. Poole. Besides," said Mrs. White, a glint in her eyes, "with me as handler to both of you, I'm certain that nothing could possibly go awry."

David and I exchanged a look. Clearly neither of us really believed that.

"Fine," he said, "but, Evelyne, I suggest that you try to learn as much as you can in training because wherever we go, I can promise you it will be a lot more dangerous than the CWR."

I straightened my shoulders and nodded. "I'm ready."

ACKNOWLEDGMENTS

I have always wanted to write a mystery novel, but the path has been a long and winding one. For that reason, I cannot thank my stellar agent Emily Sylvan Kim enough for sticking with me through every iteration of what eventually became *A Traitor in Whitehall*. I will never forget your patience and cheerleading—especially when I quit my day job and handed you this pitch a week after returning from holiday to write full-time!

Thank you to my editor, Nettie Finn, who saw a few sample pages and knew that Evelyne, David, Moira, and Jocelyn could become so much more, and Kelley Ragland, who has been such an advocate for this series from day one. Thank you also to the entire team at Minotaur, including Allison Ziegler, Kayla Janas, Paul Hochman, Diane Dilluvio, Cassie Gutman, Julia Gutin, David Baledeosingh Rotstein, and Gabriel Guma.

Thank you also to my wonderful assistant, Mark, and my social media manager, Danielle Noe.

To my fellow writers Alexis Anne, Lindsay Emory, Mary Chris Escobar, Alexandra Haughton, and Laura von Holt, thank you for your encouragement over the years.

I am truly grateful to have some of the best readers in the world. Thank you for following my journey from book to book and taking a chance on something new.

Mum, Dad, Justine, and Mark, thank you for all of your support and encouragement as I took the scary jump from writing with a day job to writing full-time. I appreciate every phone call, title brainstorming session, and early read.

And finally, but certainly not least, thank you to Arthur. You came into my life right as everything was changing, and you have never left my side for the entire wild ride. I could not have written this book without your encouragement, enthusiasm, and support—or that lunchtime run where you helped me unpick all of the problems with my draft. I love you.

1. The prologue ends with Evelyne discovering the body, whom she recognizes as a colleague but does not identify for the reader. Chapter 1 then begins with how Evelyne originally came to get her job in the cabinet war rooms. What is the effect of opening with the murder and introducing the characters afterward? How would the reading experience have been different if you knew who died from the beginning?

2. Evelyne continually brings up her interest in mystery novels and says at the beginning, "I could not abide the thought of being without books." How does her love of detective fiction help her solve the case? Do you relate to Evelyne's view of books, particularly mysteries?

3. The first mystery Evelyne read was Agatha Christie's *The Mystery of the Blue Train*. What was the first mystery you read?

4. Mr. Fletcher tells Evelyne, "This war, more than any other, is about information. Even the smallest detail could be vital to turning the tide in our favor." How do the different characters in *A Traitor in Whitehall* use information for their benefit?

5. On page 144, Evelyne says, "I find that preempting people's judgment has the delightful effect of disarming them. If you are unashamed, they don't know what to make of you." Do you agree with this assessment? How does reputation play a role in the book?

MINOTAUR BOOKS

6. Broken alliances were one of the causes of World War II. How is that represented through the characters in *A Traitor in Whitehall*?

7. The author did a lot of research into the cabinet war rooms for this novel. Her protagonist, Evelyne, had never heard of the cabinet war rooms prior to her position there. Had you heard of them prior to reading? Was there anything that you were surprised to learn?

8. How does the author utilize significant historical moments, like the Blitz, in Evelyne and David's investigation?

9. In what ways do the characters use the gender expectations of the time to their advantage?

10. Given the ending, what do you see next for Evelyne?

Turn the page for a sneak peek at
Julia Kelly's new mystery

Available Fall 2024

Saturday
November 2, 1940

ONE

The cold autumn air hit me the moment I stepped off the bus just past seven o'clock in the morning, but that didn't matter.

After six weeks away, I was home.

I strode through the faint light of dawn, my case slapping against my thigh as I rounded the corner of Bina Gardens. The moment the black door of Mrs. Jenkins's boardinghouse came into view, I broke into a sprint, an involuntary grin spreading across my face.

At the door, I dropped my case, dug into my handbag, pulled out my key, and let myself in. As I crossed the threshold, I breathed in the reassuringly familiar scent of baking bread, laundry, and a dozen different perfumes. Setting my bags aside, I shucked off my camel coat and managed to find a home for it on the rack piled high with things that Mrs. Jenkins was constantly pleading with us to keep in our rooms. From somewhere up the polished wood staircase, I could hear the faint sounds of shuffling slippers and early-morning conversation as my fellow boarders queued up for the loo, negotiating who should have the next bath. From the direction of the kitchen at the back of the house, I could hear the clank of a metal pot being placed on the hob, no doubt Mrs. Jenkins beginning the monumental task of producing one of the fortifying breakfasts she managed to turn out each morning no matter what had recently gone on the ration.

After a long train journey from Yorkshire that had been delayed several times, I was ravenous, but food would have to wait. There was one person I wanted to see more than anyone else in the world.

I mounted the stairs, grateful that the new muscle I'd acquired during my time away let me move more swiftly than ever before. As I reached my floor's landing, I spotted Cynthia, a secretary who worked in one of the government buildings in Whitehall, emerging from the room across from mine.

"Good morning," my fellow boarder said, as though I hadn't been gone for weeks. Since joining the secretive world of the Special Investigations Unit, a shadowy operation that investigated leaks, rooted out moles, and generally kept an eye on all branches of our wartime government, I'd come to appreciate Cynthia's quiet discretion. Although we lived under the same roof, she never pressed me about my job. In exchange, I never asked what department she worked for or what that work entailed.

"Hello. Have you seen her this morning?" I asked, jerking my head in the direction of my door.

Cynthia shook her head. "She's been coming home late from rehearsals, so I wouldn't be surprised if she's still asleep. Shall I tell the others you're home?"

"Thank you." My stomach growled. "And would you let Mrs. Jenkins know I'll be needing breakfast?"

Cynthia nodded and began to make her way down the stairs.

I opened the door to my room and found it dark save for a spot where the blackout curtain had folded back on itself, letting in a weak stream of morning light that illuminated the angelic face of Moira Mangan, my roommate and best friend. From Moira's twin bed came a soft, ladylike snore that made me smile. If she had late rehearsals, I should let her sleep, but I had no idea what my first assignment as a new SIU agent might be or when it might come, and I wasn't going to squander the chance to catch up with her after so much time apart.

I switched on our room's overhead light and almost immediately a rather pathetic groan came from under the bedclothes on Moira's side.

"Turn off that horrid thing or I swear on everything I hold dear that I'll despise you forever," came Moira's muffled voice.

"Well, if that's the way you greet your best friend . . ."

The duvet flew back, and Moira shot out of bed. "Evie! You're here!"

I laughed. "I am."

"But you didn't say you were coming home."

"There wasn't enough time," I said honestly. "I didn't even know I'd be on a train until a few hours ago."

Since September, my life had been focused on one thing: transforming me from an ordinary young woman into a highly trained SIU agent. At the Special Operations Executive's "finishing school" at Beaulieu in Hampshire, I'd been schooled in surveillance, weapons training, hand-to-hand combat, parachute training, wireless radio operation, evasive action, explosives—all manner of nasty things to make sure that nasty people didn't do them to me first.

For the culmination of my training, I'd been shipped up to Yorkshire where I had been expected to plan and execute an operation meant to simulate a field mission. I must have passed because as soon as I'd broken into a requisitioned house held by the army and stolen a file from a locked safe as instructed, I had been bundled onto a special train and shipped back to London to await instructions from my handler, Mrs. White.

"I was beginning to worry that you might never return," said Moira.

I tilted my head at the slight edge to her voice. "I said I would be back."

"But you didn't telephone. You didn't write. I know you warned me that I might not hear much from you, but I didn't expect six weeks of *nothing*."

I dropped onto my little bed, the mattress sagging under my weight. When Mr. Fletcher, the head of the SIU, recruited me to unknowingly work on my first mission—being his eyes and ears in Prime Minister Winston Churchill's cabinet war rooms—I had been required to sign the Official Secrets Act. The document compelled me to remain silent about everything related to my war work. That had been hard enough when I'd been shuttling between my room with Moira in Bina Gardens and my shifts as a typist in Churchill's secret underground bunker—even more so when I stumbled across the body of one of my fellow typists. However, I hadn't anticipated how strong the urge would be to pore over all my triumphs and frustrations at Beaulieu with Moira.

Still, I'd signed the document, and I took that promise seriously.

"I'm sorry, Moira. Please believe me that if I could have written or telephoned, I would have," I said.

"Why does training to be in a typing pool require six weeks of no contact with your best friend?" she pushed.

"You know I can't answer that."

I was well aware that my lie about having to go away for specialized training as a government typist was so thin Moira could see straight through it, but London was full of young women and men with vague jobs that one wasn't supposed to ask further questions about because we *all* knew that "careless talk costs lives" and all that.

"I know, I know," said Moira with a shake of her head. "It's just that I worried about you."

I swallowed. I wanted to reassure her, but she was right to worry. What I had been doing . . . well, let's just say that graduating training— or even surviving it—wasn't guaranteed.

"I'm sorry," I repeated.

Moira held my gaze for a moment longer but then slowly a little smile touched her lips. "Was it a long train journey back from your . . . typing pool training?"

"It shouldn't have been, but there were delays all along the line. I left just before midnight and only made it into London a half hour ago," I said.

"Oh, darling, you must be simply *exhausted*," said Moira.

"Mostly, I'm hungry. Hopefully Mrs. Jenkins won't mind an extra mouth to feed at breakfast."

"She'll be delighted. We all will. It hasn't been the same around here without you. Now come give me a hug," she said.

I popped up from my bed and crossed the room to let Moira pull me into a warm hug. Goodness, I'd missed my best friend's company— and the company of anyone who hadn't been learning the many varied ways there were to kill other people.

It felt wonderful to be just a little bit . . . normal again.

"I've missed you so much," said Moira, giving me an extra squeeze and accidentally hitting one of the bruises I'd sustained while sparring with a wiry but strong former professor from Durham during hand-to-hand-combat training. I winced, and immediately Moira asked, "What's the matter?"

"I bumped into a doorknob." The lie slipped off my tongue a little too easily for my own liking.

She raised a brow. "It must have been quite the rap."

"It was." At least that much was true.

Moira set me at arm's length and gave me a look over. I worried for a moment that she might press me further, but instead, she asked, "Did they feed you wherever you've been? And what's happened to your hair?"

I touched the ends of my hair, which was a good four inches shorter than when I'd left London. "It's awful, isn't it?"

She shook her head. "Not awful. Just different."

I couldn't tell her that it had become so entangled with a bramble while on a nighttime escape-and-evasion drill that I'd been forced to saw a hunk of it off and had to ask a Geordie woman to even it out for me the next morning. That and the fact that I hadn't had the energy to pin curl my hair while training meant that it was currently in its naturally wavy state, and I was beginning to look like one of the poodles my aunt Amelia had kept for a time in the early thirties.

"Well, I think the shorter length suits you. It brings out your cheekbones," she said loyally.

"Thank you, darling," I said. "Now, tell me what you've been up to. Cynthia said something about rehearsals?"

Moira stretched into a yawn. "Yes, I've been cast in a rather thin comedy of manners called *Whoever Could Say?* I doubt anyone will win any awards for it, but it's work. We open on Friday."

"If I can be there, I will be in the front row," I said.

Moira smiled. "Thank you, darling. It would mean so much to have you there."

"How is Jocelyn?" I asked. Cynthia's roommate had moved in across the hall from us when Moira had brought her in to the boardinghouse ages ago, but recently I'd found myself growing closer to the model-turned-journalist since she'd helped me track down some vital information for solving my first case.

"She's on assignment. Her editor had the bright idea that she should embed with each of the women's auxiliary services, so she's been shipped off to a base in Osterley for a week with ATS trainees to learn the ways of the army," said Moira.

"I'm sorry I've missed her," I said.

"She'll be home soon," said Moira. "Now, tell me. Did you see the delicious Mr. Poole while you were away?"

I scoffed. Despite a rocky start, David Poole and I had managed well enough as partners on the cabinet war rooms case, catching the killer and uncovering a dangerous mole in the process, but our final meeting hadn't been all sunshine and roses.

"'Delicious'? David? That's going a bit far, isn't it?" I asked.

Moira arched a pencil-thin blond brow. "What would you prefer? Handsome? Dashing? Debonair?"

"Irritating is more like it. Did you know the man actually believes that those awful American pulp authors are superior to our British detective fiction writers?"

"Perish the thought," Moira teased.

"He has abominable taste in reading," I sniffed even though I knew I was being slightly ridiculous.

"You may protest as often as you like, but any red-blooded woman with a taste for tall, handsome men would tell you you're wrong about Mr. Poole," said Moira.

I shot her a look, but she ignored me and rolled over to pull a package wrapped in brown paper out of her bedside table.

"Well, speaking of reading material, I have something for you," she said, closing the drawer.

I took the parcel and tore open the paper, revealing a book inside.

Death in the Stocks by Georgette Heyer," I said, opening the cover to examine the title page. "I've been meaning to read her detective novels."

"I'd hoped as much. You'll never believe how long it took to search rough all of your books to try to figure out whether you had any of 's."

"Thank you, Moira," I said, giving her another hug. "There is nothing like a new book to make everything right."

"Now," said Moira, "let's find you some breakfast while the queue for the bath dies down. Then we're going out because we have a very important morning ahead of us."

"Do we?" I asked.

She nodded. "We do indeed."

ABOUT THE AUTHOR

Julia Kelly is the international bestselling author of historical novels about the extraordinary stories of the past. Her
books have been translated into fourteen languages. She has
also written historical romance. In addition to writing, she's
been an Emmy-nominated producer, a journalist, a market-
ing professional, and (for one summer) a tea waitress. Julia
called Los Angeles, Iowa, and New York City home before
settling in London.